# Murder at
# Ford's Theatre

# MURDER AT FORD'S THEATRE

## A CAPITAL CRIMES NOVEL

## Margaret Truman

DOUBLEDAY LARGE PRINT HOME LIBRARY EDITION

Ballantine Books • New York

A Ballantine Book
Published by The Ballantine Publishing Group

ISBN 0-7394-3134-X

Manufactured in the United States of America

This Large Print Book carries the
Seal of Approval of N.A.V.H.

# AUTHOR'S NOTE

In 1861, John T. Ford, an American theatrical entrepreneur with successful theaters in Baltimore and Richmond, took a five-year lease on Washington's Tenth Street Baptist Church with the intention of adding it to his list of theaters. After renting it for the first year to George Christy's famous Christy Minstrels, and after a major renovation, it officially opened as Ford's Theatre in March 1862. The theater was gutted by fire nine months later. Ford's Theatre reopened in August of 1863 and went on to present 573 performances until, on April 14, 1865, it was the scene of the assassination of our sixteenth president of the United States, Abraham Lincoln.

I offer this not as a slice of well-known historical fact, but to make a linguistic point. Note that I've spelled theater two ways: theater and theatre. Although Mr. Ford was an American, the British influence in America was pervasive in those days. It still is among those of certain pretensions who, well, consider things British to be more erudite, including the spelling of words.

The British spell it *theatre.* In American English, it's *theater.*

Alas! What to do? Using alternate spellings throughout the book would prove a confusing distraction to readers, to say nothing of copy editors.

To resolve this dilemma, I turned to my editor and friend, Sam Vaughan, whose wisdom in such things is unassailable. Because the scene of the murder is Ford's Theatre, spelled with the British "tre," theater is spelled theatre throughout the book. I consider this a sensible solution, and trust you will, too. If it should cause you a problem, please take it up directly with Sam.

MARGARET TRUMAN
New York City

# Murder at
# Ford's Theatre

# ONE

Travel guides claim that the average high temperature in Washington, D.C., in September is seventy-nine degrees Fahrenheit. But on this particular Tuesday, the day after a long Labor Day weekend, the thermometer read eighty-one at seven in the morning, which meant ninety was a possibility by noon, a hell of a time for Johnny Wales's air conditioner to decide to crash. It had ground to a halt sometime during the night; it had to have been between two in the morning when Wales returned from a night of drinking with his buddies, and five A.M. when he was awakened by the sound of the vintage window unit seizing up.

He rolled his sticky body out of bed at seven and stood in front of an oscillating table fan, raising his arms to allow the moving air to wash over his nakedness. Understandably, his mood was palpably foul; his mutterings were mostly four-lettered as he poured orange juice, washed down a handful of vitamins, and entered the shower. The weather was bad enough, and you couldn't do anything about that. But Bancroft's early crew call at Ford's was arbitrary. What was the big deal? he wondered as he readjusted the faucets to add cooler water to the mix. It was only a teenage drama workshop production.

As he moved about getting ready in his room above an army-navy store on Ninth Street, not far from the Capitol City Brewing Company, the final stop on last night's toot, and only a few blocks from Ford's Theatre, where he'd been employed as a stagehand for the past two years, his size—six feet four inches tall and 220 pounds—made the cramped studio apartment seem smaller. He pulled on a faded pair of blue jeans, Washington Redskins T-shirt, slipped tan deck shoes over bare feet, attached a black fanny pack to his waist, and checked himself in the mirror. Building and erecting stage sets hadn't been his ambition when graduating from the University of Wisconsin seven years ago. He'd been a leading man in university productions, a big, handsome guy who might make it in Hollywood one day if the chips fell right. He'd tried that for a year, but left Tinseltown weary of failure and wary of tinsel and followed a girlfriend to Washington, where his stagecraft courses at Wisconsin landed him after a while membership in the union and a job at the theatre. It wasn't acting, but at least it was showbiz: No jokes about following circus elephants with shovels, thank you.

He stopped at a Starbucks, eschewing an effete latte at scandalous prices for a large coffee light and sweet, and walked through the stage entrance of Ford's Theatre at precisely eight. His pique at having to be there early was eased by the welcome blast of AC. A uniformed park ranger stood backstage with some of Wales's fellow stagehands, drinking coffee and laughing about something. The ranger in the drab brown uniform was one of many who would conduct hourly, fifteen-minute lectures for tourists later that day as they wandered into America's most infamous theatre, the three-storey, solid brick building where, not play-acting, Abe Lincoln had been shot to death by the actor John Wilkes Booth.

"Hey, big guy, good weekend?"

"Yeah," Wales said, leaning against a piece of stage furniture and sipping his coffee. "Over too soon." A pulsating headache had developed between leaving the apartment and arriving at the theatre. No sense mentioning it; he wouldn't get any sympathy anyway. "Where's Sydney?"

"Who cares?"

"I care," said Wales. "He called this stupid meeting."

"Don't speak ill of the famous Bancroft," someone said.

"Screw the famous Sydney Bancroft," Wales said, pressing fingertips to his temple. "Besides, he's not famous anymore. He *was* famous."

"I sense a hangover, Johnny."

Wales laughed. "You sense it, I feel it."

"Snap to. Our leader has arrived."

Attention turned to an open yellow door linking the theatre to the adjacent attached building in which the Ford's Theatre Society offices were housed. While the National Park Service maintained the theatre as an historic site, it was the nongovernmental

Ford's Theatre Society that used the venue to mount its ambitious schedule of theatrical productions. Heading that society, and coming through the door, was the theatre's producing director, Clarise Emerson, a former Hollywood TV producer who'd been recruited three years earlier to replace the departing Frankie Hewitt. Hewitt had been brought in almost thirty-five years before by then Secretary of the Interior Stewart Udall to help develop a plan for the theatre following its most recent renovations, and to choreograph fund-raising efforts. Hewitt was a tough act to follow. The former wife of *60 Minutes* producer Don Hewitt, Frankie had guided Ford's Theatre from being solely a government museum chronicling the Lincoln assassination to one of America's preeminent resident theatres, a living tribute to Lincoln's well-known love of the performing arts. More than twenty musicals had received their world premieres there since the beautifully restored theatre opened in January 1968, including *Don't Bother Me, I Can't Cope,* and *Your Arms Too Short to Box With God,* many moving on to Broadway. And hundreds of plays had been performed, all adhering to Ford's stated mission: "To produce musicals and plays that embody family values, underscore multiculturalism, and illuminate the eclectic character of American life."

"*Dull* theatre!" some critics said.

Certainly noncontroversial. Avant-garde playwrights need not apply. Nothing to ruffle the feathers of members of Congress who decided how much to include for the theatre in the yearly congressional budget, particularly eighty-six-year-old Alabama Senator Topper Sybers, chairman of the Senate Committee on Labor and Human Resources. Unlike some "reviewers" who never saw a play or painting or book they didn't like, Sybers had never seen a play or piece of art that wasn't lubricious. But Clarise had more than financial reasons these days for not wanting to provoke the elderly, feisty senator from Alabama. The president, Lewis Nash, Clarise's lifelong friend, had recently nominated her to chair the National Endowment for the Arts (NEA). Sybers's Labor and Human Resources Committee would conduct her confirmation hearing.

Clarise's appearance that morning was surprising to the assembled. She seldom set foot inside the theatre, delegating virtually every creative aspect to others. Her time was better spent, she often said, squeezing money out of wealthy patrons, individuals and corporations alike.

"Good morning," she said brightly to the half-dozen stagehands marking time.

" 'Morning, Clarise," they responded.

Because of her status on the Washington scene—not only was she a personal friend of the president and headed for the NEA, she'd once been married to Bruce Lerner, senior senator from Virginia, a handsome, sixty-year-old bachelor often seen on the arm of beautiful, high-profile women—there was the natural tendency for younger people at Ford's to address her as Ms. Emerson. But she'd put an end to that shortly after taking up her post there, and everyone called her Clarise.

That she was youthful in appearance and manner helped. People took her to be considerably younger than fifty-four. Good genes had given her not only beauty but boundless energy; Clarise didn't walk, she moved at an almost constant trot, up on the balls of her feet, looking as though she might suddenly decide to become airborne.

She stood military erect, like her father, who'd served twenty years in the air force, retiring to their small farm in Ohio to die of a coronary three years after exchanging his blue uniform for coveralls. She was, in fact, like her father, Luke Emerson, in almost all ways, physically and philosophically, except for her sense of humor, which was decidedly her mother's, a short, plump woman better suited to the role of farmer's wife than military spouse, subservient to her dour husband when in his presence, but wickedly prankish about him when chatting with women friends.

"Early start," Clarise said. "What's the occasion?"

"Sydney called a meeting," a stagehand said.

"Oh?"

"The teenage show, I guess," Wales said.

"Is there a problem with it?"

"Not that we know of, Clarise."

"Sydney's not even in town," she said.

"That's just terrific," Wales said, dropping his empty cup into a trash can. "Anybody got an aspirin?"

"Do you know why Sydney called a tech meeting?" Clarise asked.

Shrugs all around.

"Well, sorry you're here so early for nothing. I'll speak with Sydney when I see him."

Clarise turned and retraced her steps to the door connecting the buildings. The four men and one female apprentice watched her retreat from where they stood backstage, the men appreciating the attractive sway of her tall, lithe figure, a gazelle in an expensive, tailored gray pantsuit, neck-length reddish blond hair bobbing, hips moving in perfect rhythm with her long strides.

"That is one good-looking woman," the oldest of the stagehands said quietly. He'd been at Ford's for twenty-two years.

"Yeah, I've noticed," Wales offered.

"Hate to see her go," the older man said.

"Better Sydney should go," Wales said. "We going to hang around?"

"Might as well."

"I'm going out for a cigarette," Wales said. He'd cut back on his smoking, limiting himself to ten cigarettes a day, except when he was out drinking. He didn't keep count on those occasions.

"I'll go with you," said the young female apprentice.

As Wales and the girl headed for a door at the rear of the stage leading to a narrow area behind the theatre called Baptist Alley, the older stagehand laughed and said to the others, "She hangs around Johnny like a puppy dog. Really got the hots for him."

"He could do worse. She's a fox."

"I'll take Clarise," the older man said. "Women aren't any good until they've got a little wear and tear on them."

" 'You'll *take* Clarise?' Fat chance. She's strictly money and power."

"You never know," the older guy said, chuckling. "My wife's too good at homicide anyway. Let's put this furniture in place as long as we're here."

Wales and the girl, Mary, had paused at the door to the alley while he fumbled in the fanny pack for his cigarettes. "Just got ten," he said. "You owe me one."

She punched his arm and turned the security lock on the door.

"Got 'em," Wales said, retrieving the crumpled half pack and pulling two cigarettes from it.

"Every time I go through this door," she said, "I think of Booth."

"John Wilkes? Crazy bastard. Got his fifteen minutes of fame."

"He escaped through this door. He had his horse tied out in the alley."

"I know, I know. I've heard the tourist pitch a thousand times."

Wales grasped the doorknob and pushed on the door. It opened only a few inches. Something was blocking its way. He pushed harder, resulting in another inch or so.

"What the hell?" he muttered.

He leaned his body against the door and exhaled a rush of air as he tried again. This time the opening was wide enough through which to poke his head.

"What is it?" Mary asked.

He'd been looking straight ahead, up the long alley that forked left and exited onto F Street. He wedged his shoulder into the gap and twisted his head to look down at whatever was preventing the door from swinging open.

"What is it?" Mary repeated, envisioning some drunk sleeping it off against the door. Baptist Alley had become a downtown lovers' lane for couples looking for smooch time, drug addicts shooting up, or alcoholics deciding to nap.

"Jesus!"

"What is it?" she repeated.

"Jesus!"

"Johnny."

"It's Nadia," he managed, his voice raspy and higher than normal as though the horror on the dead girl's face had reached up and gripped his throat.

# TWO

When the call came in to the MPD's First District Headquarters at 415 Fourth Street, SW, the duty officer that morning put out a notice of a body behind Ford's Theatre. This was picked up by all vehicles in the area, including an unmarked patrol car manned by two detectives from the Crimes Against Persons Unit. Rick Klayman and Mo Johnson were parked a block from Ford's Theatre drinking coffee and comparing notes about their long weekend.

Their celebration of Labor Day had taken different turns. Johnson had had Sunday and Monday off with the family. Klayman had worked, paperwork mostly, catching up on what seemed to be a mountain of forms to be filled out. MPD's upper echelon had instituted what it termed "project paperwork simplification," which somehow resulted in more forms rather than fewer, more compli- cated, too, shades of the IRS's claims of tax simplification. Klayman really didn't care. He'd had little else to do anyway that week- end, and could use the overtime. He'd also gone over investigative files on a Congres- sional intern, Connie Marshall, who'd disap- peared a year earlier, one of many missing persons in D.C., but a case that had be- come, according to some of his colleagues, an obsession. Klayman didn't debate their view of his immersion in the case because they were probably right. His weekend re- view of the files represented the tenth time he'd done so—or thirtieth?

"You get to see your pretty little lady friend over the weekend?" Johnson had asked his partner as they sat in the un- marked car.

"Yes," replied Klayman. "We had dinner last night."

Johnson's laugh was low and deep and rumbling, like a poorly tuned outboard en- gine. "Candlelight and all that?"

"Come on, Mo, why are you always asking me about Rachel? We had dinner. No big deal."

"Uh-huh."

"Why do you care whether I get married or not?" Klayman asked.

"Just looking out for your best interests, my man," said Johnson. "Married men live longer. You never heard that?"

Klayman looked over at his partner, smiled, and shook his head. He'd been hooked up with Mo Johnson since making detective a year ago after only five years on the force. Johnson was a twenty-two-year veteran, skilled, black, a good teacher, who'd seen it all: "The kid is bright, Mo, but wet behind the ears. Show him the ropes," Johnson's supervisor had said after the veteran's partner of many years had retired, and Johnson had been told he was to be paired with the rookie detective.

Mo wasn't happy being handed Klayman as a partner. As he'd told his wife, Etta, that night, "Out of thirty-six hundred cops, most of 'em black, I end up with a skinny little Jewish kid from New York. Maybe it's time to grab the pension and walk."

Which he didn't do. The truth was, he'd come to like Rick Klayman, even respect him. Klayman had proved his mettle on more than one occasion, facing down dangerous situations with steely resolve and audacious fearlessness. "The kid may look like a nerd," Johnson told friends in the department, "but he's all right. He-is-all-right!"

That was when the female voice crackled through the speaker: "Reported unconscious person, alley behind Ford's Theatre, Tenth and F."

"Seventeen responding," Johnson barked into the handheld microphone as Klayman pulled from the curb and turned the corner down Tenth, coming to a hard stop a minute later in front of the theatre. They bolted from the car and entered, flashing their badges at two uniformed park rangers standing at an interior door leading down into the theatre itself.

"Where's the unconscious person?" Johnson asked one of them.

"Really unconscious," a ranger said. "She's stone-cold dead." He pointed to the stage. Sirens could be heard from both in front of and behind the theatre. The detectives moved quickly down an aisle, skirted the narrow orchestra pit, and bounded up onto the stage.

"Police," Klayman announced. "Where's the victim?"

The older stagehand's nod indicated the door leading to Baptist Alley.

Johnson went to it and stuck his head through the partial opening. He was faced with four uniformed MPD officers who'd driven into the alley from F Street. They were looking down. Johnson did, too, and saw the young woman whose lifeless, bloody body blocked the door. He turned to Johnny Wales sitting on a wooden chair, head in his hands. "Another way out there from here?"

"Huh?" Wales's head came up. "Yeah, over there."

Klayman beat Johnson to the second exit door and went through it, followed closely by his partner. A few people had walked up the alley from F but were kept away from the scene by one of the officers. Another uniform held a scruffy man against the brick wall with a straight-arm. The man's advanced dishevelment made it hard to determine his age. Thirty? Seventy? His hair was a helmet of matted salt-and-pepper hair, his scraggly beard hanging far below his chin and cheeks. Large, dark circles on the crotch of filthy, baggy chinos testified to his not being housebroken. Klayman took special note of his eyes; they were large, wild, and watery, giving him the look of a crazed soldier who'd just emerged from behind enemy lines. He wore a dirty white sweatshirt with ARMANI written on it.

"Cordon it off," Johnson ordered a patrolman, who went to his car for a roll of yellow crime scene tape. Klayman turned at the sound of other vehicles coming up the alley. Both were white mini-vans; one had EVIDENCE TECHNICIAN written on it, the other OFFICE OF THE MEDICAL EXAMINER. The two detectives didn't need to discuss what they would do next. Johnson returned inside the theatre to round up everyone who'd been there when the body was discovered, while Klayman took charge of the crime scene itself, making sure nothing was touched or moved, and working with the evidence technicians and ME as they went about their routines.

Klayman went to where the uniformed cop held the vagrant at bay against the brick wall. "Who's he?" Klayman asked.

"An unemployed gentleman," the cop said, grinning. "Claims he's with the FBI."

"That so?" said Klayman. "What are you holding him for?"

"Eyewitness. Says he saw who killed her."

"Ease up," Klayman said. The cop released his grip. Klayman stepped closer to the bearded man. "You saw it happen, sir?"

"You bet I did," the man said, wiping spittle from his mouth and beard. "Saw it plain as day."

"What's your name?"

"Joseph Patridge. That's the name I use undercover." His smile revealed missing teeth; the smell of whiskey curled Klayman's nose.

"What's your real name, when you're not undercover?"

"John Partridge."

"I see." To the uniformed officer: "Take him downtown, material witness."

"Okay."

The evidence technician took pictures of the deceased from many angles with a digital camera, then took positions from which he could photograph the surrounding area. Klayman crouched next to the ME, who was gently moving the girl's jaw to determine the level of rigor mortis.

"She's dead," Dr. Ong said. What was obvious to the casual observer didn't become official until the ME had decreed it so.

"What do you figure, time of death?" Klayman asked.

"Not stiff as a board yet, Detective. Legs still flexible. Less than eight hours. Maybe six."

"She look like maybe she was moved here from where she was killed? Dumped here?"

Ong pressed fingertips against the girl's abdomen, exposed because her purple shirt had ridden up to her neck. Klayman observed that there was no discoloration from pooled blood, or livor mortis, on her stomach, indicating that she'd fallen on her back when struck and had stayed in that position. Ong shook his head. "No livor on her belly. I'd say the deed was probably done right here."

Klayman stood and slowly took in the broken macadam and concrete surrounding the girl. He asked Ong from his standing position, "Blow to the head?"

"Appears that way. More than one. Head, the face. She was beaten quite badly."

Klayman summoned one of the evidence

technicians with his index finger. "See those prints over there?" he asked, pointing to areas of crumbled concrete where two footprints were visible in the gray dust. "Get those."

Inside, Mo Johnson had instructed those gathered on the stage to separate. When they were a dozen feet apart from one another, he asked the group, "Anybody know who she is? Was?"

Their reply was affirmative. "Nadia," some of them said. "Zarinski." "Nadia Zarinski."

Johnson raised his hand to cut off the chorus. "Just one at a time. You?" He nodded at Johnny Wales.

"Nadia Zarinski," Wales said.

"She work here?" Johnson pulled a small pad from his jacket pocket and started writing.

"She was an intern," someone else said.

Johnson kept his attention on Wales, his expression urging *him* to continue.

"Nadia was an intern. I mean, not really an intern. Not here. She's a paid intern in Senator Lerner's office. She sort of volunteered here once in a while, a night or two now and then. She liked being around the theatre."

"Paid intern?" Johnson said. "I didn't think interns got paid."

"Yeah. Well, she did. Get paid. By Lerner's office."

"Who could do such a thing?" Mary asked.

"Anybody got any ideas?" Johnson asked.

Silent shrugs.

"I want an informal statement from each of you. Has anybody left who was here earlier?"

"No. Well, Clarise was here."

"Who's she?"

"She's the boss."

"Where is she?"

"Up in her office, I suppose. The building next door."

Mo Johnson pulled his cell phone from his belt and called headquarters: "This is Johnson. We need backup here. Plenty of witnesses." He clicked off and told uniformed officers who'd entered the theatre to go next door and round up anyone there, including a woman named Clarise. "She runs the place, I think," he explained.

He looked down at the front row of seats. "Come with me," he told Wales, indicating the stagehand was to follow him down to the house, where they settled into adjacent seats. Johnson asked for a brief explanation of why Wales was there that morning, asking him to describe what he'd seen, and gathered his full name, address, phone number, e-mail address, and other specifics. "We'll go to headquarters after we get all the informal statements."

"What for?"

"To get your formal statement. So hang around. Don't talk to anybody except me. Got it?"

"Yeah."

"Next!"

Klayman entered the theatre after Dr. Ong had released Nadia Zarinski's body to be taken to his office and lab. An autopsy would be performed that afternoon. The members of the stage crew who'd been questioned by Johnson, or by a backup team of detectives, had been told to take seats throughout the theatre with plenty of space between them, and were instructed to not talk to one another until their formal statements had been taken at headquarters.

The slight young detective stood on the stage and stared up to the box in which President Lincoln had been assassinated, kept pretty much as it was that fateful night. Klayman was no stranger to Ford's Theatre. He'd spent many hours there soaking in its historic meaning and listening to tourist lectures delivered by park rangers. The presidency of Abraham Lincoln and his tragic death were passions of his; he'd read countless books on the subject, and attended lectures presented by Lincoln scholars. In the good weather, on days off, or when he convinced Johnson to accompany him with their brown-bag lunch, he enjoyed sitting on the steps of the gleaming white marble Lincoln Memorial, the soaring figure of a seated, serene Lincoln peering down on the millions of tourists who visited his shrine, the small children racing up and down the steps, citizens paying homage to the man who'd freed the slaves. Others simply enjoyed the view across the Reflecting Pool, inspired by Versailles and the Taj Mahal, to the Washington Monument and beyond to the Capitol.

Mo Johnson had never had a particular interest in Lincoln history—until he'd teamed up with the bookish Klayman. One day, after reading an account of the design, building, and dedication of the Lincoln Memorial on Memorial Day 1922, he asked Klayman—as they were eating sandwiches on the steps—"Did you know, Rick, that when it was dedicated, the president of Tuskegee Institute—he was black, you know—they wouldn't let him sit with the other speakers—he was supposed to speak—and made him sit across the street with the rest of the black folk?" Anger edged his voice.

"I know," Klayman replied. "Ironic, huh?"

"That's all you have to say?"

"What do you want me to say? It was wrong. If Lincoln had been there, he would have denounced it. I denounce it. Okay?"

"Okay." After a thoughtful pause, Johnson asked, "Do you think your people had it worse? You know, the Holocaust. Slavery. Who had it worse?"

Klayman stood, brushed off the seat of his pants, crumpled his brown bag, and said, "I think everybody got screwed, Mo. Everybody."

Their discussion was interrupted by a call on the police radio Johnson carried. It wasn't the first discussion they'd had about race, nor would it be the last. Johnson liked talking about it; Klayman didn't, concerned that no matter what he might say, Johnson would never fully accept that his white partner, Jewish at that, didn't harbor some deeply buried prejudice.

"Hey, Rick," Johnson called, interrupting Klayman's momentary reverie on the stage. Their attention turned to the door leading to the Ford's Theatre Society offices.

"I can't believe this," Clarise Emerson announced loudly as she strode into the theatre, accompanied by two officers; another man, whale-like and balding, wearing a white shirt, red tie, and red suspenders, tried to keep pace with her.

Johnson stood and held out his badge. "You're the—?"

"Clarise Emerson," she said curtly.

Klayman, who'd come down into the house, offered his badge, too. "Detective Klayman, Crimes Against Persons Unit, Ms. Emerson." He was well aware who she was from photographs in the Style section of the

*Post,* and from having attended productions at which she spoke.

"Is it true?" Clarise asked. "There's been a murder?"

"Yes, ma'am," said Johnson.

"It appears that way," Klayman clarified. "You've been here all morning, ma'am?"

"Not all morning. I did arrive early."

"Did you see Ms. Zarinski?"

"Zarinski? Nadia Zarinski?" Her face sagged; it was obvious she knew who the victim was, but equally apparent that she was shocked. "*She's* been murdered here?"

"Why don't we go over there and talk?" Klayman suggested, touching Clarise's arm and guiding her toward an isolated seating section. As they went, Clarise said, "She works for my former husband, Senator Lerner."

"I know, ma'am, I know," said Klayman.

"There was the scan—the rumors. What was *she* doing here?"

"We'll find that out, ma'am," Klayman said, taking a seat next to her.

"I'm Bernard Crowley," the heavyset man told Johnson, dabbing with a handkerchief at perspiration on his forehead.

"You work here?" Johnson asked.

"Yes. I'm the theatre's controller."

Johnson noted that Crowley's eyes were moist. "You and Ms. Zarinski were pretty close."

"Oh, no," Crowley said quickly. "She— oh, my God. How could this happen?"

"We'll talk over there," Johnson said, pointing to the opposite side of the theatre from where Klayman and Clarise sat.

"Does Clarise know it was Nadia?"

"I believe so," Johnson replied.

"She'll be devastated."

"She knew her well?"

"No. Knew of her. There was talk about her and Senator Bruce Lerner. That's Clarise's former husband. I told her to stay away."

"Who?"

"Nadia. The victim. When I realized who she was, I told her in no uncertain terms that it was totally inappropriate for her to be here, considering the rumor and Clarise's sensitivities."

"You can tell me all about it, sir, over there."

An hour later, the only people left upstairs in Ford's Theatre were park rangers and two uniformed MPD officers, one of whom stood in the lobby to make sure no one not officially connected with the theatre could enter—tourist lectures and tours were cancelled for the remainder of the day. Outside, in Baptist Alley, another cop stood guard over the crime scene, which was bordered in yellow crime scene tape. It would remain that way until another evidence collection team had returned to complete its examination of the alley. The stage crew that had been present that morning were at police headquarters on Fourth Street, SW, giving formal statements; Clarise and Crowley had returned to their offices, promising to show up at headquarters later in the day.

Rick Klayman had wandered out of the alley to F Street, turning every few feet to look back at the rear of the theatre where Nadia Zarinski's body had been found. He turned left and walked up F to the corner of Tenth Street, pausing in front of Honest Abe Souvenirs, which offered shirts, hats, posters, and myriad other items featuring Lincoln's likeness. Klayman grinned. If Lincoln were alive and had a piece of all the action, he thought, he'd be a very rich man.

He went up Tenth and entered the theatre through the front doors. The uniformed officer greeted him and watched as Klayman slowly went downstairs to the Lincoln Museum, where artifacts were displayed in Plexiglas cases. The museum was cool and modern in contrast to the historically preserved theatre upstairs. It was peaceful being there without the usual knots of tourists wielding camcorders and snapping at their children not to touch things. He meandered past the cases, stopping only briefly to admire their familiar contents: a pair of the president's boots, size 14, made by a boot maker in New York named Pater Kahler from tracings Lincoln had made of his own feet. There was Lincoln's overcoat stained with blood, its sleeve torn off by souvenir seekers in 1876. There was a violin played on the night of the assassination, and dozens of Playbills filled another display.

Klayman went to a life-sized photo of Lincoln on a far wall and stood before it. Red footprints were painted into the floor; the purpose was to stand in those footprints and compare your height with that of the sixteenth president, who was six feet four inches tall. Klayman placed his shoes on the prints and looked up into Honest Abe's face. "You were some big man," he muttered, "both ways," smiling and feeling shorter than his five-foot seven. "You going to help me with this one, boss?" he asked Lincoln.

He heard only the gentle whoosh of cooled air coming through a vent above his head.

Lincoln stared down at him. Did one eye move, a wink? Had a trace of a smile come and gone on his strong mouth?

"Thanks, Mr. President," Klayman said, turning to head back to headquarters.

There was work to be done, and they'd barely started. But he felt inspired.

# THREE

Klayman stood next to Eric Ong in the ME's autopsy room. The detective found the autopsy process inherently fascinating, something his partner, Mo, did not. But while Klayman didn't have any problem watching Dr. Ong work on Nadia Zarinski as the body lay naked on his stainless steel table, he was distinctly uncomfortable calling a next of kin to break the news that a loved one was dead. Mo was good at that, his deep, resonant voice calming those on the receiving end of his call or personal visit.

"What have we got?" Klayman asked Ong, a slender, edgy man wearing round, oversized glasses tethered to his neck by a psychedelic blue-and-pink ribbon.

"Cause? Subdural and subarachnoid

hemorrhages. Manner of death? Blow to the head with blunt, broad object. Definitely a homicide."

"We didn't find anything at the scene that was broad and blunt," said Klayman. "No sign of her being dragged?"

"No. But I'd say she spent a little time on her knees before dying. See those scrapes on her knees?"

Klayman leaned over the table for a closer look at the victim's legs.

"She might have gone down to her knees from the blow to her face. Whoever did it finished the job with the blow to the head."

"Or she was pleading."

Ong glanced at Klayman. "Yes, that's possible, but there's no way for me to determine that."

They went to Ong's small, crowded office, where they removed their blue hospital smocks. "Blood and tissue samples will tell us more, of course," Ong said, placing the cassette tape onto which he'd recorded his running comments during the autopsy in an envelope, to be transcribed later. "Sexual activity. A better approximation of time of death."

"If she did fall to her knees from the first

blow, was the angle of the second blow consistent with someone standing over her?" Klayman asked.

Ong displayed a rare smile. "Maybe her attacker wasn't standing over her, Detective. Maybe he was very short."

"The strange case of the murdering midget. Sounds like a Holmes novel." Klayman smiled, thanked the ME, and drove to district headquarters. Johnson was conferring with their boss, Herman Hathaway, a short, wiry man with slicked-back black hair and a silly looking tiny tuft of black whiskers on the point of his chin.

"Charlie Chan come up with anything exciting?" Hathaway asked Klayman as he entered the office and took a chair next to Johnson.

"Not much. Whoever did her hit her twice, once in the face, once on the head. Blunt, broad object. Time of death maybe between midnight and two."

"The press is on it," Hathaway said. "Got a call from Senator Lerner's office. She was an intern there."

"Got that already," Klayman said.

"You also got the rumor that the senator

might have gotten his jollies with his intern?" Hathaway asked.

"I heard something about that," said Johnson.

"Damn rumors," Klayman said. "Everything's a rumor in this town, every intern a lay."

"Sometimes they're true," said his boss. "You'll check it, of course."

"Of course." Klayman turned to Johnson. "Did you reach her parents?"

"Yeah. They live in Florida." He glanced down at his notebook. "Retired. Father taught at Purdue University in Indiana, agricultural science. Mother was a nurse. Deceased had one sister older, one brother younger."

Johnson's ability to elicit information while being the bearer of bad news always impressed Klayman. The few times he'd made such calls he'd gotten off as quickly as possible. But his partner didn't squander the opportunity to find out things, and was invariably successful. Not only was that voice calming, it held you captive.

"They're flying up tonight," Johnson said. "Got them a room at the Channel Inn."

"Our resident travel agent," Hathaway said while picking up the ringing phone.

"Figured I'd help 'em out," Johnson said. "Nice people." The Channel Inn was on the Washington Channel, close to First District headquarters, first choice when housing out-of-towners in D.C. on police business.

"How'd the formal statements go?" Klayman asked.

"Okay," Johnson replied. "Everybody claims an alibi, didn't see her last night. One guy they mentioned is interesting, though."

"Who's that?"

Another peek at his notebook. "A Sydney Bancroft."

"The old British actor."

"You know him?"

"Not personally, but I've seen a few of his films. Why is *he* interesting?"

"He works at Ford's Theatre, Rick. He was supposed to be there this morning for a meeting but never showed up. Ms. Emerson says he's out of town. But one of the stagehands claims Bancroft was always sniffing around the deceased, making a nuisance of himself, you know, touching where he shouldn't have, lewd comments, dirty old man kind of stuff."

"And they say he might have had something to do with her murder?"

"No, only that he's worth talking to."

"Why didn't he show up this morning? *Is*
he out of town?"

"I called the number they gave me. No
answer. His message on the machine
sounds like he's reciting Shakespeare or
something." Johnson's attempt to mimic
the message came out a mix of cockney
and hip-hop; Klayman suppressed a smile.

"Well, 'To be or not to be,' " Johnson said,
laughing.

"You missed your calling," Klayman said,
standing and stretching.

Hathaway got off the phone and asked
what was on their agenda for the rest of the
day.

"We'll check out where Ms. Zarinski
lived," Klayman answered. "See if we can
rustle up some friends, boyfriends, enemies. By the way, what about our FBI undercover eyewitness, Mr. Partridge?"

Hathaway snickered. "He's sleeping it off
downstairs. When he sobers up you can
have the pleasure of questioning him. Bring
your gas masks."

*   *   *

"Lincoln was a good lawyer before he became president."

Mackensie Smith perched on the edge of his desk and took in the faces of the nineteen third-year law students seated in his class in George Washington University's law building. It was the first session of a new course he'd lobbied to add to the law school curriculum, Lincoln the Lawyer, and he was enthusiastic about teaching it. Smith had been a top Washington criminal attorney until a drunk driver slaughtered his first wife and only child on the Beltway, prompting him to close up his criminal law practice and gravitate to the less violent, although sometimes treacherous, world of academia. He'd been a Lincoln buff since high school, compliments of a history teacher who always managed to weave a Lincoln story into any phase of American history being taught. It was during law school that Smith gravitated to reading not about President Lincoln but Lincoln as a young lawyer in Illinois. While Lincoln's law experiences didn't have direct relevance to other courses Smith taught to fledgling attorneys—although he had been involved in some precedent-setting cases, particularly in the area of municipal law—it was Honest Abe's attitudes about justice and the pursuit of it that Smith found compelling.

The young men and women sitting before him were the cream of the law school's crop, and Smith was flattered they'd chosen this new course as one of their few electives. He chalked it up to the subject matter. But truth was, most of them had opted for the course in order to be in another of Mac Smith's classes. Modesty precluded his acknowledging, even to himself, that he was a favorite professor among the student body.

"I wonder how many of you would have gone through what Abe Lincoln went through to become a lawyer," Smith began.

"He was self-taught, wasn't he?" a student said.

"Correct."

"Which was probably easier than going through three years of law school," said another, adding a laugh to couch the statement for Smith's sake.

"Think so?" Smith asked pleasantly. "I think not. Lincoln was driven to study law in his spare time by a devotion to justice, decency, and equality. He didn't have any money, and worked menial jobs like clerking in a store to support himself. He read constantly. There were no study guides to help him, no formalized textbooks, no lucrative job in some Wall Street law firm to motivate him."

"No brilliant law professors to mentor him," someone said.

"How nice of you to recognize that, Mr. Gormley," Smith said, mock-seriously. "My point is, Lincoln wanted to become a lawyer for what it would allow him to do for the common man. How many of you does that apply to?"

A dozen hands immediately shot up, followed by most of the rest.

"Your demonstration of altruism is heartwarming," Smith said. "Lincoln was encouraged to study law by Justice of the Peace Bowling Green, and started by reading—and memorizing—every page of *Blackstone's Commentaries.* Know how he memorized it? He wrote every page from the book on pads to help him fix the words in his mind. He did that twice, and then rewrote every page in his own words. That's dedication, wouldn't you agree?" *also, That Tells*

There were no arguments. *me he was not naturally bright*

Fifty minutes later, as the class was about *he had to put in The O.T.*

to leave, Smith announced, "I'd like each of you to spend a few hours at Ford's Theatre before we meet again next Tuesday. How many of you have been there?"

Three hands were raised.

"Take in one of the park ranger's lectures while you're there. Examine the displays in the museum. It's in the basement. We'll talk about it next time."

"What does his assassination have to do with his having been a lawyer? Or theatre?"

Smith stared at the questioner, smiled, shook his head, and didn't answer. *He'll make a good trial lawyer,* he thought. *Question everything, accept nothing.*

He added to his thought, *and an insufferable dinner companion.*

Smith packed his briefcase and headed for the faculty lounge, where he was due to meet with the law school's dean about a problem student. He entered the large room furnished with polished tufted leather couches and husky oak tables, spotted the dean sitting in a far corner, and joined him.

"How did your first class go, Mac?"

"Fine. If I can get them to view the law the way Lincoln did, it'll be a success."

"Tragic what happened at Ford's Theatre this morning, wasn't it?"

"What happened?"

The dean gave him a capsule version of events as reported on the radio: Young intern from Senator Lerner's office, and theatre aficionado—brutally murdered in the alley behind the theatre.

"Leads?"

"None that I heard. Typical all-news radio station report. We, the listeners, with our twenty-second attention spans, are told by an announcer speaking into a speech compression machine all we need to know—or can comprehend."

Smith grinned. The dean's patience with all things modern was inelastic. No song written after 1945 was worthy of recording, no piece of art failing to accurately depict pastoral scenes or the human form worthy of hanging. His hard-nosed view of the way things should be was tempered by a brilliant legal mind, a fervent commitment to turning out good lawyers, and surprising political and diplomatic skills when it came to navigating the roiling waters of a large educational institution. Smith would miss him; the dean was a year from retirement.

"Well, that is tragic news. I'm going there after I leave you."

"Board of Governors meeting?"

"No. I'm meeting Annabel—I think. Maybe after what's happened she'll have left. Clarise Emerson is coming for dinner tonight. That might be scuttled, too. Now, what about our recalcitrant student?"

# FOUR

Klayman and Johnson drove to Dupont Circle, where Connecticut, Massachusetts, and New Hampshire Avenues intersected, and parked on Eighteenth and N, a few blocks from the circle itself. Klayman knew the area well. When not on duty, he enjoyed browsing the galleries and cafés, especially Kramerbooks & Afterwords, where he would sip strong coffee and eat small but intensely rich pastries while browsing possible selections in the bookstore portion of this funky Washington landmark.

One morning, not long after they'd paired up and while cruising in the Dupont Circle area, Klayman told his partner he'd spent the previous night in that same neighbor-hood with a friend.

"A buddy?" Johnson asked.

"Uh-huh."

"What'd you do? Where'd you go?"

"We went to the movies and had dinner."

They passed a movie theatre catering to gay men. "You go there last night?" Johnson asked, his voice forced-casual, his attention out the window.

"I'm not gay, Mo."

Johnson turned and faced him. "Hey, man, I wasn't suggesting you were. It's just that—"

"Just that *what*?"

"Well, I mean, you're single and you don't seem to—I don't know, don't seem that interested in women, and this is where *they* hang out and—"

Klayman pulled to the curb and stopped. "Mo," he said, "I am not gay. But if I were, it wouldn't be any of your business."

"No offense, man," Johnson said, holding up his hands and laughing. "Just clearing the air, that's all. Wouldn't mean a damn thing to me if you were—one a' them. Live and let live, I say."

"That's what I say, too," Klayman said.

"What people do in their bedrooms is their business."

"Let's drop it, okay?"

"Okay, my man. It-is-dropped."

The subject hadn't been brought up again, although Klayman wondered whether Johnson still harbored those thoughts, and if it would, in fact, matter to him. If Johnson did think Klayman was gay, as well as young, white, and Jewish, it would severely test his partner's open-mindedness.

Johnson was married—happily it seemed—to Etta, a tall, handsome woman with strong features and a glint in her wide brown eyes, and an edge to her laugh that said she'd seen it all and wasn't surprised by anything. They had three sons—young adults a year apart, each as big and strong as their father. Klayman had been a guest at a few Johnson family gatherings, backyard barbecues, the funeral when Johnson's father died, impromptu late dinners when they'd come off a case and Etta had in-sisted Klayman have something to eat be-fore returning home.

Once, after repeated urging, Klayman brought a young woman he was seeing to a cookout at Mo and Etta's house. It wasn't a serious relationship—Klayman and Mary-jane had met at Kramerbooks & Afterwords and forged what was basically a platonic relationship based upon mutual love of certain books—although they had made love on occasion; "We're friends *and* lovers," Maryjane had liked to say. After they'd left the party, Klayman suffered guilt at why he'd brought her. It was to show his partner that he was quite comfortable around women, thank you, and you needn't question my sexual orientation.

Klayman and Maryjane stopped seeing each other shortly after that. She started dating a young, black attorney from the Department of Agriculture and told Klayman it was "a physical thing." He didn't argue, nor was he hurt. She'd lately been talking about the need to marry and to start a family—the biological clock and all, fulfillment as a woman—which had bothered Klayman. Marriage was not in his current plans.

"This is it," Johnson said, pointing to a three-storey town house on N Street. A tiny patch of English-style garden was neatly tended, bordered by a low, black wrought-iron fence. A keyhole portico covered the front door; the sun brought stained glass in the door to life.

A young, preppy woman, with silver streaked into her blond hair, wearing a pink sweatshirt and tan Bermuda shorts, answered their knock.

"Detectives from the First District," Klayman said, displaying his badge.

"Has something happened to Mark?" the woman asked.

"I don't think so, ma'am. It's about Ms. Zarinski."

"I don't understand."

"I'm afraid she's dead," Johnson said, lowering his voice beyond its usual depth. "A murder victim."

"Oh, my God. This city is—"

"You didn't know?" Klayman asked. "It's been on the news."

"I don't watch TV during the day. When was she killed?"

"May we come in?" Klayman asked. "This is where she lived, isn't it?"

"Yes. She rents from Mark and me. I . . ."

Klayman and Johnson waited patiently until she realized she hadn't responded to their request.

"Of course, please. You'll have to excuse

the mess. Our housekeeper called in sick—she's been doing that a lot lately, and I really wonder about her—and I haven't had time to neaten up."

"Don't worry about that," said Johnson as they followed her into a foyer dominated by yellow and blue tile on the floor and walls, and into a living room to their left.

"Ms. Zarinski rented a room from you?" Klayman asked.

"No, not a room. An apartment. Upstairs. The third floor. We have the first and second."

Klayman turned his head left and right. "She used this same front entrance?"

"No. There's a staircase outside, at the rear of the house. We had it installed to accommodate a tenant."

"She's your only tenant?"

"Yes." Laura Rosner sat in a tan leather director's chair and exhaled loudly. "My God, who killed her?"

"When did you last see her, ma'am?"

"Last night, I think." She screwed up her thin face in deliberate thought. "Yes, it was last night. Mark and I were cooking out in the yard. We asked her to eat with us, but she said she had a date." A slow shake of her pretty head. "Nadia always seemed to have a date."

"She saw lots of men?" Klayman asked.

"You met them?" asked Johnson.

"Just one or two."

"Names?"

"Jim, or John. I don't know. They were a little weird."

"Weird?" Johnson repeated.

"Theatrical-type people. You know."

"Last night," Klayman said. "Any idea where she was going to meet her date?"

"No. No idea. She worked for Senator Lerner. I wonder."

The detectives looked quizzically at her.

"There were those rumors. She was very sexy. Sort of liked to flaunt it. She didn't dress like an intern in a senator's office."

"How would that be, ma'am?" Klayman asked.

"Conservative. She didn't dress conservatively."

"She pay her rent on time?" Johnson asked. "Was she a good tenant?"

"Her father paid her rent. The check arrived from Florida right on time every month. A good tenant? She was all right, I guess, although Mark and I didn't appreciate how many times her male friends slept over. Not that we're prudes or anything. How can you be in this day and age? We just thought it was—well, you know, inappropriate."

They spent another ten minutes in the living room before asking to see Nadia's apartment on the third floor, and followed her up the outside staircase. Their initial impression was that Nadia Zarinski wasn't into neatness, and her landlady mirrored their reaction with a sour expression. A pile of dishes with baked-on food sat in the sink. The white tile floor had spots where food or liquid had fallen and hadn't been wiped up. Johnson opened the refrigerator. There was little in it: milk with an expired sell-by date, two slices of pizza in Baggies, lemons and limes on their last legs, half a loaf of bread, and a bottle of vodka with enough left in it for two, maybe three, short drinks.

Clothing was strewn everywhere, over the back of a chair in the kitchen, on a couch and chair in the small living room, and on the bed and floor of the bedroom. A peek in dresser drawers showed little regard for folding underwear or sweaters. The top of the dresser was covered with out-

dated fashion magazines and issues of
*People, Cosmopolitan,* and *Washingtonian.*

Klayman sat at a desk in a corner of the
bedroom and moved papers around, glancing at each before going on to the next. He
opened a drawer. In it were Playbills from
Ford's Theatre; bills from department and
smaller clothing stores; pens, pencils, and
scraps of paper with what appeared to be
phone numbers on them, but no names. A
search of other drawers failed to come up
with the address book he was looking for. At
the bottom and to the rear of the last drawer
was a jewelry box covered in powder-blue
satin. Johnson stood over Klayman as he
opened it.

"My, my," Johnson said as an array of
expensive-looking jewelry was displayed.
Klayman pulled a jewel-encrusted ladies'
Rolex from the box and held it up for Johnson and Mrs. Rosner to see. She ignored it
and leaned closer to see the other jewelry in
the box: rings, bracelets, and necklaces,
their stones gleaming in the light from the
desk lamp.

"Nice collection of trinkets," said Johnson. "You ever see her wear any of this
stuff?" he asked Laura Rosner.

She shook her head. "Never," she said.

Klayman replaced the box in the drawer, and they moved to the bathroom, the most orderly room in the apartment.

"She sure loved perfume and soap," Johnson muttered, surveying a row of at least fifteen bottles of perfume, and a large wicker basket filled with wrapped bars of scented soaps. He touched a towel hanging from a bar inside the shower. "Dry," he said. To Mrs. Rosner: "You see her this morning?"

"No. I'm sorry about the mess in here. If I'd known you were coming I'd—"

"Glad you didn't," said Klayman.

"Will this be a crime scene, with yellow tape and all?" she asked. "I wouldn't want the neighbors to be upset."

"No, ma'am. No crime's been committed here, but we will want to spend more time going through her things. No one's to come in here except police. All right?"

"Yes."

Klayman placed a call to headquarters requesting uniformed officers to secure the apartment until they'd had a chance to thoroughly examine it. "We'll be back," Klayman told Mrs. Rosner. "Some other detectives will probably swing by, too, in the next hour.

Some evidence techs. Where's your husband?"

"Mark is at work. He's with the Treasury
Department. He should be home soon."

"Did he, uh . . . did he have much contact
with your tenant?"

"With Nadia? They talked when they saw
each other, just in passing. Why do you
ask?" The answer dawned on her. "You
don't think—?"

They descended the exterior stairs from
the apartment and walked to the front of the
house. A patrol car pulled to the curb, and
Klayman told the two officers to go around
back and make sure no one entered the
third-floor apartment until he cleared it.

"Thanks for your time, Mrs. Rosner,"
Klayman said as he and Johnson went to
their car. She stood at the edge of the front
garden, arms folded across her chest, brow
furrowed. Johnson turned, took a few steps
back in her direction, and asked, "Was your
husband home last night?"

"Yes, he was. All night." Her cooperative
tone had turned to ice.

"Thank you," Johnson said, climbing in
the car with Klayman, who drove away.

"What do you think?" Johnson asked.

"I see her—the deceased—as being like half the young women in D.C., looking for action, playing the bar scene, searching for love."

"Uh-huh," Johnson confirmed. "Lots a' dates, lots a' boyfriends, all of them dorks."

"Why do you say that?" Klayman asked, laughing.

"Ah, girls like this Ms. Zarinski are always more mature than the guys they go out with. You know that. Not you, Rick. You're very mature."

"Thanks. Rich dorks."

"Huh?"

"Unless she bought all that jewelry and that watch out of an intern's pay, the guys she went out with were very rich. And generous."

Johnson laughed.

"What's funny?"

"Some cops—and you know who I mean—would be tempted to find one a' those pieces in their pocket. Where we heading?"

"Where this Bancroft lives. Maybe he's home now."

" 'To be or not to be,' " Johnson said loudly, placing his hand over his heart.

Klayman didn't respond. His thoughts were of Nadia Zarinski. He saw her battered face and wondered what could have made anyone so angry that they would beat her to death. Had it been one of her boyfriends, or a stranger? The location of her murder ruled out the latter. There was no reason to be in Baptist Alley alone at that hour of the night. Unless, of course, she was at the theatre for some official reason and went outside for a cigarette or fresh air. They'd asked people at Ford's Theatre whether anyone had been in it overnight, and had received unanimous denials that that was possible. The park rangers on overnight duty claimed no one had entered the theatre after eight o'clock. It had to have been someone she knew, probably knew well.

She hadn't been wearing a watch; at least it wasn't on her wrist when Dr. Ong had stripped her down. No purse, either. A set of keys, tissues, two folded blank checks, an American Express card in her name, a pocket comb, breath mints, some loose change, and sixty-six dollars in folding money in her jeans and white sleeveless cotton vest she wore over her blouse.

"What are you thinking, man?" Johnson asked.

"Huh? Oh, sorry. Daydreaming. I was thinking I'd like to know where she got all that jewelry."

"Maybe her daddy in Florida."

"You don't get rich teaching agriculture in college, Mo."

"Hell, he paid her rent."

"Yeah, he did."

"Daddy's little girl."

"Daddy's little *dead* girl."

"Maybe Senator Lerner was a daddy, too. A sugar daddy."

They fell silent, their thoughts the same. Solving a murder was tough enough without having a powerful U.S. senator in the middle of it.

# FIVE

"Clarise? It's Mac Smith."

"Hello, Mac. I'm sure you've heard."

"Yes. Quite a shock. I thought Annabel might be there with you."

"She is."

His wife came on the line. "I was just about to leave," she said.

"Glad I caught you. Still want me to come by?"

"No. I'll meet you at home."

"Is Clarise coming for dinner?"

"As far as I know." He heard Annabel ask Clarise the question. "She'll be there. Drinks at six okay?"

"Perfect. Hurry home."

\* \* \*

Annabel handed the phone back to Clarise
and resumed her seat across the desk from
the theatre's producing director.

Like her husband, Mackensie, Annabel
had also been an attorney, a divorce lawyer.
And like him, she'd packed up her practice
one day to pursue a lifelong love of art, particularly pre-Columbian art. With Mac's
unbridled support, she opened a pre-
Columbian gallery in Georgetown, an aes-
thetic success from the start to be sure, but
only marginally profitable. But that wasn't
the point. The Smiths were financially comfortable from their lucrative former law practices, and were blissfully free to pursue
more altruistic pursuits: the gallery; for
Annabel, being part of D.C.'s arts community; and for Mac, teaching law and lending
his vast legal experience to nonprofit activities.

Although Annabel's friendship with
Clarise Emerson was not of long duration, it
was close, having become more so over the
past few years. As often happens, they'd
met through a mutual friend—in this case, a
friend in very high places, Dorothy Maloney,
America's first female vice president.

The veep and Annabel had become

friendly when Maloney was a four-term congresswoman from Los Angeles, and the
House's most vocal proponent of the arts
and government funding for them.
Dorothy's husband seldom ventured to
Washington, preferring to remain in Los Angeles to manage a successful real estate
business, and the congresswoman had become part of the Smiths' social circle.

Once the Nash administration was up
and running, its lovely vice president took
the lead in lobbying Congress for arts funding—as well as lobbying the president for
Clarise Emerson to head the NEA. They'd
been friends since college in their native
Los Angeles; Clarise had produced
Dorothy's campaign TV spots, and the congresswoman had pushed through legislation benefiting Clarise's favorite California
nonprofit arts organizations. That this quin-
tessential quid pro quo friendship moved to
Washington—America's leading city of mutual back-scratching—when Clarise took
over the leadership of Ford's Theatre
seemed only appropriate, although there
was more to their relationship than advanc-
ing careers. They happened to like each
other, too.

When Clarise moved to Washington, two of the first people Congresswoman Maloney introduced her to were Mac and Annabel Smith. "This handsome couple knows D.C. intimately," Maloney told Clarise, "but they haven't been corrupted by it."

"I still can't believe it," Clarise said to Annabel as they sat in her office in the three-storey building attached to the theatre. "I know murders happen in this city, but here? Good Lord! And *her*?"

"Anything from the police?" Annabel asked.

"Not that I'm aware of. I told them everything I could, which wasn't much. I never even knew she spent time here at Ford's. Not that I should be expected to know. Interns come and go, volunteers, dozens of them. They work at night, helping out on productions, or in the office sometimes."

"Your office?" Annabel asked.

"At times, but not her. I assure you, if I had known she was even within a hundred feet of the theatre I'd have sent her packing." She leaned back in her chair, closed her eyes, and slowly shook her head. Annabel didn't intrude on whatever thoughts were dominating her friend. When Clarise opened her eyes, she said, "This whole business with Bruce is so distasteful."

Annabel was aware, of course, of the rumors linking Lerner to some sort of sexual relationship with Nadia Zarinski, but dismissed them as being nothing more than the result of one of Washington's favorite avocations: generating scandal. The rumor's genesis hadn't had much substance to back it up. A former aide to Lerner, who'd been fired, made the claim that the senator and Nadia had enjoyed a number of sexual episodes late at night in the office. That was it. That was enough. The seed germinated and blossomed into a full-grown "item" at bars and restaurants: "Not hard to believe," many said. "Lerner's love of the ladies isn't exactly news." "Hell, he's single. So what if he has a fling with a sexy intern?" "It's not like it's anything new in this town." And so on. Lerner, who successfully ignored the rumor until press mentions gave it legs, eventually dismissed it as nothing more than the petty grumbling of a former staffer, end of story. Nadia, too, when confronted by a reporter, said it was a filthy lie.

Some of Lerner's advisers urged him to get rid of Nadia to avoid even the appearance of impropriety, but he refused. A young woman's life, he told them, wasn't going to be ruined because of cheap innuendo and a malicious lie. And so she stayed—and was paid, which raised a few easily elevated eyebrows—until that morning in Baptist Alley, in back of Ford's Theatre.

"The police brought up the rumor about Bruce and Nadia," Clarise said. "They actually had the nerve to ask *me* about it, dumb questions, like whether I ever confronted her, or what I was feeling about her murder."

"What did they think *you* would know?" Annabel asked.

"Oh, maybe that Bruce"—she laughed—"or Nadia confided in me one dark and gloomy night to clear their consciences—who knows? It was so embarrassing, Annabel. How dare they?"

"Well, at least you have that behind you, Clarise. Being questioned by the police. I heard that there's someone who claims to have seen the murder."

Clarise guffawed. "An old drunk sleeping it off in the alley. I'm sure the only thing he sees is snakes and bugs crawling over him."

Ford's Theatre's controller appeared in the open doorway. "Sorry to interrupt," Bernard Crowley said.

"Come in," Clarise said. "You know Annabel Smith."

"Of course," Crowley said, offering his hand tentatively in the event it was bad manners for a man to do so first. He wasn't sure. Annabel accepted it and said, "We were just talking about what happened this morning."

"There's nothing else to talk about," he said, leaning against file cabinets. "Or think about. That's all I've been doing." He shifted his oversized body against the cabinets and flicked a drop of perspiration from the side of his nose with a finger. "I must tell you, Clarise, that I knew she was working here."

"You knew, and didn't tell me?"

"I didn't want to hurt you, Clarise. She helped me out a few times on some of the large fund-raising mailings we've been doing lately. She seemed like a really nice girl, willing to pitch in, not like some of the others who hang around here. All they want is the creative end of the theatre. Don't even mention the business side. But she was always willing to give me a hand when I got backed up. You know, add columns of figures, get fund-raising letters ready to go out, things like that." Tears formed in his eyes and he pulled a handkerchief from his pocket. "I'm sorry. I've never been close to a murder before. And somebody I know."

"You knew who she was, Bernard?" Clarise asked, incredulous.

"Not at first. When someone mentioned to me that she was the girl who—well, you know, was rumored to have had some sort of relationship with Senator Lerner, I told her to leave. I told her that it was insensitive and even foolish to come here to Ford's Theatre, knowing you were in charge. I'm afraid I was pretty harsh with her."

"Well," said Clarise, "at least you did the right thing. The gall, the arrogance of her, wanting to work here. It's inconceivable, but judging from what I read about her, it shouldn't be a surprise."

The phone, which had rung almost continuously while Annabel was with Clarise, was picked up by someone else in the small building. That someone else came up the stairs and handed Clarise a sheaf of phone message slips. She perused them and said, "Just about all from media wanting interviews. The ghouls are on the prowl. I'd opt for a secluded, sunny island right about now."

"I can't offer that," said Annabel, "but sunsets from our terrace are pretty nice. How about getting out of here early? Like now, for instance?"

"Good idea," Clarise said.

Crowley said, "Sunny islands don't appeal to me, not with my fair skin. I've already had a dozen skin cancers burned or cut off. For me, I'd like a quiet, dark bar where they pour big drinks."

"I can offer that, too," Annabel said brightly. "You'll have to put up with a big dog—we have Rufus, a blue Great Dane—but he doesn't drink much."

Crowley laughed.

"I mean it," said Annabel. "Clarise is coming for dinner, and you should, too."

"I wouldn't want to—"

"You work for me, Bernard," Clarise said, "and I say you join me at the Smiths' for dinner. That's an order."

"Yes, ma'am. Give me five minutes to close up my office."

"Oh, and take these," Clarise said, handing him a dozen checks she'd signed while talking with Annabel.

"He's been a godsend," Clarise said once Crowley was out of earshot. "Finances were in disarray when I got here. He arrived and quickly put everything in order. He's like a human computer. Every cent accounted for, bottom line solid for the first time in ages."

"How did you find him?"

"A search firm. He was controller for a string of movie theatres in the Midwest. He took a pay cut to come here, which concerned me. But he said he wanted to work in a place where things mattered, where money was put to good use, like this theatre. I suppose being single helped in his decision. Less overhead and obligations. He seems to spend his life here, sometimes all night, and weekends. At any rate, Annabel, having him here has certainly made my life easier. Whoever replaces me will inherit a top-notch controller."

"Once you're confirmed to head NEA."

"*If* I'm confirmed. Come on, we'll pick up Bernard on our way downstairs. An inspiring sunset and a stiff drink are precisely what I need."

# SIX

Annabel, Clarise, and Bernard Crowley had to negotiate a crowd of reporters camped outside the theatre when they left to go to Annabel's Watergate apartment. They drove in Annabel's car, which she'd put in a garage adjacent to the theatre, and parked in the space reserved for the Smiths beneath the Watergate complex, that parking privilege setting them back an additional $45,000 on the purchase price of their three-bedroom co-op in the south building. Although apartments in other Watergate buildings tended to be larger, the south building afforded stunning views of the Potomac River, and accompanying sunsets— on most days.

"I lied," Annabel said. They sat on the ter-

race, the women sipping glasses of red zin-
fandel, Crowley enjoying a glass of bourbon
over ice. Mac had called to say he'd been
detained at the university but would get
there as soon as he could.

"Lied about what?" Clarise asked.

"The sunset. Sorry about the clouds."

"Clouds seem more appropriate," Clarise
said, "considering what's happened."

"You said the young woman who's been
killed worked with you," Annabel said to
Crowley.

"Yes, I'm embarrassed to say." To
Clarise: "I hope you don't think poorly of me
for not telling you. I meant well."

"Of course I don't think poorly of you,
Bernard. You did the right thing once you
realized who she was. I'm somewhat embarrassed that I haven't paid more attention
to who's working in the theatre. And let me
say that despite my feelings about the girl, I
am very saddened by her death. Very saddened."

Clarise lightened her tone. "I'm sure you
noticed how attractive she was," she said,
sipping her wine. "I remember thinking
whenever I saw her on TV how beautiful she

was. No, make that sexy. There was a crude sexiness to her."

Annabel looked to Crowley for a reaction, whose slight shrug said he either didn't have an opinion about such things, or hadn't noticed.

"Where was she from?" Annabel asked.

"Somewhere in the Midwest," Crowley answered. "I think her folks live in Florida. I remember her mentioning that once."

"What amazes me, Bernard," Clarise said, "is that you didn't realize who she was immediately. You can't be alive in this town without reading about the flirtatious young intern and my esteemed former husband."

"I don't read that kind of junk," Crowley said, sounding as though he meant it. "Excuse me." He headed for the kitchen to refresh his drink.

"It's inevitable that the rumors about Bruce and the young girl will surface again," Annabel said to Clarise. "Had he ever discussed her with you?"

"No. Once. After all the requisite denials had been issued, I asked him straight out whether he'd slept with her. Not that it was any of my business. He's free to sleep with whomever he chooses. But I hated to see him fall into the dirty old man category. He's too good for that."

"And?"

"He gave me one of his usual charming answers. He said that at his age, talking after the act is as important as the act itself. 'What could we possibly talk about?' he said."

Annabel smiled. She and Mac had met the dashing, erudite senator from Virginia on a number of occasions, and could picture him saying that. He was a charmer, no question about that. She glanced over at Clarise, who seemed to be deep in thought, her eyes focused on the German Gothic spires of Georgetown University to the northwest, behind which the sunset had failed to make an appearance that evening. Clarise's divorce from Bruce Lerner had occurred many years before Annabel had been introduced to her, but she had seen pictures of the elegant couple, as well as attended functions at which they both made an appearance, the tall, urbane senator from Virginia and the stunning television and movie producer from Hollywood, a power couple if there ever was one—not only because of their respective positions, but the physical swath they cut when entering a room as well. They were always cordial toward each other when in the presence of others, seemingly friends who probably got along better divorced than when coupled in marriage.

Clarise had been relatively reticent with Annabel about the marriage and breakup, summing things up with flippant, offhand phrases: "No house was big enough for both egos." Or, "He wanted to be a movie star, and I wanted to be a senator. We were both failures."

"How's Jeremiah?" Annabel asked. It sounded like an obligatory question—à la *How's the kids?*

Jeremiah was the only child from the Lerner-Emerson marriage, and Clarise seldom spoke of him. Annabel knew that the young man—how old was he now, twenty, twenty-one?—was a disappointment to Clarise, and presumably to his father. There had been scrapes with the law, minor incidents—Annabel knew little of the details—and whispers among rumormongers that the kid was a foul ball, a drifter, an un-handyman type of guy with no steady employment and no future, unless the Lerner name propelled him forward.

"Oh, Jeremiah is all right, Annabel. Still finding himself."

Not an especially prideful response. Annabel withheld any follow-up questions.

But Clarise wasn't finished. "I have nightmares about Jeremiah." Her sigh was prolonged and pained. "You know, the things I did wrong, the times I wasn't there for him. Bruce and I did our best, I think, 'our best' under the circumstances of our careers and schedules. I don't know, Annabel, maybe politics and parenting don't mix."

Annabel thought it interesting that Clarise chose her former husband's career as an example rather than her own career as a high-powered movie and TV executive. Jeremiah, Annabel knew through anecdotes from people who were friends of the Lerners when they were a couple, had spent most of his youth in his father's home, with full-time nannies. Clarise, who spent each week in Hollywood, had flown home to Washington on weekends to be with her husband and son. Not the ideal parenting situation, but not as bad as some others in which poverty exacerbates single-parent homes. Who was to judge their parenting record? Not Annabel. Not anyone other than the boy's mother and father.

Crowley returned to the terrace, a fresh drink in hand. A moment later, Mac came through the door and apologized for being held up. "I see you've found the bar," he said pleasantly. "Good. I think I'll find it, too. Be with you in a minute."

When Mac joined them, the conversation turned from Jeremiah Lerner to Ford's Theatre and its upcoming productions.

"We have the teen show coming up," Clarise said. "The Stages for all Ages program has really taken off. We can't handle the number of teens who want to participate."

"The *Post* sponsors that, doesn't it?" Mac asked.

"Among others," Crowley answered. "Metro Transit, DC Commission on the Arts. The support's been terrific, thanks to our friend here." He said to her, "Clarise, you're the best arm-twister I've ever known."

"Thank you," she said lightly, "but that's what the job is all about, isn't it?"

"That, and putting on plays," Mac offered.

"The easiest part," Clarise replied. "Keeping the money flowing, and dealing with all the different personalities, are a lot harder."

"Sydney Bancroft," Crowley said flatly.

Annabel laughed. "Still the bane of your existence, Clarise?"

Clarise's smile wasn't pure pleasure. "Oh, Sydney is all right," she said. "He's directing the student play and doing a good job, I'm told."

Crowley, who was leaning against the terrace's railing, came away from it and went to take the fourth chair, which was vacant. He stumbled as he did, caught himself with a hand on the green wrought-iron table, and sat heavily. "Sorry," he said. "Lost my balance."

*A little unbalanced by bourbon,* the others thought.

"Clarise is generous to a fault," Crowley said, downing some of the shimmering amber liquid in his glass.

"How so?" Mac asked.

"Keeping someone like Sydney on the payroll. It seems to me that the only contribution he makes is trouble."

"Oh, Bernard," Clarise said, like a teacher

to a child. To Mac and Annabel: "Bernard is always keeping his eye on the bottom line. That's good. But he sometimes doesn't appreciate the more subtle aspects of fund-raising. Sydney is a valuable commodity to me. His prior fame as an actor has opened many doors, behind which have lurked generous contributors. Sydney may be difficult at times, even outrageously so on occasion, but he fulfills an important function."

"And drives everyone crazy," Crowley said.

"He always had a reputation as a prima donna," Annabel said, referring to the British Bancroft's earlier time as a stage and film actor, particularly a series of successes years ago performing Shakespeare with the Royal Shakespeare Company at Stratford-upon-Avon. "He is prickly, I must say, but he can be charming, too."

"Hardly a word I'd use," said Crowley.

Mac ignored Crowley's comment and asked Clarise what Bancroft had had to say about the murder that morning.

"I haven't talked with him," she said. "He's out of town, I think. I was annoyed this morning. Sydney evidently called a meeting on the teen show knowing he couldn't be there. That's why there was a stage crew so early. They weren't happy."

Mac excused himself to assume the role of chef. Annabel had prepared a large salad and a rice dish; Mac's task was to pop flounder stuffed with crabmeat into the oven.

"Let's talk about more pleasant things," Annabel said. "All set for your confirmation hearing?"

Clarise frowned. "That is coming up soon, isn't it? I've been making the requisite tour of Senate committee members, making nice, putting them at ease that I won't allow the NEA to support what the senators consider blasphemous or pornographic."

"Succeeding?" Annabel asked.

Clarise laughed. "Who knows? It's obvious which committee members are for me, and which ones aren't. You can put Topper Sybers at the head of the latter group."

"Good ol' Senator Sybers, champion of virtue, protector of women and children, and hypocrite nonpareil," Crowley said.

"Actually, he was endearing when I visited him. We chatted for over an hour."

"Wrapped the old reprobate around your

little finger, huh, Clarise?" said Crowley, his words slightly slurred.

"I have no illusions. Being courteous to me informally doesn't necessarily translate into his vote. We'll just have to wait and see."

"Dinner is served!"

Later, after coffee, fresh fruit, and slivers of chocolate truffle cake from Watergate Bakery, Crowley excused himself. "I don't think I realized what an impact Nadia's murder has had on me," he said. "I'm exhausted."

"I'll call you a taxi," Annabel offered.

After Crowley had departed, Mac, Annabel, and Clarise, accompanied by Rufus, returned to the terrace for a taste of rare port that Mac had recently purchased at a wine auction.

"He's such a delight," Clarise said, referring to Ford's Theatre's controller with theatrical overstatement.

"He's obviously shaken by this morning's events," Mac said.

"He's not alone," said Clarise. "I dread tomorrow. The press will be camped at the door, and I'm due to have another series of briefings for the confirmation hearings. You can't believe the possible questions my so-called handlers come up with. I'm tempted to withdraw, leave the theatre, and buy a cabin in the Maine woods."

"Wouldn't help," Mac said. "Within a month you'd be thinking up ways to get back in the race. Ambition is an attribute, and a curse."

"*You* did it," Clarise said. "The two of you. Big-time law practices abandoned for an art gallery and mortarboard."

"Guilty," Mac said. "But the NEA needs you, Clarise. Most of our clients didn't need us, or shouldn't have. More coffee? Port?"

"Thanks, no. Being here has been wonderful. An oasis. And forget what I said about cabins in the woods. 'The NEA needs me.' I like that. Senator Topper Sybers needs me, whether he knows it or not. Everything was great. You're special people, special friends."

"Give a call tomorrow?" Annabel asked after calling a cab and walking Clarise to the elevators.

"Sure. Count on it."

Mac and Annabel again settled on the terrace after clearing the dinner table and loading the dishwasher.

"She's an impressive woman," Mac said. The clouds had broken, and a full, white moon seemed within their reach.

"And beautiful."

"I sometimes think you two look as though you could be sisters."

"I feel bad for her. She was questioning what sort of mother she's been."

"Jeremiah didn't have the most stable of homes, as I understand it. Classic case of mother and father pursuing demanding ambitions and schedules without a lot of time to devote to their kids."

"Which doesn't necessarily mean the kids have to turn out bad."

"Of course not. What's her relationship with Lerner? They seem to stay in touch."

"Yes, they do. She's told me they do it for the sake of their son, which can't be faulted."

"Maybe a little late."

"Maybe."

Mac stood and stretched. "Time to walk the beast."

"Maybe we should stop calling him that in front of him," Annabel said, following Mac to the kitchen where Rufus's leash hung from a wooden peg on the wall.

"What? Calling him 'the beast'?"

"Yeah. Maybe it hurts his feelings."

Mac looked at the blue Great Dane. "Are you offended, big guy?" he asked.

Rufus replied by clamping his large mouth on Mac's wrist and wagging his tail.

"Somehow, Annie, I think Rufus's ego is intact enough to overcome any emotional trauma. Be back in a flash."

They kissed, and Mac and *their* child disappeared through the door.

# SEVEN

"So, Mr. Partridge, tell us again what you claim you saw."

Detectives Klayman and Johnson, and Sergeant Hathaway, sat with the homeless man in an austere interrogation room at First District's headquarters building. The cops had brought Partridge two candy bars and a Coke from a snack machine in the lobby, which he consumed with gusto, complaining later that he would have preferred cheeseburgers and a Pepsi.

Now, with something in his stomach other than whiskey, and benefiting from a few hours' sleep and cold water splashed on his face, he sat at the scarred oak table with the bearing of a decrepit, disheveled CEO.

"I saw the man kill the woman," he said, belching and twitching. His right shoulder kept coming up in an involuntary motion, matched by rapid blinking of his right eye.

"What were you doing back there?"

"Relaxing," he said, pleased with his answer. "No law against a man being where he wants to be and relaxing."

"You were sleeping it off," Hathaway said.

"Just a nap. Takin' a nap." As though suddenly struck with a better answer, he shifted in his chair, lowered his voice, and said, "I was working undercover."

"Is that so?" said Johnson. "Were you there in the alley all night—working undercover?"

"All night? No. Got lots of places I go to. Was there, maybe, an hour, maybe two. Got relieved, had to give my report to the director. I'm hungry."

Johnson asked, "What did the man who killed the woman look like?"

"You hear me? I said I'm hungry. You want to talk to me, you got to feed me."

"What did he look like, Mr. Partridge?"

Partridge shifted in his straight-back chair and grimaced against a pain somewhere in his body. His shoulder and facial tic intensified, then seemed to subside as he decided to answer. "He was big, a big and strong kind a' guy. Mean-lookin', too. Russian, I think."

"Russian?"

"A mole. You can't trust the Russkies. Commie bastards'll stick it to you every way."

Johnson sighed and stood. "How big?" he asked. "As big as me?" Partridge looked up at the six-foot-three-inch Johnson.

"Bigger."

"Uh-huh." Johnson sat.

"How old?" Klayman asked. He wished the session were over. He hated everything about the interrogation room, its institutional look, battered furniture, heavy metal grill over the only window, but most of all the harsh light from the twin fluorescent bulbs hanging over the table.

"How would I know how old he was?" Partridge replied. "Might have been a young punk, might have been an old one. You never can tell with them."

"Maybe he was a young punk, huh? You know, twenty maybe, something like that?"

The old drunk's face fell into a pout. His

head came forward, his scraggly beard resting on his chest. He crossed his arms defiantly, looked up, and announced, "I have nothing more to say about it." The detectives were silent. "Is there a reward?"

"Might be," Hathaway replied. "Think you'd recognize the guy in a lineup?"

"How much is the reward?"

"We don't know yet."

"I don't want to stay here anymore. They'll be wondering where I am."

"Need a drink, Mr. Partridge?" Johnson said.

"I want my lawyer."

"You've got a lawyer?" Hathaway asked, chuckling. He motioned for Klayman and Johnson to follow him from the room. "You just sit tight, Mr. Partridge. We want to go out and—talk about the reward."

Partridge had a contented smile on his face as his questioners went to an area separated from the interrogation room by a large, one-way window through which they could observe him.

"It's a waste of time," Hathaway said. "He didn't see a damn thing. He's an old drunk, that's all."

"We let him go?"

"Yeah."

"We could hold him as a material witness," said Klayman. "Give him a bed and a
few meals."

"Forget it," Hathaway said. "We're not
running a flophouse for winos. Besides, it's
not like he's going to catch a plane for Paris
or something. He's got a vagrancy and pan-
handling sheet going way back. We'll find
him again if we need him. Get him another
candy bar and show him the door. The
smell's making me sick."

"Any thoughts that *he* might have killed
her?" Klayman asked.

Hathaway looked from Johnson to Klayman and back to Johnson. "Come on," he
said. "Get real."

Partridge was escorted to the street by
uniformed patrolmen, and Klayman and
Johnson followed Hathaway to his office.

"You get hold of that Bancroft character?" Hathaway asked.

"No. Answering machine," Klayman said.
"I thought we'd give him one more try before calling it a night."

Hathaway stroked the tuft of black hair
on the end of his chain and gave out with a
small laugh. "The night is young, pal. So're

you. You say the deceased's landlady was no help coming up with names of boyfriends?"

"Right," said Johnson. "But all that jewelry says somebody took good care of her."

"Somebody's got to know who she dated. She's not out of college that long. American University. Get over there and ask around. She must have had a roommate, friends, somebody who knew about her sex life."

"Okay," said Klayman. "After we try Bancroft again."

"And check everybody who worked with her in Lerner's office."

"What about the senator?" Klayman asked.

"I need the word from up top before we contact him. Don't be strangers. Keep me in the loop. I don't want any surprises."

Klayman's and Johnson's desks butted up against each other in the detectives' room.

Johnson said to Klayman: "Ricky, got to call Etta, tell her I'll be late again."

Klayman thought it was good he didn't have to call anyone, but didn't say it to his partner. Besides, there was that fleeting moment when he wished someone were waiting for him to arrive home; that thought came and went now and then. He heard Mo say, "Hey, baby, got to put in the overtime again. That kid who got killed at Ford's Theatre." After a pause, and a sly glance at Klayman, he said, "Of course I love you. Don't wait up."

Klayman picked up his phone and dialed Sydney Bancroft's number. The British actor's live voice startled him.

"Mr. Bancroft?"

"Yes?"

"I'm Detective Klayman, First District Crimes Against Persons."

"'Crimes Against Persons'? Who else could crimes be committed against?"

"Used to be called Homicide."

"Oh, I see."

"I'd like to be able to come and talk with you."

"About the death of that dear, dear girl, Nadia."

"Yes, sir, that's right."

"How dreadful to die that way, at the hands of a madman in a filthy, barren alley. We all wish to die peacefully in a warm, dry place in the presence of loved ones, don't we?"

"Yes, sir. That would be preferable. Would it be too much of an inconvenience to come to your home tonight?"

Johnson frowned at Klayman and mouthed, Would it be too much of an inconvenience . . . ?

"To determine whether I killed her, I presume," Bancroft said slowly and with practiced diction.

"Just to ask a few questions, sir," Klayman said. "It won't take long. My partner, Detective Johnson and I, are working the case and—"

"I would love to meet you and your partner," Bancroft said, exaggerating his pleasure. "Real, live detectives. Are you like those on TV?"

Klayman laughed. "No, sir, I'm afraid not. We can be there in a half hour, if that's okay."

"That is *quite* okay," Bancroft said. "You undoubtedly have my address."

"Yes, sir, we do."

"Then come as quickly as you can. I am tingling with anticipation."

Klayman hung up and shook his head.

"He quote Shakespeare to you?" Johnson asked.

"No, but he talks like an actor. I think we're in for an interesting evening. Come on. Let's get it over with."

Bancroft lived in a well-maintained, small apartment building on tree-lined G Street, in Foggy Bottom, not far from the Kennedy Center, the Watergate complex, and George Washington University. The two men said little as they made their way across the city in their unmarked car.

"This one's yours, Ricky," Johnson said as they turned down G.

"What do you mean?"

"He's all yours. Actors make me nervous."

"Why?"

"I don't know. They're always—well, you know, always onstage. You never know whether they're being themselves or playing some part."

"Okay, I'll lead."

They parked in front and entered the lobby, where a middle-aged uniformed doorman was reading a magazine. Klayman flashed his badge: "Mr. Bancroft is expecting us."

"It's about that intern, isn't it?" the doorman said, getting up from behind his small
desk and going to the intercom board.
Johnson and Klayman said nothing. "She
worked for Senator Lerner," the doorman
said, running his index finger down the row
of buttons. "Like what happened with Condit, huh, intern and big shot politician?"

Johnson was about to tell the doorman to
speed it up when he pushed a button, and
the now familiar voice of Sydney Bancroft
came through a small speaker. "I know,
Morris, I know," he said in his distinctive
British accent. "Scotland Yard is here to au-
dition. Send them up by all means."

Johnson and Klayman smiled at each
other as the doorman opened an inside
door. "Elevator's on your right. Hope you
catch who killed her. He's on Seven.
Seven D."

Sydney Bancroft stood in the open door
to his apartment as Klayman and Johnson
stepped off the elevator. The picture he presented was unusual enough to cause the
detectives to stop in the middle of the carpeted hallway and stare. The British actor
wore a yellow T-shirt, a black, waist-length
leather jacket with silver studs, jeans, and

black cowboy boots etched in red leather. His thinning hair, worn long, had an orange tint common with male hair dyes. What especially struck Klayman was how short Bancroft was, no taller than five six, or seven. His screen presence, at least as Klayman remembered it, was that of a taller man. His face was thin and pinched, nose long and pointed, cheeks sunken, skin slightly jaundiced. Was he wearing makeup? It looked that way.

"Ah, the cavalry has arrived," Bancroft announced, his face breaking into a smile. "Welcome, welcome. You are . . . ?"

"Detective Klayman, Mr. Bancroft. This is Detective Johnson."

"As you promised you would be. Please. Come in." He stepped back and bowed slightly as he indicated with a hand that they were to enter the apartment. "As is said, sorry to meet under such unfortunate circumstances."

They passed through a small foyer and into the living room where rock-and-roll music came through speakers while a black-and-white movie played on a large-screen TV. Klayman recognized the film almost immediately. *Fool's Gold,*" he said.

"Yes," said a pleased Bancroft. "I see you are a connoisseur of fine films."

"It was a good movie," said Klayman. "You were good in it."

"Thank you. Thank you indeed. Please, make yourselves at home." He went to a table and lifted a snifter in a toast of sorts. "Join me?"

"Thank you, no," Klayman said, joining Johnson on a couch. "But you go ahead."

Bancroft took a sip. "The bartenders call it the 'stabilizer' aboard the QE2 and other ships. Half brandy, half port, quite effective for a queasy stomach. Indian food. I had Indian food tonight and should have known better. I've lectured on Shakespeare on the QE2 a number of times. Wonderful experiences. Sure you won't join me?"

"My stomach's fine," Johnson said.

Bancroft pulled up a yellow director's chair with the title of one of his movies stenciled on its back. A half dozen other such chairs were scattered about the room. The walls were covered with large posters from Bancroft's film and stage appearances; four life-sized mannequins dressed in period costumes occupied the room's shadowy corners.

"Now," said Bancroft, continuing to sip from his drink, "let us talk about Nadia." He squeezed his eyes shut and shuddered. When he opened them, he displayed a wan smile. "What a lovely young thing, so vibrant, so filled with joie de vivre."

"We understand you were out of town last night," Klayman said. Johnson pulled a pad and pen from his pocket and was poised to write.

"That is correct," Bancroft said, "unless you don't consider Alexandria to be 'out of town.'"

"You were in Alexandria last night?" Klayman said. Alexandria was only a fifteen-minute cab ride to Ford's Theatre.

"Yes. Visiting a dear friend."

"You stayed with this friend overnight?"

"Correct again, Detective."

"Your friend's name?"

Bancroft drew himself up to full height in his chair and slowly shook his head. "I see no reason to inconvenience my friend," he said, one leg over the other, the boot bobbing up and down.

"I'm sorry, Mr. Bancroft, but you'll have to give us his name."

"To see whether I was actually there at

the time poor Nadia was killed. Sorry, Detective, but—"

"Maybe you'd rather come to headquarters and discuss it there," Mo Johnson said in his big baritone.

"What a marvelous voice," Bancroft said. "Reminds me of my dear friend James Earl Jones. Have you ever considered acting, doing commercials?"

"The name, Mr. Bancroft," Johnson said in a tone that carried with it an implicit threat.

"Ah-ha," said Bancroft, draining his drink. " 'Steed threatens steed, in high and boastful neighs.' "

"Pardon?"

"Shakespeare. *Henry the Fifth.* My friend's name is Saul. Saul Jones." He laughed. "It sounds as though the only people I know are named Jones, doesn't it? Well, I assure you that Mr. Saul Jones's personality is not nearly as bland as his name."

"Address and phone number?"

After Bancroft had reluctantly given that information, he was asked about his activities the previous night, where he and his friend went, whether they were together the entire time—boilerplate questions out of the handbook on a suspect's alibi. When he was asked about his relationship with Nadia Zarinski, he said, "You do realize, I'm sure, that I have no obligation to speak with you?"

"That's right, Mr. Bancroft," Johnson responded.

"I am entitled to a lawyer."

"Of course. But we're not here because you're a suspect in the murder," Klayman said. "We're simply questioning anyone who might be able to help us understand something about the deceased, and maybe give us some leads as to any persons who might have wanted her dead."

"Who could that possibly be?"

"How well did you know her?" Johnson asked gruffly.

"Not well at all. I'm afraid I cannot possibly be of any help to you. She was simply a pretty young thing who was enamored of theatre and seemed to enjoy being close to it. I suppose there was a modicum of hero worship in it, the starstruck young woman wanting to rub elbows with the stars." His tone was world-weary.

*Stars like you, I suppose,* Johnson thought, not kindly.

Klayman had just started to ask another question when Bancroft silenced him with a finger to the lips and a loud "Shhhhhh." The actor turned to the TV, where he was playing a romantic scene with an actress. They stared at the screen, and at Bancroft, in silence. The look of disgust on Johnson's face wasn't lost on Klayman, although Bancroft was too involved with what was happening on the screen to be aware of anything else.

As Klayman watched, he was reminded of how handsome a much younger Sydney Bancroft had been, not quite a leading man, but an actor with an intensity, eyes that drew you in, a nicely modulated voice, subtle virility—an actor who was undoubtedly attractive to women in his heyday, moviegoers and offscreen romantic interests alike. Klayman tried to recall what he'd read about the actor's marital history. One marriage to a British actress early in the career, maybe another. Always lots of women, of course, plenty of drunken scenes, unpleasant public displays, a woman he slapped once in a restaurant bringing charges, an underage girl, if Klayman's memory served him right. The scandal sheets had always focused on

Bancroft's hard drinking and its impact upon his artistic temperament. He'd become increasingly difficult, the detective had read, alienating directors and producers to the extent that roles had become scarce and age diminished them further.

The scene ended, and Bancroft turned back to the detectives. "I'm sure you virile young men never have a problem when playing your bedroom scenes. But let me assure you, it is never easy with cameras and lights and dozens of people gawking at you as you attempt to portray the seductive leading man."

"Yeah, I'm sure that's true," Johnson said.

"Any further questions?" Bancroft asked, standing to signal that the visit was about to be terminated.

"Just one more," Klayman said. "We were told by people at Ford's Theatre that you showed a particular interest in Nadia Zarinski."

"Oh?"

"They said you tended to try to . . . well, become close to her. I don't know, touching her, things like that."

"And who might have made this out-landish claim?"

"That's not important."

"It is to me. I insist upon being able to face my accuser."

"Is there any truth to it?" Mo Johnson asked.

"Absolutely not. While my libido might have suffered slightly in the aging process, I assure you I am still a virile man who is blessed with numerous female companions, none of whom are below the age of thirty. I have absolutely no interest in very young women, except perhaps to enjoy them in photographs, and I further ensure you that my interest in the young Ms. Zarinski was purely as someone she could look up to. No, my new friends, I never stayed close to her or touched her, as you so crudely stated. I barely knew her. She was there only occasionally at night. This is preposter-ous. I feel like John Wilkes Booth, being ac-cused of some vile act."

" 'Accused of' a vile act?" Klayman said. "He did kill Lincoln."

"And he had his reasons, I assure you. I have studied Mr. Booth in depth. A brilliant actor and dedicated activist. I don't believe there is another person in this world who knows more about Booth, the inner man and great actor, than yours truly."

"I'm a bit of a Lincoln buff myself," Klayman said.

"Are you? How impressive. One would not expect that of a policeman."

"What do you expect of a policeman, Mr. Bancroft?" Johnson asked.

"Certainly not scholarship, sir, and I mean no offense to you personally."

"That's nice of you," Johnson said. "By the way, how come you never showed up at the theatre for the meeting this morning? They say you called it."

"And they are mistaken, I assure you. I have little to do with the technical side of things. There must have been a miscommunication."

"Thanks for your time, Mr. Bancroft," Klayman said, extending his hand. "It was a pleasure meeting you."

"I am glad to have been of help."

Johnson didn't offer his hand as the detectives left the apartment.

"He's a trip, isn't he?" the doorman asked as they walked through the lobby.

"Interesting gentleman," Klayman said.

"You ever see him bring young women up to the apartment?" Johnson asked.

"Doorman-tenant privilege," the doorman said, chuckling.

Johnson glared at him.

"Sometimes," the doorman said. "Young. Old. You mean young like the kid who got it over at the theatre? No. No teeny-boppers. At least I can't remember any."

"She wasn't a teenybopper," Johnson said sternly.

"I didn't mean anything by it," said the doorman. "He's really a pretty nice guy, polite and all, always holding the door for the women in the building."

"That's nice to hear," Klayman said, leading Johnson to the street.

"What did you think?" Klayman asked once they were in their car.

"Pain in the ass. Pretentious bastard. You catch that getup he was wearing? Man, there's nothing sadder than an old guy trying to look young."

"I kind of liked him."

"You would. You starstruck, too? Only he's no star. What's he reduced to, working with teenagers at Ford's Theatre? Some star."

"I wonder why."

"Why what?"

"Why he works at Ford's Theatre. Why he'd want to. Why they'd want him."

"We should ask."

"We will. What do you want to do now?"

"Aside from cuddling up next to Etta? Let's call this Saul Jones."

"Yeah, let's."

"You think Bancroft might have done the girl?"

"Done as in had sex with her, or done as in kill her?"

"Either one. Or both."

Klayman said nothing as he pulled his cell phone from his jacket pocket and dialed the number for Saul Jones that Bancroft had given them.

# EIGHT

Rick Klayman entered his apartment on Wisconsin Avenue, not far from the National Cathedral, turned on a floor lamp, and looked across the room to his answering machine. The message light was flashing; he counted the blinks, seven messages. He checked his watch. Almost ten-thirty. Always a dilemma; too late to return calls, or early enough? Depended upon the caller, of course. Night people or day people? Early to bed or up watching late movies?

He turned on a table lamp in his bedroom and slowly undressed, emptying pockets, blue blazer first, which he carefully placed on a hanger in the closet facing in the same direction as other jackets; then inserted wooden shoe trees into black loafers which

he returned to their designated empty
space on the closet floor; gray trousers
joined other pants in their own section; tie
carefully unknotted and nested with others
on a battery-powered rotating tie rack; and
blue button-down shirt removed and held
up to the light to ascertain its usefulness for
another day. It passed muster and was
draped over the back of a desk chair. He
deposited his underwear into a hamper, got
into pale blue short pajamas, slippers, and a
white terry cloth robe, and went to the answering machine, where he wrote down the
callers' names, numbers, and messages.
The seventh call was from Mo, which surprised Klayman. He'd seen him just a half
hour ago, when they'd signed out at headquarters.

"It's Rick."

"Yeah, Ricky, thanks for getting back so
soon. You got home okay, huh?"

"Of course."

"You alone?"

Johnson meant whether there was a
woman with him. "Yes, I'm alone."

"Ricky, you buy this guy Saul Jones's
story?"

"So far. He says he and Bancroft were

together all night, never lost sight of each other. They both said they had dinner at Duangrat's and Rabieng, in Baileys Cross-roads. Jones had the AmEx receipt to prove it."

"Yeah. So how come Bancroft said he had a bellyache from too much Indian food?"

"Meaning?"

"It's a Thai restaurant, Rick. Etta was there a month ago."

"So Bancroft got his cuisines confused. They're all the same when your stomach's on fire. We can stop by the restaurant and see if anyone remembers them together."

"I think they got together on their story. Too pat. Know what I mean?"

"Yeah, I do."

"I didn't like either of 'em."

"So I gathered. Look, I've got a bunch of calls to return. See you in the morning. We'll head over to American University and scout up her friends."

"Right, Ricky. Have a good night."

Klayman winced and hung up. He pre-ferred that Johnson not call him Ricky, al-though he never made a fuss, knowing that his partner didn't mean anything demeaning. Mo would outgrow it—hopefully.

He perused the names and numbers on the pad. Two calls from his mother in New York; his sister from Boston; a neighbor wondering whether they'd caught the person who killed the young woman at Ford's Theatre, and saying it was comforting to have a police officer living in the building; the building's super informing all tenants that there would be no hot water the following day between noon and four due to boiler repairs; and a call from Rachel Kessler, whom Klayman had been seeing on an irregular basis.

"Just wanted to touch base, Rick," Rachel's voice said, "and see if you were up to dinner or a drink some night this week. Are you involved in the murder today at the theatre? I know how much you love that place. Call me, okay?"

He dialed his mother's number.

His father answered. "How are you, Richard?"

"Fine, Dad. You?"

"Aches and pains, but I'm alive. Took a breath when I got up this morning . . ."

*. . . and it worked, so no complaints.* Rick

smiled as he silently completed the statement. It was one of his father's favorite
lines.

"Dad, Mom called and left a couple of
messages."

"I'll get her. Are you involved in the murder there in Washington?"

*Which murder?* Rick thought. There
would be a dozen murders in D.C. that day.
"The young woman at Ford's Theatre? Yes,
I am. My partner and I are working on the
case."

"Mr. Johnson?"

"Right. Mo and I are—"

"How are you two getting along?"

"Great. Why?"

"Well, you're so different, Richard. Very—
different."

He could see his father standing in their
small living room in the Bronx, thin and
stooped, wiry gray hair beyond taming,
thick glasses, a two-day growth of gray
beard; he shaved only occasionally since
retiring as a cutter in the garment district.

"Is Mom there?"

"I'll get her."

His mother and father had been vehe-
mently against Rick's joining the Washing-

ton MPD—any MPD, for that matter. His degree from City College of New York had been in history, and he'd graduated near the top of his class. The world was open to him: law, medicine, investment banking—all respected and lucrative professions, from his father's perspective, options that were unappealing to their son.

Rick had been fascinated with law enforcement since his early years, envisioning himself as a cop, a detective, questioning people, solving puzzles, and bringing criminals to justice. *Doing something.* There was a fantasy dimension to such visions when he was young. He saw himself as considerably taller and more muscular than he was in reality, athletic, able to scale tall fences in mean alleys in pursuit of bad guys, or drop on them from fire escapes. Kid stuff. Cops and robbers. But he learned early in his career as a uniformed cop with the Washington MPD that his self-perception of his physical abilities was, more accurately, self-deception.

He'd been walking a downtown beat when he came upon a mugging of an older woman. The attacker was a bear of a man, which didn't deter Klayman from leaping on his back as he tried to flee the scene. The mugger tossed Klayman off, slammed him against a wall, and was pummeling him when another uniformed cop intervened and helped subdue the mugger. Klayman broke a finger in the fracas and spent a week on medical leave. It wouldn't be his last physical challenge as a cop.

Despite his slender build, he earned a reputation as a fearless cop, willing to put his life on the line in almost any situation, especially when it involved the safety of a fellow officer. Mo Johnson was somewhat aware of that reputation when he was paired with the skinny Jewish kid from New York, and had a chance to experience it firsthand during their early months together.

They were working backup for an undercover narcotics officer involved in a buy-and-bust operation on Martin Luther King Boulevard in the Anacostia section of the city, an impoverished, hardscrabble area seething with crime, much of it fueled by drug trafficking. Their target was a young Hispanic drug dealer, Manuel "Chi Chi" Ortiz, with whom the undercover detective had forged a relationship. Klayman and

Johnson were stationed in an unmarked car parked around the corner from the buy; a small loudspeaker delivered what was being said between the narc and Ortiz.

At first, only the voices of the detective and Ortiz were picked up by a tiny microphone worn beneath the cop's jacket. But then other voices were heard, three or four, speaking rapid-fire Spanish and black street slang, sounding angry. Then the spray of voices was shattered by rapid gunshots.

Klayman peeled away from the curb and the car careered around the corner. The undercover narcotics detective was facedown on the sidewalk. Klayman barked into his radio, "Officer down! Officer down!" and gave the location. He and Johnson leaped from the car and pursued Ortiz and another dealer, who disappeared behind a row of boarded-up stores. Johnson pointed at an alley to his left; Klayman went in that direction. Johnson followed the route taken by the dealers, which led to a garbage-strewn lot separated from an auto repair shop and junkyard by a crumbling six-foot-high concrete wall.

As Johnson sprinted toward the rear of the stores, the dealers had almost reached the wall and were preparing to scale it. But Ortiz suddenly stopped, ducked behind a small Dumpster overflowing with trash, looked back at Johnson, and raised a Smith & Wesson nine-millimeter automatic. As he did, Johnson tripped over a broken, twisted bicycle frame and sprawled a few feet from the dealer, his own weapon flying from his hand and landing six feet away. Ortiz slowly stood, the pistol held steadily in both hands and pointed at Johnson. Johnson came up on his haunches and extended a hand toward Ortiz, who was dressed in a black T-shirt with the sleeves cut off, black pants, black boots, and wearing a red bandanna on his head. Ortiz smiled, and tensed, ready to fire.

"Hey!" Klayman yelled. He'd entered the area from the other direction, weapon drawn, and stood fifteen feet from the Dumpster. The dealer turned and aimed at Klayman, the smile still on his lips.

"Get down, Ricky!" Johnson called.

But Klayman began closing the gap between him and Ortiz, walking deliberately, step-by-step, weapon held out in front with both hands and aimed at the dealer's head.

"Don't be stupid," he said in a firm voice. "Drop it. Just drop it."

Johnson crawled toward his gun but never took his eyes from the face-off between Klayman and Ortiz. It was as though Klayman had hypnotized the dealer, a cat stalking a mesmerized bird. Johnson reached his weapon when Klayman was only a few feet from Ortiz. He came up to a sitting position and squeezed off a single shot. It struck Ortiz in the left temple, shattering his skull and sending a plume of blood into the air. Ortiz's finger froze on the trigger of his pistol as he fell to his right, the remaining rounds from his weapon popping like Fourth of July firecrackers.

Johnson scrambled to his feet and joined Klayman, who stood over Ortiz's lifeless body.

"You crazy bastard," Johnson muttered, his breath coming hard. "Why didn't you take cover?"

"He would have shot you," Klayman said. His eyes were still on Ortiz. He was numb, disassociated from the reality of what had just happened and its aftermath. Johnson had lowered his weapon to his side; Klayman still held his in both hands, pointed at the dead drug dealer. They heard sirens and cars coming to a noisy halt in front of the ramshackle buildings.

Johnson shook his head. "You should've taken cover, Rick."

Klayman returned his gun to its holster beneath his arm. He nodded. "I know," he said, walking away. "I know."

Because Johnson had used his weapon and a death had occurred, a department inquiry was conducted, a pro forma hearing. There was no question that the veteran detective had been justified in shooting Ortiz in order to not only save his own life but his partner's as well. When Klayman was asked during the proceedings whether he considered his actions to have saved Johnson's life, he replied in a voice so soft that the chairman of the investigative panel had to ask him to speak up: "I don't remember anything about it," he said. "It's all a blank."

He didn't have to recall the incident, for word of his bravery quickly made the rounds at First District headquarters. Johnson recounted the experience every chance he got, and Klayman basked in its glory.

\* \* \*

"Are you feeling all right, Richard?" his mother asked.

"I feel fine. You?"

"All right, I suppose, considering my age. Did you speak with your sister today?"

"No. She left a message while I was out. I'll call after we hang up."

"Please do. She isn't happy." She lowered her voice. "I don't think the marriage is going well. Harry is such a difficult man, so stubborn. I wish—"

"I just got in, Mom, and I haven't had dinner. I'll call Susan. I promise."

"Good. I worry so about you and Susan. The doctor says it isn't healthy for me to worry. How is your lady friend?"

"I—who are you talking about?"

"I don't remember her name. You mentioned her once. Rachel, maybe. Or Roxanne."

"Rachel. She's fine. Heard from her today, in fact. Have to run. Glad you and Dad are doing okay. Love you both."

He was relieved when he reached his sister's answering machine. He heated up a can of tomato soup, sliced some bread, and ate in front of the TV. Nadia Zarinski's murder was the lead story on the eleven o'clock news.

"An intern who worked for Senator Bruce Lerner was found murdered early this morning in Baptist Alley, behind Ford's Theatre. The victim, Nadia Zarinski, had been bludgeoned to death by what a police spokesman has termed a blunt object. Ms. Zarinski, who graduated from American University, had worked as a part-time volunteer at Ford's Theatre. There had been rumors of a romantic relationship between Ms. Zarinski and Senator Lerner, which was denied by all parties involved. Police say they have no leads at this point in the investigation."

Klayman clicked off the set and went to his computer in a corner of the living room, where he brought up one of many electronic folders he'd created, each devoted to an unsolved murder to which he and Johnson had been assigned. This particular folder dealt with the disappearance a year earlier of another congressional intern, approximately Nadia Zarinski's age and who looked a great deal like her: five feet four inches tall, face with prominent cheekbones (chipmunk cheeks), brown eyes and hair, full-figured. The missing girl, whose name was Connie Marshall, had interned with the House majority leader. Like the Lerner-Zarinski connection, there were rumors that the congressman and Ms. Marshall had had an affair, but that had never been proved.

He stared at the photos of Connie Marshall provided by family and friends and suffered the same emotions he always felt when opening that file. The search for her had consumed months, without results. She was a missing person, presumed dead. No one searched for her anymore.

He created a new file, **NADIA ZARINSKI,** and typed in what information the day had delivered. He made a series of notes that reflected what the next investigative steps would be, saved the file, and closed the computer.

Were the cases connected? Had Nadia's murderer also been involved with Connie Marshall's disappearance and presumed death?

With any luck, he'd play a role in answering that question.

He was physically tired but mentally alert. He took a textbook from his desk—he occasionally took courses as a nonmatriculated student at George Washington University; the course he was about to start covered the 1920s and '30s—and read until sleep came. His final conscious thoughts were of Nadia Zarinski's lifeless, battered body in a shabby alley behind Ford's Theatre.

Morning couldn't come fast enough.

# NINE

In the early twentieth century, the eminent Virginia architect Waddy B. Wood designed more than thirty elegant homes, some of them mansion size, in an area that was an extension of the exclusive Dupont Circle residential community. The area was known as Kalorama—Greek for "beautiful view"— and its stately Norman, Tudor, and Georgian homes offered stunning views of Rock Creek Park. One of the more imposing houses, in the châteauesque style inspired by Paris's École des Beaux-Arts, was the residence of Virginia senator Bruce Lerner.

Lerner and his then wife, Clarise, had purchased the house in the early years of their marriage, and it was to there they'd brought their only child, Jeremiah, home from the hospital. The previous owner had turned it into a bed-and-breakfast, a highly unpopular move with his wealthy neighbors, who were grateful when it again functioned as a private home for a distinguished U.S. senator and his family.

It was a large house, with twelve-foot-high ceilings, period moldings, and hard-wood floors throughout its sixteen rooms. There were seven fireplaces, four baths, a separate two-bedroom apartment, maid's quarters, a three-car garage with a deck above that afforded views of Washington's monuments from its front, and from its rear, the park. Senator and Mrs. Lerner paid $800,000 for it in the late '70s; its current worth was estimated to be well in excess of $2 million.

This night, Lerner sat on the deck, a glass of scotch on the rocks in his hand. His pose in the chair was relaxed, long legs in gray slacks stretched in front of him, double-breasted blue blazer hanging open, blue-and-white-checkered button-down shirt un-buttoned. Internally, he churned. The glass he held dangled at his side, hovering inches from the tile floor.

"How inconsiderate," the woman in another chair said, referring to the sound of music being played too loud from somewhere, a car perhaps.

"I'm sorry," he said, realizing she was there and turning to look at her.

"The music. I don't understand why people think others should be subjected to their taste in music."

"It wouldn't bother you so much if it were Mozart," he said, returning his attention to the city's lights visible in the distance.

"It wouldn't bother me so much if it were anything other than what it is. You were saying before about the media calls."

"Oh, yes. They won't let it go, those damn rumors about Nadia and me." His voice was low and well modulated, and he spoke with deliberate slowness, a southern pace that he tended to exaggerate at times.

The woman, Shirley Lester, had been seen frequently with Lerner at myriad social functions over the past six months. They'd been friends for years. Lerner had been especially close to Shirley's deceased husband, Vice Admiral Nelson Lester, the navy department's inspector general. After her husband died, Shirley forged a closer friendship with the bachelor senator that quickly led—too quickly, some said—to a romantic one.

"Nelson used to say Shakespeare was wrong," she said. "It isn't the lawyers who need killing. It's the journalists."

"He was right, considering I was a lawyer." He drew on his drink. "Nadia was flirtatious, Shirley. I don't doubt she would have entertained an affair with me."

"She flirted with you?"

"Yes. Hung around after hours a lot. Liked to squeeze in tight spots with me. She was damned tempting."

Shirley didn't ask how tempting Nadia had been. Truth was, she wasn't sure whether she would believe his denials, any more than she had when the rumors first started floating over Washington. It might have been important to her if she had designs on Lerner as a potential husband. But she knew that wasn't in the cards, nor did she want it to be. She was content being the attractive blond woman on his arm, reflecting in his stature, being on the A List of invitees, and enjoying the speculation that went with the role. She didn't have illusions about Bruce Lerner. He liked women, and wouldn't be content with only one. He was on the downside of life, as handsome and virile as he might be. So many women, so little time. She would enjoy his company for as long as it lasted.

"Her parents called me," he said.

"When?"

"Earlier this evening. They flew up from Florida."

"What did they say?"

"I didn't speak with them. My AA took the call. They want to meet to talk about Nadia."

"You'll have to, won't you?"

"At some point." His sigh was pained. "I suppose they want to rehash the rumor."

"You can't blame them, Bruce. They've just lost a daughter."

"Because someone murdered her. That has nothing to do with me."

"Have you heard from the police?"

"No. That's next. My press officer is preparing a statement for the press."

The sound of loud music abruptly stopped, leaving them in silent darkness, which neither of them violated. That was left to a housekeeper who came to the deck and said to Lerner, "A call, sir. In the library."

"Excuse me, Shirley." To the housekeeper: "Please refresh Mrs. Lester's drink, Maria."

Lerner's library was downstairs. He descended the wide, carpeted staircase, crossed a spacious tiled foyer, passed through open double doors, and settled behind a leather-inlaid desk. The room's only light came from a brass gooseneck lamp. One of two buttons on a phone was lighted.

"Hello?"

"Bruce, it's Clarise."

"How are you?"

"I've been better. You?"

"Just fine. You're calling about Nadia Zarinski."

"As a matter of fact, I'm not, although it's not as though it isn't on my mind. God, Bruce, what dreadful timing."

"I hadn't thought of it that way."

"I envy you, it not interfering with your life."

He laughed quietly. "Oh, it interferes all right, Clarise, but I've learned to ignore distractions. If you aren't calling about Nadia, it must be Jeremiah. Has he done something stupid again?"

"I'm calling about the hearing, Bruce. Remember? I *have* been nominated to head the NEA."

"Oh, yes. Of course I remember. Let's stop fencing, Clarise. What about the nomination?"

"I want to get together and discuss it with you. I'm worried."

"Why? You're a shoo-in."

"I don't see it that way. This unfortunate incident at the theatre might muddy things. You won't meet with me about it?"

"Of course I will. When?"

"Tonight?"

"I'm occupied tonight."

" 'Occupied.' A quaint way to put it. Bruce, please, I really do need to talk with you about the hearing. If not tonight, then—"

"An hour?"

"Where?"

"Your apartment."

"Fine. Thank you."

"The least I can do for the next head of the National Endowment for the Arts—and the mother of my child. No need to go out of your way to entertain me. I've eaten."

Shirley Lester was coming down the stairs as he left the library. She flashed a wide smile. "I know," she said, "affairs of state. High-level meeting."

"Something like that."

"I got used to it. Nelson was always fleeing the house in the middle of the night. Thanks for a lovely dinner, Bruce, and the concert. I thought the cello player's intonation was faulty, but failing that, it was enjoyable."

She kissed his cheek; he pulled her into an embrace. "I like that perfume," he said into her hair. "You should wear it more often."

"I'll try to remember." She stepped back. "Maria called a taxi for me while you were on the phone. It's in front."

"Good."

She avoided his attempt to kiss her on the lips, moved to the front door, turned, and said, "Call if there's anything I can do to help, Bruce." His expression was quizzical. "This business about Nadia Whatever Her Name Is. I mean it, darling. Just call."

# TEN

For Moses Johnson, physical fitness was an obsession. He had all the usual reasons: feeling and thinking better, relieving stress, keeping weight off, looking better, increased stamina on the job, sex appeal, an enhanced masculine image. On a deeper level, it represented a shield against mortality. There were times that he wondered whether he would be Nature's exception, never dying, which would be a good thing because as far as he was concerned, the world, more specifically his family and the Washington MPD, simply could not function without him.

He was up early Wednesday morning, before the sun, leaving Etta and their sons asleep. After splashing water on his face and exchanging pajamas for shorts and a T-shirt, he headed for the finished basement of their home in Rockville, Maryland, where an array of exercise equipment stood at attention. One wall of the room held floor-to-ceiling shelves on which Mo's extensive collection of jazz LPs and CDs were alphabetically arranged. There were more than a thousand recordings, the majority of them LPs, whose warmer sound he preferred to that of compact discs, the occasional scratch and pop be damned. Not only was Johnson a devoted collector of recorded jazz, he'd built a sizable library of books about the music and its innovators—Ellington, Armstrong, Waller, Tatum, Parker, and Goodman—which occupied their own special place in the family room. It was more than just a love of the music, however. Mo was a scholar of jazz, knew as much as anyone making a living at it, and prided himself on being able to identify a soloist after hearing only a few bars of improvisation.

His workout routine seldom varied. He perused the albums on the shelves and chose the recording of Duke Ellington's famous 1956 appearance at the Newport Jazz Festival to set that morning's pace. As the first strains of "Diminuendo and Crescendo in Blue" filled the room, he positioned himself in front of a full-length mirror and started with a few minutes of stretching exercises before getting on a stationary bike. He pedaled until the historic recording finished, his speed increasing as the band roared through a series of choruses featuring tenor saxophonist Paul Gonsalves, the seven thousand people in attendance screaming their approval until the orchestra brought the piece to a rattling conclusion. He wiped perspiration from his face with a towel, dropped the needle in the first groove of "Jeep's Blues" featuring Johnny Hodges, and lifted weights for as long as that song played.

Etta was in the kitchen when he came upstairs. "You are some sweaty mess," she said, successfully avoiding his attempt to hug her.

He laughed and poured himself orange juice. "Got to sweat out all the toxic fluids, Etta. Purify the system."

"Is that so? You sound like that Sterling Hayden character in *Dr. Strangelove,* with his vital bodily fluids. Where are you off to this morning?"

"Rick and I are heading for American University, see if we can rustle up some of her friends, lovers, anybody who knows what her private life was like."

"A boyfriend? Is that who you've decided killed her?"

"Haven't decided anything yet. But this has all the trappings of a romance gone wrong. Her landlady says she was a sexy little thing, you know, liked to flaunt it. Wore skimpy clothes, things like that."

"We're blaming the victim now, are we?"

"Of course not. You know me better than that."

"What I know is that you'll do the right thing. Go on now, get in the shower. Pancakes?"

"Eggs. Over easy. Dry toast."

He stole a quick kiss on his way from the room, showered and dressed, and joined her for breakfast in an alcove off the kitchen they'd added the previous year.

"You'll be late?" she asked as they parted on the front steps.

"Probably."

"Say hello to Rick for me. Invite him over for dinner. It's been a while."

"Yeah, I will. You have a good one."

Klayman and Johnson met up at headquarters, where their boss, Herman Hathaway, conducted a briefing.

"Okay," said Hathaway, "here's what
we've got. One dead girl, hit in the head and
face, no credible suspects. Old drunk says
he saw it happen, which is bull. Landlady
says she was a flirt, sexy, things like that.
Had a box full of expensive jewelry. Rumor
that she had an affair with Senator Bruce
Lerner. Unlikely it was a random killing. No
reason for her to be in that alley alone at
that hour. Family needs to be interviewed.
They're in town."

"We're going over to the university," Klayman said.

"*We're?* Your togetherness is touching.
We're stretched thin today. You can meet up
later. Rick, you go to her school and dig
around for friends, boyfriends, whatever.
Mo, I want you to interview the parents.
They're due here in a half hour."

Johnson walked Klayman to the parking
lot, where Klayman's unmarked car was
parked.

"Catch up with you what, around noon?"
Johnson said.

"Good. Let's meet at the Thai restaurant

where Bancroft and Jones said they'd had dinner. Make it one, okay?"

"You got it."

Klayman's first stop at American University's main campus on Massachusetts Avenue, NW, was the Hamilton Building, in which some of the school's administrative offices were located. The university had been founded in 1891 by the Methodist Church as a graduate school, and eventually evolved into a nondenominational university with strong schools of communications and education. He was ushered to the office of Wendell Jessup, vice president of student affairs. Jessup, a bald, courtly gentleman in a three-piece gray suit, warmly greeted the detective and offered coffee, which Klayman declined.

"I was shocked when I read about Ms. Zarinski," Jessup said, "and anticipated a visit from the police. I've gathered up her records for you." He slid a batch of file folders across the desk in Klayman's direction. The detective quickly flipped through them while Jessup sipped black coffee.

"I can take these?" Klayman asked.

"Of course. I had copies made."

*This guy has got it together,* Klayman

thought, returning the folders to the desk. "I'm hoping to talk to her friends on campus, Mr. Jessup, a roommate who still might be here, students she was close to, maybe even young men she dated."

Jessup shrugged and smiled. "I'm afraid those records won't help in that regard," he said. "But I can direct you to the dorm in which she lived. You might find someone there who was friends with her. Are you suspecting the murderer might have been a student here, or a former student?"

"At this stage, Mr. Jessup, we're not assuming anything. What we're doing is gathering all the information we can, from any source. No one's a suspect, although . . ."

". . . although *everyone's* a suspect," Jessup said, completing Klayman's thought and pleased that he'd thought of it. "One of my assistants will accompany you, and stay with you for as long as you need. I've provided her with a list of faculty names who might prove helpful, including Ms. Zarinski's faculty adviser during her four years here. I've instructed the person who'll be accompanying you to give you every possible bit of cooperation."

"I appreciate that, sir."

Jessup picked up his phone and asked someone named Marcia to come in. She was a stocky, thirty-plus-year-old woman in a teal pantsuit, with short blond hair, a round, open face, and whose glasses were oversized circles. After introductions, Jessup walked them into the reception area. "Please feel free to call me anytime, Detective. And good luck in your investigation."

"We'll start at Ms. Zarinski's dorm," Marcia told Klayman, leading him at a brisk pace across the street to what she described as Anderson Hall, "our largest of six residence halls. Ms. Zarinski lived there for part of her undergraduate time at the university."

"'Part of her time?' Where did she live the rest of the time?"

Marcia came to an abrupt halt and consulted papers she carried. "She lived off-campus. She'd repeatedly requested a single on-campus room, but we don't have many single-occupancy accommodations for undergraduate students."

"Do you have a record of who paid for her schooling and housing?" Klayman asked as they resumed walking.

"No, but that's easily obtainable." She

stopped again and scribbled a note on the top page.

When they reached the front of Anderson Hall, Marcia inserted an ID card into a slot, tripping the lock on the door. "Security is a top priority at American University," she proudly announced. "Each student has a coded ID card for his or her dorm. That's the only way you can gain entry."

"The only way? Students can't bring in guests?"

"We discourage it." She opened the door and allowed Klayman to precede her. "Students can only enter other residence halls with an escort from those halls."

Young men and women were everywhere, outside on the grassy knoll and in the public rooms and hallways, chatting and laughing, their energy palpable. Klayman reasoned that there were probably more students in the building that day, and at that hour, than would be the case further into the new semester when classes were in full swing.

Marcia checked her papers and led Klayman to a staircase. "Ms. Zarinski's last room was on the second floor, west wing," she announced, taking the stairs two at a time with Klayman in step behind. As they moved down the hallway, Klayman glanced right and left through open doors into student rooms where young men and women were in the process of decorating walls and unpacking suitcases, some with parents who helped, or stayed out of the way.

"Coed dorm," Klayman commented.

"All the floors in Anderson are coed," Marcia confirmed. "Some of the others have same-sex floors." She laughed. "I still can't get used to the notion of coed living. I wouldn't want it."

The room that had been Nadia Zarinski's was occupied by two young men sitting on the floor amidst a pile of half-emptied boxes. Rock music screeched from a boom box at their feet. They looked up at Klayman and Marcia; one of them waved. Marcia stepped into the room and yelled over the music, "Got a minute, guys?" They looked puzzled. "Turn that down?" she said, pointing to the boom box. They got to their feet, and one of them clicked off the recording. Marcia introduced herself, then did the same for Klayman.

"Just take a couple of minutes," Klayman

said. "Maybe you heard about the murder at Ford's Theatre yesterday."

One said, "She was a student here."

"That's right," said Klayman. "Did either of you know her?"

"I knew who she was," the other one said. "Joe used to talk about her a lot." A knowing smirk crossed his lips.

"Who's Joe?"

"Joe Cole. He used to date her."

"That's right," the roommate said.

Klayman looked at Marcia: "He's a first-year grad student," she said.

"He date her recently?" Klayman asked.

"Yeah. You don't think—"

"Where is Joe Cole?" Klayman asked.

"Other end of the hall."

Klayman took down their names in a small notebook and suggested to Marcia that they move on. As they retraced their steps down the hall, Klayman asked her, "Why do you know this Joe Cole? How many students are here, a couple of thousand?"

"Eleven thousand, Detective. Joe Cole is sort of a BMOC. You know what that means."

"Big man on campus. Popular."

"Yes. Popular. Handsome, with a great personality. He'll be something one day."

Cole's roommate told them Joe had gone off to work out at the fitness center. Marcia thanked him, and she and Klayman crossed the campus to what a sign indicated was the William I. Jacobs Fitness Center, in the Bender Sports Arena. They found Cole using a weight machine. He saw Marcia motioning for him to join them, slid off the seat, and jogged to them. He stood a solid six feet tall. His black hair was shaved into a military style crew cut. His tanned face was square, his eyes droopy and pale blue, his smile big and friendly. *The girls must trip over one another trying to get to you,* Klayman thought.

"Joe, this is Detective Klayman from the police department. He's here investigating the murder yesterday of Nadia Zarinski."

The smile disappeared as quickly as it had appeared.

"I know," Cole said. "It's all over the news. I couldn't believe it."

"You dated her," Klayman said flatly.

"Yeah, I did. I mean, it was nothing serious, nothing like that. We went out a few times, nothing heavy duty."

*He's exaggerating how casual it was.* "I'm told it was more serious than that," Klayman said.

"Who said that?"

"When was the last time you saw her?"

A bigger shrug of the shoulders than it needed to be. "A couple of weeks ago maybe. At least two weeks. Maybe three."

*Another lie.*

"What did you do . . . *three weeks ago*?"

A deeply furrowed brow to indicate serious thought. "A movie, I think."

"What did you see?"

That winning, boyish grin again. "Jesus, I can't remember. I go to the movies all the time."

Klayman lost patience. He turned to Marcia and said in a low voice, "You'll excuse us for a few minutes, won't you?"

It took her a moment to realize he wasn't giving her a choice. "I'll be right outside," she said, leaving but looking over her shoulder every few steps.

When she was gone, Klayman leaned against a padded gymnast's pommel horse, crossed his arms, and fixed Cole in a practiced hard stare. "Okay," he said, "we've got the silly answers out of the way. Now we get serious. When did you last see Nadia Zarinski?"

The big smile accompanied, "A few days ago."

"Over the weekend," Klayman said, his smile considerably smaller.

A nod.

"You have a fight?"

"A fight? No. We never fought. We got along."

"What night?"

"Huh?"

"What night over the weekend did you spend time with her?"

"Saturday."

"You went to the movies?"

Cole shook his large head. "No, we . . . ah, come on, do I have to get into this?"

"Yeah, you do."

Cole had stopped perspiring. Now, the sweat came again, and Klayman enjoyed it. It wasn't something he openly bragged about, but being a detective—being in charge and watching people squirm because of that reality—gave him at times a certain pleasure. He was investigating a murder, which made his questions a lot more important than anything Cole might be thinking or feeling at that moment. As far as Klayman knew, he was asking questions of the person who'd killed Nadia Zarinski, and he wasn't about to back off to make Cole more comfortable. He let his stare make the point that he expected an honest answer.

"We went to dinner."

"Where?" Klayman was now making notes.

"Spezie."

"In Rockville?"

"No, the one downtown, Connecticut and L."

"I didn't know there was one in town. And?"

"What? You want to know what we ate?"

"I want to know what you did the rest of the evening."

"We—we went back to her apartment and—you know, we screwed."

"A happy screw?"

He laughed. "Yeah, of course it was."

"No problems between you."

"Nope."

"You stay the night?"

"Nope. Came back here. She—"

"She what?"

"She—she wasn't feeling well and

wanted to get a good sleep. I left right after we—"

"You didn't see her again after Saturday?"

"No."

"I'll probably want to talk to you again. You're not planning to go anywhere, are you?"

"Hell, no." He let out a stream of air, shook his head, and looked to a far corner of the workout area.

"I'll be back in touch," Klayman said. He left the building and rejoined Marcia outside.

"An impressive young man, isn't he?" she said.

"Very. I'd like to go back and talk to the two young men in the room she lived in."

"All right."

When they reached the room, its occupants were playing a computer video game, the music again cranked up to an uncomfortable level. After getting them to lower the volume and to turn away from the computer screen, Klayman said, "Joe Cole says he talked to you after his date with Nadia Zarinski over the weekend."

"He said that?"

"Yeah. What did he tell you?"

The roommates looked at each other before one said, "He was bellyaching like he always does about Nadia."

"He was angry with her?"

The other roommate guffawed. "Angry? He was boiling, a volcano erupting."

"Over what?"

"Over Nadia."

"Yeah, but what had she done to make him so mad?"

The second roommate cocked his head and asked, "You sure Joe said he'd talked with us?"

"Go ask him," Klayman said, confident they wouldn't.

"She was always seeing other guys. Not that Joe was serious about her, like marriage or anything. Nobody would want to marry somebody like Nadia. But—"

"Why do you say that?" Klayman asked. He looked to Marcia, whose discomfort with the conversation was obvious.

"Because she was a round heels," the student said. "Sleeping around with everybody. I mean, that's good for fun, but serious? Nah. Joe wasn't serious about her."

"So why did he get mad if he wasn't serious?"

"Because she goes out with him, like, you know, to a fancy restaurant and all, like that, and then she hops in the sack with somebody else who doesn't spend a nickel on her. That makes you pretty mad, huh, like you're being played for a sucker."

"Joe felt like he was being played for a sucker?"

They nodded in unison, a matching pair of toy dogs in the rear window of a moving car.

"What did he tell you about the weekend?" Klayman asked.

Shrugs, then, "He took her to this nice Italian restaurant and goes back to her place to make it with her. He says the minute they were through, she starts talking about another guy she's seeing who she tells Joe is a better lover than him. What do you think of that?"

"He mention who this other guy was?"

"You don't know?"

Klayman wrote in his notebook and ignored the question.

"Big deal. So he's a senator's kid and all. He's a bum."

Klayman looked up from his notebook. "What senator?"

"Lerner." It was spoken as though the world knew. "His son, Jerry. Him and Nadia have been getting it on for months."

Klayman was tempted to correct his grammar but didn't. "Nadia was dating Jeremiah Lerner?" he said.

"Right, along with a dozen other guys. Man, what a slut."

"Are we finished here?" Marcia asked Klayman.

He nodded, wrote down their home addresses, closed the notebook, thanked them for their time, and left the building with Marcia.

"I must say I'm shocked," she said as they returned to the Hamilton Building, where Klayman had parked his car. "I trust you won't judge all our students by those two."

"Wouldn't think of it," Klayman responded. "Mr. Jessup said I could speak with Nadia's faculty adviser."

"Yes. Would you like to do that now?"

"Yes, ma'am."

*    *    *

Johnson was sitting in his car in front of the Thai restaurant when Klayman pulled up. He got into Johnson's vehicle.

"How'd it go?" Johnson asked.

"Good. Better than that. The victim was dating Senator Lerner's son, Jeremiah."

Johnson whistled. "How'd you find that out?"

"A guy who was also dating her, Joe Cole. Cole was angry because she was seeing Lerner. Cole had a date with her Saturday."

"Angry enough to do her in?"

"I'd say so. Let's go inside and check on Bancroft and his pal, Jones."

"We should have a picture of Bancroft," Johnson said, opening his door. "To show the manager."

"Yeah, but we don't have one. Maybe he'll remember him because he's—well . . ."

Johnson laughed. "Strange."

Klayman laughed, too. "I prefer 'eccentric.' "

"You would."

A picture of Sydney Bancroft wasn't necessary.

"Oh, yes," the manager of Duangrat's and Rabieng said pleasantly. "Mr. Jones is a regular. Mr. Bancroft comes here often with him."

"They had dinner here Monday night?" Johnson asked.

"Yes. Excuse me, please."

He returned moments later with the waiter who'd served them. "Sajing waited on them."

"You remember what time they came and left?" Klayman asked the small, achingly thin waiter.

He flapped his hands as though such a question were beyond the capability of mere mortals.

"Approximately," Johnson helped.

"Maybe seven. Maybe seven-thirty, they come. That table over there. Mr. Jones, he always sit at that table."

"He's a regular," the manager repeated.

"How long did they stay?" Johnson asked.

"Is Mr. Jones in trouble?" asked the manager.

"No."

"They left at ten," the manager said. "I remember because Mr. Bancroft, he—he had a great deal to drink and was entertaining people at other tables near them."

"Entertaining them?" said Johnson.

"Saying speeches from William Shake-speare, acting for them. He has done that before—when he has had too much to drink. Very funny. The other customers enjoy him."

"Yeah, I bet they do," Johnson muttered.

"Mr. Jones, he had *bhram*," the waiter said. "He always has *bhram*."

"A specialty," the manager said. "Chicken with shallots, cabbage, and peanut sauce. Very good."

"I'm sure it is," Johnson said. "So they were here from about seven until ten. They left together?"

"Yes, although—"

"Although what?" Klayman asked.

"I went with them to the sidewalk," the manager said. "They walked in separate directions."

"They say why, where they were going?" Johnson asked.

"No. I did not ask. It would not be proper for me to pry."

"Very discreet," Johnson said. "We'd appreciate you not telling Mr. Jones or Mr. Bancroft we were here asking questions about them."

"Of course."

Once outside, Johnson said, "So they weren't together all night like they claim."

"Maybe they went in separate directions to—I don't know, Mo, walk off the meal? Maybe one of them went to get the car."

"While the other one walks away? No way, Ricky. Hathaway wants us at headquarters. I told him we were meeting up here, and he said to come back when we were through." Johnson whistled, louder this time. "Lerner's kid dating the deceased, huh? Man, the plot thickens."

At a fast-food place where they stopped for lunch on the way to headquarters, Johnson filled Klayman in on his interview with Nadia Zarinski's parents.

"I'm sorry to have to meet you under these circumstances," Johnson told the parents as they sat in an interrogation room.

"We appreciate that," said Nadia's father, a short, chunky man with ruddy cheeks, and wisps of gray hair jutting at odd angles from his baldpate.

The mother, whose name was Judith— the father was Morton—was the same height as her husband, but appeared to be in better physical shape. Her features were sharp, her eyes steely. When she spoke, there was assurance in her voice, a woman used to being in charge. A nurse. No nonsense. She pulled a cigarette from her purse.

"Sorry, ma'am, but we don't allow smoking in here," Johnson said gently. No surprise to him that she was a smoker. Most nurses he'd met smoked. Salty language was next, he assumed.

"My daughter has just been brutally murdered, and you're worried about me smoking?" she said.

"It's not me, ma'am. Policy."

She shoved the cigarette back into her purse.

"Judith is upset," Morton said. "Of course, we both are."

"Who killed Nadia?" Judith asked.

"We're working on that, Mrs. Zarinski."

"Do you have any leads?"

"A few," replied Johnson. "Maybe you can help. Did your daughter share with you anything about who she might have been dating, close male friends, things like that?"

"No," Mr. Zarinski said. "Nadia didn't talk much about such things."

"With the murder rate you have here in Washington, Detective Johnson, it could have been anyone who took our daughter's life," said Judith Zarinski. "It could have been some drug addict looking for money for a fix."

"Did your daughter use drugs?" Johnson asked.

"Oh, no," Morton said.

*Typical parent's response,* Johnson thought. *"Not my little girl."*

Johnson asked the mother, "Did Nadia confide in you, Mrs. Zarinski, about her romantic life? You know, mother and daughter kind of talk."

"On occasion. When she visited us in Florida. We hadn't seen her in more than six months, though."

"She liked working at the theatre," said Mr. Zarinski. "She told me that on the phone a few weeks ago."

"What about her internship with Senator Lerner?"

Johnson asked it of both parents, and noted their reactions. The father winced; the mother met Johnson's gaze, never blinking. "I suppose you're getting at those rumors about the senator and Nadia," she said.

"I have to ask," Johnson said. "Sorry."

"They both denied it," said the mother, "and I certainly believed my daughter when she said there was nothing to it."

"Sure, I understand," Johnson said. "She ever mention an old British actor named Sydney Bancroft?"

Morton smiled and nodded enthusiastically. "She said he was a real character, really funny. She told me she thought he was abused at the theatre, not respected. She certainly respected him. That's what she said."

"She tell you that he might have made advances toward her?"

"Good heavens, no," the father responded.

Mrs. Zarinski took the bent cigarette from her purse and stood. "It's obvious there's been no real progress in finding Nadia's killer. We'd like to arrange for Nadia to be flown to Florida for burial."

"That'll depend on the medical examiner, Mrs. Zarinski. When there's been a death under unusual circumstances, we have to keep the body until—"

"Excuse me," she said, and left the room.

"Please try to understand Judith's anger,

Detective Johnson," Morton said. "This has been a terrible shock."

"I know," said Johnson. "Just another couple of questions, Mr. Zarinski. You paid for your daughter's college education. Right?"

"Yes."

"And you continued to pay her rent after she graduated. Right again?"

"That's right. We encouraged her to accept the internship with Senator Lerner because the experience would be invaluable, even though it didn't pay anything. I considered it a form of graduate school."

Johnson decided to not burst the father's bubble about the internship. Had the daughter deliberately lied, calling it unpaid, in order to continue pocketing money from her parents? It appeared that way.

"One last question, sir. What kind of a person was Nadia?"

"In what way?"

"Adventuresome? Kind of shy and retiring? A loner? Enjoy partying?"

"Nadia wasn't a loner, Detective. That's for certain. She loved people. People seemed to gravitate to her. No, Nadia was a real people person." His eyes became moist, and he wiped at one with the back of his hand. "Sorry."

"Nothing to be sorry about, Mr. Zarinski." Johnson stood and extended his hand. "Look, you and your wife try and be patient for the next few days. I'll keep in touch." He handed the father his card, on which he'd written his home phone number. "Day or night, Mr. Zarinski. Call day or night."

"Thank you," the father said, slipping the card into his shirt pocket. "You've been very kind."

"No help from them, huh?" Klayman said to his partner as they finished their grilled chicken sandwiches.

"No. Nice people. The father looks like he's confused. I don't blame him. I kept thinking about my kids and how I'd react if I got a call telling me one of 'em was dead. Probably act more like the mother. Where's the action? Who's the scum who did it? You know?"

Klayman said nothing, not because he didn't agree, but because he agreed too much. He considered bringing children into the world an act of extreme courage, and knew he didn't possess that brand of bravery. Was it selfish to have children, or to decide not to? It probably didn't matter why the thought of marrying and having babies was anathema to him. It simply was. It seemed you got married and babies naturally came as part of the deal. No decision involved. He'd met young women who'd professed agreement with his viewpoint. "I really don't want children," he'd say. And they'd respond, "Oh, I agree. I don't see why people can't get married and not have children." "You really feel that way?" he'd ask. "Absolutely," they'd reply. Somehow, he didn't believe them. You got married and the babies came. Maternal needs took over at some point. It was in the genes, in the hormones.

"Let's get out of here," he growled, his voice mirroring the foul mood that had descended upon him. Such introspection always seemed to do that.

# ELEVEN

Clarise Emerson had lunch at her desk at Ford's Theatre before heading for the final briefing session in preparation for her confirmation hearing. The meeting was held, as it usually was, in a small, seldom used conference room in the Executive Office Building, directly across from the White House.

"You certainly charmed good ol' Senator Sybers," one of three people from the administration's presidential personnel office said after Clarise had taken her customary chair across from her mock inquisitors. The woman was one of eleven people on the team the White House had assembled to whip Clarise into shape as a witness. It was informally known as the Murder Team, and the intensity of their questioning had led Clarise to consider it an apt description.

"The president had coffee with Sybers this morning," the woman in charge of President Nash's task force responsible for the arts and humanities agencies said lightly. "The senator said you were 'one damned impressive lady.'" She delivered the line the way a very old southerner would.

"That's good to hear," said Clarise. "He was charming when we met. I think he was flirting with me."

A lawyer on the team laughed. "Senator Sybers is one of the biggest flirts in Congress. He may be eighty-six years old, but he still has an eye."

"Southern shtick," said a publicist, who'd been brought in to generate positive press for Clarise and her quest to head the NEA. "The senator's charming, all right. It's a shame his politics aren't."

"How do the numbers look so far?" Clarise asked.

"Solid. Unless somebody drops a bombshell, I'd say your confirmation is a slam dunk."

Clarise sat back and smiled. "What would we do without sports metaphors?"

she asked, more of herself than of the other people at the table. She came forward. "Now, what's on tap for today?"

A young man from intergovernmental affairs spoke. "The way we see it, Ms. Emerson, the last possible sticking point could be that film you coproduced a dozen years ago, the one with incest as its theme. And these." He pulled half a dozen posters from a large black carrying case and displayed them on the table, promotional material for made-for-TV motion pictures Clarise had produced. "Senator Sybers has been circulating these to members of Congress, along with other things he considers examples of your lack of morality."

"Do I lack morality?" Clarise asked everyone with a sweep of her head. She laughed. "God, I hope not. It's no fun without morality."

"All in the eye of the beholder. As far as Sybers is concerned, he's the last bastion of morality in America."

"The film you mentioned," Clarise said. "You're talking about *that* film."

"Yes," said the White House arts and humanities czar. "Sybers pointed to it a couple of years ago as an example of why the NEA shouldn't receive an increase in funding."

"As I remember it," Clarise said, "it wasn't that he didn't want to increase government funding. He wanted to *eliminate* funding."

"He always does. Either way, he cited that movie as an example of what he considered the sort of prurient material the NEA funds."

"But it wasn't," Clarise said, extending her hands in a gesture of frustration. "That film was privately funded."

"It's all the same to the senator, Clarise. Anything that offends his moral compass gets lumped together. Did he mention the film when you met with him?"

"No."

A lawyer handed Clarise a sheet of paper with a dozen lines of type. "Talking points when that film and your role in producing it come up. Take a minute to study them. Then we'll run you through questions about it. Stick to the talking points. They represent answers that some of the senators will want to hear. If you get off-message, it will open up other questions you might not be prepared to handle."

The Murder Team's grilling of Clarise

went on for a half hour. When it was over, someone asked her about the killing at Ford's Theatre.

"Incredible," Clarise said. "A murdered young woman right at my doorstep."

"Any leads?"

"Not that I'm aware of."

There was an awkward silence at the table before one of the lawyers said, "The rumors about the young woman who was killed and your former husband, Senator Lerner. Is that liable to get messy?"

"Oh, come on," Clarise said. "Why should it? It was just a nasty rumor spread by a disgruntled former aide to Bruce. Why should it have any bearing on my confirmation?"

"It shouldn't," replied the lawyer. "But you never know what some of the committee members will dredge up, especially crafty curmudgeons like Sybers. We just don't want any surprises."

"Are any people on your staff suspects?" asked another attorney.

"I don't think so."

"You're not, are you?"

"Of course not."

"No surprise witnesses liable to show up to testify against you?"

Clarise shook her head back and forth, as far as it would go. "This is a little late for that, isn't it?" she said. "My God, you've investigated me as though I were up to head the Atomic Energy Commission. What surprise witnesses could there possibly be?"

One of two friendly senators' assistants on the team said, "Too much has gone into this process to leave room for bolts from the blue, Clarise, that's all. The murder at the theatre is an unfortunate thing. Bad timing."

"Murder," Clarise muttered. "The ultimate pornography. Look, my friends, my life has become an open book. If there is some surprise in the woodwork, it'll shock me as much as it shocks you—or the senators."

"Good," said the White House arts liaison. "You've been a real trouper, Clarise. Anything else anyone wants to raise?"

No one responded, and the meeting broke up. On her way out, Clarise was taken aside by the president's arts chief: "Vice President Maloney asked me to send her best, Clarise. She's firmly in your corner, as you know."

"Please say hello for me. I owe her a call. It's been so busy that—"

"Of course. I'll tell her you'll be in touch. Keep your chin up. It'll be over soon."

"It can't be soon enough."

Clarise headed back to Ford's Theatre, where she huddled with Bernard Crowley for the rest of the afternoon going over plans for two upcoming fund-raisers: a cocktail party for members of the theatre's board of trustees, each of whom had paid at least $10,000 for the privilege of serving; and the annual *Festival at Ford's,* a nationally televised variety show that generated large sums of money for the theatre and was traditionally attended by a who's who of Washington government officials and social leading lights, including the president and vice president and their families.

"It looks like you have things in your usual good order, Bernard."

"I try to, Clarise." He placed a hand on her shoulder. "I just don't know how you do it," he said.

"What do you mean?"

"How you manage to juggle so many things. Running the theatre society, getting ready for a senate grilling, all your social obligations, and now having to put up with a murder investigation."

"In the genes, I suppose. Dumb enough to enjoy the challenge. Have the police been back?"

"I don't think so. At least they haven't been up here in the offices. Sydney called when you were at your briefing."

"And?"

"Said he wasn't feeling well and was staying home."

"What about the teen show?"

"He said to tell you it's coming along fine. They're rehearsing tomorrow. I must say, Clarise, that Sydney is becoming more erratic. Maybe 'insufferable' is more accurate."

Hers was a gentle laugh; this time it was her hand on his shoulder. "Could we not discuss Sydney today, Bernard?"

As though not hearing her, he said, "I think you should know that Sydney is a serious suspect in Nadia's murder."

She stared. "How do you know that?"

"One of the stagehands. Wales. He told me that when the police questioned him, he told them that Sydney showed an unnatural interest in Nadia. He said Sydney was always touching her and making lewd comments. The police were extremely interested, Wales says."

"I don't believe it," she said.

"You may not want to believe it, Clarise, but it's a fact."

"I hope it isn't a fact, Bernard. Had you heard anything about Sydney and Nadia before?"

"No, of course I didn't. Are you going to ask Sydney about it?"

"Not unless I have to. I'd like to talk to the police first."

"They won't tell you anything. But I'll keep my ears open."

"Yes, do that, Bernard. I have to leave now. There's a party at the Millennium Arts Center I must stop in on, and dinner with some AT&T people. I think they might want to sponsor one of the shows next season in addition to their usual support."

As she left the building and said good night to a park ranger on duty at the desk downstairs, her thoughts were on what Crowley had told her about Bancroft. She hadn't been honest when she'd said she didn't believe the claim that Bancroft had made improper advances to Nadia Zarinski.

It was more a matter of not wanting to believe it.

"Damned old fool," she said under her breath as she hailed a cab and gave the turbaned driver the address of the arts center in southwest Washington.

# TWELVE

"I don't understand why a husband has to be in the delivery room when his wife delivers a baby," Hathaway snapped at Klayman and Johnson the moment the detectives entered his office at First District headquarters. "Wallace's wife's having a baby, so he takes off for the day. It was better when my kids were born. My wife had the kids, and I went to work."

"It's an event you don't want to miss," Johnson said.

"Were you there when your kids were born, Mo?"

"No, but I wish I had been."

Hathaway's eyes rolled up in his head. "Who wants to see that bloody mess anyway?" His eyes returned to straight and level. "So, what do you have?"

Klayman led off. "I talked to some students who knew the deceased—or knew about her. They portray her as being sexually active; one called her a 'round heels.' I didn't think anybody used that expression anymore. She was dating a student named Joe Cole. I spoke with Cole. He was out to dinner with the deceased Saturday night. They made love back at her apartment after dinner. He says he left because she wasn't feeling well and didn't see her again. Other students I talked to claim Cole was angry about the way the date turned out because, according to them—and they're quoting him—she told him that another guy she was dating was a better lover."

"That must have given his ego a hell of a boost," Hathaway said.

"Tell him who the other guy is," Johnson told Klayman.

"Jeremiah Lerner."

"Ooooh," said Hathaway. "The senator's son?"

"Yup."

"We have an address on him?" Hathaway asked.

"Easy to get," said Johnson.

"The chief was on with the senator to-day," Hathaway said, leaning back as far as his chair would allow, and rubbing his eyes. "He agrees to talk to us, but not here. They're working out a deal. Don't you love it? Somebody gets murdered, and we have to cut a deal to talk to him."

"I want to run a background on Cole," Klayman said. "According to the other students, he was mad enough to want to kill her."

"What do we do about the Lerner kid?" Johnson asked.

"Go talk to him," Hathaway said. "His old man's immunity doesn't cover the kid."

"Oh, by the way," Klayman said, "I also spoke with the deceased's faculty adviser at American. Kind of interesting what she said. She says Ms. Zarinski wasn't much of a student, just managed to get by. This adviser says she couldn't understand how Zarinski ever landed an internship in any political office, let alone with a senator like Lerner. The school's got a great reputation in political affairs and international service, and lots of good students in them. But Ms. Zarinski almost flunks the only courses she took in those disciplines, and never bothers to register with the internship department. But she ends up with Senator Bruce Lerner—"

"And with a *paid* internship, too," Johnson added.

"Right."

"I'm interested in what Johnson got out of the parents," Hathaway said. "She's getting paid by Lerner's office, but she lies to her parents and says she isn't getting paid. So they keep sending money, pick up the rent, who knows what else?"

"The jewelry?" Johnson asked. "I should have asked how much they gave her every month. Enough for the baubles?"

"Ask 'em," Hathaway said. "They're still around. Just keep the mother away from me. She's been breaking my chops since they got here. Okay. Run down the Lerner kid and see what he has to say."

"How do we handle him?" Klayman asked. "Is he a suspect?"

"If you mean do you have to read him his rights, the answer is no. Nobody's a suspect yet, at least officially. I've got a warrant out for the Partridge character to be picked up as a material witness."

"Why?"

"To cover our rear ends." Klayman's and Johnson's glances at each other were swift and discreet. *Our rear ends?* they thought in concert. Hathaway was the one who'd decided to release the old drunk.

"Maybe we run a lineup for Partridge with this Cole guy, or Lerner, or anybody else," their boss said. "For the record."

"Good idea, Herman," Johnson said.

The answer to Jeremiah's address was close at hand. He had a rap sheet, which gave his address, an apartment in the Adams-Morgan section of the city, and phone number—at least as of the date of his last arrest, which was three months ago. A girlfriend had brought charges against him for assault and battery, claiming he struck her during a domestic dispute. He'd spent the night in jail but was released the following morning after the young woman chose to not press charges. The incident had received a small mention in the Washington *Times.* Two earlier arrests involved a bar fight, and marijuana possession. Both charges were summarily thrown out; the arresting officers in each instance were never told why, although the popular assumption was that political pressure had been brought. The D.C. police prided themselves on not bowing to pressure by the highly placed; whether internal reality matched up with that public posture was conjecture. This was Washington, D.C., where almost anything was possible.

A male answered sleepily, "He's not here."

"Where is he?"

"Work."

"Where does he work?"

"The Millennium Arts Center, over in Southwest."

"He's there now?"

A loud, prolonged yawn preceded, "Five o'clock. He goes to work at five."

Hang up.

# THIRTEEN

Topper Sybers, senior senator from Alabama, slipped the mask over his mouth and nose and drew in the cold, pure oxygen. The delivery unit was on a stand next to his massive desk in his office in the Dirksen Senate Office Building, at First and C Streets. The eighty-six-year-old senator had the largest office in the building, and over the years it had turned into a museum of sorts, chockablock with mementos of his eight terms in the senior congressional body.

An aide poked her head through the door. "Senator Lerner is on his way, Senator," she said.

Sybers removed the mask. "Send him in soon as he gets here."

A lifetime of heavy smoking had taken its predictable toll on Sybers's lungs and heart. He'd "officially" quit smoking twenty years ago, but was an inveterate cheat. One of his office workers had, among other duties, the responsibility of delivering to him an occasional cigarette when the urge struck. At least he'd given up cigars, was the sentiment of those who'd been with him for years. Still, the odor of hundreds of cigars from the past had permeated the carpeting and drapes, which he refused to have cleaned. He liked that smell; it reminded him of better times.

The aide who'd announced that Bruce Lerner was heading their way had positioned herself in the doorway to the hall. When she saw the senior senator from Virginia turn a corner, she motioned to another aide, who quickly informed Sybers that Lerner was about to arrive.

"Good morning," Lerner tossed out to those in the reception area as he passed by and strode into his Alabama colleague's office.

"'Morning, Senator," he said to Sybers, who lifted himself a few inches from his chair. "No need to get up." He extended his hand across the desk, which Sybers took in what always surprised people as a firm grip. "You're looking well."

Lerner settled into a red leather chair across from Sybers, crossed one leg over the other, and checked the crease in his trousers. *Washingtonian* magazine named him among the five best-dressed lawmakers year after year, as well as one of the city's most eligible bachelors. His suits came from Savile Row's esteemed Gieves & Hawkes, his shirts custom-made at Turnbull & Asser, shoes from Trickers. His long face was attractively craggy, his full head of gray hair professionally coiffed by a barber who visited his office twice a week.

Sybers said, "I feel pretty good, Bruce, for an old man. I don't have time to feel bad."

"Good for you, Topper."

Lerner glanced at the door to ensure it was closed. He ran his tongue over his lips, examined the nails on one hand, and said, "Clarise appreciates the courtesies you extended her when she visited you."

"A fine lady, Bruce. Got some class. But then again, you'd know all about that better than me, havin' been married to her."

"You'll get no argument from me, Topper." Lerner's southern accent thickened slightly under the influence of Sybers's pronounced drawl. "As you can 'magine, Clarise is anxious about the hearin'."

"I imagine she would be, bein' grilled by a nasty old redneck like me." He let out a single-syllable grunt that passed for a chuckle. "I'll be candid with you, Senator. Always have been. I have some serious reservations about your former wife heading the NEA."

Lerner started to respond, but Sybers's gnarled, arthritic, liver-spotted hand waved him off. "I suspect that's why you come up to see me today."

"That's right, Topper. I don't want to see Clarise disappointed. She's too good for that. She'd make a fine NEA head, and I think you know that."

"Depends more on what my folks back in Alabama think. Clarise got herself wrapped up in some pretty nasty excuses for art over the years, Bruce. Every day goes by, I'm made aware of 'em. Hard to reconcile this lovely, middle-aged woman with some of the lowlifes she's hooked up with in Hollywood."

Lerner reversed legs and looked up at a photograph of Sybers with former presidents Nixon and Ford. Although Lerner and Sybers sat on different sides of the aisle in the Senate—Sybers was a lifelong Democrat, Lerner a Republican—their political views were very much the same. Sybers was more conservative than most Republicans, and often voted with them, particularly on legislation concerning military spending, judicial appointments, and social issues including abortion, welfare, and crime. He'd often been urged to switch parties by a variety of Republicans but considered that option to be anathema. He considered himself a rock-ribbed Roosevelt Democrat, viewing FDR as having used big government only in a time of extreme danger for the nation and its people. He hadn't seen a similar need since the Roosevelt administration, and had supported Republican presidential candidates ever since.

"I want to see Clarise confirmed," Lerner said quietly.

"I'm sure you do, Bruce. You bring me somethin' today to help me come to that conclusion?"

Lerner smiled and cocked his head. "Get right to the point, huh?"

"Must be my age, Bruce. Can't afford to waste time with a lot of pleasant chitchat." Sybers sat up straight, coughed, and wiggled a finger at Lerner. "You and your armed services committee are still tryin' to figure out how to slice up the budget pie for the Pentagon. Am I right?"

"When are we ever *not* doing that, Topper?"

His laugh brought on more coughing, deeper this time. "Bruce, I haven't made any secret of my fervent desire to see some of the money redistributed in the military budget. Seems to me—and it's seemed to me for a long time—that the air force keeps gettin' more and more money because of the way the damned media plays up all their smart bombs and fancy-lookin' aircraft and the like. The media doesn't like to show the dirty side of war, down in the trenches, crawlin' on bellies, and getting shot up close. Now, don't get me wrong, Bruce. Far as I'm concerned, the flyboys should get everything they need. No question about that. Desert Storm and Afghanistan made that point loud 'n' clear. But we've got to keep our ground forces up to date, too, damn it."

"I agree," said Lerner.

"You saw that presentation Accell Industries gave on its new all-terrain vehicle. That particular vehicle is one potent military machine, Bruce, and I just wonder at the sanity of some of those generals over at the Pentagon dismissin' that vehicle like it wouldn't end up savin' plenty of our boys' lives and maybe helpin' bring down scum like Hussein, and all those terrorists who're out to kill every damn one of us. Now, I know you're a reasonable man. And a smart man. You prove that every day, Bruce. And I would be very much obliged if you could use some of your influence at the Pentagon to get them to see why some money ought to rightly be shifted from the air force over to Accell to develop its military vehicle."

Lerner was well aware that Accell Industries, with headquarters in Alabama, had always been Topper Sybers's most generous campaign contributor. Accell's lobbyists seemed to be everywhere, working the halls of Congress, dropping in "just to say hello," hinting that a vote for funding its products could result in hefty campaign contributions for those senators and House members who agreed with what they were selling.

"I must say I was impressed with Accell's presentation, Topper," Lerner said. "Accurately bombing targets from thirty thousand feet is good. But you don't win wars from the air alone."

"Exactly."

"I'll be meeting with the secretary and the Joint Chiefs within the next week. I'll talk to them."

"I knew you would, Bruce."

Lerner was suddenly aware of the smell of stale cigar smoke, and wiggled his nose against it. Had it infused his suit?

He stood and reached across the desk, shook his fellow senator's hand. "Keep looking as good as you do, Topper. I'll be back in touch."

"You do that, Bruce. And give my best to that lovely lady who used to be Mrs. Lerner."

"I certainly will."

Sybers watched the long, lean Lerner open the door and disappear from view. He pushed a button on the phone, which brought an aide into the room.

"How about a cigarette, honey," he said,

smiling. "Why not bring in a couple. And then leave me alone for an hour. I've got some phone calls to make and some thinkin' to do."

She kept her smile to herself as she went to her desk and retrieved two king-size Tarryton cigarettes. *Serious thinking to do?* she mused. Nap time was more like it.

# FOURTEEN

Klayman and Johnson spent the hours of late afternoon writing reports. At a few minutes before five, they climbed into Klayman's unmarked car and drove the few blocks from headquarters to the Millennium Arts Center (MAC) at 651 I (Eye) Street, SW. The 150,000-square-foot redbrick building had been built in 1910 as Randall Junior High School, and functioned in that capacity until sold by the city in 2000 to a nonprofit group led by Washington arts impresario Bill Wooby, who began the daunting, expensive job of turning it into a true national arts center. In addition to artists' studios and large exhibition spaces, MAC was used by a variety of local theatrical groups for rehearsals and set building, including Ford's Theatre.

"Right around the corner and I've never been," Klayman said as he pulled up in front.

"A perk of the job, huh?" Johnson commented. "You get to see things you never saw before."

"And not always things I want to see. You have the picture?"

"Yeah." Johnson held up a mug shot of Jeremiah Lerner he'd taken from the files before leaving. They'd read what was in Lerner's folder and agreed that the kid came off as a foul ball, nothing major—yet—but they'd seen too many Jeremiah Lerners who'd progressed from being a nuisance to the community to eventually becoming a threat. His mug shot depicted a smug young man, the hint of a smile on his lips to make the point that being arrested, printed, and photographed wasn't such a big deal. Or, to cover the fear he was feeling at the time.

"Must be tough being a big shot U.S. senator and having a kid like this," Johnson said, slipping the photo into his inside jacket pocket.

"And a big shot mother," Klayman said. "Maybe too much for the kid to live up to."

"Thank you, Dr. Freud."

"Your forty-five minutes is up. Pay on your way out. Come on, let's see if he showed up for work today."

They climbed a short set of steps and walked through doors leading to a large, open space with white walls, a gleaming gray floor, and with artwork and sculptures lining both sides. The sounds of a cocktail party came from a doorway twenty feet to their right. A sign on an easel indicated an opening was in progress for two artists, Richard Dana and Judy Jashinsky.

They started toward the party sounds when Johnson stopped to take in a large Impressionistic painting. "What do you figure that is?" he asked Klayman.

"Looks like a head surrounded by birds to me."

"Hello."

They turned to face a slender, middle-aged man carrying a cocktail glass and wearing a purple shirt, and a wide tie from which the Mona Lisa smiled at them. "Are you here for the Dana-Jashinsky opening?"

"No," Johnson said. "Detectives Johnson

and Klayman, Crimes Against Persons Unit, First District." They showed their badges.

"Is something wrong?"

"We're looking for someone who works here," said Klayman. Johnson pulled the mug shot from his pocket.

"Yes, I've seen him before. He doesn't work for the arts center per se. He works for a contractor who does maintenance."

"Is he here today, Mr.—?"

"Wooby. Bill Wooby. I'm the center's director. He may be. I've been busy with the opening and party. Yes, I think he's the one who's been working in the garden café area."

"How do we get there?" Johnson asked.

"By following me."

He led them to a door in the middle of the building that opened out onto a grassy courtyard in need of tender loving care.

"As you can see, we're in the process of converting the space into a café," Wooby said.

The courtyard was empty. "I don't see him," Johnson said.

"I'm not sure he was due here today," the director said, sipping from his drink, "although I don't keep track of such things. I have enough to do—"

"Over there," Johnson said, pointing to the far end of the quadrangle. Jeremiah Lerner was walking in their direction.

"Hey, Jeremiah," Johnson yelled.

Lerner stopped and looked at them. He seemed unsure what to do, whether to approach or to turn. He turned and took rapid steps back toward the door he had come through. Looking over his shoulder, he saw them heading his way and broke into a run, disappearing through the door. Without a word, Klayman ran back into the building while Johnson continued after Lerner. Wooby followed Klayman inside.

"Where can he go?" Klayman asked.

"Anywhere," Wooby said. "It's a big place."

Klayman moved at a fast trot down the hall, looking left and right into artist studios and performance rooms, unsnapping the leather restraining tab on his holster beneath his armpit as he went. "Mo!" he shouted. "Mo, where are you?"

He heard his partner's voice from the recesses of the sprawling building and headed in that direction. Wooby, now minus his glass, was close on his heels. Klayman turned left down another long corridor, shouting Johnson's name as he went. He stopped, causing Wooby to almost run into him. "How many floors?" Klayman asked.

"Two, plus the attic."

They took off again and reached a staircase, which Klayman took three at a time. Johnson had gone upstairs from a different direction and was up there when Klayman and Wooby arrived.

"You see him?" Klayman asked, drawing in air as fast as he could.

"Yeah. I saw him come up here, but he had a big lead. The son of a bitch lost me. He's fast." Johnson emptied his lungs and placed hands on hips against pain.

"What's down this hall?" Klayman asked Wooby.

"Storage space. Some unfinished studios. The stairs to the attic."

They moved toward the dark confines of the hallway's end. Boxes were piled everywhere; contractor's equipment created a maze they navigated until coming to an open door.

"That's supposed to be closed," Wooby said.

Klayman went to it and looked up. A long ladder ran vertically from where he stood to another floor.

"The attic?"

"Yes."

"You say this door is usually closed?"

"Always."

Klayman looked back down the hall. There was no sign of anyone. He pulled his service revolver from its holster, stepped through the door and, slowly, deliberately began to climb the ladder, the weapon leading the way. When he reached the halfway point, he looked down at Johnson. "You coming, Mo?"

Johnson began his ascent without answering.

Klayman reached the top and carefully raised his head above the floor. Everything was silent. The attic's darkness was penetrated only by shafts of light through skylights, and a small window to his left. Particles of dust hung in the skewered light. *Why the dust?* he wondered. What had caused it to rise from the floor?

"What do you see, Ricky?" Johnson asked from directly below Klayman.

"Dust."

"Dust?"

Klayman covered the final rungs on the ladder and pulled himself up to a crouched position in the attic itself. Johnson's head appeared. He started to say something, but Klayman put an index finger to his lips to silence him. He closed his eyes and strained as he listened. It wasn't much of a sound, a slight rustle, a rubbing of something against something else. It came from across the attic, past large heating ducts that lowered the ceiling substantially, more boxes, old student desks and bookcases. A dozen blackboards were stacked side by side, inhibiting his sight line to where he was certain the sound had originated. He took a few steps to the side to allow Johnson to emerge through the floor's opening. The taller detective had to crouch even more than Klayman because of the low ceiling and paraphernalia hanging from it.

Klayman pointed to where he wanted them to go, then indicated with his hand that he would approach from the left, Johnson from the right. Johnson drew his weapon and moved away in the direction Klayman had signaled, while Klayman followed his own path. It was Johnson who first saw Jeremiah, just his head, pressed against a low brick wall that formed one of the attic's corners. A steamer trunk shielded the rest of him from the detective.

Johnson saw out of the corner of his eye that Klayman was now coming up behind Lerner. Johnson's heart pounded, his throat was dry. Was the kid armed? Were they going to end up in a shootout in the attic of an arts center, with a happy cocktail party going on downstairs? Spare me. His legs ached from the position he was in, and he felt a sudden need to go to the bathroom. That was reality, he thought. Show that side of being a cop in all the dumb TV shows and movies, having to pee while waiting to get your head blown off.

"Hey, Lerner."

Klayman's voice broke the silence, and snapped Johnson's senses into even more heightened alert. Lerner swung his head around to see who'd said it.

"Detectives, Lerner. We're armed. You can't go anywhere, so stand up nice and slow and raise your hands high."

The detectives watched as Lerner debated whether to obey.

"Don't be a jerk, Lerner," Johnson said.

The second voice brought Lerner to a half-standing position.

"Hands up, Lerner. Come on, we just want to talk to you," Klayman said.

"We don't have a lot of patience, Lerner," said Johnson. "Don't make us take you down."

Lerner slowly stood, his hands still at his side.

"Up, up," Klayman said, his voice tighter now. "Hands in the air."

Jeremiah did as instructed.

"Now, walk toward me, nice and slow," Johnson said. "Be a good boy. We don't want to hurt you."

Klayman pulled a set of cuffs from his belt while returning his revolver to its holster. Johnson, his weapon firmly engulfed in both hands, kept it trained on Lerner while Klayman prepared to cuff him.

"Hands behind your back," Klayman said.

"What do you want with me?" Lerner asked.

"Behind your back, Jeremiah," Klayman repeated, sounding as though he really meant it this time.

The young man, dressed in a U of Maryland sweatshirt, and jeans and scuffed brown deck shoes, started to comply. But as Klayman reached for his hands and as Johnson lowered his weapon and stepped closer, Lerner swung at Johnson, catching him in the cheek and sending him falling back into a pile of moldy gym mats. Klayman froze for a second as Lerner made for the opening in the floor and the ladder. Johnson flung himself on his stomach and grabbed Lerner's ankle, but couldn't hold on. Lerner was feetfirst through the hole and had gone down a few steps when Klayman reached him. He grabbed his thick, oily black hair and rammed his head against wood that framed the opening, then knocked his head in the opposite direction, banging that side of his face, too. Lerner lost his grip and footing on the ladder and slid down in a vertical free fall, his face and other parts of his body catching the ladder's rungs, generating painful grunts and anguished cries. He landed in a heap at the feet of Wooby, the arts center's director.

Klayman half fell, half scrambled down the ladder, maintaining enough control to avoid injury. Lerner was facedown, and Klayman rammed his knees into his back, jerked his hands behind, and snapped on the cuffs. Johnson arrived as his partner was pulling Lerner to his feet and pushing him against a wall. The big, heavy, black detective grabbed Lerner by the front of his sweatshirt and cocked his right hand. Klayman grabbed it.

"You are some dumb punk," Johnson snarled. Jeremiah's ring had cut Johnson's cheek; a small rivulet of blood snaked down to his jawbone.

"I didn't do nothing," Lerner said.

"Shut up," Klayman said.

"You beat me. You bastards beat me, and I didn't do a damn thing."

While Johnson continued pinning Lerner to the wall, Klayman brought his face close to the senator's son and said, "You are under arrest for assaulting a police officer, resisting arrest, and a dozen other charges I'll think of by the time we get to headquarters. And one of those charges, you moron, might be murder."

"Murder? What are you, crazy? Man, you are crazy. Crazy!"

"You have the right to remain silent . . ."

They led him down the hall while an astonished Wooby trailed behind.

"What do you think I did, kill that chick over at the theatre?"

"Now, why would you even think of that, Jeremiah?" Johnson asked, holding his handkerchief to his wound and shoving Lerner in the back with the other.

"Would you mind taking him out another way?" Wooby asked. "We have this party going on and—"

"Sure," Klayman said.

Wooby escorted them to their car, where Jeremiah was placed in the backseat.

"Sorry for the disruption," Klayman said. "And thanks for your help."

"Anytime, Detective. He's Senator Lerner's son?"

"Afraid so."

"And Clarise Emerson's son?"

"Yeah. Thanks again."

"I'm going back inside and have a drink. A double."

Wooby watched them drive away before returning to the opening party where dozens of people were milling about, enjoying drinks and hors d'oeuvres. He was on his way to the bar when the center's assistant director, Georgi Deneau, intercepted him. With her was her nine-year-old grandson, Aaron, who'd been in the young audience of an exhibit, "Through the Eyes of Children."

"Bill, where have you been?" Georgi said.

"I was, ah, showing some people around the center."

"I'm glad you're back. Clarise Emerson just arrived." She nodded toward a corner of the room, where Clarise chatted with other guests. Wooby went to her.

"Hello, Bill," Clarise said. "You're looking well."

"Thanks," Wooby said. "So is the next head of the NEA."

"Anything new here at the center?" she asked. "Besides this wonderful party and exhibition?"

"Anything new? Nothing a hefty grant from the NEA wouldn't fix. No, nothing new, Clarise. Would you excuse me? I think I have a date with a bottle of scotch."

# FIFTEEN

"Good afternoon, Mr. Bancroft."

Morris, the doorman at Bancroft's apartment building, opened the door to G Street for the aging actor and took note of how he was dressed. Bancroft was seldom seen in the same outfit, nor was he partial to conventional clothing. It was obvious to the doorman, and to others who knew Bancroft, that he costumed himself daily rather than simply dressed, which provided a show of sorts, and a mirror into what life-role Bancroft was playing on any given day. He wore a pinched-waist blue double-breasted pinstripe jacket with a floppy red handkerchief bulging from its breast pocket, white slacks in need of pressing, tan loafers sans socks, a white shirt with a high collar, and a blue-

and-green ascot. Pancake makeup had been applied with a heavy hand.

"Good afternoon, Morris," Bancroft replied, the words rolling off his tongue, each syllable enunciated. "Lovely day, isn't it?"

"Sure is, Mr. Bancroft."

Bancroft suddenly squared himself to face the doorman, hands on his hips, his face set in exaggerated anger. "Good God, Morris, how many times must I tell you to call me Sydney? Mr. Bancroft makes me sound so dreadfully old."

Morris laughed. "Goes with the job, Mr.—Sydney—referring to tenants by their last names from age three up. Polite, you know."

Bancroft inhaled as though to say that he had no choice but to accept the logic of it all. "A taxi, please."

Morris went to the corner, where he hailed a passing cab driven by someone of obvious Middle Eastern origins. Bancroft's face mirrored his dismay at the vehicle and its driver. He said, "My kingdom for a London taxi, Morris. 'The London taxi is a relic for which my zeal is evangelic . . . It's designed for people wearing hats, and not for racing on Bonneville Flats . . . A man can get out, or a lady in . . . when you sit, your knees don't bump your chin . . .' "

The doorman had heard Bancroft recite Ogden Nash's ode to London taxis countless times, but listened as though it were the first.

" 'The driver so deep in the past is sunk that he'll help you with your bags and trunk. . . . Indeed, he is such a fuddy-duddy that he calls you Sir instead of Buddy.' "

The driver blew his horn and shouted something in Arabic, undoubtedly to the effect that he didn't have all day to sit idly while some crazy man on the sidewalk recited poetry.

"Hold your bloody horses," Bancroft said, going to the taxi and entering through the door held open by Morris. "E and Eleventh Streets, Northwest," he told the driver. "And drive sanely, you bloody wog. I am in no rush."

Nor was he in a rush to tip when they pulled up in front of the Harrington Hotel, around the corner from Ford's Theatre. He added ten cents to the fare, admonishing the driver to learn better manners in the future if he wished to benefit from living in a civilized society, slammed the door, and entered Harry's Bar. A bartender, wearing a red polo shirt with HARRY'S SALOON written on it in white, announced to others at the bar, "Hey, look who's here, Richard Burton."

"Don't insult me by mistaking me for that second-rate actor," said Bancroft. "And be quick with the shandy. I am absolutely parched."

The bartender, and a waitress at the serving bar, laughed as they usually did at Bancroft's entrance. They enjoyed having Sydney as a customer; he was unfailingly polite, even when engaged in a heated debate with other regulars. "Nice guy, a little strange, but pleasant enough," was how he was summed up by others at the bar.

Bancroft took the mug of half beer, half lemonade handed him by the bartender—accompanied with a look of displeasure at having to make the drink—to a vacant high table next to the window overlooking E Street. The sidewalk was busy with people leaving their jobs and heading for home, most out of the city. It was estimated that 80 percent of those in the District during the day lived in surrounding suburbs, turning Washington into a relatively desolate place when darkness fell.

Bancroft was a regular at Harry's, although he was partial to the Star Saloon, directly across from Ford's Theatre, whose history went back to the Lincoln assassination. He chose Harry's on this day because there was less chance of being engaged in conversation than at the Star. Harry's was big enough to find some relative seclusion.

He needed time to think, along with some alcohol to steady his nerves, although he would never admit that to others. The teenage production he'd been directing, and that was to be performed that weekend, was as good as it would ever be. The cast was more willing than talented—he detested having to try to pull anything decent from a group of teens who seemed more interested in what they wore and what gossip was being spread than in following his stage directions. It had been a most unpleasant experience, one that had caused him physical discomfort, pains in his stomach, headaches, even a bout of nausea. And now the murder and the distasteful, insulting interrogation by the police.

Surely, Clarise would understand his need to get away for a few days, to escape the source of his discomfort. His assistant could carry on in his absence, as untalented as she might be. Besides, he had business in London, important meetings that could raise him out of this temporary lull in his professional career and rekindle his passion for the theatre—more important, the theatre world's passion for him as an actor.

The past two years at Ford's had been dismal, although he knew he couldn't express that to Clarise. From her perspective, she'd done him a great favor bringing him onto the staff and giving him a steady paycheck. Perhaps the most wounding thing was that Clarise viewed it, and him, in precisely that way, doing him a favor, bailing him out of what had been an unpleasant period of financial insecurity. Should he be grateful? Of course he was, but only to a point. She'd gotten her money's worth, he was certain, parading him in front of potential personal and corporate donors, Sydney Bancroft, the British Shakespearean actor—"Remember him?"—all those British movies occasionally rerun on the cable TV channels—"Tell them that wonderful story, Sydney, about when you appeared in that love scene with Margo Sinclair and dropped her on the way up the stairs"—"I could never be

an actor, Mr. Bancroft, especially Shakespeare, because I could never remember all
those lines"—(An aside from Clarise: "Just
as long as he remembers to write the damn
check.")—"Didn't you used to be Samuel
Bancroft, the British actor?"

He went to the bar and ordered another
shandy, and a shot of Irish whiskey to go
with it. Soon, fortified, he bid the bartender
a flowery farewell, stepped out onto E
Street, admired a passing young woman
whose fine figure was amply demonstrated
in the tight black pants and white sweater
she wore, and walked to the corner of Tenth
and E where young people milled about in
front of the Hard Rock Café. He walked
down Tenth and paused in front of Ford's
Theatre's box office, then looked across the
street to the Star. The saloon had originally
been where the box office was now situ-
ated, attached to the theatre, and where
John Wilkes Booth had downed a few shots
before going inside the theatre to shoot Lincoln as he sat with his wife, Mary, and Major Henry Reed Rathbone and his fiancée,
Clara Harris, who happened to be Rathbone's stepsister. General and Mrs. Ulysses
S. Grant were to have accompanied the

Lincolns to the theatre that night but had begged off at the last minute, the general citing the pressures of work. The truth was that Mrs. Grant disliked Mary Lincoln and found any excuse to avoid being in the first lady's company. Julia Grant had been on the receiving end of Mary Lincoln's jealous, volatile tirades on more than one occasion, and had been accused by the first lady of coveting the White House for herself and her famous military hero husband.

"Sydney!"

Bancroft turned to see Michael Kahn, The Shakespeare Theatre's longtime artistic director, approaching. Over fifteen years, Kahn had molded the theatre into one of the country's preeminent Shakespearean venues, its productions routinely acclaimed by local and out-of-town critics. His multiple honors, including six Helen Hayes Awards, and the coveted Will Award, testified to his preeminence. But Bancroft wasn't a fan of the theatre, or of Kahn. He'd been turned down for roles there, and he'd once approached Kahn during lunch at the Banana Café, Kahn's favorite lunchtime spot, and had been, in Bancroft's estimation, summarily dismissed by the director. His bitterness toward Kahn was palpable.

As Kahn closed the gap, Bancroft ducked into the box office and looked back out through the window to see Kahn shake his head and walk away. "Copper-bottomed bastard," Bancroft muttered, and waited until Kahn was well out of range.

"Can I help you, Sydney?" the woman in the box office asked.

"What? Oh, no, thank you. Just stopped in to see how things were."

"Everything is fine."

"Good. Smashing. Nice to hear. Well, must be going. Excuse me."

He entered the building through the front door, greeted the park ranger on duty, and walked into the darkened theatre. The last tourist tour of the day had been conducted, and a lovely calm and quiet permeated the historic room. He went down the aisle and up onto the stage where a few work lights provided muted illumination. He looked up at the presidential box in which Lincoln had been shot and began to quietly recite a line from *Othello:* "An honourable murderer, if you will; For nought I did in hate, but all in honour."

A cough emanating from the house caused him to turn. He peered into the auditorium and saw Bernard Crowley seated in a shadowy corner, on the opposite side from the presidential box.

"I thought you were home sick," Crowley said.

"I have recovered."

"That's good to hear."

The corpulent controller struggled to get up and approached the narrow orchestra pit. Bancroft glared down at him.

"Pretending you're Mr. Booth?" Crowley asked.

Bancroft pulled himself to full height and sneered. "And what would *you* know about John Wilkes Booth, Crowley? That he was a demented madman who acted upon his convictions when he shot old Abe, a lowlife lacking social grace and talent? The man was a brilliant actor, from a family of brilliant Shakespearean actors. His father, Junius, conquered the London stage at seventeen. Three of John's brothers also became fine actors, but none as fine as John Wilkes Booth. Did you know, Crowley, that just a few years before his fling at ultimate fame as America's most illustrious assassin, he was being paid *six hundred and fifty dollars a week* in New York for his stage appearances? The man was brilliant, a star of great magnitude, an interpreter without peer of Shakespeare and—" He'd been speaking to the empty presidential booth. Now, he turned to see that Crowley was gone, had had the audacity to walk away in the middle of his lecture.

"I met a fool i' the forest," he proclaimed loudly to the empty house. "A motley fool." He added softly, "And he is Crowley."

Bancroft stepped down from the stage, went through the yellow doors connecting the theatre with the adjacent building, and climbed the stairs to Clarise Emerson's office. Crowley was behind her desk.

"Where is she?" Bancroft asked.

"At a party, and then dinner with potential contributors," Crowley answered without looking up from a set of figures he'd been examining.

"Oh." Bancroft chewed his cheek before asking, "Why do you hate me so, Crowley?"

Now, the controller raised his eyes. "I don't hate you, Sydney. I just think you're on a free ride, compliments of Clarise, and wonder why. I know one thing. Paying you to do virtually nothing is a drain on the bottom line, and the bottom line is something I care very much about."

"You sound positively jealous," Bancroft said, striking a pose with one elbow on a file cabinet.

"Jealous? Of what?"

"Of Clarise's affection for me."

"I wouldn't call it affection," Crowley said, returning his focus to the numbers on the green sheets of paper. "I'd call it pity."

Crowley couldn't see the anger manifest itself in Bancroft, the pulsating vein in his neck, lips pressed tightly together, fists clenched. When the actor said nothing, Crowley sat back, hands behind his head, a grin on his face. "I'm busy, Sydney. As I said, Clarise is—"

"Tell her I've left town for a few days. Tell her I'll be in London conferring with producers and my agent concerning my one-man show. Tell her the teenage production—if it can be called that without laughing—is in as good a shape as it ever will be, and that my esteemed assistant will carry things forward. I may be back in time for the performance. I shall try to be. But if I am not—"

"Good night, Sydney. I'll pass along your message."

As Bancroft turned to leave, Crowley said, "What shall I tell the police when they want to question you again?"

"Why would they?"

"Oh, because I understand you're high on their list of suspects, considering the perverted attention you demonstrated toward Nadia."

The actor, for whom words were everything, was without them for a moment. Then, he spoke from between almost clenched teeth, "I wish you a dreadful disease, Crowley, a long, lingering, and painful one."

At Bistro Bis, on Capitol Hill, Clarise looked down at her appetizer that had just been served—galantine of duck with slices of seared foie gras in an apple-cherry compote. Her cell phone sounded.

"Sorry, but I don't think you'll mind a phone call," she told her dinner companions, two executives from AT&T. "I forgot to turn it off." She ignored a stern look from a couple at an adjoining table and put the phone to her ear. The AT&T men, busy talking with each other, didn't see her face sag as the caller, Clarise's social secretary, relayed the message that Jeremiah had left during the single phone call he was allowed from First District headquarters: "Mom, I've been arrested. They beat me. I didn't do nothing. I swear."

Clarise replaced the phone in her handbag.

"You can never get away," the female executive said lightly.

"Thanks to us," her male colleague said. "Trouble?"

"No, no trouble," Clarise said.

They'd been discussing AT&T's possible sponsorship of a play the following season when the phone had rung. "I'm afraid I will have to run right after dinner," she said. "In the meantime, this looks scrumptious." She picked up a fork and began to eat, saying between bites, "Let's get back to the show you'll be supporting at Ford's Theatre. There's a tremendous amount of goodwill for AT&T to come from your participation. Our lawmakers are keenly aware of corporations who support the arts here in Washington, and tend to look favorably upon them when specific regulatory legislation is being considered." She smacked her well-shaped lips. "This galantine is extraordinary, don't you agree?"

She raced home after dinner, flinging her raincoat on a chair as she moved through the house to her home office. Her secretary had left a note containing information from Jeremiah's call from the police station. Clarise glanced at it and was about to reach for the phone to try to reach her ex-husband when its ring jarred her. She picked up.

"Clarise, darling, it's Sydney."

"Sydney, I don't have time to—"

"I know, I know. There was just a breaking news story on the telly about Jeremiah. I'm shocked, as I know you are."

"It was on the news?"

"Just moments ago. Clarise, you know I'm leaving for London in the morning, but—"

"You are?"

"Didn't Crowley tell you? He's known about the trip for ages."

"No, he didn't."

"At any rate, darling, I'll only be away for a few days. The show is in tip-top shape.

When I come back, call on me for anything. *Anything,* Clarise. I'll be there at your side."

"Yes. Thanks, Sydney. I have to run."

"Of course. Stiff upper lip, Clarise. It's probably all a mistake."

The moment Bancroft hung up, he dialed the number on the business card Detective Klayman had given him. It took a minute for the desk sergeant to locate Klayman. When he came on the line, Bancroft said, "Ah, Detective Klayman. So glad you're there. I just heard on the news about Jeremiah Lerner being arrested. I presume it has to do with the murder of poor Nadia."

"What can I do for you, Mr. Bancroft?"

"I feel dreadful about this, absolutely dreadful, but I know I must act responsibly. It hadn't crossed my mind when you visited me at my home, but seeing the news report brought it all back. I knew Nadia had been seeing the Lerner boy, and I warned her against it. She looked to me as a father figure, I'm afraid, and I was perfectly happy to play that role. From what I know of Jeremiah, he's hardly the sort of young man a decent girl like Nadia should be involved with. And I told her that—in no uncertain terms, I might add."

"You're sure he was seeing her."

"Oh, yes. Quite sure."

"I'd like to get a formal statement from you, Mr. Bancroft."

"Happy to accommodate, although I'm sure you can appreciate how delicate this situation is for me. Jeremiah is, after all, Clarise Emerson's son, and she happens to be not only my boss but a very dear friend as well. I trust we can keep this between us."

"When can I meet you tomorrow?" Klayman asked.

"I'm afraid that will be impossible, unless you wish to join me on my Virgin Atlantic flight to London. But I'll only be away a few days. Agents, producers, meetings day and night. They wish to speak to me about a one-man show I'm mounting."

"When will you be back?"

"Saturday, if all goes well."

Klayman hesitated before responding. Should he press to see Bancroft tonight? He wouldn't have time until much later. He didn't need a statement to use that night when questioning Jeremiah Lerner; knowledge that there was someone to verify Lerner's involvement with Nadia Zarinski in the event he denied it was good enough.

"Please check in with me when you come back, Mr. Bancroft. And . . . do come back."

"Of course. You'll be the first call I make upon my return. Good night, sir. Keep up the good work."

# SIXTEEN

"Why did you run? Why did you hit my partner?"

Rick Klayman sat with Jeremiah Lerner in an interrogation room. A uniformed officer stood in a corner, arms folded across his chest. Firearms had been left outside the room; the only weapon in the room was a hefty nightstick suspended from the officer's belt.

Lerner slouched in the straight-back wooden chair, his coal black hair in disarray. Bruises on his left cheek and temple were turning from red to blue-green.

"Why?" Klayman repeated. "All we wanted to do was talk to you, ask you a few questions."

"I didn't know who you were. For all I knew, you were a couple of hit men."

Klayman looked up at the cop in the corner, who smiled.

"Hit men? Come on, Jeremiah. That's a dumb answer. We identified ourselves."

"You beat me up."

"You beat yourself up going down that ladder."

The door opened, and Herman Hathaway motioned for Klayman to join him outside.

"What's he saying?" Hathaway asked.

"He's claiming police brutality. Nothing about the murder, and no questions from me about it. He made a comment when we brought him in, asked if the murder was why we came after him. I thought it was strange he thought of it."

"You didn't rough him up, right?"

"Right."

"Look, Rick, this is a potential mess. The kid may be a suspect in the Zarinski murder, but now he's here on charges of assaulting an officer and resisting arrest."

"Which he did."

"Yeah, I know. I saw Mo's cheek. And we can hold him on those charges. But the murder is another thing. He's got a senator for a father. His mother, Mrs. Emerson, called. She says there's a lawyer on his way. He *ask* for a lawyer?"

"No."

"Mo's talking with the family, see if the daughter ever mentioned dating the Lerner kid."

"I had a confirmation."

"Huh?"

"A call from the actor at Ford's Theatre, Sydney Bancroft."

"What'd he say?"

"He claims he knew she was dating Lerner, and says he counseled her against it."

"Thanks for sharing it with me, as they say."

"It just happened a couple of minutes ago, Herman."

"Get a statement from Bancroft."

"I will. He'll be in London till Saturday. I'll catch him when he gets back."

"Okay. We can hold Lerner on the assault-and-resisting charges until the preliminary hearing tomorrow. That'll give us twenty-four hours. Maybe we can get him to talk about the murder, provided the lawyer doesn't shut him up. Remember, he's not a suspect in the murder, Rick. We just want to ask a few questions."

Johnson joined them. "The parents say she never mentioned Lerner," he said, "the kid, that is. Their daughter talked a lot about the senator, what a great guy he was to work for."

"The affair with the senator? That come up again?"

"Yeah. The mother thinks the kid is being brought into it because of the rumors about her daughter and the senator. She's blaming the media."

"She's way off base."

"Tell me about it."

"By the way, Gertz in Public Info wants to know how the press got hold of it so fast. Any ideas?"

"Wasn't us," Johnson said.

"What about the guy at the arts center who helped you find Lerner?"

"Wooby, the director? Possible. Doesn't seem the type to go running to the press."

They looked through the one-way mirror into the room where Lerner still slouched in his chair, defiance etched into his narrow, swarthy, brooding, unshaven face. A few years ago, it would have been the face of a thug, or villain. Today, it was the face of a male model.

"Read him his rights again, Rick," Hathaway instructed, "and see how much you can get out of him before the lawyer arrives."

Klayman and Johnson entered the room and took chairs on either side of Lerner. Johnson took his time sitting, glaring at Lerner as he did.

"It was an accident," Lerner mumbled.

Klayman read Lerner the Miranda warning again, slid a copy of it in front of him, and told him to sign as verification that he'd received it. Lerner pushed it back unsigned.

"Suit yourself," Johnson said. "How long were you and Nadia Zarinski dating?"

"What are you talking about?"

"Nadia Zarinski, the murder victim behind Ford's Theatre. We know you were dating her, Jeremiah. Keep evading our questions and you just dig a deeper hole for yourself," Klayman said.

"I never dated her. I never even knew her."

Klayman and Johnson looked at each other before Klayman said, "We have two witnesses who say you did."

"They're—lying."

"I don't think so," said Johnson. "Make it easy on yourself, Jeremiah. What'd she do, break it off? Tell you she had another guy, and you lost it?"

"I want a lawyer," Lerner said. "I'm not answering any of your questions."

"Suit yourself. You'll need a lawyer when you're up on murder charges. Of course, you're lucky you live in D.C. No death penalty, just the rest of your life in prison. The other inmates should find you attractive."

Lerner folded his arms across his chest, sunk his chin into his breastbone, and said nothing.

Klayman left the room to join Hathaway on the other side of the one-way glass.

"Lerner's attorney is here," Hathaway announced.

A minute later, Mackensie Smith was escorted in. He introduced himself and asked, "What's he being charged with?"

"Assault of a police officer and resisting arrest, Counselor," Hathaway replied.

Smith peered through the window at Lerner. He didn't want to be there any more than Lerner did.

*   *   *

He'd been relaxing at home when the call came. She sounded uncharacteristically panicked. "Mac, they've arrested Jeremiah," she said.

"I'm sorry to hear that, Clarise. What was he arrested for?"

"That's what has me so upset. If it was just one of his silly antics, marijuana, getting into a fight, I wouldn't be so concerned. But his message—I was out at a dinner meeting and my secretary took it—his message said he thought it had to do with the murder of that poor girl at the theatre."

"Had he known the girl?"

"I don't think so. Even if he had, that doesn't mean he'd kill her. Jeremiah is a handful, Mac, but he's not a murderer."

"You might be jumping the gun, Clarise. Questioning him doesn't mean he's a suspect. At this stage, the police will be wanting to talk to anyone who might have some information to help them."

Her distress turned to anger. "What information could Jeremiah possibly have, Mac?"

"I don't know, Clarise. Have you called an attorney?"

"I'm calling you. I deal with lots of lawyers, but none who handle criminal cases."

"And I'm one of those who doesn't, Clarise—at least not anymore. I'm just a college professor now. Remember?"

"Please, Mac. I don't want to beg. Help me. I have my confirmation hearing coming up—Good God, it's almost here—and—please!"

"I'll call someone, Clarise."

Although Smith hadn't practiced much criminal law since resigning from his practice, he was still a member of the D.C. Bar, and active in its functions. Those times that he had heeded the call to action had been because of unusual circumstances, a friend in need, or a challenge too compelling to ignore.

"No, Mac, I want you to go. I know this is an imposition, and I wouldn't think of dragging you away from Annabel, but—"

"Annabel's out at a meeting."

"Will you? I'm sure it won't amount to much. Just say whatever it is you lawyers say and get him out of there."

It was good that Smith's sour expression couldn't be seen over the phone line.

"Do you know where he's being held?" he asked.

"Yes. First District headquarters, on Fourth Street, Southwest."

"All right, Clarise. I'll see what I can do. But I won't go beyond this. My former law partners are the best in the city. I'll put you in touch with them tomorrow. Does Senator Lerner know?"

"Yes. I reached him. He's on some damn retreat in Virginia and said he couldn't do anything until tomorrow afternoon. A big help."

Smith let it pass.

"But he did say that he agreed with me about calling you. He's always been impressed with you, Mac. He's told me that on several occasions."

"Are you at home?" Smith asked.

"Yes."

"I'll call you there later."

He considered after hanging up to attempt reaching one of his former partners to see if he'd handle matters that night, but decided that would be going back on his word to Clarise. There was also a current running through him that he recognized from previous calls to action. He didn't miss being a criminal trial lawyer, and was quite content, thank you, teaching law, and being Annabel Lee-Smith's devoted husband. But all the adrenaline hadn't drained from him; he was still capable of feeling the rush of being needed by someone in the rough-and-tumble world of the criminal justice system.

He left Annabel a note, retrieved his car from the garage beneath the building, and headed southwest.

"This is Detective Klayman," Hathaway told Smith. "The detective in with your client is Detective Johnson. They're the ones who arrested him. Detective Johnson was the victim in the assault."

"I understand there's some question of you wanting to talk to him about the murder at Ford's Theatre," Smith said.

"That's right," replied Hathaway. "He hasn't been designated a suspect. We just want to know whether he knew the victim, had dated her, and whatever else he might be able to provide."

Smith said nothing as he stepped to the door and waited for Klayman to open it.

Johnson and Lerner looked up at Mac's entrance.

"This is Mr. Smith, the accused's attorney," Hathaway said.

Lerner's puzzled expression indicated he had no idea who Smith was. Mac introduced himself: "I'm a friend of your mother," he explained. "She asked me to represent you." He said to the three detectives and the uniformed officer in the room, "I'd like some time alone with him." He'd almost said "my client," but caught himself.

"We'll leave," said Hathaway.

"No," Smith said, nodding at the one-way window. "I mean alone. Could we use an empty office?"

"Your client's already tried to get away, Counselor."

"I assure you he won't try again," Smith said, fixing Lerner in a hard stare.

Hathaway was reluctant to allow Lerner to leave the interrogation room, but decided that considering who he was, he'd play ball. "Sure," he said. He told Klayman and Johnson to escort Smith and Lerner to his own office. "Stay there," he told them. To Smith: "Fifteen minutes, Counselor?"

Smith nodded.

With Johnson and Klayman stationed directly outside the office, Smith sat Lerner down in a swivel chair, and perched on the edge of the desk. "Let me tell you the facts of life, young man. First of all, I'm no longer a practicing attorney, although I'm licensed. I used to practice criminal law. Now, I teach it. I've known your mother for quite a while and consider her a friend. I'm here because she asked me to come. In the morning, I'll get a hold of some top attorneys I used to work with and they can take over.

"Right now, I'm here to help you through the initial phases of the trouble you've got yourself in. You're charged with resisting arrest and assault on a police officer. Did you do those things?"

"I didn't know who they were."

"Bad answer, son. Did you run from them?"

"Yeah."

"When they tried to arrest you, did you resist?"

"They beat me up."

It was as though he'd never been away from criminal law. How many times had he sat in a police station with young punks, many of them from affluent families, who considered themselves—increasingly, young women, too—tougher than the system, and who were effusive in their answers, thinking they could lie their way out of the trouble in which they'd found themselves? The oppressiveness of such situations, the futility of it all, coupled with the tragic death of his first wife and only child, had pushed him away from the system as it was, and into a less bellicose life.

"Are you saying that the officers who arrested you lied, Jeremiah?"

"Whose side are you on, man, theirs or mine?"

"I was told they came to where you worked because they wanted to ask you questions about the young woman who was murdered last night at Ford's Theatre."

He guffawed. "Man, that is ridiculous. I didn't even know her."

"Do you know her name?"

"Yeah."

"Why?"

"I—I read it in the papers."

"I see. Well, let me sum up what's going on here, Jeremiah, and give you some solid lawyerly advice. They'll hold you overnight because they can. Sometime tomorrow, there'll be a preliminary hearing where the judge will decide whether there's probable cause to charge you with resisting and assault. The lawyer who represents you at the hearing will ask for bail, which you'll be granted. I suggest you have one of your parents with you at the hearing. I'll tell your mother that.

"But from this moment on, Jeremiah, I suggest you keep your mouth shut. That means offering nothing, saying nothing about the charges against you unless your lawyer is present. As for their interest in you regarding the murder, my best advice is to remain silent on that issue, too. Do you understand?"

"I don't want to spend the night in jail."

"You don't have much choice in the matter. Any questions?"

"Man, this sucks!"

Smith knocked on the closed door, which was opened by Mo Johnson. With him outside the office were Klayman and Hathaway.

"Have you booked him?" Smith asked.

"Not yet," Hathaway said.

"Where will he be, in Central Lockup at D.C. headquarters?"

"That's right, Counselor."

Smith said, "There'll be a different attorney for him tomorrow."

"I can't wait," Hathaway said. "Show Mr. Smith out, Rick."

The attorney and the cop went to the lobby and out to the street.

"Mind if I ask you something, Mr. Smith?" Klayman asked.

"As long as it doesn't have to do with the young man inside and the charges against him."

"Are you the Mackensie Smith who teaches the course at GW on Lincoln and his law career?"

"Yes."

"I thought so. I'll be in your class Saturday morning."

"Oh?"

"I take courses at GW, nonmatriculated. I'm already enrolled in a history course, but when I saw you were teaching a second section of the Lincoln course on Saturday mornings, I signed up quick."

"You have a special interest in Lincoln the lawyer?"

"In Lincoln, period. I guess you could say I'm a Lincoln buff. I'd like to say Lincoln scholar, but I'm a long way from that."

"You might be closer than you think, Detective. I'll look forward to seeing you Saturday."

"Thanks. Nice meeting you—Professor."

Smith drove back to the Watergate, where Annabel and Rufus were waiting.

"I can't believe you did that, Mac," Annabel said.

"I'm having some trouble believing it, too. Clarise was very upset, and I thought . . . well, I wanted to help out. I'll call Yale first thing in the morning and turn it over to him." Yale Becker, one of Smith's former partners in the criminal law practice, was considered a top criminal attorney, perhaps the District's best now that Mac Smith was no longer in the saddle.

"Clarise called," Annabel said.

"I said I'd call her. She should be at Jeremiah's hearing tomorrow. Being in a parent's custody is helpful when setting bail."

"Is he in big trouble?"

"Yeah, I'd say so. They're charging him with resisting arrest, and assault on an officer. Those are serious felonies, as you know. What really concerns me, though, is that they want to question him about the murder at the theatre."

"Clarise didn't mention that. Did he know the girl?"

"He claims not to, but he's lying."

Annabel didn't ask how her husband knew Jeremiah was lying. His instincts about such things were uncannily accurate.

"I'll get hold of Yale and see if he'll take the case."

"Maybe Clarise or the senator won't want him. The way Clarise talked, she won't settle for anyone but you."

"Out of the question. By the way, one of the detectives involved in the case—a nice young man named Klayman—is signed up for my Saturday session. He says he's a Lincoln buff."

"Conflict?"

"Not as long as we keep any discussions to Lincoln, and avoid any talk about the Lerner case. Know what bothers me, Annie, besides not believing Jeremiah?"

"Tell me."

"Clarise seemed more concerned about her confirmation hearing than what was happening to her son."

"She's an ambitious woman, Mac. We know that. And I suspect she was never much of a nurturing mother. I don't mean a loving mother. She obviously loves Jeremiah. But she's spent her life chasing a career, not motherhood."

"She was annoyed that Senator Lerner was away at some retreat and wouldn't bother coming back until tomorrow."

"Sad. I dealt with a lot of parents like that when I was handling divorces, and kept in my desk a copy of something Dickens wrote. He said, 'I am the only child of parents who weighed, measured and priced everything'—and went on to say that what couldn't be weighed, measured, or priced didn't exist."

"Let's not be too judgmental, Annie. Lots of kids are brought up in such circumstances and end up solid citizens. I had too many young people in trouble with the law, and with generally screwed-up lives, who blamed their parents. It's a convenient excuse for avoiding responsibility. Speaking of responsibility, I'd better walk the beast."

"Mac!"

"Sorry. I forgot about his fragile ego."

# SEVENTEEN

Sydney Bancroft exited the Delta Shuttle at New York's La Guardia Airport, went to a large electronic board on which airport hotels were displayed, and called one. Ten minutes later, he boarded a shuttle bus and checked in at the lowest price offered, which included a senior citizen discount.

"Tricked you," he told the dour young woman at the check-in desk. "I'm actually thirty-five but made myself up to enjoy your old fogy rate."

She handed him his room key without breaking a smile.

Shame. He had tried to brighten her day. Young fogy. The room was small. It had one window, which faced a highway, beyond which jet aircraft arriving and departing could be seen—and heard, though muted. He freshened up, checked himself in a mirror cracked in one corner—he was wearing jeans, a black turtleneck, and a tan safari jacket, his usual flying outfit—and went downstairs to the restaurant and bar. It was empty except for the bartender, a waitress whose fatigue showed through her heavy makeup, and two men in business suits with an attractive, middle-aged woman who Bancroft immediately decided was a prostitute.

"Yes, sir?" the bartender asked.

"Scotch whisky, a double, sir, with water on the side."

After a second round, he took a table and ordered a shrimp cocktail, and another drink. "And please bring rolls," he told the waitress. "And butter. Lots of butter."

He was drunk when he returned to his room, and a little queasy, which was fine with him. Without the alcohol as a sedative, sleep would elude him. He called the desk to reserve the shuttle to Kennedy Airport the following morning, but was told the hotel didn't provide that service. The severe young woman who'd checked him in said he'd have to take a taxi. Bancroft didn't argue. He placed a wakeup call with her, stripped off his clothing, and stood naked in front of the bathroom mirror, trying not to notice the folds of skin on his slender body that obeyed gravity. He smiled at his mirror image, yellowing teeth returning the affection. He vowed to use one of the teeth-whitening products on the market the minute he got back, a pledge he'd made to himself countless times.

"Ah, Harrison, how very good to see you again," he said to his mirror image. "Me? . . . couldn't be better . . . top of my game . . . how's things here in the West End? . . . ah-hah, as I suspected . . . yes, I heard Mendes was leaving Donmar Warehouse . . . and Trevor is leaving the Royal National . . . see, Harrison, old chap, I've been keeping up with things while in Washington . . . how are things progressing with sprucing up the West End? . . . it's been looking shabby for years . . . the last time I was here it was positively slummy . . . what it needs, Harrison, is a bit of the old glitter . . . that's what I intend to bring in with my one-man show . . . I tell you, Harrison, it will be the talk of London . . . and the touring potential is absolutely marvelous, dear chap . . . now, I know we've had our little spats over the years, but isn't that supposed to happen between client and agent? . . . the creative always butting heads with the money end of things . . . Ford's Theatre will be absolutely devastated with my leaving . . . I sometimes think I'm the only person in Washington who knows *anything* about Shakespeare and how to present him . . . I—"

His eyes became heavy in the mirror; he shook his head to no avail in an attempt to revive. Exhausted, he sprawled on the bed and fell asleep to the sound of a jet taking off across the highway. *Thank God for sleep,* he thought, *anesthesia for tormented souls.*

The following morning, an insufferably talkative cab driver drove him across Queens to the larger airport, where his Virgin Atlantic flight to London would depart. Bancroft had bought the cheapest available coach seat and tried to charm the ticket agent into upgrading him to what Virgin called Upper Class. "You may have seen my films, dear girl," he said. "I'm heading for London to negotiate my one-man show, and I'd be delighted to tell audiences that I only fly Virgin Atlantic. Wonderful press for you, you know."

"I'm sure it would be, sir, but I don't have the authorization to upgrade you. Perhaps when you get to London you should call our executive offices and propose something to them about your show."

"Oh, I certainly intend to do that. But surely in anticipation of it happening, you could find me one of your empty seats in Upper Class. I'm afraid my back has been acting up, and—well, I really need to work on my show and would find it terribly difficult to be in the back with crying babies and—"

"Sir, there is nothing I can do for you," she said. Coughs from those behind him in line expressed their displeasure at his holding things up.

"Yes, well, cheerio, my dear. I understand. Yes, I understand."

He slept most of the way to London. When awake, he kept going over what he would say to his agent, and to theatre people from his past. It had been almost six months since his last trip to London, and that had been a disappointing visit. This time it would be different. This time he had something tangible to offer, a one-man show featuring the former great Shakespearean actor Sydney Bancroft, whose return to the stage had "lifted the theatre world to new and refreshed excellence. His very presence on the stages of the world has audiences howling in their seats, and shedding tears as this gifted thespian presents the words of William Shakespeare as no other actor of his generation can."

He was in the midst of creating this self-review, saying the words aloud to the chagrin of an elderly woman seated across the aisle, when the flight attendant asked if he wished to purchase another drink.

"No, no thank you, my dear. I believe I've had enough. But thank you for asking. It was sweet of you."

He rode the underground's Piccadilly line from Heathrow Airport to Piccadilly Circus and walked to Beak Street, only a few blocks away, where he stopped in front of an Italian food shop. Sausages of every size and description hung in the window of the closed store, illuminated by red bulbs strung haphazardly from the ceiling. He looked up. Lights were on in the apartment above. He went to a door next to the shop and pushed the buzzer. A gruff male voice came through a tiny speaker: "Who's there?"

"It's Sydney. Open up."

There was a harsh metallic sound as the lock disengaged. Bancroft opened the door and looked upstairs leading to the apartment. Standing at the top was the silhouetted figure of a burly man. "Well, come up, for God's sake," he said. "Don't just bloody stand there."

Bancroft slowly ascended the stairs and followed the man, whose stage name was Aaron Kipp—a variation of his birth name, Aaron Kipowicz—into the flat. Now, Kipp was fully visible—well over two hundred pounds, black-and-green flannel shirt hanging loose over baggy tan pants, frayed carpet slippers, his full beard as wild and woolly as his salt-and-pepper hair.

"Damn, Sydney, you're as skinny as a pole," Kipp said as Bancroft dropped his bag to the floor and collapsed on a couch. "What the hell have you become, one of those anorexic types?"

"The result of healthy living, Kipp, and a busy schedule. Got a drink, or are you on the wagon again?"

"Fell off that months ago, Sydney, but there's no booze in the flat. Thought we'd pub it. Hungry?"

"As a matter of fact, I am. Been working much?"

"Nah, just a bloody voice-over now and then. Hardly enough to keep the larder stocked. I'm up for a cartoon character. Imagine that. You?"

"Can't keep up with it, although Washington is not like London, not for a serious artist. Come on, Kipp, I'm absolutely famished."

They walked to The Round Table Pub, in St. Martin's Court, a narrow, pedestrian-only cut between St. Martin's Lane and Charing Cross Road. The Round Table was a popular watering hole for cast and crew from the Albery and the Wyndham Theatres, whose stage doors opened onto the court. The downstairs bar was packed, so they went upstairs and found a single empty table in a corner. Patrons were three-deep at the bar, some of whom greeted Kipp as he and Bancroft passed through the room. A chunky waitress with orange hair and a heavy Cockney accent took their orders— bangers and mash for Kipp, shepherd's pie for Bancroft, and a two-pint jug of cask ale for each. Their beer had just been served when two men and a young woman approached. "Well, well, well," said one of the men, "what have we here? The famous Aaron Kipp and the infamous Sydney Bancroft."

Bancroft had seen them coming and had silently prayed they would pass. No such luck. He knew the two men; the woman was unknown to him. The older of the men, Philip Wainsley, was a relatively successful actor-turned-director, who years ago had worked with Bancroft on two Shakespearean productions, *Titus Andronicus,* with the Royal Shakespeare Company, in which Bancroft played the arrogant Saturninus, and Iago in *Othello,* at the Royal Shakespeare Theatre in Stratford-upon-Avon. Reviewers had not been kind to him in either role, although he had fared better with the critics in some of Shakespeare's comedies, including the roles of Antonio in *Much Ado About Nothing,* the well-born but penniless lover, Fenton, in *The Merry Wives of Windsor,* and the treacherous Oliver de Boys in *As You Like It.* Perhaps the most scathing review he'd received had come toward the end of his stage career when an out-of-town reviewer, who'd followed Bancroft from his earliest days, wrote of his performance in *Julius Caesar:* "Sydney Bancroft, appearing in the minor role of Cinna, managed to remember his lines." This came after years of reports in London tabloids of Bancroft's bouts of heavy drinking, womanizing, and lack of professional reliability.

The younger man was Sam Botha, an Algerian-British playwright who'd been making his mark in avant-garde London theatre circles. He'd been introduced to Bancroft at a party the last time he'd been in London, and Bancroft had attended one of his plays, which he'd detested, terming it to Kipp "an exercise in arrogant self-indulgence. The man is obviously without talent."

"This is Kitty Wells," Botha said after Kipp, to Bancroft's dismay, had invited the trio to join them at the table. "She'll be appearing in my next play. In fact, I've written it for her."

"How wonderful," Bancroft muttered.

"And how are you, Sydney?" Wainsley asked.

"Couldn't be better, Philip."

"What brings you to London?" said Botha.

Bancroft's first words of response came out in a stammer. "I—I—well, I suppose there's no harm in letting the cat out of the bag, is there? Truth be to tell, I'm here putting the finishing touches on my one-man show."

"How impressive," said Kitty Wells. "A one-man show. What will it be about?"

"About me, dear girl," Bancroft said as the waitress delivered their food. "It will be—well, let me say that it will encompass various highlights of my career, particularly my experiences performing Shakespeare."

"Obviously a brief play," Wainsley said. "If it depends upon highlights—"

"Are you suggesting I have had so few, Philip?"

"No, no, of course not, Sydney. I'm simply saying that few of us have amassed enough high points in our careers to sustain an entire evening on a stage—alone."

"Speak for yourself, Philip," Bancroft said, digging into his meal.

"Will you be opening in London?" Botha asked.

"Oh, yes, of course, London. London it

will be. Is there any other place on earth to open?"

"Have a theatre yet, Sydney?" Wainsley asked.

"Purpose of my trip, make those sort of decisions on the spot. I thought I might incorporate film clips of the Bard's plays on the silver screen. Zeffirelli and I go back a long way. I—"

"Is it already written?" Kitty asked. "Your show."

"No, not quite finished," Bancroft said through a full mouth.

She placed long, slender fingers tipped with red on his arm and said sexily, "Any room in your show for me?"

"I'm offended," said Botha with mock seriousness. "Here I've written you a starring vehicle and you cozy up to him."

"Maybe you could make it a father-daughter show, Sydney," Kipp said, laughing. "Or an examination of how old men make fools of themselves falling for pretty young things and—"

As they bantered back and forth about how Bancroft's show could be reconfigured to explore relationships between old men and young women, Bancroft fell silent. No, it was more than that. He'd slipped into what might be called a trance state, his eyes fixed on Kitty, his lips pressed tightly together. Their voices swirled around him like noisy insects, punctuated by her high-pitched laugh that seemed to become shriller by the second. She had long, silky black hair worn straight that reached her waist. Her lips matched the crimson of her nails; her eyelashes were long and curved, and her chalky white face was becoming ghostly. She came in and out of Bancroft's focus, like someone manipulating a zoom lens. He rubbed his eyes. It was no longer the pretty face of a young woman he'd never met. It was Nadia's face, smiling, then laughing at him after he'd patted her rear end backstage at Ford's Theatre . . . a sharp, cruel laugh.

"Jesus, Sydney, keep your hands off me. I don't get off on old farts."

Her words, and laugh, stung. He was embarrassed. Others had heard, including a handsome young stagehand named Wales in whom Nadia seemed to have an inordinate interest.

"Just a slip of the hand, my dear," Bancroft said, bowing and forcing a laugh.

"Hey, Pops, hands off. She's young enough to be your daughter," Wales said.

Sydney regained his composure. "Practiced hands, sir, gentle, caressing hands that have brought pleasure to the world's most beautiful actresses."

Wales and Nadia now laughed together.

Bancroft adopted a pose, one hand placed jauntily on a hip, head cocked, a thin smile on his lips. He placed his other hand over his heart and said in stentorian tones, " 'Fair flowers that are not gath'red in their prime rot, and consume themselves in little time.' "

Wales and Nadia looked quizzically at him.

"From the pen of the Bard, my dear, young, ignorant friends. Waste not your youthful beauty, Nadia, lest it turn to rot. Good evening, all. I suddenly crave the company of the more enlightened. Or other old farts."

"You all right, Sydney?" Kipp said, slapping him on the shoulder and feeling the bones through his clothing.

"Yes. Quite. Why shouldn't I be?"

Their visitors left the table, saying they were meeting people at the Ivy. Bancroft hailed the waitress and ordered double shots of scotch.

"Drowning your sorrows, Sydney?" Kipp asked, joining him in the harder stuff.

"Sorrows? You're daft, Kipp. After tomorrow, you'll be able to brag to your chums that the next star of the West End, Sydney A. Bancroft, was a houseguest."

"What's tomorrow?"

"Meeting with Harrison about my show."

"He still your agent?"

"You bet he is."

"I thought you had a falling out, how many years ago, ten, twelve?"

"Nothing like bringing an agent a brilliant idea and talent to make him stand up and take notice. Have you ever known one, Kipp, who didn't respond with open arms when someone waltzes into his office to offer the chance of a lifetime?"

"You?"

"Good for you, Kipp. You're still quick on the uptake."

They said little over the next round of drinks. When they were ready to leave, Kipp said, "Since you're about to make a bloody fortune, Sydney, drinks are on you."

Bancroft's words were slurred. "You'll have to put up some money, Kipp, add it to the pot. I am unfortunately short of funds, but only a temporary situation. Only temporary."

Bancroft slept soundly that night on Kipp's couch. But Kipp lay awake for hours, mulling over the night at the pub. "Poor, deluded bastard," he said in a whisper before drifting off. "Poor, deluded bastard."

Harrison Quill's offices were on the second floor of a four-storey office building on Shaftesbury Avenue, across from the Lyric, Apollo, Globe, and Queen Theatres. He'd been a theatrical agent for forty years, and his small suite of offices reflected it, as did Quill himself. He was a short, moderately structured man with a hawk-like nose, thin black mustache that curved down around his mouth Oriental style, and whose hairpiece was shiny black. He wore a red-and-blue awning-striped shirt with white collar, a wide black tie, and a gray wool tweed suit. He was reading the morning papers when his receptionist announced Sydney Bancroft's arrival. Quill lowered the paper, closed his eyes, opened them, drew a bracing deep breath, and instructed her to send him in.

"Ta-ta," Bancroft said, striking a pose in the open doorway. "Raise the curtain, Harry. Sydney Bancroft is back!"

Quill stared at the actor for a moment before getting up, coming around the desk, and accepting Bancroft's outstretched hand. "Hello, Sydney," he said.

"Come, come, Harry, you can do better than that. I've flown across an ocean specifically to see you and all I receive is that lukewarm greeting?"

They shook hands again, with more energy this time. "Please, sit down," Quill said. "Coffee, tea?"

"A cup of tea would be wonderful," Bancroft said. Quill passed an order for two teas to the receptionist.

"Well, Sydney, how have you been?" He said it as though filling a space. Bancroft often thought that Quill would make a good ventriloquist; his lips barely moved when he spoke.

"Quite well, thank you, Harrison Quill. And you? You look prosperous enough." He extended his hands to take in the cluttered, overstuffed office.

"If you mean the business, absolutely dotty. Insane. Not due to overwork, I assure you. The theatre scene here is grim, Sydney, absolutely grim. Everything is retro, dragging out old shows. Good God, we've got *South Pacific* and *My Fair Lady* playing to packed houses, even old Coward works like *Private Lives* and *Star Quality.* Nothing new. Absolutely nothing new!"

"Sounds promising for older actors and actresses, Harry."

"And good for agents who represent them, which doesn't include this agent. They've all gone to the conglomerates, the big agencies with Hollywood connections. It's depressing, I tell you, bloody depressing. I'm thinking of getting out of the business, settle down in the Dorset cottage with the missus, tend the garden, and flip the bird at the whole bloody mess."

Quill had been talking this way for all the years Bancroft had known him, even when his agency was prospering. He raised poormouthing to new heights, and had the first pound he'd ever earned, Bancroft was sure.

"How would you like to turn things around, Harry, old chap?"

Quill's response was a belch.

"My one-man show."

"Your what?"

"One-man show, Harry. It's been percolating for years inside me, and I know the time is right."

"What sort of show, Sydney?" He didn't know what else to say.

"A show about me, Harry, Sydney Bancroft. Oh, don't misunderstand. There will be lots more to it than simply a nostalgic look at my career." He stood and began pacing the office. "You can't believe, Harry—you simply cannot believe how many people remember my performances on both the stage and screen. They come up to me all the time, wanting an autograph, or just to chat about a favorite film of mine. Young people, too. Last night at the pub, Phil Wainsley and Sam Botha made a point of coming to my table to pay respects, and I could sense a buzz at the bar when I entered."

He stood in the middle of the room and raised his hands high. "Think of it, Harry. A show in which one of Willie Shakespeare's

leading interpreters brings audiences into
the Bard's world as no one has ever done
before. The humor most people—and, I
might add, most actors—miss, new inter-
pretations of famous scenes as they should
have been played, some inside gossip
about Shakespeare. He was as much of a
scheming businessman as he was a writer.

"There'll be plenty of sex, Harry. Shakespeare was the master of the double enten-
dre, wasn't he? You know, of course, of the
American comedian George Carlin."

Quill nodded.

"He's packed them in night after night
with his list of forbidden words. Very clever
the way he does it. Made millions, I suspect.
I'll do the same with Shakespeare, let the
audience in on all the words he used that
sound innocuous but have come to have
sexual meanings."

Quill tried to say something, but Bancroft
was not to be interrupted.

"I call this section of the show 'The
Bawdy Bard.' Here's but a small sample.
Romeo and Juliet." He assumed a forlorn
expression as he slipped into character. "I
must another way to fetch a ladder by the
which your love must climb a bird's nest

soon when it is dark. I am the drudge, and toil in your delight, but you shall bear the burden soon at night."

Quill stared.

"'Bear the burden,' Harry. The man on top of the woman. Can you picture the publicity the show will generate with an insider's look at how bawdy Shakespeare could be? That was the nurse."

"Pardon?"

"The nurse speaking to Romeo."

He returned to his chair.

"Now, let me sketch out the entire show for you. The production costs will be low, Harry, the beauty of a one-man show. Here's how I see it."

Ten minutes later, when Bancroft had finished his presentation, Quill yawned and went behind his desk.

"Well?" Bancroft asked.

"Sydney, I do not believe a show as you envision it has a chance here in London. Or anywhere else for that matter."

"Nonsense!" Bancroft jumped up and prepared to perform another scene. "Let me—"

"Sit down, Sydney!"

Bancroft did as he was told, staring help-lessly at the agent.

"I understand that actors and actresses who have fallen out of the public limelight for many years think that the same public can't wait for them to return. I understand that, Sydney, as much as I consider it sad. The truth is, your career was predictable, an actor with modest talent and fierce determi-nation who managed to earn a living for quite a few years on the stage, and then in films. But Sydney, for God's sake, be realis-tic. The critics didn't rally to your cause ex-cept in a few instances. The films I man-aged to get you roles in certainly never set the world on fire at the box office. You've had a good run, Sydney. Enjoy having had it. Accept your age gracefully and revel in the fruits of having been—of having once been an actor."

"Your cruelty has been duly noted, Harry." Bancroft swallowed hard and turned to avoid having Quill see the wetness in his eyes.

"Now don't be coming down hard on me, Sydney. I'm just an agent." He forced light-ness into his voice. "Tell you what, old friend. We do go back a long way, and I must admit a certain fondness for you, as well as respect for who you are and who you were. Raise the money for your show, Sydney. Go back to the States and hit up all those who've made fortunes in boring, probably illegal endeavors, and who would like to end their lives having rubbed elbows with the arts." His snicker was his excuse for laughter. "Come up with the money to mount the show, Sydney, and *then* come back to me. As you say, it shouldn't cost too much to produce your show, a couple of hundred thousand pounds. Costs are up. You wouldn't believe what it costs these days to put on even a modest play with a small cast. You live in Washington, Sydney. There must be all sorts of funds available for the arts. What about that bird you had a fling with in your drinking days? What was her name? Claire, was it? She heads that theatre you're working at these days, doesn't she?"

"Her name is Clarise, Harry."

"Ah yes, Clarise. Well, use your consider-able charm and get her to back your show. Get someone, Sydney, to fund it. Anyone! Once you have, I'll be delighted to help you find the right producer and director in the

West End." He came around the desk and offered his hand. "See? I never forget an old and valued client. Off you go now. I have— ah—I have an important meeting across town."

Bancroft seemed unsure whether to take Quill's hand, or even to get up from his chair. He looked down at the worn carpet at his feet, fingers working his chin. Finally, he rose, smiled at the agent, went to the door, turned, and said, "You shall hear from me again, Harry, despite your need to insult me. You shall hear from me when all of the West End and Broadway are clamoring for my show, outbidding one another for the privilege of being involved with it. And when that happens, Harrison Quill, I shall seriously consider allowing you to represent me."

The receptionist came into the office after Bancroft was gone.

"Who the hell is he?" she asked.

"A sick man, my dear. A very sick man. I need another tea. And pour a spot of brandy in it. I'm feeling very depressed."

# EIGHTEEN

While Sydney Bancroft's Thursday morning flight to London winged its way across the Atlantic, Mac Smith and his former law partner, Yale Becker, were passing through the metal detector in the lobby of the H. Carl Moultrie District of Columbia Superior Court. With six divisions—Criminal, Family, Civil, Multi-Door Dispute Resolution, Probate, and Special Operations—its Indiana Avenue building is one of the busiest courts in the country, with six hundred cases adjudicated each day; thousands of people flood its lobby, hallways, and courtrooms in search of justice, or to find themselves guilty of having denied justice for others.

Smith and Becker rode the escalator to the second floor and headed for one of the building's seventy courtrooms and hearing rooms. They'd almost reached their destination when a rotund black man with a close-cropped gray beard, coming from the opposite direction, stopped them. He wore a black suit, black shirt, flamingo-pink tie, red lizard boots, and wide-brimmed Spanish hat. He carried an oversized, bulging-at-the-seams, elaborately tooled, well-worn leather briefcase. "Mac Smith?" he said.

Smith smiled. "One and the same, Horace."

"What are you doing here, slumming?" the man asked with a chuckle.

"Wish I were," Smith said with equal pleasantness. "You know Yale Becker."

"Of course I do," Horace said. "You two back in business together again?"

"For the moment," Smith said. "Actually, I'm more along for the ride."

When Smith had reached Becker the previous night and asked him to represent Jeremiah at the Presentment hearing, Becker agreed, but only if Smith would accompany him. "You know the family," Becker had said. "Besides, I'd enjoy working with you again, Mac. Good to keep your hand in."

And so Smith agreed, but not before Annabel urged him to. She'd seen it before with her husband, a vague restlessness that wouldn't go away until he'd taken some action to satisfy it. It came in cycles, once, maybe twice a year, something, someone, luring him with a challenge too compelling to arbitrarily ignore.

"It'll take too much time, Annie," Mac had said. "I have my classes and—"

His weakest excuse, she knew. Mackensie Smith was one of the most efficient time managers she'd ever known. "I'll help you," she said.

"All right," he'd said.

And that was that.

"The bad guys keeping you busy, Horace?" Becker asked the flamboyant black attorney.

"The numbers say crime in D.C. is down, but you'd never know it by me. Never been busier. But you two wouldn't know about that. Got another high-profile, big-money case on the docket today?"

"You might say that," Becker said. "Half right—on the profile, not on the money. Good seeing you, Horace."

"Always a pleasure." To Smith: "Still turning out bright-eyed young lawyers over at GW?"

"Doing my best, Horace. You take care."

As they resumed navigating the hundreds of people coming and going in the hall, Smith said, "How many cases do you figure Horace is handling today, Yale? Six? Ten? A dozen?"

"Too many, I'm sure. Drugs. Domestic abuse. Petty thieves. He's a hell of a good attorney, Mac, nobody better at cutting deals. Love his style. Can't overlook him in that getup."

*No more of a getup than we're wearing,* Mac mused, *Yale's three-piece suit and my tweed-and-button-down outfit perhaps not as flamboyant, but every bit as much of a uniform as Horace is wearing.*

A clerk escorted them from an outer office into where the magistrate judge sat at a table examining the Lerner files provided by the police. With him was a U.S. Attorney who was introduced as Alex LeCour. He was young, black, and obviously on the rise.

The judge, Jerry Millander, got right to the

point. "So, here we are. Why are we meeting?"

"There's a complication in this case,
Judge," Becker said.

"There always is," Millander said. "You're
talking about the murder at Ford's Theatre."

"Yes, sir," Smith said. "The hearing today
on the assault and resisting charges is one
thing. But the police want to question our
client about what he might know of the murder."

"So?"

"So, it puts our client in the position of
possibly being coerced," Becker responded. "The police have already pres-
sured him to answer questions about the
murder, which he declines to do. He claims
he didn't even know the victim. I'm uncomfortable having the assault and resisting
charges used as a wedge to get him to say
things he wouldn't under ordinary circumstances."

U.S. Attorney LeCour said, "He was read
his rights twice, Counselors."

"About the charges against him," Smith
quickly said. "Not concerning the murder."

LeCour said, "According to the investigating officers, two people have confirmed

that your client not only knew the deceased, he'd dated her."

"You're making my point, Mr. LeCour," Smith said. "We're not here to try a murder case." He glanced at Becker. "These so-called confirmations that Jeremiah knew the victim is news to us. I'd like a copy of the file."

"No can do, Counselor," said LeCour. "Not the murder investigation file. The other charges? Sure." Millander handed one of two files to Smith.

"Our concern," said Becker, "is that today's Presentment hearing will confuse the issue, as Mr. LeCour has just done. We want to be sure that the murder plays no part in the proceedings, or in your decisions, Judge."

If Millander was offended at the suggestion that his decisions might be based upon anything but hard fact and judicial propriety, he didn't demonstrate it. He said to LeCour, "They're right. Let's not mix apples and oranges."

"The detectives went out to the Millennium Arts Center, Judge, to question the defendant *about* the murder," LeCour said. "That should be brought into the equation."

"They went out there to question him," said Smith, "not to arrest him. He couldn't have resisted arrest if the officers weren't there to arrest him in the first place. As for assaulting the detective, they both ended up with bruises. Sounds like a wash to me. The kid was scared. He saw two strange guys in suits looking for him. He swung on them and bolted. The preponderance of evidence just isn't there."

"Save that for the Presentment, Mr. Smith," Millander said. "By the way, Senator Lerner is here in the building. He's asked that the hearing be closed. I can't accommodate him with that, but we have arranged for him, and any others involved, to enter and exit the building through a door not available to the public. He's also asked that I impose a gag order on all participants. I choose not to do that, but ask that all of you exercise restraint, particularly with the press. They're here in force."

"I don't wonder," Smith said.

"See you downstairs in an hour," Millander said, dismissing them.

Smith and Becker went to the cafeteria, where they carried coffee to a small table far removed from others.

"What do you think, Mac?" Becker asked.

"Like the judge says, apples and oranges. I think he's committed to separating the charges from their interest in Jeremiah as a potential suspect in the Zarinski murder. I'm sure we can plead out the charges. What concerns me, Yale, is what LeCour said: that the police have two confirmations that Jeremiah knew the deceased, and possibly even had some sort of a relationship with her."

"If he did, he's not doing himself any favor denying it."

"They got him to deny it before I arrived last night. I told him, of course, to say nothing. But he's an arrogant kid."

"We'll ask for no bail. You know Senator Lerner. I suggest we get him to accept responsibility for his son and agree to have the boy live with him while this gets sorted out. The judge'll certainly waive bail if that's the case."

Smith nodded.

"That still leaves the kid subject to investigation for the murder. What's your read on him, Mac? Capable of it?"

Smith agreed, but added, "Capable of it

the way almost everyone is, given provoking circumstances. You'll represent him through to the end?"

Becker smiled. "On two conditions. One, that the defendant and the family request that I represent him. And two, that you're in for the duration."

"I can't promise that, Yale."

"Then I can't promise I'll take the case. Look, Mac, this goes beyond my simply wanting you on the team because, frankly, I enjoy your company. It also has to do with your connections with the family. We're dealing with two highly visible parents, the senator, and his ex-wife. And you well know that in that situation, the attorney ends up with three clients, none of whom will see eye to eye on anything."

Smith smiled. "That was one of many reasons I got out of the business, Yale. Criminal law is easy, provided you don't have to deal with people. Like most everything else in life."

"Like most everything else in life," Becker repeated. "Well?"

"Annie wants me to."

"Smart lady. You won't go against her wishes. Right?"

"Not a prudent thing to do. Yes, I'll assist. Of course, that assumes he ends up charged in the murder. Failing that, you don't need me to plead out the assault and resisting charges."

"Fair enough. Introduce me to the senator when we get there. Is he as much the playboy as the media paints him to be?"

Smith shrugged. "I'm really not that friendly with Lerner. Clarise is our friend. But I've met him on a number of occasions, and shared a dinner table with him a couple of times. He's always had an attractive woman at his side. And I read the papers."

"Any inside knowledge about the rumors that the senator had a fling with the murder victim?"

A shake of the head.

"Will your friend, Ms. Emerson, end up heading the NEA?"

"I suspect so, unless some bombshell explodes in her face."

"Like her son being charged with the murder of a young woman rumored to have been sexually involved with his father? Juicy!"

"And unlikely. Let's go. I have a feeling Judge Millander doesn't abide lateness."

Magistrate Judge Jerrold Millander, now wearing a black robe, sat at the bench of a first-floor hearing room. U.S. Attorney LeCour occupied one of two tables. With him were Detectives Rick Klayman and Mo Johnson. Seated at the second table was U.S. Senator Bruce Lerner and a young female aide. They stood as Smith and Becker approached.

"Good to see you again, Mac Smith," said Lerner, shaking hands and introducing the aide. Smith did the same for Yale Becker. With everyone seated, they pulled their chairs close together and spoke in whispers.

"We'd like you to take personal responsibility for Jeremiah," Smith said. "If he can be released to your custody, we're sure the judge will waive bail."

Lerner's expression said either that he wasn't sure that was possible, or that he wasn't accepting of the suggestion.

"A problem?" Becker asked.

Lerner looked around before confiding, "Jeremiah and I have been estranged for a long time, gentlemen. I'm not sure he would want to live with me, no matter for how short a duration."

"Let's ask him," Smith said as they all turned to see Jeremiah being led into the room by a court bailiff and a U.S. Marshall. Jeremiah saw his father seated at the table and frowned, as if to say, "What are *you* doing here?"

He was brought to the table and directed into the only unoccupied chair, next to Lerner.

"Hello, son," the senator said.

Jeremiah ignored him.

Smith, who sat on Jeremiah's other side, leaned close and said, "We're going to ask that you be released to your father instead of asking for bail. That means you're to live with him until the next phase comes up, a probable cause hearing in ten days or so."

"I don't want to live with him," Jeremiah said defiantly.

"I suggest you rethink that, Jeremiah," Smith said. "You're in serious trouble here. Don't make it harder on yourself."

"I'll live with my mother."

"She isn't here to warrant to the judge that it's all right with her, and that you'll abide by the court's order. Your father is here. Take advantage of it."

The court clerk's reading of the charges

against Jeremiah Lerner, and his citing of the case number, interrupted them. Judge Millander looked down from the bench and told LeCour to proceed. The young U.S. Attorney spelled out the circumstances of the defendant's arrest and incarceration, and indicated the arresting officers were present. Klayman looked over at Smith and nodded a greeting, which Smith ignored. The two detectives were sworn in separately, and under questioning by LeCour explained what had happened at the Millennium Arts Center the previous evening. Their collective testimony took only fifteen minutes. Smith and Becker had decided not to ask the detectives why they'd gone in search of Jeremiah. Raising the question of how he could have resisted arrest when he wasn't being arrested was better saved for the trial, if that became reality, or better yet, to be used as ammunition in attempting to persuade the U.S. Attorney's office to drop that charge. Becker asked a few routine questions for the record, and sat down. Millander announced that a probable cause hearing would be scheduled within the ten days mandated by law. Becker stood and requested an extension: "I've just been brought in on the case, Judge, and will need more time to prepare."

"Granted. Talk to my clerk about a date. What about bail?"

"The state requests bail of two hundred fifty thousand dollars, your honor," LeCour said.

Millander's expression reflected the absurdity of the amount.

"He has a previous criminal record, your honor," said LeCour. "And he's already attempted to avoid custody as evidenced by his flight from these officers."

Millander asked the defense for its comments.

"Your honor," Becker said, "his previous criminal record involves three minor charges, one of which was dropped." He looked down at Jeremiah. "As you're aware, the defendant comes from a distinguished family, pillars of the community. His father, Senator Lerner, who is here this morning, has agreed to take personal responsibility for his son, and will ensure his attendance at any future legal proceedings. Under the circumstances, we feel bail is not only inappropriate, it's unnecessary."

Millander addressed Jeremiah, who was

prodded into standing by Smith. "If you are released to the custody of your father, Mr. Lerner, you understand the conditions of that release. You are to live with him, live by his rules, and otherwise stay out of trouble. Do you agree to those terms?"

There was silence at the defense table as Jeremiah hesitated before responding. Finally, he said, "Yes, sir."

"Good," said Judge Millander. "Work out a date for the hearing." He slapped the gavel on the bench, stood, and left the courtroom.

"My car is outside," Senator Lerner said angrily to Jeremiah. "Come on, before he changes his mind."

"We'll need some time with you," Smith said. "Mr. Becker has agreed to handle Jeremiah's defense—and let's not forget the police want to speak with him about the Zarinski murder."

"Whatever you say, Mac," the senator said. He handed him a card with his home number written on it, shook Becker's hand, and said, "Your reputation is well known to me, Mr. Becker. I know Jeremiah is in good hands."

"We'll be in touch," Becker said.

Smith and Becker watched the father fairly push his son away from the table and in the direction of a doorway held open by the bailiff.

"Touching family scene," Becker mumbled.

"No father likes to see his son in trouble," Smith said, "and doubly so when the father is a U.S. senator."

Klayman approached. "Professor Smith," he said.

"Hello, Detective. This is Yale Becker."

"A pleasure, sir," Klayman said.

"I'll see you Saturday," Smith said.

"Yes, I'll be there. I'm looking forward to it." He walked away and left the room with his partner.

"What's Saturday all about?" Becker asked.

Smith told him about the second section of his course on Lincoln the Lawyer.

"Uncomfortable about having one of the detectives in the case sitting in your classroom?"

"No. All we'll be talking about is the honesty of Abe. Drop in. I think you'd enjoy it."

"Another time. We need to meet with the senator and his son as soon as possible."

"I'll set it up."

"And the mother, too."

"I'll call her."

"And we should check on the two people who've allegedly confirmed that the kid was dating the murder victim."

"Maybe having the detective in my class isn't such a bad idea. The professor might learn something from the student."

Becker laughed. "You wouldn't take advantage of him, would you, Mac?"

"Of course not. Speaking of classes, I've got to get to the university. Faculty meeting. Too damn many of them."

"Call me the end of the day?"

"Of course. Good being with you again, Yale."

"Yeah, I like it, Mac. I really didn't know how much I missed you."

# NINETEEN

"He's staying with Bruce," Clarise Emerson said to Bernard Crowley.

It was seven-thirty on Friday morning. Clarise had come to Ford's Theatre especially early to prepare for a luncheon meeting with the finance committee from the theatre's board of trustees, and was surprised to see Crowley already there, in shirtsleeves and sweating, putting final touches on a financial report for the meeting.

"Did you see him?" he asked.

"No. But I spoke to him. He's not happy, of course, and claims the police beat him. God, to imagine it happened at the Millennium Arts Center when I was there. I mean, a few minutes before I arrived."

"Horrible," said Crowley. "Coffee?"

"Yes, please."

Clarise removed her beige linen jacket and draped it over her chair as he filled two mugs and rejoined her at the small conference table.

"You say Mac Smith handled his defense," Crowley said.

"Yes, bless his heart. He didn't want to— I can't say I blame him—he and Annabel have forged a pleasant, quiet life together. But he's such a good friend. He brought along a former law partner, Yale Becker. At least Jeremiah is in capable hands. What I can't deal with is why the police want to talk to Jeremiah about Nadia Zarinski. He didn't even know her."

"Why are they interested in him, Clarise? They must have a reason."

"Jeremiah wouldn't discuss it with me. Bruce tried to explain, but he's so damned preoccupied. Evidently, someone has told the police that Jeremiah knew Nadia and had dated her. What rubbish! Had you ever seen them together, Bernard? I mean, had you ever seen Jeremiah hanging around the theatre?"

"No. Never."

"You said Nadia helped you out on a couple of mailings. Did she ever say anything, hint at knowing Jeremiah?"

He shook his large head.

"It's all a mistake, I'm sure. I talked to Mac last night after speaking with Jeremiah and Bruce. He wants all of us to meet as soon as possible. How do I find the time? The hearing is days away, it's the busy season here at the theatre, and there just doesn't seem a spare minute. How do the numbers look?"

"Excellent. I think the finance committee will be impressed." He handed her a file folder containing checks to be signed.

"Speaking of numbers," she said, "my dinner with the AT&T contingent went especially well. I'm sure they'll underwrite one of next year's shows."

Crowley's mouth tightened and his brow furrowed; there was something he wanted to say, but wasn't sure he should.

"Yes?"

"I know this isn't my business, Clarise, and if I'm treading where I shouldn't, please say so."

"All right."

"I think you should find a way to spend the necessary time with Jeremiah, even if it means letting things go here at the theatre for a few days. We're in good shape. *Festival at Ford's* is falling into place—it should be the best ever, I'm told, thanks to all the preliminary work you did in conceiving its program—the president and first lady and the veep and his wife have confirmed, along with anyone who's anybody in Congress. And look at this." He handed her a fax that had been in the machine when he arrived. It was from a New York talent agency confirming performers committed to that year's *Festival at Ford's,* the annual gala televised nationally by the ABC television network.

". . . Tony Bennett. Diana Krall—I really like her—Alan King, Placido—is he bringing others from the Washington Opera?—Natalie Cole—impressive." She handed the fax back to Crowley. "About taking time for Jeremiah. Yes, I agree with you. Damn him! Don't children realize that when they misbehave, they wreak havoc with their parents' lives?" She laughed. "I don't really mean that. He needs me, and I'll be there. And I appreciate your concern for him, Bernard. And for me. Thank you."

"Heard from Bancroft?" Crowley asked,

trying to sound as though he didn't care whether she had or not.

"No."

"The teen show is Saturday. Sydney, who's supposed to be directing it, hasn't been putting in a lot of time."

"I'll check on it," she said, standing and stretching.

He got to his feet and helped her on with her jacket. "No," he said, "I'll check on it. Why don't you go back home for the morning? I've put together a complete presentation for the finance committee that'll knock their socks off. Go home and get things in order with Jeremiah, Mac Smith, anyone else you need to confer with. Come back, have a pleasant lunch, and enjoy the presentation. You'll feel better having that *other* problem in tow."

Clarise drew a breath, smiled, and kissed him on his cheek. "You are absolutely right, Bernard." How pasty his face was. If he didn't lose weight soon, she'd be going to his funeral. "See you at lunch," she said.

"Don't worry about a thing," he called after her as she walked from the room and headed downstairs.

Clarise's home was a nondescript, narrow gray town house in Georgetown. It was three storeys high, and had a small enclosed backyard with a studio at the rear. She'd purchased it shortly after moving to Washington from Los Angeles, and had decorated it in a slapdash manner, filling the space with hotel-like furniture and accessories, creating the look of temporary housing for a traveling executive. She seldom entertained there; when she did, it was small gatherings, dinner for six, sometimes eight, or cocktails and hors d'oeuvres with friends before going out for dinner. There were times when she would look around and wish she'd taken the time to apply a more caring hand, or perhaps had used a professional decorator, or just plain looked longer and harder for a couch or chair or wall hanging. Time. There never seemed to be time for such reflection. A housekeeper occupied the third floor and kept things running, serving breakfast each morning to Clarise in a cramped solarium at the rear—always fresh fruit, dry toast, and tea—and picking up after the lady of the house, who seemed always to be in perpetual motion, clothes dropped and shoes kicked off as she passed from room to room, papers and files piled up on the desk to be filed another day, a cellular phone permanently cradled between jaw and ear.

She'd no sooner entered her home and waved to the housekeeper, who was vacuuming the living room, when her cell phone sounded.

"Hello, Mac," she said. "Your timing is good. I just walked in."

"Good," Smith said. "I've just gotten off the phone with Yale Becker. A source has told him that a student at American University is the one claiming that Jeremiah dated Nadia Zarinski."

"Why would he lie like that, Mac?"

"We'll have to find that out," Smith said. "There's evidently a second source about Jeremiah's relationship with the deceased, but we don't know yet who that is."

"This is all so preposterous," Clarise said.

"It'll get sorted out. Have you spoken with Senator Lerner?"

"Last night. Briefly. I spoke with Jeremiah, too."

"I hope he understands, Clarise, that he's got to behave himself while living with his father. Judge Millander won't tolerate any misbehavior."

"You sound as though you expect Jeremiah to act badly. Why?"

"Just based upon my brief time with him, Clarise. He seems to be an angry young man, a defiant young man."

"Aren't they all these days?"

"He didn't seem happy being told he'd have to live with his father."

"Of course he isn't happy. He and Bruce have been estranged for a long time. At least he's stayed close to me." She shook her head. "Mac, I'm sure this business with Ms. Zarinski is all one great big stupid mistake. My concerns are the charges against him for—what was it?—assaulting an officer and—"

"Resisting arrest," Smith filled in. "The resisting arrest charge will probably be dropped. I'm confident of that, and so is Yale. As for hitting the detective, I—"

"They beat him, Mac. He told me that."

Smith realized it was futile to continue to try to present the reality of the situation to her. She was reacting the way most parents do when confronted with criminal charges against a son or daughter. It must be a mistake. Their child's rights were violated. *Just make it go away,* they tell their lawyers.

Instead, he said, "Yale and I need to meet with you, Senator Lerner, and Jeremiah, and we need to do that quickly, if possible today. I tried to reach the senator, but no luck. One of his aides said he's tied up in meetings at the Senate all morning, but thought he might be free at lunchtime. Will you be available to meet then?"

Her sigh was prolonged and anguished. "Lunchtime? No, I'm not free, Mac. I have a luncheon with the board's finance committee. I can't miss it."

Smith's silence said much.

"Please, Mac, try to understand. This is an especially trying time for me. How about later today? This evening?"

"Maybe," Smith said. "Whether you're free or not, Yale and I need to sit down with Jeremiah and get the whole story from him. I'll let you know when we set that up." He tried to keep pique from his voice at her lack of cooperation, but wasn't sure he'd succeeded. He hadn't.

"Mac," she said, "I must admit a certain disappointment that you don't seem to understand the situation I'm in."

"Your son is in trouble, Clarise," he replied. "If there's any truth to his alleged relationship with the murder victim, his troubles are just beginning."

"I'm sorry," she said. "I'm not thinking clearly. Forgive me."

"Nothing to forgive."

"Set up your meeting with Jeremiah whenever it's convenient for you and Mr. Becker. I don't want to impede the process. I'll try to free myself up to be available whenever you need me."

"Good. I'll keep in touch."

"Best to Annabel."

She clicked off the phone and went to her bedroom, where the bed was still unmade. The housekeeper hadn't gotten to it yet. *How many times have I told her to start with the bedroom?* she thought, closing the door and sitting atop the rumpled bedclothes. She suddenly felt cold, and wrapped her arms about herself. *Don't let this happen now,* she thought, referring to the feeling of confusion that was beginning to envelop her. It was a sensation she seldom suffered, and when such episodes struck, she was usually capable of controlling it, willing it away, negotiating with her emotions: *Think it through, Clarise. Don't allow yourself to be over-*

*whelmed. Compartmentalize. There's noth-
ing you can't handle.*

What she hated at that moment was her
lack of control over events. The police, the
lawyers, and the courts would control Jeremiah's fate. Topper Sybers and his Senate
Committee on Labor and Human Resources
would determine whether she became the
new head of the NEA. She'd managed to
control her destiny since the time she left
the family farm in Ohio to attend college in
California, and to forge what had been a
winning and rewarding career, first in television, and now in the nation's capital as head
of Ford's Theatre Society. She'd made all
the decisions during her transformation
from teenager to successful business-
woman. They weren't all good ones, she
knew. Marrying Bruce Lerner, which had
seemed a dream come true at the time, had
been a mistake, and her sense of relief and
freedom after the divorce was palpable.
Giving birth to Jeremiah was—no, she
would never label it a mistake—hadn't filled
her with the sort of joy other mothers experienced when having a child.

She preferred to not dwell on memories
of the day Jeremiah arrived in the world, the

tiny, helpless infant handed her in the hospital by a beaming nurse, her emotions clashing, joy tempered with fear, exultation sliding into resentment at what having a child would mean to her career and life. She was almost afraid to love this son born to her, and a keen sense of responsibility became the overriding commitment.

Her husband, Bruce, wasn't there for the birth. He'd been on the road campaigning for weeks leading up to the day, and learned he had a son from a phone call from an aide. That night, he called Clarise at the hospital.

"So," he said brightly, the sound of a party in the background, "little Jeremiah Lerner has officially arrived. Is he as handsome as his father?"

She laughed and confirmed that he was. They chatted for a few minutes. As they did, Clarise's cheerful mood deteriorated into bitterness toward her husband. That he wasn't there, that he seemed to be discussing the arrival of a new car or delivery of a rug, said to her—promised to her—that he would not allow the child, their child, to impact his career and schedule. And she grimly, silently pledged to herself that she would not allow that to happen, either.

The housekeeper knocked on the door.

"In a minute," Clarise said, getting up from the bed and going into the bathroom, where she was surprised to see that she'd welled up, and that two teardrops had run down her left cheek, streaking her makeup. She made the necessary repair, opened the door for the housekeeper—"Please, do the bedroom first!"—and went downstairs, where she sat on the patio in the yard, enjoying the sun's warmth on her face. She dialed her ex-husband's house. The call was answered by an aide.

"This is Clarise Emerson. Is the senator there?"

"No, ma'am."

"Is my son there?"

"Please hold on."

It seemed an eternity before Jeremiah picked up the phone.

"It's Mother, darling. Are you all right?"

"Sure."

"What are you doing?"

He snickered. "Just hangin' out. Nothing else to do here."

"Jeremiah, has Mr. Smith talked to you today?"

"Just a little while ago. He and the other guy are coming here this afternoon."

"I spoke with Mr. Smith this morning. Can you tell me about this claim that someone has told the police that you dated the poor girl who was murdered?"

"He's a liar."

"Do you know who he is?"

"No. I just mean that whoever said that is a liar."

"Of course. Have the police spoken with you again?"

"Uh-huh. They're coming here."

"When?"

"This afternoon. That's why the lawyers are coming."

"What did they say when they called?"

"I don't know. They want to ask me questions again."

"About the murder?"

"I guess so. Why don't you tell Smith and the other lawyer to sue the city for police brutality? That's what they ought to be doing."

"I'm sure they'll consider that in due time. Now listen to me, Jeremiah. It is vitally important that you do what the lawyers tell you to do, and that you not do anything wrong. Your father and I cannot have you doing things that put us in a bad light. Do you understand?"

"Sure."

"Good. Jeremiah, unfortunately this is an especially busy time for me. You know I have to go through a hearing in the Senate about heading the NEA, and there's so much going on at the theatre. But when it's all over, you and I are due to go away on a long, well-deserved vacation. Just the two of us. You pick the place—the Caribbean, Mexico, Europe, wherever you say. How does that sound?"

"Okay, I guess. Sure. Whenever you're not so busy."

"Fine. I'll call later today after you've seen the police and the lawyers. Just be good, Jeremiah. This all will be over soon, and we can go away and laugh about it."

"Okay. Bye."

The click was loud in her ear.

She placed a series of calls from the patio, including one to Mac Smith, whom she reached at home.

"I just spoke with Jeremiah, Mac. He says

the police are coming to question him this afternoon."

"That's right. I'll be there, too. Yale is tied up with a deposition. Can you be there?"

"I don't think so, although I'll try."

"Well, it's not urgent that you be there. The senator will be."

"Oh. Well, that's good. Will you let me know how it goes?"

"Of course."

"Mac."

"Yes?"

"There isn't any possibility, is there, that they might actually accuse Jeremiah of the murder?"

"Anything is possible, but let's not even consider that at this juncture, Clarise. I'll be in touch later today."

She felt satisfied after the call. She left the house and returned to Ford's Theatre where, in the structured refuge of work, things seemed to be less confusing on the personal front. What she didn't know was that after she and Smith had concluded their conversation, he'd turned to Annabel and said, "When this is over, I don't think I'll ever view Clarise the same way as before it happened. I knew she was ambitious, and admired that ambition and her successes, but she is one cold woman, Annie. She's ice."

"And we've seen her when that ice has thawed, Mac. Let's not rush to judgment."

He smiled and kissed her. She was right, of course. He'd spent most of his professional life fighting prosecutors who'd jumped to judgment in indicting some of his clients, and secretly considered himself to be a thoughtful and not-too-quickly judgmental person.

"I'm glad you decided to become involved," she said, returning the kiss.

"The jury is still out on that, Annabel. But I'm glad you're glad. See you tonight."

# TWENTY

"Impressive, Clarise. Most impressive. I just wish all the groups with which I'm involved had their financials in order the way you've managed."

"I'd love to take the credit, Sol, but I can't. The credit belongs over there." She pointed to Crowley, who stood in a knot of members of the finance committee. "I hired smart."

"The sign of a good administrator," Sol Wexler, chairman of the theatre's finance committee, said. "Well, no matter where the credit belongs, the numbers look solid."

Another member of the committee interrupted to offer congratulations. The woman, barely five feet tall, expensively dressed, tanned, and with silver hair expertly arranged—and whose life was a series of meetings of boards and committees to which she belonged—took Clarise aside. "I just want you to know, my dear, that the board stands solidly behind you in this dreadful mess you've found yourself in."

Clarise's blank expression prompted the woman to say, "The business with your son."

"Oh, yes. It's all a mistake. I'm sure it will be settled shortly."

"I certainly hope so. We'll miss you once you've gone over to the NEA, but I know your heart will still be here at Ford's."

"You can count on that, Melinda."

The finance committee member leaned closer and became conspiratorial. "Is it true that your son is suspected of—"

"No, of course not. As I said, it's all a mistake, bureaucratic fumbling."

"Well, as long as it doesn't jeopardize your confirmation to the NEA. You know how politicians can twist things and use them for their partisan advantage. We're with you, Clarise." She squeezed Clarise's arm as physical affirmation of her support, and left to speak with someone else.

An understanding and supportive Crowley filled the void at Clarise's side.

"Pleased?" he asked.

"Oh, yes, Bernard. The presentation was top-notch. Truly professional. Everyone is impressed with your efforts in getting our finances in order. Well done!"

"Thank you. By the way, I spoke with the assistant director on the teen show, Ms. Riva."

"And?"

"She says that despite Sydney's absence"—he chuckled—"in fact, she said it might be *because* he's not here, the show is in good shape. No hitches. I just wanted to put your mind at ease on that front."

Truth was, Clarise hadn't given that production a thought. But she thanked him for following up as he'd promised, and excused herself to go to the rest room. Once there, she checked her watch. One-thirty. The police and Mac Smith would be on their way to her former husband's house to question their son. She was tempted to jump in her car and drive there to be present during what would surely be an ordeal for Jeremiah. But knowing Bruce was planning to be on hand led her to abandon that idea.

She had unbridled confidence that Mac Smith would provide all the necessary legal protection for her son, and prevent any abuse of his rights.

She went to her office, closed the door, and began poring over the possible questions that Senator Sybers and his committee might raise at her confirmation hearing, and the kind of answers she'd been instructed by her handlers to give.

*Compartmentalize.*

It worked. Her only thoughts were of the hearing, and how she would breeze through it, Sybers and his outdated view of art, morality, and women be damned!

"You ever been to a U.S. senator's house before?" Johnson asked.

Klayman turned a corner and said, "Oh, sure. Once a week at least."

They'd left First District headquarters at 1:45 to drive to Senator Bruce Lerner's home in Kalorama.

"Hathaway says the senator'll be there, loaded for bear."

"So I hear. Mac Smith, too."

"The lawyer?"

"Yeah. I'm going to his class tomorrow."

"You are? How come?"

Klayman explained the nature of Smith's class, and why it appealed to him.

"Man, you'd better be careful."

"Why?"

"Don't talk to him about the case."

"Of course not. I'm not stupid."

Johnson said nothing; Klayman looked over at him.

"No, no, Ricky, I didn't say you were. Just be careful, that's all. You have the warrant?"

"Uh-huh. Right here." He patted his jacket's breast pocket.

They were escorted into the house by a maid and led to Lerner's study, where the senator, Mac Smith, and Jeremiah Lerner waited. After introductions, they were invited to sit on a couch across from two leather armchairs occupied by Jeremiah and Smith, on the opposite side of a coffee table. The senator, dressed in a British-cut dark blue suit, white shirt, and burgundy tie, stood at the edge of the desk, a dispassionate expression on his craggy, handsome face.

"A question," Smith said to open the discussion. "Has Jeremiah been targeted as a suspect in the murder of Nadia Zarinski?"

"No, sir," Klayman answered. "We just want to ask him some questions about his relationship with the deceased."

"I told you I didn't have one!" Jeremiah said.

Smith put his hand on the young man's arm to quiet him, and said to the detectives, "Any questions about the assault or resisting charges are off the table for now." He looked pointedly at Johnson, who'd been on the receiving end of Jeremiah's punch at the Millennium Arts Center. Johnson nodded.

"Okay," Smith said, "ask away."

Smith, Jeremiah, and Senator Lerner had met before the detectives arrived. During that meeting, Smith told Jeremiah that he did not have to answer any of the police's questions, and suggested that he not— ". . . in the event you have information about the victim, or the murder itself, that might be incriminating."

Jeremiah had assured Smith he had no reason to not answer questions: He did not know Nadia Zarinski, had never even met her.

"Why, then, Jeremiah, are people—the

police say there are two people—saying that you not only knew her, but that you'd had some sort of a romantic relationship with her?"

"I don't know. Whoever they are, they're liars."

But Smith was now convinced that the only lying was coming from Jeremiah's lips. What was the young man thinking, that by denying it, he could will it to be the truth? Deny, deny, deny, and you'll eventually be believed? Had growing up in Washington, D.C., contributed to Jeremiah's belief, a city where lying was routinely indulged in, and plenty of people got rich teaching others the subtle art of misinformation, so-called?

Klayman asked the same questions while Johnson noted the answers in a small spiral pad, and received responses identical to what Jeremiah had told Smith.

"Who are the people who claim that Jeremiah knew the deceased?" Smith asked. He knew the answer about one of them, a student at American University.

"We're not at liberty to divulge that at this point in the investigation," Klayman replied.

"I thought you could face your accusers,"

Jeremiah said. "That's the law or some-thing, isn't it?"

Klayman ignored the comment and asked, "Where were you last Monday night, Mr. Lerner?"

Jeremiah didn't respond.

"Answer the question, son," the senator said, the first words he'd spoken since the questioning began.

"I don't remember," said Jeremiah. "I was home, I think."

"In your apartment in Adams-Morgan?" Klayman asked.

"Yeah."

"Anybody there with you, your room-mate, a date, anybody?"

Jeremiah shook his head.

"Nobody to confirm you were there? Did you leave the apartment that night?"

"I don't think so. No, I stayed there all night."

"Last night of the long weekend?" John-son said, looking up from his notebook. "No partying?"

Smith injected, "This isn't a trial, gentle-men. This isn't cross-examination. You've asked your questions, and he's given you his answers. Move on."

Klayman and Johnson glanced at each other; both were thinking the same thing: *The kid's lying.*

Klayman continued. "Would you be willing to appear in a lineup, Mr. Lerner?"

"No, he wouldn't," Smith said. Did they have a witness to the murder? he wondered. "Next?" he said.

Before Klayman could ask another question, Senator Lerner left the desk, came around behind Jeremiah, and placed his hand on his son's shoulder. "I believe we've been extremely cooperative, gentlemen," he said in measured tones, as though beginning a speech on the Senate floor. "But I think it's time for this to end. Are there any last-minute questions you have, any final pieces of business? If not, I'd appreciate my son and I being left alone."

Klayman and Johnson said nothing for a few moments. Klayman looked at Smith, whose posture and expression were noncommittal. Finally, Klayman pulled a piece of paper from his pocket and said to Jeremiah, "We have a warrant for your shoes, Mr. Lerner," realizing as he said it that it sounded like a joke.

"His shoes?" Smith said, taking the warrant from Klayman.

"That's correct," said Johnson. "Are those the only pair of shoes in your possession, Jeremiah?"

"This is ridiculous," the senator said.

Klayman and Johnson stood. "Sir," Klayman said, "the warrant is valid. It extends to your son's apartment, too. Officers are there as we speak." To Jeremiah, who'd gotten up and walked to a window overlooking a garden: "Are those Ecco shoes you're wearing?"

"What?"

"The shoes you're wearing. They're Eccos. Right? Are they the only Eccos you own?"

"Yeah. So what?"

"Please remove them and give them to me."

Jeremiah looked to his father, then to Smith.

"The warrant is valid," Smith said. "You'll have to turn them over, Jeremiah."

"What room is he staying in, Senator?" Johnson asked.

"Upstairs. A guest room."

"Please take me there, sir."

As Senator Lerner led the imposing black detective from the study and to the staircase, Jeremiah sat on a window bench and slowly removed his shoes. Klayman picked them up from the floor, careful to hold them by the tongues and to not touch the soles.

Johnson returned a few minutes later and announced, "He doesn't have any other shoes upstairs, Rick. Let's go."

Smith accompanied the detectives to the front door and out to where they'd parked.

"You're skating on thin ice," he told them.

"Oh?" said Johnson.

"You said he wasn't a target in the investigation, but you obtain a warrant for his shoes. How many other pairs of shoes have you gotten a warrant for? How many other possible suspects are walking around barefoot?"

"We just want to—"

Smith cut Johnson off. "I assume you've gotten footprints from the scene, and your forensic people say they were made by Ecco shoes."

"I can't discuss it, Mr. Smith," Klayman said.

"Neither can my client. He's off-limits from now on."

"Sure," said Johnson. He looked up at the home they'd just left. "Nice house," he said.

Smith looked hard at Klayman. "Maybe you'd better reconsider attending my class tomorrow, Detective. I'm liable to flunk you on general principle."

Klayman grinned. "I'll take my chances, sir," he said. "Tomorrow, I'm not a cop, just a student interested in Lincoln the lawyer, and you're not a defense attorney, just a learned professor. See you then, and please thank the senator for his time. I'm sure he's a busy guy."

Smith lingered outside for a few minutes, processing what had transpired, before returning to the study where father and son sat in silence.

"Is there any reason why your footprints would be behind Ford's Theatre, Jeremiah?" Smith asked.

No one spoke. Then, the senator said in a tone so low, it was difficult to hear him, "Yes, there is."

Smith took them in, going from one to the other.

"Jeremiah has something to tell you," the senior Lerner said.

Now, Smith focused his eyes on Jeremiah.

"Yeah, I knew her," the young man said. "Yeah, I dated her." He came forward in his chair. "But I didn't kill her, dude. I did not kill her!"

# TWENTY-ONE

"Maybe you'd better tell me about it, Jeremiah," Smith said. "The truth this time. And do not call me 'dude.'"

Senator Lerner could barely contain his anger. He stood at the window, his back to the room, taking in air to calm himself.

"How close were you to Nadia?" Smith asked Jeremiah.

"Just a couple a' dates. That's all."

"What's a couple?" Smith asked. "Two? Four?"

Jeremiah responded angrily. "How the hell do I know? It's not like she was my girlfriend or something. She was wild, man, hot, loved a good time, so, like, I showed it to her a couple a' times."

"Damn it, Jeremiah, show some respect,"

Senator Lerner growled. "Why did you lie to the police?"

" 'Cause they'd think I had something to do with her murder. Man, what is this, some kind of railroad job?" He turned to Smith, his face red with anger. "What kind of lawyer are you, huh? They beat me up. How come you're not suin' them for police brutality?"

Senator Lerner approached. He looked down with disgust at his son, and Smith wondered if he was about to strike him. Lerner asked Smith, "How serious is this?"

"Very serious," Smith replied. "The detectives who were here will write their report, reflecting what Jeremiah has told them. If he ends up charged and goes to trial, they'll use these lies against him. My suggestion is that I call them, ask them to come back, tell them Jeremiah wishes to correct some misstatements he made, and get him on the record with the truth."

Smith said to Jeremiah, "But I have to know the whole story, Jeremiah, before I can proceed in your defense. Did you kill her?"

Jeremiah erupted. He jumped up, smashed his fist into the back of the chair, knocking it over, and stormed from the room. His father called after him to no avail.

"Damn kids!" Lerner spewed, taking the chair behind his desk.

"Some kids are their own worst enemies, Senator. They think they know everything, and don't realize the ramifications of their actions. It's obvious that your son is going to face some tougher times in the weeks ahead, whether he had anything to do with the girl's death or not. His attitude won't help."

Lerner started to reply, but Smith said, "I don't have your son's faith as an attorney, which is necessary. It would be better if you found someone else to represent him."

"Absolutely not," Lerner said with a slap of his hand on the desk. "Clarise says you're the best defense lawyer in town, and—"

"Clarise is being kind. I retired from criminal law years ago, and have been teaching at GW. My former law partner, Yale Becker, has agreed to become involved, too."

"Of course. I knew you were a professor, and Mr. Becker's reputation is certainly known to me." He'd calmed down and was again the senator, in charge and sure of himself. "I appreciate your agreeing to help us. I'm sure it wasn't an easy decision."

Smith righted the chair Jeremiah had toppled and sat in it. What had been a sunny sky was now overcast; light through the windows was flat and gray. Lerner looked older than when Mac had first arrived. He sat behind his desk, chin resting on clenched hands, eyes focused on the desktop but thoughts elsewhere. He asked absently, "You have kids, Mac?"

"I did. A son. He and my first wife were killed by a drunk driver on the Beltway."

Lerner's voice didn't change in response to that grim statement. "They break your heart, don't they?" he said.

Smith didn't know how to respond. Yes, his heart had been broken, but not by his son—by an irresponsible drunk who ended up being convicted of negligent manslaughter. Where was he now? What was he doing? Did he wake up in the middle of the night as Smith sometimes did and recoil at the horrible memory of that rainy night?

"What'd the drunk get, a slap on the wrist and probation?"

"Four years."

Lerner snickered. "Obviously some wimp of a judge put on the bench by the liberals."

Smith sat in silence.

"You give all you can to your kids, Mac, and they turn on you. Like Jeremiah. He wanted for nothing, was taught to be a good citizen, work hard, make something of himself." He suddenly straightened, as though struck by an important thought. "Is this indicative of where young people are heading today?"

"Not all young people," Smith said, thinking of the Lee J. Cobb role in *Twelve Angry Men,* the vengeful juror who'd been disappointed by a son and took it out on a young defendant.

"They've got their values wrong, Mac. They get twisted messages from the media, movies, TV, those damn video games. The liberals don't seem to care what kind of garbage they fill kids' heads with these days. There's a lot of blame to be laid there."

Mac hadn't expected to be on the receiving end of a political speech. Lerner's conservative politics were well known. Had his right-wing beliefs butted heads with Clarise's more liberal thinking, and con-

tributed to the breakup of their marriage? It
didn't matter. Politics, and any discussion of
it, seemed grossly out of place at that moment.

"I'd like to spend more time with Jeremiah, Senator, before I leave."

"Yes, I'm sure you would. So would I.
Maybe this situation has rammed enough
fear into him that he'll sit down and listen to
reason." He slowly got up and came around
the desk. "I'll get him."

But before he could leave the room, the
sound of a powerful automobile engine was
heard from downstairs. A garage door
opened, a car door slammed shut, and the
vehicle noisily left. Senator Lerner peered
out the window and saw his black vintage
Jaguar head down the street and disappear
around a corner.

"He's gone," Lerner said.

"That's a shame," Smith said. "Any idea
where he might go?"

"None at all. I'm sorry, Mac, for the trouble he's causing you. Maybe you can see
what Clarise and I have had to put up with
all these years."

"Well," Smith said, standing, "at least he
must have found another pair of shoes."

"Oh, he had another pair upstairs. That detective didn't see them, and I didn't see any reason to mention them to him."

*Just answer the questions, offer nothing.* Smith had delivered that sage legal advice to countless criminal defendants over the years. Evidently, the senator had received the same wisdom, or naturally came by it.

"I'll be going," Smith said. "I suggest you do everything possible to find Jeremiah and bring him back here."

"I'll do that, Mac. Everything that's happened stays in this room."

"Of course."

The phone rang. Lerner picked it up and launched into an animated conversation with the caller. He waved good-bye to Smith, who left the house and headed home, stopping on the way at Annabel's gallery, where she was taking inventory of pre-Columbian pieces displayed on the shelves, and those stored in a back room.

"How did it go?" she asked.

"Not well."

He'd realized as he drove there that since meeting, falling in love with, and marrying Annabel, he'd been faced only a few times with the dilemma of balancing attorney-client confidentiality with a need to discuss things with her. When married to his first wife, he'd made the decision whether to discuss a case on an individual basis. Most lawyers he knew, depending upon the solidarity of their marriages—as well as their faith in their wives to keep secrets—would discuss certain cases in which they were involved. You had to talk to someone. He decided early on that he would bring Annabel in on everything that was occurring. She, too, was a lawyer, and had been instrumental in convincing him to help Jeremiah and his parents. She knew the players. Most important, he hadn't the slightest fear that what he told her would escape the confines of the gallery, or their apartment.

"He's in trouble," he said. "He now admits that—"

The door opened, and a well-dressed couple came in to browse.

"I'm going to run by the school, Annie," Mac said, kissing her on the cheek. "Feel like dinner out?"

"Sure."

"Meet you at home at six. We'll go from there."

He'd no sooner settled in his office at the

university when Dean Mackin looked in. "Got a minute, Mac?" he said.

"Sure."

"We've been getting calls from the media wanting to interview you," said the dean.

"They're on the prowl, huh?" Smith said with a small laugh. "Sorry if they're bothering you. Give me their names and numbers and I'll get back to them. Maybe."

"More than you bargained for," Mackin said.

Smith's expression invited elucidation.

"You didn't think you'd end up on a murder case, did you?"

Smith leaned back and held up his hands. "Wait a minute," he said. "Where did you hear this?"

"On the news a few minutes ago."

"On the news? What did they say?"

Mackin assumed an announcer's voice: "A highly placed but reliable source has told this station that Jeremiah Lerner, the son of Senator Bruce Lerner, and of Clarise Emerson, who's been nominated to head the NEA, has emerged as a suspect in the murder earlier this week of a young woman at Ford's Theatre. This is the same young woman rumored to have had an affair with the senator . . . etc., etc., etc."

"The MPD is a sieve," Smith said.

"It's true, Mac?"

"He's been questioned about it, Ralph. That's all."

"The newscast makes it sound more serious than that."

"Trust the press to get it wrong," Smith said.

He didn't want to mislead the dean, but also was reluctant to share what he knew. What *did* he know? Only that despite earlier protests to the contrary, Jeremiah had dated Nadia Zarinski. No crime in that, although denying it could do nothing but raise suspicions. The police had asked whether Jeremiah would participate in a lineup. That could only mean they had someone claiming to have witnessed the murder, or events closely allied with it. And what about obtaining a warrant for Jeremiah's shoes? Undoubtedly, footprints had been lifted from the scene of the murder, and the police wanted to match sole patterns with those prints. What concerned him most was his conviction that Jeremiah's shoes were the only ones seized under warrant. He hoped he was wrong. But if he was right, it meant Jeremiah was now the prime suspect in Nadia Zarinski's killing.

Where had Jeremiah gone? Hopefully, he'd drive around a while to cool off, and return to his father's house. But if he'd decided to flee, his problems would be compounded. He'd been released to his father's care. The court would be calling to check on him. The police would undoubtedly want to interview him again. The hole he was digging was getting deeper; soon, it might be too deep to climb out of.

"Mac."

"Yes?"

"Sure you don't want to reconsider?"

"No, I'm not sure. I've been questioning it ever since I first became involved."

"My recommendation?"

"Shoot."

"Leave the matter to Yale Becker. I know you want to help friends, and I admire that. But by bringing in Yale, you've already done your friends a huge favor."

Smith nodded.

"There's also the question of the university, Mac. Becoming embroiled in a scandalous murder case, especially one involving such high-visibility people, could kick back on us, on our fund-raising efforts, to say the least."

Smith wished Dean Mackin hadn't injected fund-raising into the equation. A young woman had been brutally murdered, and a young man, as unpleasant as he might be, faced possible indictment as the murderer. Smith knew, of course, and was respectful of any university's need to raise funds, and was not reacting personally to Mackin's comment. Among the dean's many responsibilities was the need to generate contributions to further the law school's programs. Mac had taken part in his share of events designed to do that.

*But we teach the law here,* he thought, *not fund-raising.* He'd made a commitment to Clarise Emerson and to Yale Becker, and commitments were important to Mackensie Smith.

"Think about it, Mac," said the dean.

"I will, Ralph. Thanks."

Dean Mackin left the office, stopped, returned, and said, "I'm getting nothing but positive feedback on your Lincoln course. The Saturday session had to be closed."

"The Saturday session," Mac repeated. "That's tomorrow. I'd almost forgotten."

"Mustn't do that, Mac. You'd have a classroom full of very unhappy students."

Smith realized he wasn't in the mood for paperwork, packed up, and left the building for home. As he did, Klayman and Johnson were at American University talking again with the student, Joe Cole.

They began by asking a series of questions similar to what they'd asked during their previous visit, and received basically the same answers. Yes, he'd dated her; yes, they'd been together the previous Saturday night; yes, they'd made love at her apartment; and yes, he'd left and returned to his room in the dorm.

"You were pretty pissed, weren't you?" Johnson said, leaning against the closed door.

Cole displayed his most charming smile from where he sat on his bed. "Why should I be pissed? Come on, guys. We had a great roll in the sack. What would I be mad about?"

"The other guy she talked about," Klayman said. "That's what."

"What other guy?"

"The one she compared you to," said Johnson. "The one she said was better in bed than you."

The smile faded. "How do you know that?" Cole asked.

"What'd she do, laugh at your sexual performance?" Johnson asked. "If some woman did that to me, I'd be pretty mad, too."

"She never said anything to me about that. I mean, about the other guy being better."

Klayman, who'd been content to allow Johnson take the lead, spoke. "So she *did* talk about another guy," he said.

Cole nodded.

"Who?" They'd decided on the way to the campus to not offer that they knew about Jeremiah and his alleged relationship to Nadia. Hopefully, the other students who'd told them about Cole dating Nadia, and being angry over her comments about Lerner, wouldn't have shared it with him, considering his BMOC status.

"Lerner. Jerry Lerner."

When they didn't respond, Cole added, "He's already a suspect, right? I heard it on the news."

"What did Nadia say about him?"

"Have you talked to him?" Cole asked.

"Mind if we ask the questions, Joe?" said Johnson.

"Do you know Jeremiah Lerner?" Klayman asked.

He shook his head.

"Ever see him together with Nadia?"

"No."

"What did she tell you about him, Joe?"

He made an embarrassed false start before saying, "She thought he was some kind of a stud. I guess she'd know, huh, considering what a slut she was."

Johnson came from his position at the door and stood over Cole. "Let me give you a little good advice, my man," he said in his best baritone. "I am getting tired of hearing you trash the victim. I am getting tired of hearing you talk like you're the original macho man and slandering a young woman who was beaten to death. Is my message getting across?"

"I didn't mean anything. It's just that—"

"So you were angry with her. Right?" said Klayman.

"Yeah, I was, and I told her so."

"How did she react?"

"She laughed and told me to get out."

"And this was Saturday night?"

"Right."

"Not Monday night."

"Monday? No. Hey, look, if you think I got mad enough to kill her, you're all wrong."

"You own a pair of Ecco shoes?" Klayman asked.

"What's that?"

"Mind if I look at your shoes?" Johnson asked, opening the closet door.

"No. Why should I mind?"

"Which shoes are yours, and which ones are your roommates?"

Cole showed them his shoes. No Eccos among them.

Klayman opened the door, and he and Johnson stepped into the hall, with Cole following anxiously.

"So you know I didn't kill her. Right?"

Johnson replied, "You just remember what I said about slandering the dead, Joe."

"Okay."

On their way back to First District headquarters, Johnson said, "Man, I don't like that smug bastard."

"Think he's lying? Think he was with her Monday night?"

"Wouldn't surprise me. We should check the restaurant he says he took her to."

"Right."

"You know, buddy, I've got to give it to you about the shoes."

"What do you mean?"

"Noticing that the Lerner kid was wearing a pair when we brought him in, and remembering it when forensics came back with a match of the prints to that sole pattern."

They stopped at a light, and Klayman raised his right foot off the accelerator. "Eccos," he said, returning his foot to the pedal. "My parents bought me this pair last time they visited."

Johnson chuckled. "I'm impressed. Yeah, I am impressed."

"I was more impressed with the judge who gave us the warrant. Hardly compelling evidence to base it on."

They pulled into the parking lot at the rear of the building.

"What about Bancroft, the old actor?" Johnson asked. "We know Lerner lied to us about knowing the victim because of what Cole says. We get Bancroft on the record about it and the kid is dead meat. He's due back tomorrow?"

"That's what he said. I figured we could check him out tomorrow afternoon, after my class."

"How'd you get Hathaway to give you the morning off? He's got us on twenty-four/seven until we break this case."

"Herman's a believer in education," Klayman responded wryly.

Johnson chuckled. "Like Lincoln, huh? Hey, by the way, since you've become a shoe expert, what kind of shoes did Lincoln wear? Eccos?"

Klayman said without hesitating, "He wore size fourteen boots made by a New York boot maker named Kahler. Lincoln made tracings of his own feet and sent them to New York."

Klayman opened the rear door to head-quarters and held it for Johnson, who'd stopped a few feet away.

"Coming?" Klayman asked.

"I should have known better than to ask," Johnson said.

# TWENTY-TWO

"Clarise. It's Bruce."

"I just walked in the door." She cradled her cell phone between shoulder and cheek as she kicked off her shoes and moved through the Georgetown house. "I have guests arriving in a half hour and—"

"Have you heard from Jeremiah?"

"No. Oh, the interview with him this afternoon. I'd almost forgotten. I meant to call you. How did it go?"

"Badly. He lied to the police when he said he didn't know the girl. He did know her. He dated her."

"Oh, my God. Are you sure?"

"I was there, remember? He admitted it to me, and to Mac Smith. The police took his shoes."

"What?"

"His shoes. They had a warrant for his shoes."

"Why?"

"As evidence, of course. He left, drove off in my Jag. You haven't heard from him?"

"No. I told you I hadn't. Where did he go?"

"Damn it, Clarise, if I knew that I wouldn't be calling you. Look, this is serious. He's obviously in big trouble with the law and—"

"Can't you do something?"

"Such as?"

"Such as—you're a U.S. senator, for Christ's sake. Maybe it's political, a way to get at you—and at me. My confirmation hearing is looming and—"

"I don't give a damn about your hearing, Clarise. Jeremiah is—"

"Thank you very much, Senator Lerner. What do you want me to do about Jeremiah, get in my car and cruise the streets looking for him?"

She felt her internal thermostat rising, becoming hotter. She could see her ex-husband sitting in his study, probably wearing one of his dozens of custom English suits, debonair and smug, viewing her as a hysterical woman unable to control herself and not making sense. She prided herself in her ability to manage her anger, to force cognition to trump emotions, to use any anger she might feel in a positive way, channeling it to achieve whatever goal was in her sights at the moment. But she hadn't always been successful in doing it.

There was the time less than a year ago when rumors had begun to circulate about a possible sexual affair between her former husband and Nadia Zarinski. Clarise had first heard about it when a friend, who consumed gossip and thrived on it the way health fanatics consume and thrive on sprouts and personal trainers, called.

"Clarise, dear, how are you?"

"I'm fine. How are you, Sissy?"

"Well, I must admit I'd be considerably better if my very good friend, Clarise Emerson, wasn't being trashed the way she is."

"I'm sorry, Sissy, but I have no idea what you're talking about, and I have an appointment I'm already late for."

"Oh, I'm sorry. Maybe I'm speaking out of turn. You haven't heard?"

"Heard what?" Her pique was palpable.

"About Bruce and his intern."

"What about them?"

She lightened her voice to soften her response. "About them having . . . well, I suppose there's no delicate way of putting it . . . having a thing."

Clarise's immediate reaction was muted. Politicians becoming involved with female interns was nothing new in Washington. She laughed and said, "Don't you just love this city's rumor mill, Sissy? Thanks for sharing the latest with me. Have to run. Bye, sweetie."

But after hanging up and chewing on what she'd been told, she found herself becoming increasingly agitated. And when, an hour later, she turned on all-news radio WTOP and heard mention of the rumor about Bruce and the intern, she experienced a painful wave of disgust, which quickly escalated into rage. She considered calling her former husband but held back— until the rumor developed legs and seemed to dominate every newscast. Worse, it soon became the centerpiece of whispers all over Washington. When she walked into a room, the sudden silence, then the shift to any inane subject other than what had been being discussed, was transparent.

Of course, she was asked about it by those who considered themselves close enough to tread on such delicate ground, and honed lighthearted answers that she considered sophisticated but that in no way truly reflected what she was feeling. Her favorite line was, "At Bruce's age, talking after making love is as important as making love itself. Having sex with an empty-headed twenty-two-year-old isn't his style." She'd said it so many times, to so many people, that she sometimes thought she believed it.

She finally confronted him about the rumor after a Washington *Post* writer questioned what impact his affair with Nadia Zarinski would have on *her* future in Washington. He wrote:

*Despite the adamant denials by Senator Lerner and the intern, Nadia Zarinski, that they'd engaged in sex in his Senate office after hours, the story just won't go away. Obviously, the extent to which it has sullied his reputation as it might affect a future presidential run is worthy of serious discussion. But what of his high-powered former wife, Clarise Emerson, who heads the oh-so-staid and proper Ford's Theatre, and who has recently been nominated to head the controversial agency, the National Endowment for the Arts? Pundits say the ripple effect might swamp her, Hillary Clinton's successful 'divorce' from her husband's shenanigans aside.*

"You bastard! How could you?" she demanded as they stood in his study. It was night; landscape lighting in the gardens beyond the windows tossed ribbons of white light across the room. The senator was dressed in suit, tie, and white shirt: "I have a dinner appointment in an hour," he'd told her when she arrived unannounced at his door.

"I don't give a damn about your dinner dates," she said. "What were you thinking, playing doctor-nursey with some kid bimbo? You couldn't find a mature woman to satisfy your goddamn sexual urges?"

"Calm down, Clarise. Hysteria doesn't become you."

She tried, tried very hard to get hold of

her emotions, and partially succeeded, at least to the extent that her voice lost some of its shrillness, and her hands shook less.

"Don't you realize what this is doing to me, Bruce? To you? We're not a couple of slugs whose life isn't impacted by this kind of cheap scandal. Our futures are at stake."

"Clarise," he said calmly from where he sat behind his desk—she paced the room—"Who I choose to sleep with is my business and my business alone. I'll worry about my future, thank you, and you take care of yours."

She was speechless. She stopped pacing and grabbed the back of a chair to steady herself. She'd expected a denial from him, a blanket refutation of the rumor. Instead, he seemed to be saying—

"Are you admitting to me that you *did* sleep with that little bitch?"

"I think it's time you left, Clarise."

"No, I will not leave, Bruce. Has it ever occurred to you the embarrassment Jeremiah must feel about his father taking up with a woman his son's own age?"

"She's older than Jeremiah, Clarise. It would help if you'd deal with the facts, not flashes of imagination. Besides, I'm sure

Jeremiah is worldly enough to not fall apart, as his mother seems to be doing."

She suffered the sort of frustration she'd always felt when engaged in an argument with her ex. He was unflappable, low key, his law training of many years ago still ingrained, a stolid wall of seeming reason and wisdom. Infuriating!

She fell silent, pulling herself together, searching for the right words to say next, words that would penetrate his armor.

He came around the desk and reached to put his hands on her shoulders. She recoiled and stepped back. "I heard she's still working for you," she said softly, tentatively.

"Yes. I won't allow rumors and the press to destroy a young woman's life."

"How princely."

"Let it go, Clarise. You've got more important things on your plate than to fixate on something this trivial."

"Trivial?"

"Insignificant. Go home. I have to leave. Maybe we can discuss this at another, calmer time. Have you heard from Jeremiah?"

"Yes."

"He's well?"

"Yes."

"One of these days, he'll come around and realize how silly he's been acting. He'll grow up. They take longer these days to grow up, don't they?"

She smiled and said, "And some never do, Bruce." A welcome steely resolve had replaced her previous frenzy. "I'll tell you this, Bruce Lerner," she said. "I will never allow you, or one of your young sluts, to ruin my life."

The amused grin on his face as she turned to leave made her want to kill him. It wasn't the first time she'd felt that.

"Call me if Jeremiah shows up at your house, Clarise," Lerner said.

"And you do the same."

Klayman and Rachel Kessler met at ten at the Georgetown Café, one of Washington's few restaurants open all night. Rick and Mo Johnson had finished their day at nine-thirty interviewing Nadia Zarinski's parents, particularly about their deceased daughter's financial situation.

"The parents claim they didn't know that their kid was being paid by Senator Lerner's office," Klayman told Rachel over chicken salad sandwiches and iced tea. "They paint her as a young woman struggling to make ends meet in a big city, you know, always writing or calling home and asking for money. I hated to burst their bubble by telling them about her being a paid intern, but there was no choice. I mean, she probably didn't get paid much and needed extra to live on. Interns don't get paid much, right?"

"I didn't know they got paid at all."

"That's right. Anyway, the father took it well, but the mother actually accused Mo and me of lying about it. She's a tough lady, and who can blame her? Her daughter gets murdered in an alley and it sounds like we're prosecuting her."

"I don't envy what you have to do in your job," Rachel said. "I couldn't do it."

Rachel Kessler was a large girl, with strong features, prominent nose and cheekbones, and a wide mouth. She wore her brunette hair short, which tended to exaggerate her broad face. She worked as a statistical analyst at HUD, a job she described as deadly dull but without pressure. She wore an oversized, midnight blue sweatshirt, jeans, and a lightweight white windbreaker. Klayman liked many things about her, particularly her quiet nature and infectious laugh. And, like her job, dating her didn't apply pressure to him in their fledgling relationship. She was easy to be with, like a welcome weekend houseguest who immediately falls into the flow of things and doesn't cause problems or create tension, someone who eats anything and helps clean up.

"You said she had a lot of jewelry," Rachel said.

"Yeah. We asked the parents whether their daughter had any independent source of money. They claimed she didn't, at least not that they knew of. They'll get the jewelry at some point. Right now it's evidence."

"Are there any leads?"

He shook his head. There were some things he was willing to share with family and friends, but most aspects of an investigation were off-limits.

"Amazing," she said, shaking her head.

"What is?"

"You being a detective. I mean—don't misunderstand—what I mean is that I think of cops as"—she laughed heartily—"as big and not especially bright. That's not you."

"Thank you," he said.

"I didn't mean it to compliment you, Rick. I suppose what I'm doing is admitting to my own stereotyping, my own occupational profiling. You know, all Irishmen drink, and all Greeks dance like Zorba." Another laugh. "I'm not making sense, am I?"

"Sure you are. We all do that. What counts, I think, is whether we recognize what we're doing and don't let it affect how we treat others."

"I agree," she said. "Feel like dessert?"

"Sure. Ice cream."

They'd reached that awkward moment when it was time to decide how they would spend the remainder of the night. Klayman had read in some magazine that women make up their minds whether to go to bed with a date far in advance of being asked. While she dipped into her bowl of choco-late–peanut butter ice cream, he went through the internal debate of whether to suggest they extend the evening at his apartment, or hers. His emotions were mixed. On the one hand, he was sexually attracted to her; their few previous episodes of lovemaking had been pleasurable. On the other hand, he was still operating on police time, his mind filled with thoughts of what had transpired that day, and what future days might hold.

"It's been a tough day," he said.

"And a long one for you," she said.

"Yeah."

He tried to read her: Would she be disappointed if he called it a night, to the extent that she would decide to look elsewhere for male companionship? Or, if he transformed himself from cop to lover and suggested they spend the night together, would she turn him down because she'd decided she wasn't interested in sex that night, and make him feel foolish?

She answered his questions by saying, "You have your class in the morning. What did you say it's about, Lincoln as a lawyer?"

He nodded. "Taught by one of the lawyers for—"

Her eyebrows went up.

"Mackensie Smith. He used to be a criminal lawyer, but now he teaches at GW."

"You started to say—"

"Nothing. Yeah, I have his class tomorrow, and then back on the investigation. You should meet my partner, Mo Johnson. A great guy."

"You've mentioned him before."

"He's got a nice family. He's a big jazz buff."

She laughed. "Another stereotype."

"Why do you say that?"

"Jazz is a black music. That's the stereotype. It's wrong, I know, but—"

"He's serious about it. A real scholar. I never see Mo as being black. I mean, sure, I know he's Afro-American because his skin is darker than mine, the way I know you're a female, or somebody is short or tall. But he's just my partner, a guy. When I was in college, I voted against allowing a black student into my fraternity, not because he was black, but because he was a jerk, a real pain in the butt. I figured that represented true racial equality because I would have done the same for a white pain in the butt."

"That's nice," she said.

"I suppose he views me a little differently. He brings up the black-white thing every once in a while. Can't blame him. I understand."

She finished her iced tea and said, "I

think it's time we head home. I have a busy morning, too."

They parted on the sidewalk with a light kiss on the lips, then a more passionate one but not so engaged that *the* question would have to be resolved again.

# TWENTY-THREE

"In eighteen fifty-six, Lincoln drew up some legal papers for a client. This was after he'd served one term in the U.S. Congress, and had returned to practicing law. The client sent Lincoln a check for twenty-five dollars for the work he'd done."

Smith surveyed the faces in his classroom. There were grimaces and grins at the mention of Lincoln's fee. Rick Klayman sat at the back of the classroom. He'd quietly slipped into his seat before the start of class and hadn't attempted to greet Mac.

"Do you know what Lincoln did?" Smith asked. "He wrote his client and said, 'You must think I am a high-priced man. You are too liberal with your money. Fifteen dollars is enough for the job.' He sent the client a ten-dollar check."

"Did you ever do that when you were practicing, Professor Smith?" a young woman asked. "Send money back to clients?"

"No," Smith said. "And I don't cite this anecdote to suggest you should, either. Good law and good lawyers cost money, and good lawyers, practicing good law, should be adequately paid. But maybe that story says something about why Lincoln rose to the top of the legal profession, and was considered an attorney without peer. Maybe that attitude of fairness contributed to his courtroom successes."

"I don't understand," said another student. "Courtroom law is an advocacy situation, isn't it? There really isn't a lot of room for fairness when you're fighting for your client."

"Ah-ha," said Smith. "You are right. A good lawyer fights for his or her client, and does whatever is necessary within the law, and courtroom rules and decorum, to win. But let's not confuse fairness as a moral issue, with fairness as an effective courtroom tactic."

He could see by the looks on their faces that they weren't following.

"Let me explain," he said, "using fairness as practiced by Abraham Lincoln. He was famous in courtrooms across Illinois and Indiana for seldom challenging the opposing lawyer, or the judge, in court. He was known for saying countless times during a trial, 'I reckon it's fair to let that piece of evidence in,' or, when an opposing lawyer really couldn't prove something, Abe would say, 'I reckon it's fair to admit that to be the truth.' "

"Pretty passive," a student said.

"And effective. You can all learn from it. Maybe it'll head you off from becoming a trial lawyer always jumping up to object, or conducting interminable cross-examinations of witnesses because you like the sound of your own voice, even when it's obvious you're turning off judge and jury alike. The fact is, Lincoln focused on what was important. He'd concede six issues but hammer hard at the seventh—because he knew it was the seventh issue that was really important in the jurors' eyes."

Smith shifted into an in-depth discussion of some of Lincoln's more famous cases, which included murder, civil actions, and extensive involvement in litigation between the railroads and municipal and state governments. Lincoln was not, Smith pointed out, a lawyer with a cause. He deftly represented defendants and plaintiffs alike, switching from one side to the other depending upon who paid for his services.

He closed the session with an anecdote about Lincoln's most celebrated criminal case. The son of a friend had been accused of murdering another man during a religious camp meeting in 1857, and the accused's mother, Lincoln's friend, pleaded with him to defend her son. He agreed, and represented the young man, William "Duff" Armstrong, at no fee to the family. The chief witness for the prosecution during the trial was Charles Allen, who claimed to have seen Armstrong strike the victim, causing his death. Although the incident took place at eleven o'clock at night, and Allen admitted to being more than a hundred feet away, he testified under oath that he could see the assault clearly because of a full moon that illuminated the area. During cross-examination, Lincoln had Allen repeat his story numerous times on the witness stand. Then, in a Perry Mason moment, Lincoln produced an almanac from 1857, which showed that the moon had already set on the night in question, provoking loud laughter in the courtroom.

"This was a rare case in which Lincoln became emotional during his closing argument to the jury," Smith said. "He actually had tears in his eyes as he played on the jurors' sympathies. It was unusual because Lincoln was known as an attorney who presented low-key closing arguments, clearly stating what facts he knew would lead jurors to the logical conclusion he sought. Of course, Armstrong was acquitted."

Smith ended the class with, "Thank you for being here this morning. I'd like you to spend some time at Ford's Theatre before we meet again next Saturday. If you haven't already done so, time spent in the Lincoln Museum downstairs in the theatre is time well spent. Enjoy the rest of your weekend."

Klayman approached Smith, who was packing notes into his briefcase, and waited until other students had finished their post-class discussions with the professor.

"Enjoy the class, Detective?" Smith asked.

"Very much. I didn't realize Lincoln was such a successful lawyer. My study of him has pretty much been limited to his presidency and assassination."

"That makes sense," said Smith. "If President Lincoln had had a few good cops protecting him the night Booth decided to kill him, he might have lived."

"Incredible," Klayman said, "how little protection there was for him that night. There was only one uniformed cop assigned to protect him—his name was Parker, I think, John Parker—and he left his post just outside Lincoln's box. And his valet—someone named Forbes-—let Booth into the box because he recognized him as a popular actor. Couldn't happen today with all the Secret Service surrounding a president."

"But it has, too many times. You know, of course, that the Secret Service had been established prior to Lincoln being shot, but its duties hadn't been expanded to protecting presidents."

"Yes, I did know that. Lincoln hated bodyguards, didn't he?"

"Evidently."

"Just a week before he was killed, he was walking down a main street in Richmond,

Virginia, without any protection at all." Klayman laughed. "He's reported to have said that since nobody took a shot at him there, he didn't have to worry for his safety in Washington."

"He was obviously wrong. How are things with you?"

Did he mean with the investigation? "Good," he said. "How's the senator holding up?"

"Senator Lerner? Quite well, but that's to be expected. Well, Detective Klayman, it was good seeing you. I assume it won't be the last time."

"Oh, no, Professor, I'll be back next Saturday."

"I didn't mean that. Enjoy the weekend."

Klayman left the law building and went to headquarters, where Johnson sat with Hathaway in the chief's office. With them was Wally Wick, an MPD forensic specialist.

"Bingo!" Hathaway proclaimed as Klayman took a seat. "Catch what Wally's come up with."

Wick handed Klayman a written analysis of the comparison he'd made between latent footprints found at the murder scene, and color photographs of the soles of Jeremiah Lerner's Ecco shoes.

"Look at the left shoe, Rick," Wick said. "The class characteristics match perfectly, sole design, size, everything. But the individual characteristics are even more telling. See the wear pattern on the outside of the sole?" Klayman examined the photo carefully and saw what Wick meant. "Same as the latent print. And there's that nick on the toe. See?"

"Yes, I do."

"Perfect match," said Wick. "That shoe was behind the theatre. No question about it. Whether the Lerner kid was wearing it is conjecture."

"Conjecture, hell," Hathaway said. "What do you think he did, lend his left shoe to somebody that night?"

Wick chuckled. "I just match 'em, Herman. You and the lawyers decide who was wearing 'em. Always a pleasure to do business with you."

"Okay," Hathaway said after Wick had left, "looks like we're getting there. The shoe matches, and we've got witnesses who claim Lerner was dating the girl. When are you getting a statement from Bancroft?"

"Hopefully this afternoon," Klayman said. "He said he'd be back from London today."

"Well, get on it. I think we've got enough to charge Lerner. I'll run it by LeCour over at the U.S. Attorney's office. Get a statement from that actor and do it fast."

"What about the senator himself?" Johnson asked. "Any progress on setting up an interview?"

"Not yet, but I'm not especially concerned about that. The kid did it. I'd bet my pension on it."

"How was your class?" Johnson asked as he and Klayman went to the lobby, where Johnson used the ATM to get cash.

"Great. He's a good teacher. I learned a lot."

"You learn anything about the Lerner kid?"

"From Smith? No. We never got into that. He asked me how the investigation was going. I said slow. That was it."

Klayman used a phone at the desk to dial Bancroft's number.

"Hello?"

"Mr. Bancroft, Detective Klayman."

His announcement was met with a moan. "Sir?"

"I just walked in the door, Detective, and am suffering terminal jet lag. My circadian rhythms have positively crashed, although I'm pleased the plane didn't."

"Sir, could my partner and I come by and get a statement from you regarding Jeremiah Lerner having dated the murder victim, Nadia Zarinski?"

"Oh, my, that sounds so official. A statement. Written, I presume."

"Yes, sir. Just a short statement. Won't take more than a few minutes."

"I find this terribly dismaying."

"Yes, sir, I'm sure you do, but—"

"Ms. Emerson mustn't know I told you about the boy dating Nadia. I won't have to testify at his trial, will I?"

"That's not my decision, sir."

"Perhaps another time."

"Sir, I'm afraid this can't wait."

"What if I refuse to give you your statement? What if I deny I ever said anything about Jeremiah and the girl?"

"That wouldn't be the truth, would it?"

Klayman glanced at Johnson, whose expression clearly mirrored his annoyance at his partner's placating of Bancroft.

"Mr. Bancroft," Klayman said, "I would really appreciate it if—"

The actor's voice, more studied and theatrical now, said, "Take note, take note, oh world, to be direct and honest is not safe."

"Pardon?"

"The hypocritical Iago, Detective, to Othello. Honesty isn't always the best policy, I fear. People unfortunately have a habit of blaming the messenger. But come if you insist. Your servant awaits."

Klayman couldn't help but smile and shake his head as he hung up.

"He's a whack job," Johnson said.

"I like him," said Klayman.

"You would. Because he talks that way?"

"Talks?"

"You know, with that British accent. Anybody with a British accent sounds smarter than the rest, cultured. Know what I mean?"

"Yeah, I do, but it's not his speech. I just—I guess I feel a little sorry for him. Once a star, now a has-been. The underdog. I always root for the underdog."

"We're going there now?" Johnson asked.

"Yeah. And be nice to him, Mo."

"Oh, I will be, Ricky. I-will-be-nice."

Bancroft was waiting for them in the hall-way when they reached the seventh floor. This day he wore a red silk bathrobe and sandals.

"Thanks for seeing us," Klayman said.

"I just hope we can make it quick, gentle-men. As I told you on the phone, I am ex-hausted, absolutely exhausted."

"Won't take more than a few minutes, sir."

They settled in his living room. A small overnight bag lay open on the couch, its contents piled on the floor.

Klayman said, "You said you knew that the deceased, Nadia Zarinski, had been seeing Jeremiah Lerner, and that you'd warned her not to. Is that correct?"

He nodded.

Klayman gestured toward Johnson: "De-tective Johnson is writing a statement for you to sign, sir. Is that all right?"

"You don't trust me to write my own?"

"That's not the reason, sir. Just trying to make it easier on you."

"And I speak in jest. Please, write what you will."

"When did you warn her, Mr. Bancroft?

Do you remember when it was, the day, or night, the time?"

"Oh, no. How could I possibly?"

"Over the long weekend?"

"Long weekend? Labor Day, you mean. No. It was before that. Yes, the week before, possibly two weeks."

"During the day?"

"No. At night. Definitely at night. A rehearsal, I'm sure. Nadia, poor thing, only came to the theatre at night. Yes, that was it. At night. A rehearsal."

"How did you come to know she was seeing Jeremiah Lerner?"

He touched his fingertips to his mouth and assumed a wicked expression. "I eavesdropped," he said. "I know, I know, that isn't very nice. But you will admit it can be fun. You learn the juiciest of secrets."

"Go on."

"I heard her complaining about the Lerner boy to some of the other young people backstage. Frankly, I was shocked to hear she was dating him. I mean, after all, his mother, Clarise, runs the theatre, and considering the rumors about Nadia and Senator Lerner—well, I was shocked, that's all, simply shocked."

"So you were shocked," Johnson inter-jected, more to break the boredom he was feeling. "What did you do?"

"I took her aside." He feigned extreme concentration. "No, actually she took me aside, which wasn't unusual. She valued my advice, I'm sure." A laugh. "Once you reach my age, you have more advice to give than certain other things." His arched eyebrows asked whether they agreed.

"She asked your advice about Jeremiah Lerner?" Klayman asked.

"Not so much asked for advice as com-plained to me the way he was treating her. I will tell both of you gentlemen something. Any man who lays a hand on a woman is, in my estimation, a scoundrel of the first or-der."

Klayman thought about having read years back of Bancroft's arrest for assault-ing a woman in London, but didn't raise it. He asked, "She told you Lerner had hit her?"

"Yes."

"And that's when you suggested she not see him anymore?" Johnson asked.

"Exactly."

"Did she agree with you?" Klayman asked.

"Absolutely. But she evidently didn't follow through, saw him one final, fateful time. I have a theory about the murder, gentlemen."

"Is that so?" said Johnson.

"I believe that she decided to do what I said, break off their relationship, and met with him behind the theatre for that purpose. It sent him into a rage and he battered her to death."

Klayman stood and said, "Well, Mr. Bancroft, thanks for your time and for being so forthcoming."

Johnson handed Bancroft the brief statement he'd written—it said only that the actor knew that Jeremiah Lerner had engaged in a relationship with the murder victim, Nadia Zarinski, and warranted that his statement was true.

"Must I?" Bancroft said.

Klayman nodded, and Bancroft scratched his signature on the paper.

"Thanks again," Klayman said. "By the way, how are things coming with your one-man show? You went to London for that, didn't you?"

"Yes. Oh, yes, it's coming along famously. I'm very excited about it."

He walked them to the elevator.

"One thing I will never understand," he said as they waited for the car to arrive.

"What's that?" Johnson asked.

"Why Clarise stood for having Nadia at the theatre, even as an occasional helper."

The doors opened, but Johnson held them that way with his hand. "You say Ms. Emerson *knew* the girl hung around?"

"Yes."

"Mr. Crowley says she didn't," said Johnson.

"*Mr.* Crowley?" Bancroft said, guffawing. "That fat excuse for a man?"

"I take it you and Mr. Crowley aren't friends," Johnson said.

Bancroft said to the otherwise empty hallway, " 'Sweep on, you fat and greasy citizens.' "

"Shakespeare, I suppose," Johnson said.

"Very astute, sir. *As You Like It.*"

"You're sure she knew?" Klayman asked.

"Have I said something I shouldn't have?"

"No, not at all," Klayman said, stepping into the elevator.

"Have a nice day," Johnson said as the doors slid shut.

They waited until reaching their car.

"What do you make of it?" Klayman asked. They were headed back to head-quarters.

Johnson answered, "Why would Ms. Emerson claim she didn't know the girl was working at the theatre?"

"It was Crowley, the controller, who said that. Right?"

"Yeah, but she also put on the big surprise act when she found out. How come?"

"Maybe to not look foolish," Klayman offered.

"Or maybe to take herself out of the running as a suspect."

"We'll ask," said Klayman.

"Yeah, let's do that."

# TWENTY-FOUR

Immediately following his Saturday morning class, Smith went to his office at the university and dialed Senator Bruce Lerner's unlisted home number. The housekeeper who answered informed Smith that the senator was gone for the day on official business.

"Is his son there?" Smith asked.

"No, sir, I don't believe he is."

His next call was to Clarise Emerson's Georgetown home. Again, a housekeeper answered: "Ms. Emerson isn't feeling well, Mr. Smith. She's resting."

"It's important I speak with her," Mac said.

"Sir, I—"

"Put her on."

"One minute, sir."

Clarise eventually came on the line.

"Sorry to disturb you, Clarise, but I tried the senator's house and was told Jeremiah wasn't there."

"Oh, God," she said. "I'm sorry, Mac. I have a splitting headache. It came out of the blue and my head feels as though it's exploding. Jeremiah! I know he left the house yesterday. I spoke with Bruce about it."

"Do you have any idea where he might be?"

"Not the slightest. I'm sorry, Mac. I wish I could be more helpful."

"We have to find him, Clarise."

"What do you expect me to do, Mac? Bruce said the same thing, as though I can snap my fingers and he'll appear."

She was right, of course. From a pragmatic point of view, she couldn't be expected to produce her son. But she might speculate on where he'd go. Smith just wished she sounded a little more concerned; he needed company to share the frustration he felt, and the sense of pending trouble. Although he didn't have firsthand information, he was convinced the police were narrowing in on Jeremiah for the murder. Obviously, Jeremiah had sensed it, too, and fled his father's home in a foolish attempt to avoid facing it.

He also found it inexplicable that Lerner would be gone for the day knowing the situation. Yes, he was a United States senator, and undoubtedly had pressing matters of state with which to contend. Then again, maybe he had decided to absent himself to avoid having to deal with the increasingly active media. But their son was in deep.

"Clarise, do you know any of Jeremiah's friends we can call, anyone who might know his whereabouts?"

"No, I don't. Jeremiah never shared such information with me. I assume his roommate has been contacted."

"Roommate?"

"Yes. In the apartment they share in Adams-Morgan."

"Give me the number."

"I—all right. Hold on." She returned a minute later and gave him the number.

"Will you be at the house for the rest of the day?" he asked.

"I hope not. I'm supposed to meet with a corporate sponsor later today, and then with the producers of the festival. And

Bernard and I need to meet. We're getting ready for the annual outside audit. What a dreadful time to come down with a migraine."

Smith sighed. If he had his way, he would have insisted that Jeremiah's mother and father meet with him to help find their son before the police tried to contact him and discovered the boy had violated the court's order by leaving his father's home.

"You have my cell phone number, Clarise, and my other numbers. Please, if you hear from Jeremiah, let me know immediately."

"I promise I'll do that, Mac. I can't thank you enough for all your help."

His next call was to the apartment where Jeremiah had been living. The roommate answered.

"I'm looking for Jeremiah Lerner," Smith said.

"He's not here, man."

"Has he been there in the last twenty-four hours?"

"Who is this?"

"His attorney."

"Oh, man, right. He's in some trouble, huh?"

"Here's my number. Please have him call me if you see him."

"Sure. I guess he's famous. I already talked to some reporters who called."

"Maybe you shouldn't," Smith said. "Thanks."

Next was a call to Yale Becker at home. He filled his colleague in on the situation, and they agreed that unless Jeremiah elected to return, his problems were magnified tenfold.

"Dumb kid," Becker muttered.

"If he doesn't return of his own volition by tomorrow, maybe we'd better put an investigator on it."

"If we have to. What about the parents?"

Smith related his conversations with Senator Lerner and Clarise Emerson.

"They don't sound terribly concerned."

"I think they're so consumed with their professional lives, there isn't a lot of room for concern about anything else. Besides, these are people used to having their way. Bad things don't happen to them."

"Their luck may have run its string. I'm heading out, Mac. My cell will be on."

Smith realized that he, too, had developed a headache, and took a Tylenol from his desk drawer before heading home.

Clarise Emerson had been doctoring herself with Tylenol since getting up that morning. She hadn't showered or dressed when taking Smith's call, having spent the morning drinking black coffee and applying cold compresses to her forehead. Now, with time running out before her first appointment of the day, she ran as cold a shower as she could tolerate, chose a peach-colored pantsuit outfit and white blouse, dressed, and prepared to leave the house. Her departure was delayed a few minutes by a phone call from a reporter, whom she summarily dismissed.

"Ghouls," she mumbled as she grabbed her purse and briefcase and made for the door. A sharp knocking stopped her.

She flung open the door and was face-to-face with Jeremiah.

"Where have you been?" she shouted.

He responded by pushing past her and slamming the door behind him.

"Jeremiah," she said, following him from the foyer into the living room. "What are you doing here?"

He collapsed on the couch, arms spread wide, legs extended in front of him. His eyes were dilated as though artificially propped open, and ringed with dark circles. He wore black jeans, a black T-shirt, and sandals; his clothes and breath reeked of marijuana.

"Do you know they're looking for you?" she asked, standing over him, one hand on her hip, head cocked.

"Yeah, I know." He was out of breath.

"You took Daddy's car?"

He nodded.

"Where is it?"

"Around the corner. I didn't want to park in front of the house."

She exhaled in frustration and took a few steps away, turned, and resumed her posture. "Jeremiah, did you have some sort of relationship with that young woman, Nadia?"

"Stop asking questions," he said. "Jesus, all everybody does is ask me questions. I didn't do nothing to her. I swear."

"Where have you been?"

"Hangin' out at a friend's house." He jumped to his feet, went to the windows, and pulled the drapes aside in order to see the street. She came up behind and placed her hand on his shoulder, causing him to start. He turned and looked at her with eyes she hadn't seen since he was a small child, pleading, frightened eyes glistening with moisture. "What am I gonna do?" he asked. "You have to help me."

She hesitated, then wrapped her arms about him and pulled him close. "We'll take care of it, darling. I promise."

He stepped back; she checked the lapel of her jacket for stains from his tears.

"I don't want to go to jail," he said, resuming his seat on the couch.

"And you won't have to."

The housekeeper entered the room.

"Not now, Isabella. Not now! Please, go to your room and leave us alone."

Clarise joined Jeremiah on the couch.

"Mac Smith is very worried," she said softly. "He says the court allowed you to go free only if you lived with Daddy."

"Mac Smith!" he said scornfully. "He doesn't care what happens to me. He's one of them."

"No, no, Jeremiah, he's not. He has your best interests at heart. He's my friend. He wouldn't do anything to anger me. I promised him I'd call if I heard from you."

"No, you can't," he said. "Please, don't call him. Don't call anybody."

"What do you want me to do then? What do *you* intend to do?"

"I just need a little time to think, that's all."

"But Mr. Smith and—"

"No!" His voice was strong and emphatic, as though it carried physical weight. "I just want to stay here for a while."

Her brow furrowed. "I don't know," she said. She glanced at a grandfather clock in a corner of the room. "All right," she said. "I have to be somewhere, but I'll be back as quickly as I can. You stay here. Don't answer the phone or the door. Do you understand?"

"Uh-huh."

"But only for a little while, Jeremiah. Maybe overnight. Then, tomorrow, we'll talk to the right people and make this whole nightmare go away."

"Okay."

She went to the door, where she stopped, turned, and said, "Mr. Smith told me they had a warrant for your shoes. Is that right?"

"Yeah." He shook his head. "Really stupid, huh?" He looked down at his sandals. "My friend's. He lent them to me."

As though struck by a sudden thought, she crossed the room, leaned down, kissed him on the forehead, and left the house.

"We're bringing him in," Hathaway said to Klayman and Johnson.

"LeCour buys it?" Johnson said.

"Yeah. But he doesn't want us to take him from the senator's house. Lerner's image and all that. He's getting ahold of the kid's lawyers, Smith or Becker, and offering to have them surrender him here at headquarters."

"Rank does have its privilege," Johnson said.

Hathaway laughed. "We can't ruffle a senator's feathers."

"Think they'll do it?" Klayman asked.

"Sure, why not?" Hathaway replied. "I don't know much about Becker except by reputation, but Smith is wired in all over town. He's too savvy to not play along."

"So, what do we do now?" Johnson asked.

"I wait to hear from LeCour. You two go to the senator's house and keep an eye on it in case the kid tries to run. Stay out of the way, low-key. Keep your distance. You've done a good job lining up those two witnesses who say Lerner was dating the victim. And you, Klayman, you with the shoes. What are they called, Eccos?"

"Right."

Hathaway shook his head. "Sometimes you get lucky," he said. "A pair a' high-priced shoes. Who'd have thought? Nice job, guys."

Annabel was spending that Saturday visiting Annapolis galleries with a friend, and Mac took advantage of her absence to catch up on reading at their Watergate apartment. He was in the midst of his papers when the call came.

"Mr. Smith? U.S. Attorney LeCour."

"Yes. How are you today?"

"Just fine, sir. We have a warrant for the arrest of your client, Jeremiah Lerner, on charges of murder."

"I see."

"We're sensitive to the family situation, Mr. Smith, and don't wish to inflict any undue pain on the senator or Jeremiah's mother, Ms. Emerson."

It sounded to Smith as though LeCour were reading a prepared statement.

"I'm sure that will be appreciated," Mac said.

"We'll give you and your client the opportunity to surrender voluntarily at First District headquarters, Mr. Smith, rather than send officers to make the arrest at the senator's home."

Smith heard the words, but was thinking of other things, namely how to finesse the fact that Jeremiah wasn't available to turn himself in. He wouldn't blatantly lie to LeCour, but he needed to buy some time, any amount of time, in the hope Jeremiah would return to his father's house of his own volition within the next few hours.

"You understand," Smith said, "that I'll have to confer with my client."

"There's not much to confer about," LeCour said. "Either you bring him in, or we go get him." This didn't sound scripted.

"I'm an attorney, Mr. LeCour. I don't make decisions for my client. My assumption is that he'll agree to what it is you're suggesting. But I'll need time to"—he almost said "locate him," but caught himself in time—"I'll need time to explain your offer, which I might add is generous. He'll need time to put some things in order before surrendering. Nine o'clock tomorrow morning?"

There was silence on the other end, and Smith heard LeCour speak with another person, the words not clear. Obviously, that someone else was superior to the U.S. Attorney and would be the one to agree to Smith's suggestion.

LeCour came back on the line. "Nine o'clock sharp," he said.

Smith added, "Give me until six this evening. How can I reach you to confirm that my client agrees to this?"

LeCour started to respond, but Smith said, "And if he doesn't agree, you can come and arrest him."

"I'll be here at six, Mr. Smith." He recited the number. "Let me just say that if, at six, you call and tell me your client does not agree to voluntarily surrender, officers will immediately be dispatched to Senator Lerner's house."

"I understand. You'll hear from me at six. And thank you for your courtesy."

Smith's priority was to attempt to reach Clarise and Bruce Lerner in a last-ditch effort to find Jeremiah. His call to Lerner's home was again answered by the house-keeper. The senator was away on official business and wasn't expected home until the next day. He tried two numbers at Lerner's senate office, finally reaching a staff member who was reluctant to give out a way to contact her boss.

"Look, Miss," Smith said, "this is ex-tremely important. It has to do with the sen-ator's son. I assure you that the senator will thank you for putting me in touch with him—and will be very unhappy if you don't."

She absented herself from the phone for what seemed a long time. When she re-turned, she asked Smith for a number at which he could be reached. "The senator will call you there," she said.

"Thank you. And please tell him to do it fast."

Lerner called within a minute of Smith hanging up.

"Sorry to disturb you, Senator," Smith said, "but this is urgent. The police are about to arrest Jeremiah for Nadia Zarin-ski's murder."

"That's absurd."

"Maybe it is, and it doesn't necessarily

mean they have a sufficient case to indict. But they've offered to have me surrender Jeremiah voluntarily to avoid having cops swarming all over your house. I have until six to get back to them. Have you any idea, any notion, where he might be?"

"Not a goddamn one, Mac. Not a one. Have you tried Clarise?"

"Yes, earlier. She came up blank, too."

"So, Counselor, what do we do now?"

Smith found the use of "we" to be inappropriate. As far as he could see, the only person doing anything was himself.

"Senator," Smith said, "I'm way out on a limb here. As an attorney, I have a code of conduct that doesn't include lying to the authorities about the whereabouts of my client. I asked to have until six in the hope Jeremiah would return. Obviously, that's not about to happen. I have no choice but to call the U.S. Attorney handling the case and tell him Jeremiah has violated the court order, and is not available to be surrendered. That's my obligation as an officer of the court."

"I know all about that," Lerner said. "I'm a lawyer, too."

*You gave up law years ago,* Mac thought.

"Can we meet to discuss this, Mac?"

"Of course."

"Will you come to the house tonight? Say, seven?"

"All right. But I must call LeCour, the U.S. Attorney, at six and tell him of Jeremiah's disappearance."

"If you tell them he's not there, they won't have to come, will they?"

Mac managed a small laugh. "I'm not sure they'll believe this attorney about that, Senator. They'll want to see for themselves."

His was a pained sigh. "Well, do what you can, and know I appreciate your efforts. Damn him! He must be sick in the head."

Mac was tempted to say that too many people were labeled "sick" when they behaved badly, giving legitimate mental illness a bad name. The truth was, Jeremiah Lerner was a surly, rudderless young man, and it didn't matter what made him that way. If he'd murdered the young woman, he'd have to pay for that, although he was entitled to the best possible defense if charged and brought to trial.

They ended the conversation and Smith went to the terrace, Rufus at his side. It had clouded up; rain was imminent, which was good. Washington and its environs had been in a drought all summer, unusual for a city whose summers were characterized by wet, humid, heavy, hot weather.

He realized he was conflicted at that moment, reminiscent of that period of his life when he came to the conclusion that he no longer wished to practice criminal law, and had resigned his partnership and abandoned what had been a love for many years. It hadn't been the reality of the criminal justice system that he enjoyed as much as it was a reverence for the law and his country's system of jurisprudence, as flawed as it sometimes was.

He'd spent time in London at its Old Bailey, where he engaged in long talks with British attorneys and judges. The U.S. legal system, which Smith revered, had been based upon the British model, although he'd pointed out to his British counterparts that there were some aspects of their approach that unfortunately had been ignored. The prepping of witnesses before trial, a common and, Smith thought, flawed practice, was anathema in England. Any attorney doing it there faced severe censure. On the other hand, there were English legal practices that he felt were best left behind, particularly the rule under which an English judge summarized for the jury the evidence as he or she saw it.

Mackensie Smith loved the law and its importance in creating and maintaining the American democratic system. Had his wife and son not been killed, he perhaps would have continued practicing, although that tragedy had coincided with a fear that he was becoming burned out, and that the time had naturally come when it was time to shift gears in his life.

At the same time, the more mundane, less stressful life of college professor did not always provide the brand of stimulation to which he'd been accustomed. That, he knew, had been at work when Clarise had drawn him into Jeremiah's troubles with the law. And Annabel knew the signs, too, recognized when her husband was restless and craving the sort of action and challenge that only the adversarial structure of the criminal justice system could provide. For other men, it was driving fast or engaging in some athletic activity, climbing a mountain or diving off a charter boat in the Bahamas.

For Mac Smith, it was standing up to the formidable resources of prosecutors and fighting for a client, using every bit of knowledge, experience, and skill he possessed. Despite his initial reluctance when contacted by Clarise, he knew that by taking that first step and representing Jeremiah the night of his arrest, he'd made a commitment. He was in for the duration, and reminded himself as he stood on the terrace that late Saturday afternoon that he owed his best to his young client, as unpleasant and unattractive as he might be.

"Mr. LeCour, please."

"LeCour."

"Mac Smith, Mr. LeCour."

"You're early."

"Yes. My client, Jeremiah Lerner, hasn't been available to me since you called."

"Oh? Why not?"

"He's not at his father's home."

"He's supposed to be. Where is he?"

"I don't know."

Smith knew he'd placed himself in a precarious position. Although he'd known about Jeremiah leaving since the previous day, he was under no legal obligation as his attorney to inform the authorities. But when told that the interest in his client had been elevated from assault and resisting arrest to murder, he'd been evasive to LeCour, leading the U.S. Attorney to assume, by inference, that Jeremiah was still at his father's house. Not exactly a lie, but not exactly truthful, either.

LeCour then asked the question Smith hoped he wouldn't.

"When did he leave the house?"

"Late yesterday afternoon."

"You knew that?"

"I didn't know he'd absent himself overnight. He and his father had an argument, and he left in anger, took his father's car. The assumption was that he'd cool off and return. He didn't."

"I should have been notified."

"Why? The judge didn't specifically state that he couldn't leave the house. He was free to go to the store and buy a newspaper and a cup of coffee."

LeCour's pique entered his voice. "He's wanted for *murder*, Mr. Smith."

"As of this afternoon," Smith said, his momentary questioning of his legal culpability now gone. "Last night he wasn't wanted for murder, Mr. LeCour. Now, concerning his whereabouts: You'll obviously want to send officers to verify that he isn't at Senator Lerner's house, and that's fine. But I'm meeting there at seven with the senator. I'm certain your previous offers of courtesy to the senator can be carried over for a few more hours. There's nothing to be gained by turning a search of the house into a circus."

Except, Smith knew, that prosecuting such a high-profile case, and reaping the publicity fallout, wouldn't be unappealing to LeCour—or to any U.S. Attorney, for that matter.

"Send those two detectives who were there previously. Give me an hour with the senator. Make it eight. All right?"

"Absolutely not, Mr. Smith. We want Jeremiah Lerner. He's already gone, who knows where, maybe out of the area. I'll be honest with you. I consider your decision to not be forthcoming to be a breach of legal ethics."

"You're entitled to your opinion, Mr. LeCour. And you're entitled to take whatever action you choose regarding sending officers to the house. We'll be speaking again soon."

# TWENTY-FIVE

Sol Wexler headed his own CPA firm in Washington, and listed an impressive roster of politicians and business leaders as clients. He was, of course, sought after by a number of nonprofit D.C. organizations and agencies to lend his financial knowledge to their boards, and managed to deftly turn down most of them. But he'd been an aspiring actor early in his life—before reality trumped youthful dreams—so when asked to join Ford Theatre's board of trustees, he'd readily accepted. Naturally, he ended up chairing its finance committee, and had become close to Ford's producing director, Clarise Emerson, as well as other trustees, including Annabel Smith.

Clarise's brief confab with the director of

philanthropic programs for American Express had gone well. The company pledged to continue its support for the theatre's productions, and entertained Clarise's suggestion that it up its pledge. She went directly from that meeting to one with the producers and the director of *Festival at Ford's.* Everything was proceeding as planned, she was told, no hitches.

Now, she huddled with controller Bernard Crowley in her office. The independent auditors had been there all day poring over the books and reconciling income and expenditures. They seemed pleased, Crowley said.

"It's going smooth as silk," he told her after the auditors had departed, taking with them additional records needed to complete the audit.

"That's no surprise," she said. "I can't tell you what a relief it is for me to not have to worry about finances. I—"

A phone call interrupted.

"Hello? Yes, how are you? . . . What? . . . I see. . . Yes, of course . . . All right . . . See you then."

"A problem?" Crowley asked after she'd ended the call.

"Problem? No, no problem."

"You looked concerned."

She smiled. "It's all this nonsense with Jeremiah. You've heard, of course, that the media is reporting that he's a suspect in that girl's murder."

"Yes, Clarise. I didn't mention it because—"

"Because you are a gentleman, that's why, and I appreciate it."

"He's still with Bruce?"

"Ah, yes. He's still with Bruce."

Crowley looked quizzically at her.

"Now *you* look concerned," she said.

"I am, Clarise. I know you. You'll take on everything yourself, never seek help, and overload your system. When they question Jeremiah, I'm sure they'll realize that they're barking up the wrong tree."

"And I'm sure you're absolutely right."

Crowley swiveled in his chair, which he overflowed, and looked out the window. Clarise took the opportunity to observe him.

She knew so little about him outside the confines of the office. He was a tragic figure in her eyes, grossly overweight, perpetually flushed, and with thin, wet strands of hair covering the expanse of his baldhead. He was only forty-three years old; at least that's what he'd claimed on his employment application. Was he gay? It was unfair to make that assumption based only upon the fact that he'd never married. Asexual? There was more of that than people realized, Clarise theorized, men and women so busy pursuing their professional dreams that taking time out for sex was simply too intrusive.

She'd never been to his apartment, which she knew was in a large building in Silver Spring, Maryland, nor had she ever met any of his friends. He talked of having friends, male and female, and occasionally related what he'd done with them over the weekend, a movie, dinner out or in, a monthly low-stakes poker game at which he claimed he invariably lost but enjoyed the evening nonetheless.

Her interest in his extracurricular activities wasn't especially keen, no more than a natural human desire to know how other people live. As far as she was concerned, the thing that mattered was the job he did for the theatre, which was splendid. If only he didn't wear that dreadful cologne, she thought as he turned in the chair again and faced her. He struggled from the chair. "Nature calls," he said.

"And I have to leave. I'm already late for my next appointment."

"Go home," he said. "Spend a quiet night in, Clarise. Recharge the old batteries."

"*Old* batteries?" she said, laughing.

"Just a figure of speech," he said, joining her laugh. "Excuse me."

She watched him leave, packed things into her briefcase, then picked up the phone and dialed her home number. Isabella answered.

"Is Jeremiah there?" Clarise asked.

"Yes, ma'am."

"Good. Tell him to stay, not to leave for any reason. I'll be home in an hour."

"Yes, ma'am."

Crowley stood at the door.

"That was quick," Clarise said, smiling.

"One advantage of being a man," he said. "It's always quicker."

"One of many advantages," she said, standing and walking past him to the tiny hallway. "Don't stay too late. And thanks again, Bernard, for all your fine work. Having the auditors come in to a shipshape operation takes a lot off my mind."

"Clarise."

She'd already gone down a few steps. "What?"

"When the pressure is off—when things calm down a little—I'd like some of your undivided attention."

"Meaning?"

"A chance to sit down and talk."

"Sure. About what?"

"Oh, many things, my future here, nothing more important than that."

"Absolutely. When the pressure is off, you can buy me a drink and talk about anything, Bernard. Absolutely anything."

She'd no sooner retrieved her car from the garage downstairs and started the engine when her cell phone rang.

"Ah, Clarise, darling," Sydney Bancroft said. "So glad I caught you."

"What is it, Sydney?"

"We absolutely must talk. I'm back from London, rejuvenated and revitalized and—"

"I don't have time now, Sydney. I'm running late for an appointment."

"Of course. What about Jeremiah? Anything new and exciting while I was away?"

"No, nothing. Your teen show went well this afternoon, I'm told."

"Wonderful! I knew it would. When can we talk? Seriously talk?"

"Monday. At the theatre."

"Ah, if it must be. I'll be home all day tomorrow if you change your mind. Tomorrow would be better, at my apartment. Not the theatre. It's—well, it's highly personal, Clarise."

"Yes. All right. I'll think about it, Sydney. Good-bye."

She checked her watch as she turned onto Pennsylvania Avenue, drove to the entrance of the Four Seasons Hotel, on the edge of Georgetown, and turned her car over to a parking attendant. She entered the lobby and looked through to the Garden Terrace, where a pianist in a black gown applied a light touch to show tunes on a black grand piano.

"Clarise."

She turned to see Bill Wooby of the Millennium Arts Center. "Join us for a drink?" he asked.

"Thank you, no, Bill," she replied, looking past him to the terrace. "I'm meeting someone."

"Best of luck with your hearing."

"My—oh, goodness, I've forgotten all

about that—at least for the moment. Have a nice evening."

"You, too, Clarise."

"A table?" she was asked when entering the room.

"No, I see who I'm meeting."

As she crossed the room, Sol Wexler stood and offered his hand, kissed her on the cheek, and indicated the spot next to him on a love seat. A glass of ginger ale sat untouched on the table. A waitress took her order for diet Coke. After she'd been served, and small talk had been gotten out of the way, Wexler leaned close and said, "I know how busy you are, Clarise, and I appreciate you meeting with me like this on short notice."

She sipped her Coke.

"I felt the matter was serious enough to warrant this meeting," he said.

"Yes, you indicated that on the phone, Sol. Now, what's this all about?"

Klayman and Johnson sat in an unmarked car a considerable distance from Senator Lerner's home, but within viewing distance. It was six-thirty. No one had entered or left the house since their arrival.

"The kid is dead meat," said Johnson between bites of a chicken burrito they'd picked up on their way from headquarters.

"Seems like it. Not a hell of a lot of evidence, though."

"Looks solid to me," said Johnson. "The kid lied. And the shoes."

"All that evidence says is that one of the shoes made an imprint in the alley behind the theatre. Doesn't mean he killed her."

"Then why would he lie about knowing her?"

"Scared."

"Man, you are something," Johnson said. "You sound like the lawyer. Smith get to you?"

"Don't be ridiculous. I just get the feeling that somebody's putting on the pressure to arrest somebody—anybody."

Johnson finished the burrito and wadded up its paper wrapper.

Klayman continued. "They've dropped interest in everybody else, Mo. That grad student, Cole, at American, was mad enough to kill her. At least his friends say so. All the people at the theatre, stagehands, the like. Maybe Senator Lerner had reason to want her out of the way."

"The senator? Come on, man. You saw him. He's not the type to hang around back alleys beating some chick to death."

"Maybe he had somebody else do it. That was the speculation about Congressman Condit. And what about what her landlady told us: that she dated lots of guys. The only two we know are Lerner and Cole. Who were the others?"

Johnson downed the remains of an orange soda. "Nah, Ricky. It was Lerner, Lerner the younger."

Klayman laughed. "Because he cut your pretty face?"

"I forgot about that, but—"

"There's the senator," Klayman said, indicating Lerner's car that was entering the garage after the automatic doors had been activated.

A few minutes later, Mac Smith drove up, parked in the short driveway, and went through the front door.

"The troops are gathering," Johnson said.

Klayman's cell rang.

"Klayman."

"It's Herman. Change in plans. Lerner

skipped from the house last night. He's gone. At least that's what the lawyers say."

"Not too bright," Klayman said.

"He look like a genius to you?"

"The senator and Mackensie Smith just arrived," Klayman said. "What do you want us to do?"

"Sit tight for a few minutes."

"The free press is here," Johnson said, pointing to a remote truck from a local TV station pulling up in front of the house. Its arrival prompted two people, a man and a woman, to exit a car they'd been sitting in at the other end of the block, and approach the house.

"Yeah, well, the kid blew the offer to come in quietly, provided he really did skip last night. I've got two cars on their way. The uniforms in them will block off the street at both ends in case the kid's still there and decides to show us how fast he is. Stay until they're in place. When they are, you two go into the house and make sure our little friend isn't there."

"Okay."

Hathaway clicked off, and Klayman filled Johnson in.

A minute later, the two marked patrol cars

arrived, and their uniformed occupants took up positions at the ends of the street.

"Might as well get out, "Johnson said, yawning, stretching, and opening the door. "No big secret the gang's all here."

Klayman's cell phone sounded again.

"Go," Hathaway instructed. "Be nice, but don't take any B.S. from Smith or the senator. I figure Smith was telling the truth about the kid running, but you never know what these goddamn lawyers will pull. Let me know what goes down."

The two print reporters who'd been in the car, and a reporter from the TV station, approached Klayman and Johnson as they walked to the house.

"Are you here to arrest Senator Lerner's son?" one asked.

The detectives ignored the question, stepped up to the front door, and rang the bell. Questions continued to be asked as the housekeeper opened the door and allowed Klayman and Johnson to enter. The senator and Smith were waiting in the study.

"We're here to arrest Jeremiah Lerner," Johnson intoned, "on the charge of the murder of Nadia Zarinski."

"He's not here," Lerner said.

"We'd like to take a look," Klayman said.

"Be my guest," Lerner replied.

A half hour later, the four men again gathered in the study.

"Any idea where he might be, Senator?" Klayman asked.

"I'm afraid not, gentlemen. I wish I did."

"It would have helped him if he'd surrendered," said Klayman, rhetorically. He looked at Smith. "There'll be an all-points out for him, Professor."

"We're aware of that," Smith said.

"I suggest that if his whereabouts become known, he be encouraged to turn himself in."

"Any other advice, Detective?" Lerner asked.

"None at the moment, sir. Thank you for your cooperation."

When the detectives left the house, the number of media representatives had increased. They hurled questions as Johnson and Klayman went to their car.

"Is the senator in there?"

"Where's Jeremiah Lerner?"

"Is he being charged with the murder?"

Klayman and Johnson said nothing in response, climbed in the car, and drove away until they'd distanced themselves. Johnson used the car's radio to call Hathaway at headquarters. "No sign of him at the house," he reported.

"That's because he's not there," Hathaway said.

Johnson and Klayman looked at each other quizzically as their chief's words came through the speaker.

"We've got a lead on him. His mother's house." He gave them Clarise Emerson's address in Georgetown.

"How'd you come up with that?" Johnson asked.

"A little bird told me. It doesn't make any difference. Get over there. Cars have been dispatched. You two bring the little bastard in—in one piece. Got it?"

"Got it," Johnson said as Klayman gunned it and turned the corner.

By the time they arrived, the street had been blocked off to traffic. TV remote trucks and journalists on foot were kept at bay, some berating officers about being unjustly kept from the scene, and loudly proclaiming their First Amendment rights.

Johnson and Klayman left their car, identified themselves to a uniformed cop, and were allowed to approach the house, where a contingent of a dozen officers waited for instructions. Two powerful halogen searchlights had been hooked up to a portable generator and were positioned to brightly illuminate the front of the three-storey home. Another cop with an electric-powered bullhorn was among the gathered.

"Who's that?" Johnson asked, pointing to a downstairs window where the drapes parted for a moment. A woman's face was seen, but disappeared as the drapes closed again.

"We're ready to go in," the officer with the bullhorn told Johnson.

"Let's hold up," Klayman said. To Johnson: "Come on."

They went to the door, pushed the button, and heard chimes inside. Johnson banged on the door. "Police!" he shouted. "Jeremiah Lerner? If you're in there, open the door and come out with your hands raised."

This time, Klayman kept his thumb on the bell, causing the chimes to tinkle rapidly, while Johnson continued to knock.

"We take the door down?" Johnson asked.

"I hate to do that," Klayman said. "Stupid kid. Why doesn't he just open the damn door?"

"Please," a woman's voice said from behind.

Clarise Emerson had been allowed through the barricades, and had been escorted to the door by an officer.

"Oh, Ms. Emerson," Klayman said.

"Is your son in there?" Johnson asked.

"I don't know. I mean, he was, but—"

"Can you get him to come out?"

"Is all this necessary?" she asked. "This spectacle?"

"We're here to arrest him, ma'am, for the murder of Nadia Zarinski," Johnson said.

"Good God, this is a nightmare, an absolute nightmare." She looked down the street to where reporters and TV camera crews vied for a better vantage point. "The press is everywhere. Jeremiah didn't kill anyone. Don't you see that?"

"Ma'am," Klayman said, "whether he did or not will be determined by others. Right now, our orders are to bring him in. We'd rather do it quietly, but—"

"You call this 'quietly'?"

"If you can get him to surrender himself,

it'll be over," Johnson counseled. "Otherwise, we're going to have to go in and get him."

"I want his lawyer present," she said, her voice reflecting the modicum of control she'd managed to muster.

"Mr. Smith?" Klayman said. "He's at your former husband's house. We just left there. But I suggest we take care of getting your son first."

"I'll make that decision," she said, fumbling in her purse for her cell phone. She found it and dialed.

"Bruce, a horrible thing has happened. Jeremiah is here, and . . . what? . . . Here, at my house . . . he's here and the police are here, too, and the press are everywhere and—is Mac Smith still with you? Put him on."

She told Smith what was occurring, thanked him, and ended the call. "He'll be here shortly," she told the detectives.

"Look, Ms. Emerson, we don't have time to—"

Klayman's cell rang.

"What's going on there, Rick?" Hathaway asked.

Klayman explained.

"Go in and get him," Hathaway said. "The hell with the lawyer. Read him his rights and bring him in."

"Okay," Klayman said, not happy with the order. He saw no reason to not wait until Smith arrived, which would undoubtedly be in minutes. He said to Clarise, "Ms. Emerson, why don't you go inside and talk with Jeremiah? It would make things a lot easier if he just came out nice and peaceful."

"What do you intend to do, shoot him down like some rabid dog?" she growled.

Klayman or Johnson didn't respond. Clarise removed a set of keys from her purse, inserted one in the door, and pushed it open.

"Jeremiah?" she yelled. "It's Mother. Jeremiah, please, you must talk to me." She vanished into the foyer's darkness; a light came on in a room to the right.

"We go in?" Johnson asked, sotto voce.

Klayman indicated patience with a raised hand.

Mac Smith arrived with a uniformed officer, who said, "He says he's the lawyer for the perp."

Smith's facial reaction was worth a thousand words.

"Sorry, Professor," Klayman said. "If he'd only—"

"I know, I know," said Smith. "Ms. Emerson is inside?"

"Yes."

Smith walked past them and entered the house. They heard him call Clarise's name, and she responded. Klayman and Johnson stepped into the foyer. The voices from the room on the right were distinct.

"You've caused a lot of trouble, Jeremiah," Smith said.

"I've been telling him that," Clarise said, her voice shrill.

"You told them," Jeremiah said.

"No, I did not tell them, darling," she said. "I don't know how they knew. Reporters are everywhere. This will be front-page news tomorrow, on every TV station."

"Look, Jeremiah," Smith said, "there's nothing to be gained sitting here. You can't go anywhere. If you don't allow me to bring you out, they'll storm in here and take you by force. Nobody wants that, including the police. If this is a mistake—and the police do make mistakes—we'll sort it all out, and you can go home. Until then, my best advice is to cooperate. I'll be with you every step of the way. No one will abuse you or your rights. I promise you that."

There was silence, broken only by what sounded like sniffling.

"Ready?" they heard Smith say.

Smith came from the room to the foyer, followed by Jeremiah and his mother.

"He'll cooperate," Smith said. "He's not running anymore."

# TWENTY-SIX

The apprehension of Jeremiah Lerner as the targeted suspect in the murder of Nadia Zarinski was, in fact, the lead story on every TV and radio newscast that evening. In a sense, it was refreshing news. Washingtonians, like the rest of the country, had been numbed by a daily dose of unpleasant war stories from the Middle East, tales of childish squabbling among members of Congress, and countless pundits carrying form-over-substance to new heights. The arrest of a U.S. senator's son for murder was almost palliative.

Smith had to wait until the eleven o'clock news to see reports of the scene with which he'd been involved. He'd accompanied Jeremiah to First District headquarters, where Jeremiah was booked, and then to the central cellblock, where he was placed into a cell. He would remain there until a probable cause hearing could be scheduled, within ten days of his arrest if established procedure was honored. At that hearing, the U.S. Attorney's office would present evidence it felt was sufficient to charge the defendant with murder. Whether the government would opt to indict directly, or take its case before a grand jury, was its call.

Mac had called Annabel from police headquarters to tell her he'd be late. He didn't have to explain why. TV had told her all she needed to know.

He walked into the apartment a little before eleven. The strain of the day and evening was readable on his face. Annabel made him a drink while he changed from his suit into shorts, a T-shirt, and sandals, and they sat on the terrace.

"It's bad, isn't it?" she said.

"Yeah, it is," he said. "Jeremiah made it a lot worse than it had to be by running. I don't think they have that strong a case against him, but it doesn't matter, does it? He's been convicted by the press, and Senator Lerner and Clarise have been thoroughly trashed."

"What *is* the evidence against him?"

"A couple of people who say he'd dated the girl, and his lying about it. And one of his shoes matches a print found at the scene. And, there are the accusations that he'd roughed up previous girlfriends. We'll be able to keep that out—it's more prejudicial than probative—and all the pretrial publicity raises some due process issues. But, yes, the damage has already been done." His sigh was long and pained. He closed his eyes, slowly shook his head, opened his eyes, and smiled at his wife. "Just think, Annie, a few days ago I was a dumb and happy, low-profile professor turning out future Supreme Court justices, or at least well-trained ambulance chasers."

"Want to give up?"

"Did you have to put it that way? No, I'm in this to the end. Yale will carry much of the burden, write the motions and pleadings, handle all the preliminary hearings. I think there's been a classic rush to judgment here, Annie, by the police and the U.S. Attorney. Jeremiah hasn't made it easy on himself. Cops love to nail unpleasant people, and juries tend to convict abrasive, arrogant defendants. Jeremiah Lerner fits all those categories, and more."

"The political fallout has to be big," she said.

"Big and nasty. As you know, Lerner has spoken of possibly running for president next time around. What his son might have done shouldn't have any bearing on his qualifications, but it will, if only by extension."

"What about Clarise and the NEA?"

"Same story. Those on the committee who are against her will use this messy family situation to indicate she's—well, imply that she's been a bad mother, raised a bad child, has victimized her own son through her defense of questionable art and movies—you name it."

She reached across the short space between their chairs and placed a hand on his arm. "So, Counselor, what's next?"

"Let's see," he said. "I'd better speak tomorrow with Dean Mackin. I can always get someone to take my regular classes, but I'll have to keep the Lincoln sessions. Hopefully, I won't have to miss any classes, but I need to pave the way in case I do."

He went on to relate to Annabel the conversation he'd previously had with Mackin, and how the law school dean had questioned the pragmatic wisdom of becoming involved in the Lerner case.

"You can't blame him, I suppose," Annabel offered.

"And I'm not."

"I'm going to lunch Monday with Clarise and others involved in her NEA bid. The vice president is hosting it at the Lafayette."

"Don't count on it."

"Don't count on what?"

"On the VP being there, considering what's happened, or on Clarise showing up, for that matter. The VP might not consider it politically expedient."

"What about Clarise? You don't think she'll withdraw from the NEA nomination, do you?"

"Annie," he said, getting up and leaning on the railing, the black waters of the Potomac flowing silently below, "there is nothing, absolutely nothing, that surprises me in this town these days. Ready for bed?"

"I'm always ready for bed with you, Mackensie Smith."

# TWENTY-SEVEN

Sunday, as everyone knows, is a day of rest, except for those in jobs demanding their presence. Across the country, men and women enjoy Sunday as a day to reflect and relax, to sleep late, go to the beach, barbecue, nap in a hammock, or catch up on reading the book that seemed impossible to get to during the workweek. For some reason, this is especially apparent and visible in Washington, D.C. Maybe it's the sprawling Mall, where the briefly leisurely congregate, tossing Frisbees to willing dogs, displaying the latest jogging outfits guaranteed to lessen the pain, and lovers leaning against each other on benches and thinking their individual thoughts about whether this relationship is worth pursuing.

But that reflects Washington's common folk. For the city's uncommon residents—and they probably represent the majority—Sunday might appear to be a day of rest, but even their most recreational of activities have a purpose. Someone is invited to the barbecue because that person might prove helpful. The phones continue to be worked. Seemingly social brunches offer both eggs Benedict as well as the scrambled eggs of negotiation. Slaps on the back confirm deals made by people in shorts and wearing straw hats. The dark suits and fashionable pantsuits will be de rigueur on Monday. For Sunday, while the uniforms might change, it's business as usual in the nation's capital, albeit with pale legs showing and midsection bulges revealed.

For Mac and Annabel Smith, this Sunday revolved around brunch at Yale Becker's house in Bethesda. They'd had to politely brush off a couple of reporters camped in the Watergate's lobby, one of whose aggressiveness raised Mac's temperature a few degrees. But after a dip in the Beckers' pool, it dropped back to 98.6. Following a low-calorie lunch, Smith and Becker sat in a corner of the patio to discuss their next moves. Becker had been on the phone that morning with U.S. Attorney LeCour.

"I told LeCour that if they intended to formally charge Jeremiah with murder, we wanted the assault and resisting arrest charges dropped," Becker told Smith. "He refused, which leads me to believe they have questions about supporting the murder charge. They'll keep the other options open in the event the murder charge collapses."

"Did LeCour tell you who's claiming that Jeremiah dated Nadia?" Smith asked.

"No, but we know one of them is a student at American University, a Joe Cole. LeCour knows he legally doesn't have to disclose anything to us until the probable cause hearing. He cited all the usual cases, Brady, Weatherford—he sounded like he was giving me a lecture."

"We'll have subpoena power."

"Eventually."

"Any hint as to whether they'll seek a grand jury?"

"None, but they're liable to. Gets them off the hook if twenty-three grand jurors vote to indict a senator's son instead of the politicos having to make the decision on their own."

"Did LeCour mention a lineup?" Smith asked.

"He says the police want one. What do you think?"

Smith grimaced and looked back to where Annabel and Sue Becker were admiring Sue's award-winning rose garden. The police obviously had what they considered an eyewitness. According to what Smith had heard, though, he was an alcoholic street person, hardly what a savvy prosecutor would want to present at trial. Still, Smith had tried enough criminal cases in which a so-called eyewitness identified his client, and despite the witness's shaky character and debatable reliability, the jury had believed him.

"We really can't stop them," Smith said. "If we try, they'll use it as an example of our having something to hide, of consciousness of guilt on his part. I'll make sure it's a legit lineup. And if it isn't, we can use that to our advantage if this ever goes to trial."

The Beckers' yellow Lab joined the two attorneys, laying his head on Mac's lap and giving his hand a lick. Yale left to refresh their iced teas. Mac massaged the dog's neck as he sat back, closed his eyes, and enjoyed the sun on his face.

He'd been troubled when he'd gone to bed the previous night. Now, engaged in a strategy discussion with another attorney for whom he had great respect and personal affection, he realized how much he was enjoying the experience. He loved teaching, found it immensely challenging, particularly when dealing with an especially promising student who forced him to dig deep into his intellect and knowledge. But so much was theoretical.

Being part of Jeremiah Lerner's defense team was real, nothing theoretical about it. This was criminal law as the textbooks never described it. Yes, there were time-honored, Constitutionally guaranteed principles to be adhered to, and local laws to be followed, and Smith knew them like the back of his hand, and taught them. But lecturing, and navigating them as an advocate for a young client facing a lifetime behind bars, was another matter.

In Georgetown on this sunny Sunday, Clarise Emerson stayed at home with her drapes drawn, and an answering machine screening callers. She'd chosen to not answer most calls, including three from Sydney Bancroft, but had picked up at the sound of her ex-husband's voice.

"How are you handling things, Clarise?" he asked.

"Dreadfully," she said.

"The press camped at your doorstep?"

"Of course. A TV crew, too."

"I think we'd better talk."

"About what?" she snapped, anger on the rise.

"About our only son, goddamn it! Look, I know we have differences, and I'm not suggesting we discuss them. But we've got to present a united front as his father and mother, stand behind him publicly, take the initiative with the press, and express our belief in Jeremiah and his innocence. I met late last night with Andrew and Janice, and we—"

"Your staff?"

"Yes. We believe that sitting back and waiting for things to happen is the wrong approach. Andrew is drafting a statement for the press to come from both of us. We'll put that out tomorrow morning. We'll hold a press conference a day or two after that, when we'll make a joint statement. That'll be drafted, too, and we'll hold a briefing session prior to it to try to anticipate questions that might be asked."

"A briefing session." She said it as though it were a guilty plea. "That's all I seem to be doing these days, Bruce, being grilled at briefing sessions for the NEA hearing. I don't think I can take another."

"Well, Clarise, I suggest you suck it up and make yourself available for what I've put together. Don't forget, this is for our son. I'll be at the house for the rest of the day. Call me. Make it five. I'll have more details then."

The next call she took was from Joyce Drummond, President Nash's White House aide responsible for the administration's task force on arts and humanities agencies, and who'd been in charge of prepping Clarise for her hearing.

"I hate to call you on a pretty Sunday, Clarise, especially because of what you're going through with your son. But this has to do with that."

"Should I sit down?" Clarise asked, wishing she had a cigarette. She'd quit smoking twenty years ago.

"Maybe."

"Go ahead, Joyce. I'm in a chair, not far to fall."

"I just got off the phone with Ken Shoenlein, Topper Sybers's chief of staff. We go back a long way together on the Hill. He called me as a courtesy to an old friend. I'm sworn to secrecy."

"And?"

"He called to tell me that Senator Sybers is going to call for the president to withdraw your nomination—unless you offer to do it."

"Because of what's happened to my son?"

"Yes. Sybers, according to Ken, feels your personal troubles would make it too difficult for you to devote sufficient time and attention to the NEA. That's nonsense, of course, nothing more than an excuse to get rid of you."

"At least he's not claiming I corrupted my son through the TV shows I produced."

"What?"

"Nothing. Will the president do that? Withdraw my nomination?"

"Not according to the VP. I called her

chief of staff to tell her what Sybers is threatening, and she got hold of Vice President Maloney, who said the president will do it over her dead body, an overstatement, but reflective of her position."

The day had been a cocktail of emotions for Clarise, anger, sadness, frustration, and only fleeting moments of resolve to stand tall against whatever was flung at her. Now, that resolve consumed her.

"I can't control what President Nash decides to do, Joyce, and can only hope he won't bow to Senator Sybers. But I know one thing: No one is going to force me to withdraw my name. I'm in it until I'm told I'm not."

"That's what I wanted to hear, Clarise," she said, a happier note replacing the seriousness that had permeated her voice.

"What do you suggest I do?"

"Nothing. Enjoy what's left of the day. We'll be working behind the scenes with the president. See you tomorrow at the luncheon?"

"Of course. It's for me, isn't it? The guest of honor has to be there."

Joyce laughed. "The guest of honor," she

repeated, "and the next head of the NEA. See you tomorrow."

"What an arm," Rick Klayman said.

He was at Mo Johnson's house enjoying a family Sunday barbecue, and ended up playing catch with the middle son, eighteen years old, an outstanding pitcher for his high school baseball team.

"Big-league potential, Ricky," said the proud father, dressed in green Bermuda shorts and yellow T-shirt, and wearing a large white apron with KING OF THE BAR-B-Q written on it in red letters. "Had his fastball timed last week. Ninety plus. Scouts are showing interest."

Klayman handed the glove to Johnson, rubbed his palm where the pitches had stung, and joined Etta, Rachel Kessler, two other couples, and the Johnsons' other sons on the patio. The sounds of an early Miles Davis quintet came from small, wireless outdoor speakers.

"I'm so glad you could join us," Etta said to Klayman and Rachel. "We've been wanting to get you here for a cookout for months now."

"There never seems to be time for anything that's fun," Rachel said with a laugh. "It's work, work, work."

"All work and no play makes for a dull child," Mo commented as he unwrapped plastic from a large platter containing marinated rib steaks. "Who said that?" he asked Klayman, "and don't say Abe Lincoln."

Klayman threw up his hands. "Maybe it *was* Lincoln," he said lightly.

"James Howell," Rachel said. "And the dull child was named Jack."

Everyone laughed; Klayman applauded and said, "Only Rachel would know something like that. She's a treasure trove of trivia."

"You should go on *Jeopardy!,* Rachel."

"Rick is a Lincoln scholar," Mo said, preparing to place the steaks on the gas grill.

"Not a scholar," Klayman said, "but I do read a lot about him."

"You must have been fascinated with the murder at Ford's Theatre," someone said.

"I wouldn't say fascinated," Klayman said. "I've spent a lot of time there. You ever been?"

One of the couples had, and discussion ensued about the Lincoln Museum in the theatre's basement, and the tour they'd taken with a park ranger.

"Is it true that John Wilkes Booth originally hadn't planned to kill Lincoln?" Klayman was asked.

"Yes, it is," the young detective replied. "Booth was a die-hard Confederate supporter and hated Lincoln, considered him uncouth and a traitor for advocating freeing the slaves. He originally intended to kidnap Lincoln, take him to Richmond, and trade him for Southern prisoners, but that plot failed. He was in the audience during Lincoln's last public speech in April 1865. Lincoln gave it from a second-storey White House window and proposed that some blacks be given the right to vote."

"*Some* blacks?" There was much laughter.

"I think he meant well," Klayman said in defense. "At any rate, even suggesting that some blacks get the vote was too much for Booth. He tried to get a colleague to shoot Lincoln on the spot, but he refused. That's when Booth told his friend, 'That's the last speech he'll ever make.'"

"He was right, wasn't he?"

"Unfortunately."

Johnson took orders—rare, medium, or well done?—and the grill flared up as he slapped the meat on it. Rachel went with Etta to fetch accompanying dishes from the house, and Klayman followed Johnson into the family room, where Mo replaced the Miles Davis CD with one by pianist George Shearing.

"You still thinking Lerner might not have killed her?" Johnson asked his partner.

Klayman shrugged. "I'd just feel better if we were following other leads, talking to other people."

"Like who? The senator? That crazy old actor? Cole? Somebody at the theatre?"

"I suppose so. I—"

"Ooh, better get out and turn those steaks."

They were in the middle of dinner on the patio when Klayman's cell phone sounded. "Sorry," he said, standing and walking a few feet from the table.

"Rick, it's Herman."

"What's up?" Klayman asked his boss.

"Nothing to pull you away—how's Mo as a chef?"

"Five-star."

"Look, I know you've been dogging the

Connie Marshall case since she disappeared. What is it now, two years?"

"Yeah."

"They dragged a floater from Chesa-
peake Bay early this morning. Some fisherman snagged the body—skeleton, I
guess—and the ME was called in."

"It's her? Connie Marshall?"

"Looks like it. They used dental records
on file, brought in a forensic dentist from
Virginia. It matches up."

Klayman said nothing.

"Rick?"

"Yeah. Sorry, Herman. I'm glad they
found her."

"I just thought you'd want to know."

"I appreciate the call. Is Ong still there?"

"Yeah. He's doing his number on what's
left of her."

"I'll swing by."

"Nothing you can do."

"I'd just feel better. Thanks again."

"That was Herman," Klayman told Johnson as he rejoined the other guests. "They
found Connie Marshall."

"Who's that?" someone asked.

"An intern who went missing a couple of
years ago, the one supposedly having an

affair with the House majority leader, Tomlinson. A fisherman found her in the bay."

"Rick's been following the case," Johnson announced.

"Is there a connection with the intern at
Ford's Theatre?"

"I doubt it," Klayman said. He turned to
Rachel: "I need to stop by headquarters."
To the others: "Hate to eat and run, but I
really have to go."

"You didn't *eat* and run, Rick," Etta said.
"You've barely touched your food."

He stood, and Rachel did, too.

"No, you stay," Rick said. "I'm sure
someone will drive you home."

"No," she said pleasantly, "I'm old-fash-
ioned. I leave with the guy I came with."

"Take a doggie bag home," Etta said,
jumping up and disappearing inside the
house. She emerged seconds later with
plastic food bags into which she placed
their steaks and a few other items. Mo
walked them to their car.

"I'm sorry, Mo, to cut out like this," Klayman said. "It's just that—"

"Hey, buddy, no apologies necessary. I
know how much this case means to you."

He said to Rachel, "Just don't let my main man here get too bent out a' shape over it."

"I promise," she said, kissing him on the cheek.

Rick wanted to drop her at her apartment, but she insisted on staying with him, stipulating it didn't mean accompanying him into any room where there were dead bodies.

As Rachel sat in a reception area reading a paperback book, Klayman entered Dr. Eric Ong's office, where the ME sat at his desk writing a report. "Sit down, Detective," Ong said, motioning toward a chair. "I'll only be a minute."

Klayman passed the time questioning his decision to leave the barbecue. It wasn't very polite, he knew, and certainly wasn't necessary. The Marshall case was two years old. The fact that her remains had been found was good; at least it might bring her family some measure of closure. Funny, how important it is to families to have someone to bury, he thought. It didn't bring them back to life. In a sense, it was an exclamation point to their grief. He sometimes wondered how he would react if a loved one disappeared, and murder was the suspected cause. As long as there wasn't a body, there was hope, as unreasonable as it might be as time dragged on, that the person would one day surface healthy and happy, and hopefully embarrassed at having caused so much consternation and worry.

He'd interviewed Connie Marshall's parents on a few occasions when the crime was fresh, and saw in them the same expression of confusion, sadness, and anger as Nadia's parents had exhibited. Constance Marshall's disappearance had been big news for months, fueled by rumors that she'd been involved in a sexual relationship with the married House majority leader, Willard Tomlinson. But media attention eventually and predictably drifted to other stories, and only an occasional call to Klayman from one of the parents to ask whether anything was new had kept him in direct touch with the case. The C. Marshall folders had been placed in the unsolved homicide files—this was when homicides in D.C. were called homicides, not "crimes against persons"—and the active investigation ceased.

The Marshall case had become borderline obsessive for Klayman; he'd volunteered on weekends and days off to follow up on leads that became less frequent as the months went by. And his interest had waned, too, as leads dried up and his only link to the case was the computer file he kept at home. Accessing it gave him a feeling of still being connected, a poor substitute for the real thing.

"So, Detective Klayman, the missing person is no longer missing," Ong said in his shrill voice.

"The ID is definite?"

Ong laughed. "With reasonable medical certainty, as the lawyers like to say in court. Yes, it's Ms. Marshall. The dental records confirm it. And there are the general physical characteristics of the skeleton, length, approximate weight and age—a female, of course. There are also the facial characteristics as shown in photographs provided by the family when she disappeared. There are three basic facial types, you know, square, tapering, and ovoid. She's an ovoid."

*So was Nadia Zarinski,* Klayman thought. And she was approximately the same height and weight as Constance Marshall, same color hair and eyes. Not that that was especially significant. Lots of young women in Washington fit that description.

"Any evidence of how she died?" Klayman asked.

"Oh, yes," Ong replied. "There's a nasty crack on the left side of her skull."

"Could it have happened when she went into the water, hit a rock or the side of a boat?" Rick asked.

"Anything is possible, Detective, but I would say not. I need to do further examination, but my opinion at this moment—"

"With reasonable medical certainty," Klayman said with a smile.

"Yes, with reasonable medical certainty. She died from the blow to the head and was placed in the water sometime thereafter."

Klayman stood and extended his arms into the air against a backache. "Well," he said, "this opens the case again. Anything else?"

"Whoever did it wasn't interested in robbing her."

"Why do you say that?"

"The jewelry she was wearing. We're fortunate that it didn't disintegrate over time, or get ripped off by the crabs."

"What sort of jewelry, Eric?"

"An expensive wristwatch, gold ring, and gold chain."

Klayman leaned on the desk. "She was wearing those?"

"Oh, yes. Of course, the watch had stopped, and everything is badly corroded. Not much value to them."

"Yeah, not much value. Thanks, Doc. I appreciate the time."

"Anytime, Detective. Always happy to contribute to the cause of justice."

# TWENTY-EIGHT

"How does the defendant plead? Guilty or not guilty?"

"Not guilty," Jeremiah muttered.

"Speak up. Guilty or not guilty?"

"Not guilty."

U.S. Attorney LeCour had filed written murder charges against Jeremiah, and went on to verbally present the State's formal charges against him at the Monday morning Presentment hearing. The charge was murder in the first degree, with a lesser-included charge of murder in the second degree. The murder-one charge assumed malice aforethought and premeditation. The lesser charge contained all the ingredients of first degree, but without premeditation. LeCour had presented only two witnesses

to corroborate his allegations, Herman
Hathaway, MPD's chief of the Crimes
Against Persons Unit, who testified about
Jeremiah's lies to detectives concerning a
prior relationship with the deceased; statements from unnamed witnesses who had
knowledge of that relationship, and who
LeCour promised would testify to that fact;
and the defendant's previous assault on a
police officer, resisting arrest, and violation
of a court order placing him under the custody of a "family member." Becker objected
when Hathaway mentioned previous complaints against Jeremiah, including assault
on a woman, and was sustained. Not that it
mattered at this juncture. There was no jury;
the judge alone would make the decision
whether the State had ample grounds to
formally charge Jeremiah with the murder.
LeCour and the U.S. Attorney's office had
the option of presenting the case to a grand
jury, but had informed Smith and Becker
that they did not intend to do that.

Forensic expert Wallace Wick gave testimony about the shoe print matching the
pattern of the defendant's sole.

On most mornings, Presentment hearings drew few spectators, usually retired

men and women whose favorite avocation was hanging around the courthouse and sitting in on legal proceedings. They knew every judge and court officer, and zealously debated the merits of each case.

This morning, however, the visitor benches were filled, including a large contingent of press. Judge Walter Jordan, a veteran on the bench, had to admonish the crowd more than once to be quiet or risk being expelled from the room. He was a kindly looking older black man with a sweet smile, soft voice, and kind eyes, but with a reputation for running a tight ship. He was considered a fair judge, although he had little patience with defense attorneys who practiced theatrics in defending their clients.

Yale Becker's cross-examination of Hathaway and Wick was cursory. Such hearings were an opportunity for lawyers on both sides to gain a sense of their opponent's projected tactics, and the evidence they might present at trial. The advantage was clearly with the defense. It was incumbent upon the prosecution to lay out its case in detail in order to justify the charges against a defendant. Becker and Smith knew that

unless they had a bombshell that would de-
rail the proceedings, it was prudent to keep
their cards close to the vest. They'd submit-
ted a pro forma Motion to Dismiss earlier
that morning in order to have it on the
record. There would be multiple motions
filed before trial, all to make a record in the
event an appeal was in the works somewhere down the road.

"Let's deal with the matter of bail," the
judge said. "Mr. LeCour?"

"Under the circumstances, your honor,
the state feels that no bail should be set for
the accused. He's being charged with a
heinous crime, the murder of an innocent
young woman. He's already proved to be a
flight risk. Bail would be highly inappropriate."

Smith responded, "Your honor, Jeremiah
Lerner is from a distinguished family. His
father is a highly respected U.S. senator,
and his mother heads Ford's Theatre and is
in line to head the NEA. The U.S. Attorney's
claim that he's already demonstrated a tendency to flee is unfounded. It isn't as
though he left his father's house and winged
off to South America. All he did was go from

his father's house to his mother's house. He stayed well within the family."

"He was charged with resisting arrest and—"

"Objection, your honor," Smith said. "We've asked that those charges be dropped by Mr. LeCour's office."

"I'm well aware of that, Mr. Smith," said the judge. "Anything else, Mr. LeCour?"

"Just that we ask that no bail be set, Judge."

"Under the circumstances, I don't see the need for an excessive amount of bail. Two hundred thousand." He rapped the handle of his gavel on the bench.

"Your honor."

"You aren't about to argue with me and upset me, are you, Mr. LeCour," the judge said softly, and with a smile.

"I wouldn't think of it, Judge."

"Good. It's the opinion of the bench that the state has presented evidence sufficient to hold the defendant over for arraignment a week from today, same time, same station. Who's putting up bail?"

"The family, your honor," Smith replied.

"Well, work it out with the court." He leaned forward and glared at Jeremiah.

"You, young man, have two of the best lawyers in this city, and you're being allowed to spend your time with them and your family while you prepare yourself to face these charges. I suggest you wipe that snarl off your face and count your blessings. Dismissed."

Smith and Becker watched their client be led from the courtroom. LeCour came to where they stood. "You got off with pocket change," he said.

"Seems fair to me," Becker said.

"Where's his family, the distinguished senator and his lovely ex-wife?"

"Attending to affairs of state," Smith said. "Why do I have the feeling that you don't have much of a case, and that the judge thinks so, too?"

"Enough to arraign him," LeCour said. "That is, if he shows up next week."

"Oh, he will," said Becker, gathering up papers.

*I hope so,* Smith thought.

LeCour took a few steps, turned, and said, "If you want to discuss pleading this out, give me a call."

"Thanks," said Smith, "but don't take it personally if you don't hear from us."

"I would have felt better if one of his parents were here," Becker said as he and Smith left the courthouse.

"I would have, too, although it really didn't matter. I spoke with the senator last night and told him we were hoping for a reasonable bail. He said he'd come up with whatever was needed. I'll call and let him know what it's going to cost him, unless he wants to use a bail bondsman, which I doubt. He doesn't need to. Frankly, I'm just as happy having Jeremiah cool his heels a while longer. Maybe it'll get through to him that being behind bars isn't fun."

"That would be nice. Let me know when the senator wants to post bail, and I'll handle it. Where are you off to?"

"School. I need to talk with Dean Mackin about missing classes."

"How do you want to divvy up the depositions? You work around your other commitments. I'll handle most of them."

"No, Yale, I'll make myself available. Now that I'm in, I want to be all the way in. Hello to Sue, and thanks again for the swim and barbecue. Refreshed us both."

He went to his office and made calls, including to Annabel.

"How did it go?" she asked.

"Fine. Two hundred thousand bail. A bargain."

"I'd say so. You caught me going out the door."

"Oh, that's right. The luncheon. I tried Clarise, but no answer. She's probably already on her way. I've got to call Senator Lerner and inform him of the bail arrangement."

"Neither of them was there this morning?"

"No, which is no longer a surprise. Plenty of press, though. Maybe it's just as well they stay away."

"Jeremiah will be staying with his father?"

"Or mother. The judge didn't stipulate, but it's got to be one or the other. Going back to that apartment he shares with some roommate won't do. He'll have to be available at all times to the police, to say nothing of for Yale and me. At any rate, enjoy the luncheon. Tell Clarise what's transpired. Should put her mind at ease a bit—if that's necessary."

"I will. Love you."

"The feeling is entirely mutual. See you this evening."

* * *

Rick Klayman had spent a sleepless Sunday night.

After leaving the ME's office, he'd taken a hungry Rachel Kessler for a burger before dropping her home.

"Come in?" she asked as they sat in the car in front of her apartment building.

"No, thanks," he'd said. "I really have to go."

"Where are you going?"

"Work."

Voicing his thoughts for the first time, he'd told her of what he'd learned from Dr. Ong, that there were similarities between the two slain young women that might indicate the same person had killed them. Nothing definitive, but the possibility existed.

"That's comforting," she'd said. "There's a murderer walking around Washington who preys on young women, one of them two years ago, and now another. Gives me the chills."

"May not be true," he'd said, "but I want to follow up on it. Sorry I dragged you away from Mo's house and a steak."

"You made up for it with the burger. Besides, I have the steak for tomorrow. Sure you won't come in?"

"I'd just be lousy company."

"Okay," she said, "but I think my mother was right."

"About what?"

"About not falling in love with a cop or fireman."

"She said that?"

"Yeah. Her father was a fireman, and she had a cousin who was a cop."

"And she told you not to get involved with either."

"No, Rick, she told me never to fall in love with one."

"Oh. And you're—?"

"Go to work. Solve all the city's crimes. Save us all. When you're finished, call me."

"Hey, don't be mad."

"You're too cute to get mad at." She grabbed him by the ears, pressed her lips tightly to his, lingered there, released him, left the car, and ran up the steps to the building, leaving a befuddled detective sitting in his car.

He drove to First District headquarters, went to the records room, and pulled out the Constance Marshall files, which he pored over until past midnight, making notes, drawing diagrams linking names of people who'd known her and trying to inject order into a fragmented mind.

He went home to sleep but found that impossible. Among many thoughts and questions was what every veteran cop had told him, that the minute you became personally involved in a case and with a victim, you lost your ability to think clearly and rationally. You lost your impartiality. They said the same about doctors, particularly surgeons. A patient was a body, an anatomical unit to be opened and its disease cut out and discarded.

But wasn't that the problem with too many cops and doctors? he mused as he sat in his living room. He knew cops, too many of them, who carried the notion of detachment to an extreme, dismissing victims as just another case with a file number on it, and approaching victims' families, or anyone else with something to offer, as moronic, congenital liars.

If that's what it took to be a successful cop, his parents were right. He was in the wrong business.

*    *    *

He was preparing to leave the apartment at six Monday morning when a call from his sister in Boston stopped him.

"Rick, it's Susan."

"Hi. How are you?"

"Not too good. Harry had a heart attack last night."

"I'm sorry. Is he okay? I mean, is it serious?"

"Is any heart attack not serious?"

"I just meant that—"

"It was a mild one, a good early warning. He'll be fine if he watches his diet and exercises and starts living a more healthy life."

"That's good to hear."

"I just thought you'd want to know."

"Yeah, I'm glad you called. Where is he? I can send, I don't know, flowers or something."

"We don't want flowers. It's a waste. Maybe you could send him a book, something on golf. That's his hobby, you know."

"Sure. I'll send a golf book or something."

"He'll have to recover at home for a while. He'll need things to read."

"I imagine. I'll send it to the house. How are you?"

"How can I be, with a husband who's a cardiac cripple at forty-five?"

She cried; he waited.

"I have to go," he said finally. "I'm sorry about Harry. Will call you shortly."

Which was true, although he'd never particularly liked his sister's husband, who sold insurance and constantly boasted about his prowess on the links. For Rick, Purgatory was watching golf on television. The last time they'd been together, Harry had asked, "What's it like playing cops-and-robbers as an adult, Ricky?"—followed by a hale and hearty laugh. Later that day, Harry had tried to sell Rick life insurance, pointing to a variety of statistics indicating that his brother-in-law's projected life span was lower than others' because of his line of work. Rick had said he'd think about it, but didn't.

"I'll tell Harry you were concerned about him," she said.

"Yeah, do that. Tell him I—tell him to eat right and get some exercise. Thanks for calling, Susan."

"Hey, Rick, I thought this was your day off," a detective said as Klayman sat at his desk.

"It is, but I've got things I want to catch up on."

"What'a you think about finding the Marshall body?"

"I'm glad they did."

"Opens it up again, huh?"

"Yeah, it does."

"Could it figure to be the same guy as the Zarinski case?"

"Could be. Too early to tell. Both victims young women, interns, same general physical characteristics, both killed by blows to the head. If it is the same guy, he's gotten sloppy. First time around, he takes the trouble to dump the victim in the river. This time, he leaves her in the alley where he killed her."

"Yeah, well, whoever did it is long gone, Rick. It's too cold, man, too cold."

Klayman worked at his desk until eight, when he went to the lobby, withdrew cash from the ATM, and was on his way out the door when Mo Johnson arrived.

"What are you doing here, man?"

"Catching up on stuff."

"It's your day off."

"I know. Yours, too."

Johnson grinned as though being there

when he wasn't required to be was embarrassing. "That's what I'm doing, too, catching up on things. Where are you going?"

"Out to American University. I want to talk to Joe Cole again."

"I'll tag along."

"Great."

They found Cole in his room studying for an exam.

"Glad you nailed the guy who killed Nadia," he said. "What a sick-o."

"He hasn't been convicted yet," Johnson said, perusing posters of rock stars on the walls intermingled with magazine pages of pretty young girls in bikinis.

"But he will be. Right?"

"Maybe, maybe not," Klayman said. "There's not a lot of evidence against him."

"I heard on the news you found his shoes in the alley."

"You should listen more closely," Johnson said. "They found a shoe *print,* that's all."

"That matches him, right?"

"Let's talk again, Joe, about the Labor Day weekend. You say you were with Nadia on Saturday night, had dinner, made love back at her place, and she kicked you out after telling you she'd had better lovers. Correct?"

"That's right. Hey, are you asking me the same questions because you think I had something to do with her murder?"

"Nice pictures," Johnson said. "You like brunettes, huh?"

"What? Oh, I don't know. I never thought about it."

"Most young guys like blondes," Johnson said. "All these pinups are brunette."

"So what?"

"Just making a comment, that's all. Feel like taking a ride, Joe?"

"A ride? To where?"

"The restaurant, Spezie, the one you said you took Nadia to Saturday night." Klayman pulled a color photo of Nadia from his pocket and flashed it at Cole. "Let's see if they remember you from that Saturday night."

Cole forced a dismissive laugh. "No-body'll be at the restaurant this morning."

"Sure they will, Joe," Johnson said. "Tough business, owning and working in a restaurant. Long hours. I have an uncle owns a ribs joint in Baltimore. Spends his life there."

"I have to study."

"Only take a half hour, Joe," Klayman said. "You don't want to disappoint us."

"Don't you have to have a warrant or something?"

"A warrant? To take a pleasant ride with somebody? Hell, no. Come on, you're wasting time. Let's go."

Spezie's manager, and most of his staff, were at the restaurant when the detectives and Cole arrived. Klayman showed them Nadia's picture and asked whether they remembered seeing the young man with them, and the girl in the picture, Saturday night. No one did. Cole became overtly and increasingly nervous.

"You said you paid cash," Johnson said when they'd left the restaurant and were back in the car.

"That's right."

"Do you have credit cards?"

"Yeah, an American Express. My father got it for me."

"Nice father. How come you didn't use it at the restaurant?"

"I don't know. I guess I didn't want to run up too many charges on it."

"You *guess* you didn't?" Johnson asked. "Can't remember?"

"I'm not saying anything else," Cole said, folding his arms across his chest and assuming an expression intended to confirm it.

They dropped him back on campus.

"We'll be in touch again, Joe," Johnson said. "Good luck with your exam."

"What do you think?" Klayman asked as they drove downtown.

"I wouldn't rule him out," Johnson responded. "Of course, I don't like him, but I don't like Lerner, either. No, Cole's a possibility—assuming Lerner didn't do it. I'm not convinced."

"Neither am I, but I thought it was worth touching base again with some of the others."

"Like Mr. Shakespeare?"

Klayman laughed. "Yeah, I'd like to talk with Sydney Bancroft again. And some of the people at the theatre. I just have this feeling we didn't ask all the right questions. Know what I mean?"

"No, but I'll go along. Give the actor a call. Etta gave me a hard time this morning about coming in on my day off. I could use a good laugh about now."

Mac Smith managed to track down Senator Lerner and arrange for him to contact Yale Becker regarding Jeremiah's bail. That detail out of the way, Smith met with Dean Mackin to discuss the possibility of missing an occasional class, depending upon how the case against Jeremiah developed. Mackin had evidently accepted Mac's decision to take part in Jeremiah's defense; he didn't raise again the question of whether his colleague had erred in that decision.

After meeting with the dean, Smith closed the door to his office and quickly went through professional journals that had piled up over the past week. It was almost noon when a colleague knocked. "You pulled off a coup this morning," he said. "Two hundred thousand for bail. I would have bet a million."

"To be honest," Smith said, "I wouldn't have been disappointed if the judge had denied bail. At least I'd know where my client is."

"You'll be at the press conference?"

"What press conference?"

"Senator and Mrs. Lerner. I mean, the former Mrs. Lerner."

"When is it taking place?"

"Five this afternoon, according to the radio. At the senator's home."

Smith wondered if Becker had been informed about it. At this juncture, Mac wasn't sure holding a press conference was a good idea, especially if an attorney wasn't present to field potentially damaging questions. Then again, Lerner considered himself an attorney, no matter that he hadn't practiced for most of his adult life. *A fool for a client* . . .

There was decided arrogance in deciding to hold such a press conference without having notified their son's attorneys, but Smith wasn't surprised. Arrogance, it seemed, was a natural outgrowth of power, especially for those who equated the popular vote with a mandate to practice self-importance beyond reason. Then again, was the arrogance there to begin with, a requisite for anyone seeking high office?

Such thoughts were gone as quickly as they'd formulated. He checked his watch. Annabel would be arriving at the luncheon for Clarise Emerson at the Lafayette. Would

Clarise show up? Would Vice President Dorothy Maloney? He'd find out soon enough. In the meantime, there were his classes to prepare for, including the next session of Lincoln the Lawyer, and within minutes he was immersed in analyzing cases in which the sixteenth president of the United States had been involved.

"I don't know how she does it."

Fifteen women had gathered in the Federal-Baroque–style brick town house on Sixteenth Street, NW, home from the 1950s to the 1980s to the Gaslight Club, a retreat for wealthy Washington men, now a combination residence, office building, and opulent small catering facility. The luncheon honoring Clarise took place in the downstairs banquet room, an attractive space with Queen Anne chairs, floor-length swag drapes, and an elaborately set table.

Clarise was the last to arrive, which broke with protocol. Under ordinary circumstances, Dorothy Maloney, vice president of the United States, would be afforded the privilege of making her entrance after the others were there, like the champion in a boxing match climbing into the ring only after the challenger has arrived. Not that it mattered to Maloney. A large, square woman who was often described as being "handsome" rather than pretty, she was known for not standing on ceremony, except, of course, when there was something official on the line. She had a laugh that was contagious, bubbling, and knowing, and a perpetual glint in her emerald-green eyes.

Until Clarise arrived, most talk had been of Clarise and the problems she faced with her son. The city now knew that Jeremiah had been formally charged with the murder of the young intern, and there was the expected potpourri of theories, alleged "inside" information, and rampant, reckless speculation. The misanthropic proposed that because of Jeremiah's father's role, charges would eventually be dropped and swept under a political rug. Others expressed hope, in hushed whispers to those deemed safe to confide in, that justice would be served and that warped young men like Jeremiah Lerner would be kept off the streets. Said one: "We have enough crime in this city without young punks like him running around killing young women."

"Clarise, darling, how wonderful to see you."

"I don't know how you do it, with everything that's happening."

"You look—wonderful, Clarise. Our next head of the NEA."

Annabel sat between Vice President Maloney and Clarise during the catered lunch. Lunch consisted of light food and conversation consisted of light banter, and there was much laughter as Dorothy Maloney told tales out of school, in this case the White House.

When not participating in the chatter, Annabel tried to zero in on what Clarise must be feeling at that moment. She certainly seemed to be in control of herself, put together, gregarious, and tuned in to what everyone was saying. Could she be capable of parking her problem with Jeremiah in some neutral area of her brain while focusing on the moment? Not easy for anyone to do, but Annabel knew a number of people who had that practice down to a science, and she admired them. It was a requisite of success, the ability to sever personal problems from professional demands, handling each on its own merits, and never the twain should meet.

The vice president toasted Clarise at the end of the luncheon: "Clarise and I have been close friends for many years," Maloney said, standing and raising her champagne flute. "She is, as we all know, a friend and staunch supporter of the arts in America, which, Lord knows, we need at this moment. There are those in positions of authority who view funding for the arts as money down the drain, money that could be put to better use—weapons, tax cuts for the rich, and other agendas that certainly cannot be labeled 'artistic.' Clarise has stood up against these other interests—and will continue to do so as our new head of the National Endowment for the Arts."

There was applause around the long table.

Maloney announced she had to leave, and was escorted from the room by an aide and Secret Service agents. When she was gone, Clarise stood and said, "I'm blessed with friends like all of you here in this room." She wiped away a tear. "Thank you so much for being here, and for being who you are."

As people filed from the room, Clarise took Annabel aside.

"Can I ask a huge favor of you, Annabel?"

"Of course."

"Bruce and I are giving a joint press conference this afternoon at five."

"Concerning Jeremiah?"

"Yes. Bruce has scheduled it. I'm heading to his house from here to prepare."

"Does Mac know?"

"I don't think so. Bruce doesn't want any of the attorneys to be there. He doesn't want it to appear to be a conference about Jeremiah's arraignment, or the trial, if there is one. He wants us to state our support for Jeremiah, that we're with him one hundred percent."

Annabel didn't say what she was thinking, that the self-serving nature of the press conference was transparent. Instead, she said, "How can I help?"

"Be there with me? Offer moral support?"

"Sure. I'm not sure it's wise having a conference without at least one of Jeremiah's attorneys present, but that's not my decision. How are things otherwise?"

"Dreadful. This business with Jeremiah is a nightmare. My hearing comes up later this week. *Festival at Ford's* is Thursday night. On top of all that, Sol Wexler thinks there's a problem brewing with Ford's finances."

"Oh?"

"That's between us, Annie. I'll try to get to the bottom of it when I find a spare minute."

"Your plate, as they say, is full," Annabel said, placing a comforting hand on her friend's arm. "Anything I can do before the press conference?"

"No. Just knowing you'll be there is enough. Thanks for everything."

"Mac, it's Annabel. I'm at the gallery."

"How was the luncheon?"

"Good. Dorothy looks great, and Clarise seems to be holding up nicely. Did you hear about the press conference?"

"Secondhand."

"I promised Clarise I'd be there."

"Why?"

"Moral support."

"It's a mistake."

"Me being there?"

"Having a press conference. Yale called a few minutes ago. It's taken him by surprise, too. Interesting development, though. LeCour—he's the U.S. Attorney prosecuting

Jeremiah—he called Yale to tell him they want to meet to discuss a plea bargain."

"Really? So soon? Sounds as though they're not very confident in their case."

"Exactly. They're running a lineup this afternoon."

"With the street person?"

"Yeah. It's at four-thirty. I'll be there."

"Well, I suppose we'll catch up later. Mac?"

"Yes?"

"Let's book a vacation."

"Now?"

"For when this is over."

"It's a deal," he said. "Where are we going?"

"Any place that doesn't have 'D.C.' after its name."

Mac laughed and said good-bye.

# TWENTY-NINE

John Partridge, the homeless man claiming to have seen the murder of Nadia Zarinski, had been picked up the night before from a church-sponsored shelter. He'd smuggled in a pint of cheap brandy to top off a day and night of heavy drinking; when the officers arrived, he stumbled to his feet from his cot and dropped the half-consumed bottle, sending it smashing to the concrete floor.

"Nice move, Mr. Partridge," one of the cops said. "Smooth."

"I didn't know he had a bottle with him," the shelter manager said.

"Yeah, yeah," said the cop. "Nobody knows nothing anymore."

Partridge was allowed to sleep off his

inebriation in a cell. He was fed a hot breakfast, sandwiches for lunch, and was urged
to clean up before the lineup took place. He
was sequestered in a small interrogation
room when Smith arrived.

"This is your eyewitness?" he asked
Hathaway as they observed Partridge
through the one-way mirrored glass.

"Hey, Counselor, you know you don't get
to pick your witnesses," Hathaway said. "If
you did, they'd all be choirboys and kindly
grandmothers."

Smith had reviewed Constitutional case
law regarding lineups before leaving his office at GW. It had been decided in numerous court rulings that a defendant's Fifth
Amendment right against self-incrimina-
tion—not to be "compelled in any criminal
case to be a witness against himself"—did
not apply to pretrial identification proce-
dures, including fingerprinting, photograph-
ing, measurements, speaking or writing for
identification, and lineups. A defendant's
rights under the Fifth Amendment applied
only, as one court put it, to protecting one
from being compelled to express the "contents of his mind." Smith knew he was pow-
erless to prevent the lineup; his presence

would serve to ensure it was done as fairly as possible, and to be an official observer who could refer to prejudicial practices when examining witnesses at trial.

He was pleased that the alleged eyewitness was a man like Partridge. It wouldn't be difficult to challenge his reliability in court. Hathaway, he was certain, was well aware of this. Why, then, was he going through the motions of a lineup so blatantly tainted? Obviously, to fail to use Partridge, who claimed to have seen something, would place the police and U.S. Attorney in an awkward position. Chances were, they wouldn't reference the lineup during trial, which posed another problem for them, the rock versus hard place argument very much present. Depend upon a drunken homeless man and you're laughed out of court. Fail to mention the lineup during the trial and have to answer why to a blistering cross-examination before judge and jury. Either way, the lineup would work in Jeremiah's favor.

"Who are the others in the lineup?" Smith asked.

"Cops," Hathaway responded, "dressed like your client, and two guys from administration."

"Fine," said Smith. "Let's get to it."

Hathaway, Smith, Partridge, and a stenographer stood in a darkened room. On the other side of one-way glass was a large chart on a white wall; red lines marked off heights in six-inch increments, behind seven spots where the lineup participants would stand.

"You ready, Mr. Partridge?" Hathaway asked. Partridge was dressed in a torn red-and-yellow flannel shirt, baggy chinos, and sandals. Despite not having had a drink for hours, his breath filled the small space with the odor of alcohol and bile, probably oozing out of his pores, Smith thought.

"Do I get the reward?" Partridge asked.

"We'll see," Hathaway said, looking at Smith with a please-try-to-understand expression. Smith understood perfectly. The steno had taken down Partridge's comment. If the homeless man testified, it would be easy to make the point with the jury that he was motivated by the promise of money.

"Ready, Counselor?" the detective asked Smith.

"Bring 'em in," Smith said.

Five men of approximately Jeremiah Lerner's height and weight filed into the lineup room before Jeremiah entered, leaving the seventh man to stand at his right. Hathaway hit a switch that flooded the room with harsh white light, causing everyone to shield their eyes with their hands.

"Okay," Hathaway said into a microphone, "hands down. Come on, get those hands down."

Smith focused on Lerner. He looked bewildered and frightened. He moved from foot to foot, his eyes scanning the room as though seeking an escape hatch.

"Take a look, Mr. Partridge," Hathaway said.

Partridge stepped closer to the window and squinted.

Smith approved of the men chosen by the police to join his client in the lineup. A witness would have to be especially astute and observant to pick Jeremiah from the seven.

"Well, Mr. Partridge?" Hathaway asked. "Recognize anyone in there who you saw behind Ford's Theatre when the girl was killed?"

"That's him!" Partridge said excitedly.

"Which one?"

"The one over there." He pointed to

the left side of the lineup, where Jeremiah stood.

"What number?" Hathaway asked.

"Six. That fella there, Number six."

He'd identified Jeremiah.

"Number six, step forward," Hathaway ordered through the speaker system.

Lerner took a single step.

"You sure?" Hathaway asked.

"Oh, yes, sir. Year of training taught me how to spot 'em. Never forget a face."

"What kind of training is that, Mr. Partridge?" Smith asked.

"CIA. Been all over the world."

"Okay, that's it," Hathaway said. He picked up a phone and said, "Come get Mr. Partridge. We're finished with the lineup."

Partridge was led from the room, the seven men in the lineup left, and the stenographer departed, leaving Smith and Hathaway.

"I know, I know, Counselor," the detective said. "But he was sober when he made the ID, and he sure didn't hesitate."

Smith smiled and picked up his briefcase. "I'm sure with his Central Intelligence Agency credentials, he'll make a fine wit-

ness for the prosecution. Good to see you
again, Hathaway."

Smith arrived home too late to catch the
Lerner press conference live, but watched
excerpts on the news.

*". . . Clarise and I, Jeremiah's par-
ents, are understandably concerned
and sad about what has happened to
our son. But he is innocent. The supposed evidence against him is extremely weak and misleading, and I'm
confident that once everything is
sorted out, he will be found to have
had nothing whatsoever to do with this
tragic murder, and we can get on with
our lives. I'm sure Clarise wishes to
add something."*

She delivered her set speech as it had
been handed her at the house before the
conference.

*"A dreadful mistake has been made,
which I have no doubt will be rectified
soon. Our son is a gentle, caring young
man; hurting another human being
simply isn't in his makeup. I ask that*

*you in the press give us the courtesy of*
*respecting our privacy during this try-*
*ing time, and not judge our son until all*
*the facts are known. Thank you."*

Questions flew from the assembled reporters, most of them about the alleged affair between the senator and Nadia Zarinski.

"I won't dignify those questions with an
answer," Lerner said sternly.

"Will you take a lie detector test, Senator?"

"About what?"

"About the murder of the young woman
from your office."

Lerner ignored him and turned to the next
questioner.

"Have you met with Nadia's parents?"

"Unfortunately, no. My schedule has
been especially busy, and they had to return
to their home in Florida. But I look forward
to meeting them in the near future."

"Ms. Emerson, do you think any of this
will jeopardize your chances to head the
NEA?"

"No. Now, if you'll excuse us."

Clarise and her former husband disappeared inside his home. Mac had seen

Annabel standing behind and to the left of Clarise, and was anxious to hear her perception of how it had gone. He didn't have to wait long. She called on her cell phone.

"How was the lineup?" she asked.

"Amusing. I just saw some of the press conference. As awkward as it looked?"

"Yes. I need soul food."

"Ribs and rice?"

"Spaghetti and meatballs."

"Café Milano in an hour."

# THIRTY

"That's a wrap."

Ford's Theatre's stage crew had spent much of the day preparing for Thursday's *Festival at Ford's* telecast. Tours of the theatre had been cancelled for that day and the rest of the week leading up to the show. Sydney Bancroft had arrived at one that afternoon and attempted to inject himself into the process, to the chagrin of others.

"Why doesn't he just go to a bar and get drunk, get out of our hair?" Johnny Wales muttered to a colleague as they completed erecting a flat. "He's not worth a damn around here."

"That flat should be moved a titch to the right," Bancroft said from where he stood at the edge of the orchestra pit. The musicians had run through musical scores and were packing their instruments.

Wales ignored Bancroft.

"To the right," Bancroft repeated, louder this time.

The director of the show, who'd been brought in from New York by ABC-TV, came to Bancroft's side and said, "It looks good the way it is, Sydney. I think it's fine."

Bancroft failed to disguise his anger. "I've spent my life in the theatre," he said, lip curled. "I know the way a stage should be dressed."

"Yeah, well, this is TV, Sydney. Time to undress. We're finished here for the day. See you tomorrow."

Bancroft watched him walk away and involuntarily clenched his fists at his sides. "Television, indeed," he mumbled. "Fools!"

Disdain for him and his suggestions were in abundant evidence that day. All his suggestions had been summarily dismissed, and the snide comments whispered behind his back weren't lost on him. Clarise had told him he was associate director of the festival, which should have carried with it at least a modicum of respect. The truth was, she'd thrown him another bone, and he'd had to lobby even for that. He was impotent; he might as well be invisible.

He'd stayed in bed until almost noon, although he'd awoken early and wasn't tired. He lay under the covers paralyzed by fear, afraid to step out of bed and face another day of frustration and defeat. It was insufferably hot in the apartment, yet he shivered, and cried once when thinking about his childhood in England during the war.

He was three years old when his mother sent him from London to a safer place, a farming community two hundred miles north of London, where he stayed with a distant relative for the duration of the war. Even there, the roar of German planes on their way to bomb Liverpool struck fear into the hearts of everyone in the community, and Sydney and his surrogate family routinely took shelter beneath a large oak kitchen table whenever the planes were heard.

His bedroom in London had had wallpaper with a frieze of lions and tigers resting in a jungle setting, and they would come alive in his dreams as a small boy living with strangers, coming down from the walls and clawing and ripping at him. He would wake up screaming, bringing Mrs. Watterson running into his small room beneath a stairwell and holding him until the nightmare had passed.

After the war, he was brought back to London to reunite with two sisters who'd also been provided safe passage to areas outside war-torn London. His father had been killed in one of the nightly raids, and his mother had died of natural causes, he was told, of an unspecified kidney disease. An uncle and aunt had completed the raising of the Bancroft children; he'd stayed with them until leaving to attend a theatre school in Manchester, and then to hit the road with a traveling Shakespearean troupe that appeared throughout the British Isles.

He thought of his childhood more often these days, never pleasant, happy thoughts.

"You have a call, Sydney," a theatre intern told him.

"Oh? London?"

"I don't know. It's a man who said he wants to speak with you."

Bancroft went to the phone dangling

from its cradle on a backstage wall. "Hello?"

"Mr. Bancroft, this is Detective Rick Klayman."

"Oh, yes, that nice young man who asks all those questions."

"Mr. Bancroft, I'd like to get together with you again."

"To do what, ask more questions? I can't imagine what there is left to ask. You've admirably solved dear, poor Nadia's murder, and I applaud you for that, you and your charming partner with the mellifluous voice. But I am very busy, as you can imagine. I'm directing the show to be televised Thursday on the ABC network. You're aware of it?"

"Ah, yes sir, I am. That's quite an assignment."

"Well within my capabilities, I assure you."

"I'll try not to take too much of your time," Klayman said.

Johnson sat across the desk from Klayman at headquarters, where he made the late-afternoon call to Ford's Theatre. Attempts to reach Bancroft at home had failed. Johnson's amused grin summed up his reaction to the call.

"I'm really not interested in the murder anymore," Klayman said, sounding sincere. "As you say, we've solved it. Actually, I'd enjoy chatting with someone like you about Abe Lincoln."

"Lincoln? You wish to discuss President Lincoln with me?"

"Yes, sir. I'm a bit of a Lincoln buff, and I know you're quite an expert on his assassination. You told us you'd made a study of John Wilkes Booth and his role in the assassination."

"Oh, yes, Detective, that is quite true, quite true, indeed. And I do recall you saying you had some minor interest in Lincoln. An unofficial visit is it, then?"

"Yes. Unofficial."

Johnson's thick salt-and-pepper eyebrows went up.

"Let me see. Yes, I shall find the time for you, Detective. Shall we say at six?"

"Okay. At your apartment?"

"No. I'm suffering—what is it you call it?—cabin fever? I've been working here at the theatre all day. The incompetence surrounding me is staggering. I intend to treat myself to a proper drink at the Star Saloon, and a spot of dinner. Will you join me?"

"I'd love to have dinner with you, Mr. Bancroft. Six it is, the Star Saloon."

"I'm appalled," Johnson said when Klayman hung up. "An officer of the law lying to a citizen."

"I wasn't lying. I'd enjoy having dinner with him."

"An 'unofficial' visit?"

"Exactly. It's my day off. I'm not on duty."

"Shameless!" Johnson said with exaggerated disgust. He laughed. "I'm going home," he said. "Told Etta I'd take her out to dinner. If you change your mind about Bancroft, come join us. We'll be at B. Smith's in Union Station."

"Bancroft says you have a mellifluous voice."

"Then give him my best, by all means."

Klayman arrived at the Star Saloon, across the street from the theatre, a few minutes before six, and took a seat at the bar. He would have ordered a Coke but decided at the last minute to have something alcoholic to indicate he was off-duty. A white wine was placed in front of him.

Bancroft arrived twenty minutes late.

"So sorry, dear chap, but I had to run home for something before coming here."

He wore the tan safari jacket usually reserved for when he traveled, jeans, and a
blue button-down shirt open at the neck.
Theatrical makeup had been heavily applied, giving his face the color of a gnarled
tree trunk. A well-worn leather satchel hung
from his shoulder, which he placed on an
empty stool next to the one he took at Klayman's side.

"The usual, Sydney?" the bartender
asked.

"Yes, yes, please."

The restaurant was sparsely populated.
The cancellation of tours at Ford's Theatre
because of preparations for Thursday's *Festival at Ford's* had been bad for business in
the area, the Star no exception.

Bancroft lifted his glass: "To my new
friend," he said. Klayman touched rims with
him. "I assume you know the historic meaning of where we sit, Detective."

"I think so," Klayman said. "And please,
it's Rick."

"Of course. And I am Sydney."

Bancroft took in the room with a sweep of
his head. "The infamous Star Saloon," he
said. "It was originally across the street, you
know, where the box office now stands.

Owned by a chap named Taltavul. After the president had been shot, it was suggested he be carried into Taltavul's saloon, but the barkeep said it wouldn't be fitting for the president of the United States to die in such surroundings."

Klayman nodded and took a tiny sip of wine.

Bancroft took a healthy swig of his drink and wiped his mouth with the back of his hand. He turned and looked Klayman in the eye. "Historians have it all wrong, Rick. They say John Wilkes Booth had a few drinks before shooting Lincoln in order to fortify himself, to fill him with needed confidence. The truth is, young man, he went into Taltavul's establishment to enjoy celebratory drinks for the heroic act he was about to engage in. Whiskey and water, unusual for him. He generally drank brandy."

"Heroic? Booth was demented."

Bancroft finished his drink and ordered another. "No, my new friend, he was not demented." He placed his hand on his chest. "Though this be madness, yet there is method in't."

Klayman looked quizzically at him.

"Hamlet. Do you know what he said at the bar that night?"

"I've read various accounts."

"A drunk said to Booth, 'You'll never be the actor your father was.' And Booth smiled"—Bancroft adopted what Klayman assumed was a facsimile of that smile— "and said, 'When I leave the stage, I will be the most famous man in America.' "

A second scotch in front of him, Bancroft continued to lecture Klayman on Booth and his actions leading up to the assassination. He had a few facts wrong, Klayman knew, but didn't bother to correct him. Bancroft claimed that a German named Atzerodt, one of two conspirators working with Booth, had been assigned to assassinate Secretary of State William Seward, but Klayman knew that Atzerodt's target was Vice President Andrew Johnson. Seward was to be killed by a brawny, violent man, Lewis Paine. Booth reserved Lincoln for himself. All three assassinations were to occur simultaneously, at 10:15 P.M.

"You haven't touched your wine," Bancroft said, taking a break from his sermon.

"I'm not much of a drinker," Klayman

said, "but I am hungry. Can I buy you dinner?"

"That's very generous of you," Bancroft said. "Yes, much obliged."

They took a table and placed their orders, a shrimp cocktail, onion soup, broiled bay scallops, salad, side orders of French fries and spinach, and custard pie for Bancroft, pasta and a salad for Klayman.

"Let me pick your brain a little about the Nadia Zarinski murder," Klayman said. "Why do you think she would go out with a lowlife like Jeremiah Lerner?"

Bancroft seemed pleased to be asked his opinion. He replied, "Who can ever determine why pretty young things take up with the men they do?" He slipped into his thespian mode. "Rebellious hell, If thou canst mutine in a matron's bones, to flaming youth let virtue be as wax and melt in her own fire."

"Shakespeare?"

"Hamlet again. Youthful lust. Nadia was a sensuous woman, Rick. I'm afraid it led to her unfortunate and premature demise."

"Do you feel—I mean, really feel in your bones, Sydney—that Jeremiah killed her?"

"No question about it, sir. You and your

colleagues should be immensely proud of your accomplishment in bringing him to justice. I salute you." He motioned for another scotch.

"Did Nadia seem to have money, Sydney? I mean, lots of available money?"

One of the actor's eyebrows arched impossibly high; Klayman was tempted to try it but knew he'd fail, and look foolish in the process.

"Money? Oh, yes, she always seemed to have money, Rick, flashing it around. I often wondered about it."

Klayman came to the conclusion during dinner that Bancroft pretended to know a lot more about Nadia than he actually did. He'd seen that same tendency in other people he'd interviewed about crimes. For whatever reason, perhaps to inject interest into otherwise mundane lives, they offered testimony far beyond their actual knowledge, necessitating caution on a detective's part in culling truth from fanciful thinking.

"What about other young men working at the theatre?" Klayman asked over Bancroft's dessert, and two coffees. "Any chance one of them had something against Nadia?"

"I thought you had your man, as they say."

"Oh, we do, but that doesn't mean we don't keep looking, if only to come up with witnesses to use at trial."

"She died in Baptist Alley, where Booth's horse was tethered," Bancroft said absently, as though not hearing what Klayman had said. He became animated, and leaned into the table. "Are you aware, my intelligent and curious young man, that Booth had accomplices at the theatre who aided him in his escape—his getaway, as you would say?"

"I've heard that," Klayman said.

"And John Wilkes Booth would have made a faster getaway had he not broken his leg leaping from the presidential box after putting a hole in Mr. Lincoln's head."

Klayman looked away and adjusted himself in his seat. Bancroft's description of the killing of Abraham Lincoln was almost joyful. He'd termed Booth's murderous act "heroic." It caused Klayman discomfort.

"Come," Bancroft said after Klayman had paid the bill. "We go to the theatre, where your lesson will continue."

"My lesson?" Rick asked, laughing.

"Yes. Your lesson in how one great man was slain at the hand of another."

As they crossed Tenth Street, Klayman asked how Bancroft's one-man show was shaping up.

"Splendid, Rick, splendid. I am on the verge of obtaining significant financial backing. Unfortunately, money rules, even in the arts. The learned pate ducks to the golden fool."

"Translation?"

"Even geniuses must toady to rich idiots. *Timon of Athens.* Of course, Shakespeare was a genius *and* rich. Pity I can't say the same—about being rich."

"Neither can I," Klayman said pleasantly as they entered the theatre, where a park ranger sat behind the tiny ticket window.

"Good evening, Mr. Bancroft," the ranger said.

"Good evening."

The ranger came from his position to ask Klayman for identification.

"A detective," Bancroft said with authority.

Klayman showed his badge.

"Working late?" the ranger asked, returning to his perch.

"A learning experience," Bancroft said, "for my young but learned friend."

The theatre was empty. A few work lights illuminated the stage, and wall sconces provided minimal lighting for the rest of the house.

Bancroft dropped his leather shoulder bag on a front-row seat and bounded up to the stage. Klayman watched with amusement as the aging actor walked left and right as though surveying his working surroundings. Rick sat in the front row. He was obviously about to be treated to a performance, perhaps a sneak preview of Bancroft's one-man play.

Bancroft went to the large electrical board and pulled levers, sending spotlights into action. "Let me set the scene," he announced. "It is Friday, April fourteenth, eighteen sixty-five, Good Friday. Lee has surrendered the South, and there is a celebratory atmosphere in the city. The theatre is full, one thousand, six hundred and seventy-five festive theatregoers sitting everywhere, clogging the aisles, sitting on the floor, and lining the walls. But they aren't all happy, Rick. Oh, no. Many had paid scalpers a bloody fortune for their tickets because it was rumored that the president and General Ulysses S. Grant, fresh from his victories in Virginia, and their spouses would attend that evening. Imagine, tickets that regularly cost seventy-five cents going for two-fifty. Scandalous!"

Klayman found himself settling into his seat and enjoying what he was seeing and hearing. Much of what Bancroft was relating was familiar to him from his reading, but even those elements came to life when presented by this tragic-comic actor whose best days were long gone.

"Lincoln loved the theatre, particularly opera, and had seen John Wilkes Booth perform in *The Marble Heart.* He was also a lover of Shakespeare, Rick, being especially fond of Macbeth. Lincoln was rather like Macbeth, wasn't he? A tragic figure in his own right.

"The play had started, a dreadfully pedestrian British work, *Our American Cousin,* starring Laura Keene, America's so-called leading lady. She was to receive a portion of the proceeds that night, not bad for a mediocre actress. The public's taste must never be trusted. Are you with me, Rick?"

"Yes, I am," Klayman responded from where he sat.

"Good."

Bancroft was becoming increasingly antic on stage, pacing its entirety as he replayed the night of the assassination.

"Booth, clever devil that he was, had no trouble prowling this theatre that day. He was known, and revered by everyone. That afternoon, he'd gone up to the presidential box and, using a penknife, cut a hole into which to wedge something against the outer door behind the presidential box to keep others from interrupting his plan."

Klayman knew that whenever Lincoln attended performances at Ford's Theatre, two small upper boxes to the audience's right were made larger by removing a partition between them. Each box had its own door, both of which opened into a tiny vestibule. Booth's plan was to gain entry to that vestibule, wedge the door shut, and wait for a particular line in the play that invariably generated loud laughter from the audience. A peephole just above the doorknob afforded him visual confirmation that the president was in his rocking chair, and allowed him to hear the action on the stage in anticipation of the famous line.

"The president and his party were late," Bancroft continued. "The play had been on for an hour when they arrived. Laura Keene saw the president moving through the Dress Circle up there." He pointed to the balcony jutting out over the rear of the theatre. "She motions to the orchestra leader—he stops what the orchestra has been doing and they launch into 'Hail to the Chief'—Lincoln, his wife, and Major Henry Reed Rathbone and his fiancée, Clara Harris, reach the box and take their seats." Bancroft now crouched onstage. "The time is getting close, Rick. President Lincoln takes his wife's hand, which she shakes off, concerned that it would be too—too public a display of affection. A hard woman, Mary Lincoln."

Bancroft was moving about the stage like a man possessed. He went to the door leading to Baptist Alley and opened it.

"Booth is here, Rick, when the play resumes. His steed waits outside to whisk him away. He asks a stagehand if he can cross behind the scenes to the side where the presidential box is, but is told he can't. He's not deterred. He opens a trapdoor leading down to a basement beneath the stage, goes down the steps, and feels his way along the dark underground passageway, the sounds on the stage above reverberating in his ears, reaches the other side, and comes up through a second trapdoor."

Bancroft ran across the stage to position himself beneath the presidential box. He motioned for Klayman to join him. The detective, transfixed by the bizarre performance unfolding onstage, got up and went to where Bancroft stood.

"Come with me," Bancroft said, leading Klayman down into the orchestra and up a staircase to the Dress Circle. "Booth moves easily through the throng. He's recognized; he's almost as famous as the president. A woman comments that John Wilkes is the handsomest man she's ever seen, which he was. So handsome, so dashing."

They went to a narrow hallway leading directly to the presidential box. A red velvet rope hanging from two stanchions barred their way.

"This is off-limits to the public," Klayman said.

"But we are not the public, Rick. You are an officer of the law with every right to be

here, and I am an important part of this theatre."

Bancroft moved the rope and led Klayman to the door leading to the vestibule. He
opened it and stepped back for Klayman to
enter.

"See, Rick, see how he carved the wood
to allow him to wedge the door shut behind
him with a piece of a wooden music stand
he carried upstairs with him?"

They stepped up to a Plexiglas partition
that had been installed in place of the door
to the box. The door itself was displayed in
the basement museum.

"Alas, we won't be able to enter the box,"
Bancroft said. "But imagine what Booth
was feeling as he approached, his forty-four
caliber, single-shot Derringer concealed beneath his clothing." He pulled an imaginary
weapon from his waistband and pointed his
index finger at Klayman. "Who's here to protect the president of the United States?" He
waited for a response. "Come now, Rick,
you certainly know that part of the story."

Klayman smiled and nodded. "He was
supposed to be guarded by a member of
the D.C. police force, a John Parker. Parker
was here outside the box that night, but dis-

appeared once the show started. The only person between Booth and Lincoln was the president's personal valet, Charles Forbes."

"Well done, Rick, well done. Booth comes here and hands Forbes his calling card. Forbes recognizes the famous John Wilkes Booth, of course. Booth says he has a message to deliver to the president, and Forbes ushers him into the vestibule. Once here, Booth wedges the outer door closed and views the president through the peephole. And he presses his ear against the hole and listens to the play being performed, waiting for that fateful line. Do you remember what it is, Rick?"

"Not precisely."

Bancroft straightened and intoned, " 'Do you know the manners of good society, huh? Well, I guess I know enough to turn you inside out, old gal—you sockdologizing old man-trap.' "

Bancroft's face lit up, his eyes widened. "Do you hear it, Rick, the uproarious laughter at that line? Perfect! Booth enters the box and—" He pressed his index finger against Klayman's head and said loudly, " 'Boom! You're dead, Mr. President.' "

Klayman stepped away from Bancroft. A

cold sweat had formed on Klayman's brow and upper lip, and his stomach churned. Bancroft was staring at him, a maniacal smile on his pinched face. He was sweating profusely, causing his makeup to streak.

"It was so simple, Rick," the actor said. "Were it not for that Plexiglas panel, I would leap from the box as Booth did, tangling my feet in the infernal bunting and breaking my leg on the stage in front of thousands witnessing the most memorable performance of my career."

They returned downstairs. Klayman stayed by the seat he'd been in when Bancroft's theatrical re-creation had begun. The actor wasn't finished. He went to the stage, faced the empty house, raised his hands, and shouted, "*Sic semper tyrannis!*"

*Thus always unto tyrants!*

Lincoln had been Julius Caesar, the tyrant, and Booth saw himself as Brutus, killing the tyrant.

"I have to be going," Klayman said when Bancroft came down from the stage.

"Yes, of course. Did you enjoy your little lesson?"

"I, ah—it was an interesting evening."

"Cheerio, Rick. You've been a very good

audience, indeed. And thank you for a lovely dinner. We must break bread again together soon."

As Klayman turned and started up the aisle, the park ranger quickly moved away from where he'd been eavesdropping on the action. By the time Klayman reached the lobby, the ranger was again seated in the ticket booth.

"Mr. Bancroft not leaving with you?" he asked.

"I guess not."

"Glad to see you nailed the guy who killed the girl, even if it is Ms. Emerson's kid. I feel sorry for her."

"Yeah, I do, too. Good night."

"Working late, Mr. Bancroft," the park ranger said when Bancroft came to the lobby a few minutes later.

"The festival is coming up in three days. Frankly, I'm not sure I should have accepted the offer to direct the bloody thing. Well, too late now. Cheerio."

The ranger shook his head and laughed when Bancroft was gone. He'd heard all the complaints about the aging, eccentric British actor from others at the theatre. He wasn't directing anything, just getting in the way. He picked up the magazine he'd been perusing before eavesdropping on the impromptu performance inside, and resumed reading. Another long, uneventful night ahead of him, and six years to the pension. Oh, well, other people had it worse.

# THIRTY-ONE

"How was dinner?"

"Great. You should have joined us. The Swamp Thing was first-rate."

"The what?"

"At B. Smith's. Shrimp and crawfish flavored with mustard, and collard greens. Funny name, but tastes good. How about you? Bancroft admit he killed her?"

"No, but it wouldn't matter if he did. He'd get off on an insanity plea. He's nuts."

"It took you this long to figure that out?"

"I didn't realize I was talking to the great American psychiatrist, Dr. Moses Johnson. When I say he's nuts—hardly a clinical term—I mean he's pathetic, a sad man. He turned me into his audience, re-created the

Lincoln assassination for me, called me his pupil, acted out a history lesson."

"The Swamp Thing is sounding better every minute. So you're satisfied he didn't do the deed."

"I wouldn't say that. How'd the lineup turn out? You talk to Hathaway?"

"Yeah. The old drunk nailed Jeremiah right out of the blocks. No hesitation. Herman says you're wasting your time chasing other suspects."

"I hate to disagree with our leader, but—"

"Hey, Ricky, you don't have to convince me. Save it for Herman. By the way, you should be happy. We're pulling duty at Ford's Theatre Thursday night for that TV show."

While security for the president and vice president and their families was the responsibility of the Secret Service, their efforts were routinely augmented by local law enforcement whenever they appeared outside the confines of their official residences and workplaces. Johnson and Klayman had been assigned to such duty on other occasions in the past, working closely with the Secret Service, the FBI, and other organizations.

"Know what still bothers me most?" Klayman asked.

"What?"

"Lerner's mother. She claimed she didn't know the victim was hanging around her theatre, but that's not what Bancroft says. Crowley, the controller, too."

"Forget it," Johnson said. "Like I said about the senator, Ms. Emerson doesn't strike me as the type to be beating some girl's brains out."

"Maybe she had somebody do it for her. Ever think of that?"

Johnson didn't say what was on his mind at the moment, that his young partner had fallen into the trap Johnson had seen with other young detectives: a belief that they could single-handedly solve every murder in town and save the world in the process. With a felony crime index in D.C. more than four times the national average, and 250 murders a year, to go with assaults, rapes, and other crimes against persons, you didn't have time to be a white knight. Nor was it your decision as a detective to determine guilt or innocence. You developed what leads and evidence you could, turned it over to the courts, and moved on to the next case.

Klayman didn't express his inner thoughts, either, to his veteran partner. He'd testified in a number of murder cases on which he'd worked, and had seen it first-hand—shrewd defense lawyers claiming a rush to judgment on the part of the police, zeroing in almost immediately on a suspect to the exclusion of others. Isn't that what had happened with Jeremiah Lerner? he reasoned. The questioning of Senator Lerner had never happened, nor had anyone followed up with Clarise Emerson, the boy's mother. Employees of Ford's Theatre had given their original statements, and that was that. Once they knew Jeremiah had dated Nadia despite his denials—and because of those denials—and his shoe print had been found in the alley, it was case-closed. Add to that the fact that Jeremiah Lerner was easy to hate. And now, a lineup ID by an alcoholic homeless man reinforced the belief that they had their man. It was all too quick and easy.

"See you in the morning?" Klayman asked.

"Sure. Hathaway's putting us on that

drug rubout that went down yesterday in Southeast."

Klayman didn't voice his displeasure at being assigned to another case. He was an MPD soldier, not a general. He took orders, didn't give them. But there would be other days off, and other nights to pursue the truth in Nadia Zarinski's murder.

"Glad you enjoyed the Swamp Thing, Mo. I had pasta. It was delicious."

"You're all meat and potatoes, Rick. Bye."

# THIRTY-TWO

Clarise was drained of energy and emotion as she walked through the door of her home, locked the door behind her, dropped her bag and shed her shoes in the foyer, and walked numbly into the living room. Monday was the housekeeper's night off. Although Clarise welcomed the solitude, the live-in maid's absence cast a cold, empty pall over the house as though no one had ever lived there, an empty shell without the smell or heat of another human being. She looked at the furniture, and the drapes, down at the carpet and up to a chandelier. What were those things? They silently surrounded her, mute, inanimate witnesses to the hollowness she felt.

She fell on a couch and stared up at the

ceiling. She'd dreaded the press conference but had managed to get through it. She resented her former husband's aristocratic, staunch stance at the microphone, in charge and cocksure, the practiced inflection of his voice honed by thousands of speeches over the course of his political career. She was aware of Annabel's presence but realized asking her to be there had wasted her friend's time. No distant moral support could have helped ease her fears and anxiety, nor her anger at having been placed in such an untenable position.

Once they were in the house, she'd suggested to her former husband that they visit Jeremiah in the jail, but he dismissed the notion as having come from a demented mind. "That's all we need," he'd said, "having our pictures splashed all over front pages going into a jailhouse. Stop and think, Clarise. Damn it, stop and think before you say or do anything."

Now, at home, she closed her eyes and was on the verge of unconsciousness when the phone rang. She hadn't bothered checking the answering machine, although she'd thought about it. There would be dozens of messages, most from the press, and from others with whom she had no interest in speaking.

Her eyes snapped open, and she absently reached for an extension near her head.

"Clarise. It's Sydney."

She couldn't stop the words: "Oh, my God, what do *you* want?"

"To see you."

"Sydney, I—"

"Don't put me off, Clarise. Do not do that."

Was he drunk? She'd never heard him use that tone of voice.

"What do you want, Sydney? Can't it wait?"

"No, Clarise, it cannot wait. Your confirmation hearing looms, does it not?"

"Wednesday."

"I'm certain you don't want to do anything to lessen your chances of confirmation."

"Are you threatening me?"

"I'm speaking common sense, Clarise, giving you good advice. Is anyone there at the house with you?"

"No. The maid is—"

"I will be there in twenty minutes."

He hung up hard.

A sense of panic consumed her. She wouldn't let him in. She turned off the lamp and stood in darkness, in the middle of the room. Lights from the street played on the drapes; muffled car horns could be heard—the nighttime sound of a freight train behind the family farm in Ohio came and went, as though she were a girl again lying in bed dreaming of being somewhere else.

A jolt of resolve replaced the panic. She turned on lights all over the house, frantically going from room to room, turning knobs and flipping switches, and listening for the doorbell to sound. When it did, she was in the foyer, a few feet from the door. She drew a series of deep breaths, unlocked the door, and opened it.

Bancroft entered without saying anything. He walked past her and went into the living room, where he went to the fireplace mantel on which photographs in oval frames were displayed along its length.

"What do you *want*, Sydney?" she asked from the doorway.

Bancroft picked up one of the photos: Jeremiah standing with his mother in a garden setting.

"How old was he in this picture, Clarise? Ten? Eleven?"

She said nothing. He replaced the picture on the mantel, turned, and said, "I need your help."

"You have a strange way of asking for it, Sydney, barging in here like this. I've had a very trying day, and wish to go to bed. Now, what is it you need that couldn't wait until tomorrow at the theatre?"

His smile was crooked as he sat in a red leather wing chair to the side of the hearth, crossed his legs, and motioned for her to take a matching chair on the opposite side of the fireplace. She hesitated, unsure of whether to leave the room or to take the chair. Her legs felt heavy, and her heart raced. Slowly, like an IV, the reality of why he might be there, and what he intended to say, dripped into her consciousness.

"Now, Clarise," he said calmly after she was seated, "it is time for us to rearrange our lives and put them in order. I assure you I have nothing but your best interests at heart in coming here tonight and explaining why you should be open and generous to what I am suggesting."

"Go on," she said, not wanting to hear more.

"I met in London with my former agent, who is absolutely dying to represent me and my one-man show. He's extremely excited, Clarise. He feels it will take the West End by storm. There'll be a world tour, of course."

"I—that's wonderful, Sydney." She relaxed somewhat. He was exaggerating, lying about his so-called show. What he was claiming was preposterous. Poor, demented Sydney. Was that his purpose for coming there, to spin his fanciful yarn about a one-man show that existed only in his imagination?

"I knew you would be thrilled for me," he said. "In a sense, I have you to thank for this good fortune."

"Oh?"

"I have no illusions, Clarise, about why you've kept me on at Ford's. On the one hand, it has been demeaning to be patronized, to be the object of scorn by those inferior to me. I shan't say it hasn't hurt, Clarise, hurt deeply."

She started to speak but he stopped her.

"On the other hand, 'he is well paid that is well satisfied.'" He observed her for a reaction. *"The Merchant of Venice,* Clarise.

Keeping me in pocket change must have given you immense satisfaction, my benefactor, my savior."

Another attempt to say something was interrupted.

"Or should we more properly term it hush money? A bribe to poor, old Sydney Bancroft, to keep his infernal mouth shut."

Clarise shifted in her chair. She had sensed he would eventually get to this, and deeply resented him for it. She said, "I suggest we drop this right now, Sydney. Right now!"

"Of course you do, dear, sweet Clarise. It makes you uncomfortable, doesn't it? Makes you squirm a bit, hey? Well, a bit of squirming might be in order right about now. Of course, we can avoid all this by coming to a sensible agreement."

"Get out!" she said, half rising from the chair.

His hand went up, then made circles in the air. "I suggest you relinquish your important, powerful woman stance for a moment, Clarise, and listen to me. Yes, you had damn well better listen to me."

The force of his words pushed her down.

"What do you want, Sydney? Money?"

"Yes."

"I have been giving you money for years. Your salary at Ford's, the extras, paying for trips—"

"Trips for me to charm some rich, fat bloke into giving money to you and your precious Ford's souvenir shop. How humiliating." He leaned forward. "Don't you realize how humiliated I've been all these years, or don't you care?"

"I've done what I felt was right," she said defensively. "I've done what I considered decent, considering the circumstances."

"Oh, come now, Clarise, claiming patron saint status doesn't become you. You define the word 'pragmatic,' and I respect you for that. The pragmatic, dynamic Clarise Emerson, formerly wife to a titan of government, and mother to a son named Jeremiah." He paused and cocked his head; his smile said he considered himself on the winning side of the confrontation. "Did he ever know, Clarise? I mean, did your senator-sweetie ever really acknowledge what we know to be the truth?"

A sense of divine resignation set in. They hadn't had this conversation for years. The last time was three years ago when she'd assumed the leadership of Ford's Theatre, and she hadn't heard from him for at least four years prior to that. He'd shown up unannounced at the theatre, gaudily dressed like a 1920s vaudevillian, a caricature of a British theatrical performer—comical, but not funny.

"Congratulations, Clarise, on your new post," he'd said that day, only a few weeks into her new job.

"This is quite a surprise," she said, not at all happy at seeing him.

"I flew here straightaway from London when I heard the news. My, my, I said to myself, my favorite lady is giving up the glamour of Hollywood for the staid, stodgy world of live theatre."

"I'm excited about it, Sydney. Ford's Theatre has a rich history, but not only because a president was killed here."

"I suspect I know a great deal more about that than you, Clarise. Yes, indeed. John Wilkes Booth has been a passion of mine for years. Don't you remember when we were in London together? I talked your ear off about him."

"Vaguely. Well, Sydney, it was good of

you to come all the way from London to congratulate me."

"And you now wish me to leave."

"I—"

"Clarise, I need a favor, a big one from you. Things have—how shall I say it?—things have slowed down for me in England. Professionally, that is. I fired my agent, Quill, that bloodsucker. Absolutely worthless, he was, out of touch with the theatre scene there, a bumbler of the first order. He'd make a better fishmonger than theatrical agent."

"I'm sorry to hear that, Sydney. Now, what's this favor you're asking of me?"

"You will admit that I've been admirably discreet all these years."

"Sydney, I—"

"*And,* I might add, have been noticeably absent from your life."

"Yes."

"Well, dear girl, as that famous line in *My American Cousin* went when Mr. Booth put a bullet into Honest Abe's head, 'Well, I guess I know enough to turn you inside out, old gal—you sockdologizing old mantrap.'"

She stared at him.

"I'd like to bring my considerable theatrical talents here to the good old U.S. of A., to this venerable theatre known as Ford's."

He didn't let her respond.

"You owe me, Clarise. I'm sure you agree with that. I shan't need much, just enough to find an agreeable flat, buy a new suit now and then, enjoy what culinary arts are practiced here in your nation's capital, and to be kept in good scotch whisky. I'm a modest man. I assure you that once those needs are met, I shall never again raise the little secret we both hold so dear."

Her anger was expressed in her mouth, drawn tight, a slash.

"Now, don't be angry, Clarise. Actually, I think you'll find me quite useful around here. Oh, and with your considerable political connections, arranging for the proper paperwork to allow me to stay here shouldn't be a problem. I'm staying with an old friend, Saul Jones. He lives over in Alexandria or Arlington or one of those bloody places across the river." He wrote out Jones's phone number and handed it to her. "Don't keep me waiting long with the good news, Clarise. I'm afraid my patience has worn thin with age, to say nothing of other things wearing thin, or out. Planned obsolescence by the man upstairs. Cheerio. It is wonderful seeing you after so long. And again, congratulations on your new post. Well deserved, my friend, well deserved."

Clarise stood and looked at the array of family photographs on the mantel. Fury was what she now felt. Had she a weapon in her hand, she would have gladly turned it on him.

She faced him; he cocked an eyebrow and smiled.

"What do you want?" she asked, working to keep her voice from quavering.

"A contribution to the arts, Clarise. Soon—very soon—you will have at your disposal a large sum of money, compliments of your taxpayers. You'll sit at the head of America's preeminent arts funding agency."

He stood and approached, reaching out a hand to touch her. She recoiled: "Get away from me," she said.

"I see you haven't lost your sense of the dramatic," he said. "I am not asking for anything illegal or unethical, Clarise. Your NEA is in the business of funding worthy artists.

I am a worthy artist. All you need do is fund my show, give me enough money to launch it in London. You might even justify it as an example of hands across the sea."

"And if I don't fund this one-man show of yours?"

"Oh, I don't think that's a possibility, Clarise. By the way, I must have your answer no later than tomorrow evening."

"Why?"

"Your hearing. Bad enough that your son has been accused of murder. If the distinguished men and women sitting in judgment of you were to learn that your equally esteemed husband, the senator from Virginia, isn't even the boy's father, that would really send them into a tizzy, wouldn't it?"

"And you think anyone would believe you?" she asked, now more in control of herself. "You've never been sure, nor have I. Bruce has never questioned it. Jeremiah looks like Bruce."

"I'd say he looks like you, Clarise. And will I be believed, you ask, in this day of DNA testing? Come, come."

He made another attempt to close the gap between them and to touch her. This time, she allowed his hand on her shoulder.

"This never should have come to this, this—this adversarial situation between us. I'm not asking you to rob a bank. The NEA's money will be put to good and proper use, to fund an important artistic undertaking: Sydney Bancroft, alone on the stage, regaling audiences with his insights into the great Willie B."

A second hand reached her, on the opposite shoulder.

"There's no need for rancor between us, Clarise. We loved each other once, at least for one night, and what a joyous night it was, glowing and warm from all the good wine we consumed, the silly giggling—remember the laughter?"

"Yes," she said. "I remember." She offered a petite smile.

"Of course you do."

He stepped back and rubbed his hands together.

"I would say that things are in jolly good order, wouldn't you?" he said.

She nodded.

"I promise you, Clarise, that I will put your NEA's money to very good use, very good use indeed. You shall be proud of me, Clarise; front-row center seats shall be yours at my London opening, and the bubbly shall flow afterward."

"That will be nice, Sydney. Now please, you must go."

"Of course, dear. You've been through so much, but you're strong, always have been."

Her kiss on his cheek was unexpected.

"Good night," she said.

She watched him leave the room, pausing in the doorway to throw her a kiss, and he was gone.

She went to a small bar in the family room, grabbed the nearest bottle, and poured some of its contents into a water glass. She drank half of it, coughed against its harshness, slammed the glass down causing some of the alcohol to spill over the rim, and picked up the phone.

"Annabel, it's Clarise."

"Hi."

"I need to see you and Mac."

"Of course. I have a relatively free day tomorrow and—"

"I need to see you now. I need—please. Can I come over?"

"Yes. We're both here."

"I'll be there as soon as I can."

# THIRTY-THREE

The breaking news graphic appeared on the screen at nine-fifteen the next morning, Tuesday. The CNN anchor explained.

*"CNN has learned that Clarise Emerson, whose confirmation hearing was scheduled for tomorrow, has withdrawn her name from consideration as the next head of the NEA. Emerson, the former wife of Virginia Senator Bruce Lerner, whose son, Jeremiah, has been charged with the murder of the senator's intern, Nadia Zarinski, released a prepared statement through White House chief of arts and humanities agencies, Joyce Drummond. In it, Ms. Emerson states that she's with-*

*drawn her name because of pressing personal commitments, and a desire to return to California to resume her career in television and movies, which she gave up three years ago to become producing director of Ford's Theatre.*

*"In a second White House statement, President Nash said, 'Claire Emerson would have made a superb leader of the NEA, and while I'm saddened at her decision, I certainly respect it, and wish her well in her future endeavors.'"*

While the announcement came as a surprise, it did not send shock waves throughout official Washington, at least not initially. Interest in the National Endowment for the Arts, and who would lead it, did not rank high on the political meter. Of course, those for whom the arts were a passion, or who toiled in its vineyards, took Clarise's decision seriously, but D.C.'s general public yawned. Eventually, by early afternoon, the talking heads began showing up to discuss not what her decision meant to the arts community, but whether it represented a refutation of President Nash and his administration, Washington being a place where nothing, not even the most mundane event, can escape potential political meaning and ramifications.

Mac and Annabel had discussed Clarise's decision with her for hours, and as they talked, her resolve seemed to harden by the minute. She told them repeatedly how burned out she felt, and how the situation with Jeremiah had drained every ounce of ambition from her. "When this is over, I want to take Jeremiah back to California with me," she said. "Lord knows I'll feel better there, and I think he will, too."

It was almost midnight when she placed a call from the Smiths' Watergate apartment to the home of Vice President Dorothy Maloney's chief of staff. That put into motion a series of other calls involving various White House staff, culminating with a call from the vice president herself.

"There's no way I can get you to change your mind?" Maloney asked.

"No, hon. It's got to be this way. Someday, when we're a couple of tottering dowagers looking back over our lives, I'll tell you everything behind my decision. But for now, let's just say I'm tired, beaten down, and in desperate need to leave this city. I thought Hollywood was bad, but it's a fairyland compared with Washington. My only regret is letting you and the president down. You'll just have to find a way to forgive me."

"Okay," the veep said. "I've spoken with the president. Naturally, he's disappointed, but he says he understands how personal pressures can override career decisions, and wishes you nothing but the best."

"That's good to hear," Clarise said, glancing at Mac and Annabel while wiping at a tear rolling down her cheek.

Clarise and the VP agreed that it would be Joyce Drummond who would release the news in the form of a written statement to the media. When the call from Maloney was ended, Clarise called her ex-husband, woke him up, and informed him of her decision. He didn't sound especially disappointed, although it was hard to distinguish between true feelings and grogginess. Their conversation was brief and unemotional.

Annabel asked Clarise, "You'll be leaving Ford's Theatre, too? No chance of deciding to stay on there?"

"I meant it when I said I wanted out of

Washington, Annie. The resignation I turned in to the board stays in effect. I'll remain until they come up with a successor, as long as that process doesn't drag on too long. I've got the *Festival at Ford's* on Thursday night, and the financial question to be settled."

"What financial question?" Mac asked.

"Irregularities the outside auditors have come up with. I'm not certain of the details, but Sol Wexler promised to fill me in once he has a better grasp of it. Exactly what I needed at the moment."

"What's your first step?" Mac asked.

"My first step?" Her laugh was rueful. "My first step is to go home, shower, and change. I feel like I've been in this outfit for weeks. Then head for the theatre and do my usual juggling act."

Clarise offered to call a cab, but Mac insisted on driving her. It was after three in the morning. When he returned, he and Annabel sat on the terrace. Sleep was out of the question.

"Did she say anything in the car about what put her over the edge?" Annabel asked. "I keep having the feeling that there's something beyond the ordeal with

Jeremiah that prompted her decision to back away."

"No, she didn't, and I agree with you. We'll probably never know."

"What about Jeremiah, Mac? Why is he still in jail?"

"I spoke with Yale earlier today. Lerner is obviously dragging his feet with the bail, but he assured Yale that he'd have it to the court tomorrow afternoon—which happens to be this afternoon. The prosecution convinced the judge to place a lot of restrictions on Jeremiah, including an electronic monitoring ankle bracelet, but Yale managed to kill that. Clarise asked whether I could arrange for him to stay with her until the trial, instead of with his father."

"Can you?"

"I'll submit a motion today. The last thing Senator Lerner wants is to have Jeremiah living with him again. I'm sure he won't balk at Clarise having custody. Let's grab a few hours' sleep."

A few hours were all the sleep they enjoyed. The rising sun two hours later saw to that.

# THIRTY-FOUR

Bernard Crowley had been up for hours at his apartment in Silver Spring. A call from Clarise at five-thirty had not only jarred him awake, it had sent him into a prolonged bout of anxiety.

"You woke me," he'd said.

"And I've been up all night. I received a call from Sol Wexler a few minutes ago."

"Oh? So early?"

"Bernard, we have to talk, and I mean now."

"On the phone?"

"No. At the theatre. What time were you planning to come in today?"

"The same time I always do. Nine."

"It will have to be later. Noon. In my office."

"Clarise, I—"

"Noon, Bernard," she said firmly, and hung up.

Crowley sat stunned, staring at the phone. She'd sounded so angry, so uncharacteristically harsh. He'd often marveled at her even temperament when under pressure, at least where he was concerned. He'd seen flashes of anger directed at others, but those incidents were infrequent and usually of short duration.

After showering and dressing in suit and tie, he went to the kitchen, where he sat at a small table, a small glass of orange juice in front of him, a small radio tuned to an all-news station.

He called the theatre at nine and told the person who answered that he wouldn't be in until noon: "No, I'm not ill, just personal things to catch up on."

Which wasn't exactly true. His stomach churned, and acid rose to his throat. He thought he might vomit, but the waves of nausea came and went. He made himself a cup of tea and a slice of dry toast, hoping that would calm his stomach, and it seemed to help.

Until . . . the voice from the radio's tiny

speaker announced that Clarise Emerson had withdrawn her name from consideration to head the NEA, intended to honor her resignation as producing director of Ford's Theatre, and return to California.

Crowley was stunned. The newscaster's voice, now intoning another story, hung in the kitchen like smoke from a burning pan. He wanted to turn a dial on the radio to hear it again, to confirm it had ever been said.

*Why hadn't she told* me? Was that why she had demanded a noon meeting? No, of course not. He knew why, and it had nothing to do with her leaving. The larger question was how her announcement would impact her reason for demanding—yes, she'd demanded it, hadn't suggested it—that he meet with her.

As he watched the minutes pass on a wall clock, he fought to keep his emotions in check. Sol Wexler kept coming to mind. Crowley had been convinced from his first day on the job that Wexler had disliked him, and was working to undermine his authority. He was certain the accountant had counseled Clarise to not hire him. "That bastard!" he exclaimed to the empty room.

He turned on the TV and again heard the

news about Clarise and the NEA, although
the stories were now considerably shorter
than when first announced, and were buried
deeper in the newscasts. He ignored his
ringing phone, left the apartment, went into
the basement parking lot, got in his 1996
Honda Accord, and went up the ramp. It
was ten-thirty, an hour and a half before the
meeting. He drove aimlessly, eventually
parking in the almost empty lot of a seafood
restaurant on Water Street in the city's
southwest quadrant. If there was ever a
time for clear thinking, it was now.

Bernard Crowley wasn't the only person in
Washington who'd been deeply affected by
the news about Clarise.

Sydney Bancroft became absolutely fran-
tic.

He'd started the morning in an ebullient
mood.

After leaving Clarise's home and receiving what he perceived to be her agreement
to fund him through the NEA, he'd considered calling his former London agent,
Harrison Quill. But it was the middle of the
night in England. He waited until three that
morning—eight A.M. in London—and called

Quill's home number. The agent's wife answered.

"Sydney Bancroft here," he happily announced, "with good news, very good news indeed, for your hubby. Put him on."

"He's sleeping."

"Wake him up, woman. I am about to make him the most important agent in London—again."

It seemed an eternity before a sleepy Quill came on the line.

"What do you want, Sydney?"

"I have the money, Harrison, old boy. I have the money for my show."

There was silence.

"Did you hear me, Quill? I said I have the backing for my show."

Quill responded with a fit of cigarette-induced morning coughing. When it had subsided, he said hoarsely, "That's wonderful, Sydney. Congratulations."

"That's what I wanted to hear, Harry. It will take a few weeks for the funds to flow. When they do, I'll be in London and we can begin lining up a theatre, production team, the works."

"Sydney, I'm out of the bloody agenting

business. I'm closing up shop. You'll have
to—"

"Fine," Bancroft said. "Just as well. I'll
need someone fresh and with more energy,
a young Turk with vision. No hard feelings,
Quill. But remember, I gave you first shot."

Quill's announcement didn't diminish
Bancroft's sense of jubilation. He'd meant
what he'd said, that his former agent was
over the hill, a dinosaur from another era. It
was time for new blood to be infused into
Sydney Bancroft's return to the stage and
stardom.

His elation lasted until nine-fifteen, when
he heard the news on TV about Clarise. At
first, he sat slack-jawed, unable to process
what he'd heard. *Not heading the NEA?* But
she'd told him she'd give him the money
once she was ensconced as head of the
arts agency. *She'd bloody well promised!*
He screamed at the TV, his words decidedly
not Shakespearean. He shook his fist at the
tube, and at one point fell to his knees and
cursed not only Clarise but the whole human race as well.

His first attempt to call Clarise resulted in
a misdial; his hand shook as he sought the
numbers on the keypad. He drew deep

breaths to calm himself and correctly dialed her number. Her voice on the answering machine spoke to him: "Leave a message if you wish."

He slammed down the receiver and paced the living room before calling Ford's Theatre: "Clarise isn't here, Sydney," he was told.

"When is she coming in?"

"I really don't know. She has a noon appointment with Bernard."

"Does she? I must speak with her."

"About the news?"

"Yes. Is she serious?"

"I think so. Yes, of course she's serious."

"She mustn't do this."

"I don't think we have anything to say about it."

"Well, I do. Oh, yes, I certainly do have something to say about it. When you see her, tell her I shall be there within the hour, and I must speak with her."

"All right, Sydney. I'll tell her."

He spent the next half hour rehearsing what he would say to her, the words he would use to persuade her to change her mind, the emotions he would evoke, the reasoning he would employ to reach her

senses. But while he engaged in this exercise, the futility of it was apparent, and his
mood and tone gradually evolved into
anger, then rage at her. The truth was, he
told himself, she'd lied to him, knowing
she'd never intended to go through the confirmation process and provide him the funds
needed to launch his comeback. She'd
played him for a fool, as she'd been doing
all along. The question of whether Jeremiah
was his son, or Senator Bruce Lerner's boy,
was now moot. She'd stripped him of whatever potency he might possess, and had
probably laughed loudly the minute he'd left
her house.

He poured himself a large water glass of
scotch and downed it, and then drank
another as he walked into his bedroom,
opened the closet door, and frenetically
shoved clothing in his closet back and forth
on the rod, pulling out an occasional piece
and disgustedly throwing it to the floor. He
settled on a pale green linen jump-suit, and
white loafers, stripped off his pajamas, and
dressed. He brushed his teeth, popped a
breath mint into his mouth, and grabbed his
leather shoulder bag from where he'd
dropped it near the bed the night before. He

ran his hand through the bag's contents, talking to himself, not making any sense, speaking nonsense, lines he intended to use to convince Clarise to change her mind, coupled with obscenities, curses at a God he didn't believe in, snippets of Shakespearean dialogue, mumbles and grunts, the ranting of a man consumed by frustrated fury.

He returned to the closet, got down on his knees, and pulled shoes and shoeboxes from its floor. He finally reached what he was seeking: a cigar box wrapped in a discarded shirt. He removed the shirt and opened the box. In it was a Colt .32 caliber revolver. He stood, stared at the weapon for a moment, held it at arm's length, placed it in the shoulder bag, and hurried from the apartment.

"A beautiful day, Sydney," Morris, the doorman said as Bancroft crossed the lobby.

"What? Yes, lovely day. I need a taxi."

Bancroft was dropped in front of Ford's Theatre. He handed the driver a twenty-dollar bill, far more than the fare, but didn't ask for change. He stood on the sidewalk and looked up and down the nearly deserted street. The cancellation of tours at the theatre had sent tourists elsewhere in search of history and culture.

"Hello, Mr. Bancroft," said the park ranger on lobby duty.

"Hello, hello. Splendid day out there."

"So they say but you can't prove it by me, cooped up here inside."

Bancroft didn't continue the pleasantries. He entered the theatre, where the stage crew and TV technicians were hard at work preparing for the telecast of *Festival at Ford's* the next night. They ignored Sydney, which was fine with him. He went backstage and into a small room used for props. He paused inside. Confident no one was about to join him, he closed the door and stood before floor-to-ceiling metal shelving holding labeled boxes: WIGS, GLOVES, JEWELRY, SHOES, BOOKS, GLASSWARE, DRIED FLOWERS, KNIVES, TABLECLOTHS, PHOTOS WITH FRAMES—and FIREARMS. He took the firearms box down from where it sat on a top shelf, opened it, again checked that no one was about to come through the door, removed the Colt .32 from his shoulder bag, and placed the revolver in with the replicas of pistols and other handguns, nestling it beneath them at the box's bottom. He returned it to the shelf, stood on his toes, and delivered to the otherwise empty room one of Brutus's lines from *Julius Caesar* in a deliberate, harsh whisper, " 'Between the acting of a dreadful thing and the first motion, all the interim is like a phantasma or a hideous dream.' "

Waiting would be the hardest part.

# THIRTY-FIVE

Annabel realized she hadn't been paying enough attention lately to the gallery, and decided to spend Wednesday in Georgetown catching up on paperwork and other administrative chores. Despite having had only a few hours' sleep, she and Mac felt surprisingly awake and alert that morning. They breakfasted on the terrace, with Rufus at their feet.

"What's on your plate today besides eggs over easy?" she asked.

"Deliver the motion for Clarise to take custody of Jeremiah after his bail is paid, and meet with Yale. We need to sit down with Jeremiah and start from page one. I want to know why his shoe print was found in that alley. Yale is contacting a forensic expert in St. Louis who specializes in shoe prints. The science isn't all that scientific; we may need testimony to that effect at trial."

"I can see a battle of the experts looming large in your future," she said lightly.

"Guaranteed to confuse even the best of juries. Experts usually cancel one another out, and the jury ends up using what common sense it brings into the deliberations. I also want to set up a meeting with LeCour, the U.S. Attorney."

"To discuss a plea possibility?"

"To hear what he has to say. You can always tell how strong a case the other side has by how lenient they're willing to be in pleading out a case."

"You've gotten dozens of defendants off who had much tougher cases against them."

"I wish you wouldn't put it that way. I prefer thinking that justice prevailed despite strong cases on the other side." He smiled and looked at his watch. "I'd better walk Rufus and be on my way. I envy you a quiet day with your friends."

"My friends?"

"Tlatilco and Teotihuacán and—"

She laughed and placed her hand on his. "The humor is in the mispronunciation," she said playfully. "But you are right. I will enjoy spending the day with my pre-Columbian friends. I do intend to try to catch up with Clarise. The fallout from the announcement has got to make for an overfull day for her."

"Her decision pleases me," he said, standing and carrying his dishes into the kitchen, with Annabel close behind. "I think it might be good for Jeremiah—provided, of course, he doesn't end up behind bars, and provided, of course, she means what she says about taking him with her back to California. It could be the first time she actually becomes a mother to him."

Mac stopped at the H. Carl Moultrie D.C. courthouse and handed his motion to Judge Walter Jordan's law clerk before heading for the downtown law offices of Yale Becker, on K Street.

"Where do we stand with bail?" Smith asked after Becker's secretary had served them coffee.

"Senator Lerner had the funds wired to the court overnight. I'm picking up Jeremiah."

"*You*? Not the senator?"

"He's on some junket." Becker didn't attempt to disguise his scorn. "You delivered the motion about the mother taking custody?"

"Yeah. The judge has it. Just have to wait for a decision."

Smith tasted his coffee. It wasn't as good as what he made at home—he was an inveterate coffee snob—but it would do. He asked, "Have you worked out your fee schedule with the senator?"

"*Our* fee schedule, Mac. No, but it's on my list."

They spent the next twenty minutes going over details of the case and determining what pretrial motions to develop. In papers filed with the court, LeCour indicated he wanted to introduce prior acts of violent behavior by the defendant, which Smith and Becker would challenge on the basis of its prejudicial impact outweighing any probative value. Asking for a change of venue based upon the intense media coverage was being debated when Becker's secretary interrupted: "Judge Jordan's clerk for you," she said. Becker took the call.

"The judge has granted your motion, Mac, to allow Jeremiah to reside with his mother," Becker said after hanging up. "But there's a caveat. Senator Lerner has to sign off on it."

Smith shook his head. "The judge doesn't want to cross a U.S. senator, huh? Not that it makes much difference. Lerner doesn't want the kid living with him. The problem is getting hold of him. Where's the junket?"

"Mexico City."

"Can he be reached?"

Becker instructed his secretary to attempt to make contact with Lerner through his Senate office. He said to Mac, "Jeremiah will just have to cool his heels in jail until this gets straightened out."

"I don't want to wait until it is to sit down with Jeremiah and see if we can get a straight story from him."

"I agree," said Becker.

A call to the jail resulted in an appointment to meet with their client at two that afternoon.

"Changing the subject," Becker said, "what's the inside scoop on his mother dropping out of contention to head the NEA? You know that was coming?"

"Yes. Annabel and I were with her last

night until the wee hours this morning." He briefly recounted part of the discussion that had taken place with Clarise at the Watergate apartment.

When Mac was finished, Becker said, "She didn't seem like the type to cut and run."

"We've all got our breaking points, Yale," Smith offered. "We both know people who are rock-solid on the surface but turn to jelly when the spotlight is off. There's something else involved here that prompted her to drop out, but I don't know what it is. I do know that her decision makes me more determined than ever to ride this thing through to an acquittal for Jeremiah. As I told Annie, she might one day actually have a shot at enjoying a real mother."

"That's nice to contemplate."

Before leaving, the two attorneys agreed that Smith would visit Jeremiah alone. He left the office and went to the university where he worked on his next Lincoln-the-Lawyer lecture until time to head for the jail.

Detectives Klayman and Johnson were busy, too, that Wednesday. They met for most of the morning with U.S. Attorney

LeCour, going over evidence against Jeremiah Lerner to be used in his trial. They reviewed written reports of interviews conducted with American University students, particularly Joe Cole, and Klayman's conversation with Sydney Bancroft in which the actor claimed he was aware that Nadia Zarinski had been dating Jeremiah, and had counseled her against it.

"What kind of witness will Bancroft make?" LeCour asked.

Johnson replied with a snicker, "Oh, he'll be terrific. He'll spout Shakespeare and put on a great show. Of course, he's liable to show up wearing a leopardskin leotard or dragon costume."

"What is he, nuts?" LeCour asked.

"No, he's not nuts," Klayman said, "but he is strange. The problem you'll have is getting him to simply answer your questions. He's always on. Kind of pathetic, you know?"

"Has Lerner ever said how his shoe print ended up behind the theatre?" LeCour asked.

"Not to us," Johnson replied.

"What about the jewelry found in her

apartment?" LeCour asked. "Any link to Lerner?"

The detectives shook their heads.

"We're running down the serial number on the Rolex," LeCour said. "We should come up with where it was purchased. Hopefully, they'll have a record of who bought it."

It was toward the end of their meeting that Johnson said, "Rick here doesn't think Lerner did it."

His comment brought a worried expression to LeCour. "What's this all about?" he asked the young detective.

"It's not that I don't think he did it," Klayman responded, "but it just seems to me that we haven't taken a hard enough look at other possible suspects."

"Such as?"

Klayman wasn't sure whether he should walk through that door opened by LeCour. It wasn't his responsibility to make such judgments. But now that it was opened, he didn't have much choice.

"Lots of people," he said. "Anybody working at the theatre. Her landlord, the husband. Senator Lerner."

"Oooh, let's not go there," LeCour said.

"Why not?" Johnson asked; Klayman was pleased to see his partner step into the conversation. "He was rumored to have been having an affair with her. He wouldn't be the first high-and-mighty politician under the gun from some young mistress."

"Blackmail," LeCour said absently.

"Exactly," Klayman said. "And what about Jeremiah's mother? She lied when she said she didn't know Nadia was hanging around the theatre."

"Says who?"

"Says Bancroft, the old actor, and Bernard—what's his name?—Crowley, the theatre's controller. It's in our report. There are those stagehands, some of them young, her age. And there's the similar M.O. in the Connie Marshall killing, and the jewelry she was wearing."

"What same M.O.?" LeCour scoffed. "Marshall was dumped in the river. Zarinski was left in an alley. No similarity whatsoever."

"Look," said Klayman, "I don't know that somebody else killed her, but if I were you—"

"Yes?" LeCour said.

"If I were you, I'd be prepared for the defense lawyers, Smith and Becker, to make a big deal out of the rush to judgment."

"You should enroll in law school, detective," LeCour said. "And I think you watched too much of the O. J. trial." He stood to indicate the meeting was over.

Klayman was tempted to say he hadn't watched any of that infamous murder trial, but didn't bother. Good soldiers, good cops, didn't argue with superiors. He'd said his piece, and it was time to go. The afternoon would be spent again trying to find witnesses to the drug shooting that had occurred in Southeast, no easy task. Anyone who was in a position to have seen the killing go down was adopting the all too familiar see-and-hear-no-evil posture. You couldn't blame them. Word got around fast when someone from the neighborhood snitched on a friendly drug dealer. Still, sometimes you got lucky. You had to try.

Smith sat with Jeremiah Lerner in a room reserved for attorney-client conferences. The young man was subdued, although not without an occasional demonstration of testiness. He asked almost immediately why he was still in jail. "I was bailed out, man."

"That's right," Smith said, determined to not allow his client's volatility to deter his own professional demeanor. "But I've applied to the court on your mother's behalf to have her take responsibility for you while you're out on bail. The judge wants your father to sign off on that. We're trying to reach him. He's on a trip to Mexico City."

"He won't care," Jeremiah said glumly.

Mac didn't offer his agreement. Instead, he said, "You'll be out of here as soon as that hurdle has been cleared. Now, let's get down to business. There are things I must know from you in order to mount a proper defense. Let's start with why you lied about knowing the victim."

Jeremiah repeated that he was afraid such an admission would lead the police to suspect him. Smith made notes as Jeremiah talked, not offering his own comments about how that lie had dug a deeper hole for him. After a series of other questions, he got to the shoe issue.

"The imprint of your shoe was found in the alley, Jeremiah. There's a possibility that we can defuse that through expert testimony. But my question to you is, why was it found there in the first place? Remember, what we say to each other here today is protected by attorney-client privilege. It doesn't ever go beyond us."

"I was there, man."

Jeremiah's blunt statement caught Smith by surprise. He removed his half-glasses and sat back. "You *were* in the alley that night?"

Jeremiah nodded.

"With Nadia?"

"Yeah." He leaned into the table. "But I didn't kill her, man. I swear it."

"Why were you there?"

"I came to see her. I knew she was at the theatre that night and figured we could go out, get something to eat, you know, then—"

"Don't assume I know anything, Jeremiah. What did you intend to do, get something to eat and go somewhere to make love?"

"Right. Correct."

"So, what happened then?"

"So, she gave me a hard time. Man, she could be a bitch sometimes. She said she'd go with me if I had any loot."

"She wanted money?"

"Right. I got really pissed off. I hit her once, nothing hard, like a slap."

"What happened then?"

"She yelled at me and went into the theatre."

"What did you do?"

"I split."

"Where did you go?"

"Some bar. I don't remember."

"So you weren't at your apartment as you said previously."

"What difference does it make?"

"It can make all the difference in the world in a murder trial, Jeremiah. Was anyone else in the alley when your confrontation with Nadia took place? Anyone else see it?"

"No."

"What about the man who identified you in the lineup?"

"Him" He guffawed. "Maybe he was the old geezer sleeping it off back there."

"Then there *was* someone else."

"Yeah, the old drunk. He was out like a light."

"Maybe he wasn't out as much as you think. Is that the last time you saw Nadia?"

"That's right. And she was alive, man. I swear it on a Bible."

The meeting lasted an hour. When he left, Smith got into his car and dialed Annabel's gallery.

"Mac, I'm so glad you called. I've got to talk to you."

"Sure. I can swing by now. I just finished up with Jeremiah."

She lowered her voice to barely above a whisper. "Clarise is here, Mac. She's in the back office using the other line. What she's told me is—well, it's upsetting, *and* important."

"How long is she staying?"

"She said she'll be leaving in a few minutes. She came here to get away from the theatre. Look, I'll leave as soon as I can after she's gone. I'll meet you at home."

"All right. Annie, are you okay?"

"I think so. Have to run. See you soon."

# THIRTY-SIX

The media devoted considerable space and airtime Thursday morning to Clarise's decision to not seek leadership of the NEA. It wasn't front-page news; the articles were treated more as feature stories, with boilerplate descriptions of her career, beginning with college and tracing it through her Hollywood years and eventual position as producing director of Ford's Theatre. The *Post* ran a wedding photograph of Clarise and a young Bruce Lerner, and a picture of Jeremiah, "the now divorced couple's young son currently being held on charges of murder." President Nash's comment about personal needs trumping career decisions was duly reported, and Vice President Dorothy Maloney, billed as a friend of long-standing, said the NEA had lost a superb future leader but wished Clarise all good wishes for whatever she chose to do in the future. "Ms. Emerson declined to respond to repeated requests for a comment for this article," the writers wrote, although there were plenty of others more than willing to weigh in on why they thought she'd made her decision, regardless of whether they knew anything about it or not.

Klayman and Johnson had worked late Wednesday night, scouring the neighborhood in Southeast for witnesses to the drug murder, and writing their report at headquarters. "It's almost ten," Johnson said as they prepared to leave. "Come on back to the house for a nightcap and something to eat."

"No, thanks, I—"

"You've got to eat, man. Don't argue with me."

Etta whipped up leftovers, and Mo poured beers. Klayman was glad he'd agreed to come. He found himself relaxing more than he'd been able to in recent days, and by the time he left—almost midnight— he was enjoying a drowsy reverie; he wouldn't have trouble sleeping that night, and looked forward to a leisurely morning. Because they'd been assigned to duty at Ford's Theatre Thursday night, they weren't required to sign in until noon.

Wednesday was another late night for Mac and Annabel Smith. He'd met her at the apartment late in the afternoon and they talked for hours, interrupting their confab twice, once for Mac to fill in Yale Becker about the subject of their discussion, and to learn that his colleague had personally delivered Jeremiah to his mother's house after Senator Lerner's verbal assurances to the court that he approved of Jeremiah being with Clarise. The second intermission was to order in dinner from the Watergate Hotel's Aquarelle restaurant.

Later in the morning, Mac went to GW to teach a class while Annabel met with a wealthy Japanese collector of pre-Columbian art at the gallery who'd flown to Washington specifically to examine items she had for sale.

In the afternoon, Mac worked out at his health club, and Annabel attended a tea honoring the retirement of a friend from the Library of Congress. They met back at the apartment at five, took a nap, showered, dressed in formal wear befitting the occasion, and headed across town to attend *Festival at Ford's.*

Security at the theatre was rigorous. After submitting their invitations to members of the Secret Service, Annabel's purse was sent through an X-ray machine and searched by hand after it had emerged. Mac set off bells when passing through the portable metal detector that had been positioned in the lobby. The culprit had too many keys. Uniformed members of the Washington MPD, especially and hurriedly trained in security following the attacks on the World Trade Center and the Pentagon, waved wands over the couple, apologizing as they did for any inconvenience they might be causing.

As they were about to be ushered into the theatre by park rangers with special clearances, Rick Klayman, who'd come to the lobby to deliver a message to an officer, stopped them and said hello.

"Hello, Detective Klayman," Mac said. "This is my wife, Annabel Reed-Smith."

"Nice meeting you," Klayman said. "All set to enjoy the show?"

"If we ever get inside," Mac said.

"I didn't mean to hold you up."

"I wasn't referring to you," Mac said. "Rule number one in Washington, D.C.— never attend an event when the president will be there, too."

"He's not coming," Klayman said.

"Really? Why? I thought this was a yearly command performance."

"It usually is, I guess, but there's some last-minute crisis." Klayman shrugged. "The vice president will be here, though."

"Well, that's one less person for you to protect. See you in my class Saturday?"

"Wouldn't miss it, sir. Oh, would it be possible for my partner, Moses Johnson, to attend with me? Just this once? I was telling him last night about the class and he said he'd enjoy it."

"Sure. Happy to have him."

They were shown their seats on the aisle, stage-right, halfway back from the orchestra pit and stage. As the house filled they were greeted by a number of people. When they found a moment of privacy, Mac asked in Annabel's ear, "Will Clarise be welcoming the audience?"

"She's supposed to," she replied, "although judging from her state yesterday, I wouldn't be surprised if she begged off."

Mac glanced up at the empty box in which Abraham Lincoln had sat the night he was murdered by John Wilkes Booth. You couldn't be in Ford's Theatre without experiencing some feeling, some thoughts of that tragic night more than 130 years ago when America suffered its first presidential assassination.

The presidential box, of course, was empty, and had been since the assassination out of respect for the slain president—and because, in reality, it was a poor location from which to watch what was occurring on the stage. It had been faithfully re-created, replete with white lacy curtains framing two openings through which the box's occupants could see two American flags draped over the balustrade, a large engraving of George Washington—there was no presidential seal at the time, and the more famous first president's likeness was displayed rather than Lincoln's, the sitting president—and a reproduction of the red rocking chair in which Lincoln had sat that fateful night; the original was on display in the Henry Ford Museum, in Dearborn, Michigan.

The building had suffered another day of infamy almost three decades after the assassination when the government gutted the theatre and turned it into an office building, three floors of which collapsed in 1893, killing twenty-two people. It wasn't until 1965 that the property was again restored to a working theatre.

Petersen House, the boardinghouse across the street in which the president died at 7:22 the morning after he'd been shot, was also maintained as a National Historic Site by the National Park Service, another monument to the tragedy that had befallen the nation's leader, and the nation itself—so much sad history to digest surrounding a man who, it was said, had been chosen by God to do unequaled work, "not only for America, but for all mankind."

"It's about to start," Annabel said.

They directed their attention to the stage where final preparations were underway for the live telecast that would begin in a half hour. The vice president arrived and was escorted to her front-row seat by a knot of Secret Service. She turned to the crowd and waved, generating a round of applause. A few minutes later, with every seat occupied, Clarise walked from the wings to center stage and was handed a microphone.

"You have to give it to her," Annabel whispered to her husband.

"The show must go on."

Clarise flashed a wide smile and said, "Welcome, welcome, to all of you." She looked at Dorothy Maloney. "And especially to you, Madam Vice President, my friend." She took in the wider audience. "The show will begin in just a few minutes. Your presence here is heartwarming. This theatre is important, and your support of it testifies to that. President and Mrs. Nash send their regrets, and I know that whatever occupies them this evening must have been very important to miss this gala evening at Ford's Theatre. So please, sit back, relax, and enjoy."

"There's Sydney Bancroft," Annabel said quietly to Mac. The actor had crossed backstage and disappeared into the wings.

"Hmmm," was Mac's response, his jaw firmly set.

The countdown began. At precisely eight

o'clock, an off-stage announcer proclaimed in a voice resembling a one-man gang, "Ladies and gentlemen, this—is—Festival—at—Ford's—Theatre!"

Klayman and Johnson stood in the wings stage left. Other plainclothes detectives were dispersed throughout the theatre, some fortunate enough to have been assigned seats in the audience. They all knew how easy it was to become distracted by the performance and lose sight of the reason they were there: to be aware of everything and everyone within their sight and hearing. Those with seats had been given funds with which to rent tuxedos in order to better blend in, although it wasn't difficult to identify them, solitary and silent men more interested in their seatmates than in the action on stage.

Earlier, in the midst of the seemingly frenetic yet orderly hustle-bustle on the stage, Klayman had spotted Bancroft and stopped him as he hurried past.

"Exciting night, huh?" the detective said.

"What? Oh, yes, hello, Detective." He nodded to Johnson.

"Should be quite a show," Klayman said. "I really enjoy Diana Krall."

"Who is that? Oh, yes, Ms. Krall. Quite good, I hear. Excuse me. I have—I'm—I'm frightfully busy."

Johnson laughed as they watched the British actor scoot away from them. "He's wired, or high," he said.

"High strung," said Klayman.

"Showbiz hysteria."

"I guess."

"Hate to get stuck next to him on a long plane ride."

"You don't have to worry about that, Mo."

Klayman was unable to take his eyes off Bancroft as backstage preparations continued. Although their encounter had been brief, there was a look in the actor's eyes that both detectives had picked up on, and that Klayman hadn't noticed during their earlier meetings. Yes, Bancroft was a manic personality, with eyes constantly in motion, emoting through them, using them to provide punctuation. But this was different. Was it fear Klayman had observed? Or something else?

Diana Krall and her quartet opened the show, the popular Canadian jazz singer and pianist setting an upbeat mood for the audience. As she romped through her first number, a pulsating version of Gershwin's "The Man I Love," Bancroft stood on the opposite side of the stage from where Klayman and Johnson were posted. He'd avoided members of the stage and TV crews since arriving at the theatre late that afternoon, and had come in close proximity with Clarise only once when she'd come down to the theatre from her office to check on something with the house manager. They locked eyes, but she turned away, which didn't especially nettle Bancroft; his anger at her unwillingness to even speak with him had peaked the previous day when she'd refused, through her secretary, to meet. It took every ounce of self-restraint to keep from physically barging in.

He'd left the theatre after being rebuffed by the secretary and had spent the afternoon in Harry's, downing scotch with beer chasers until he was sufficiently drunk to anesthetize the pain. A cab delivered him to his apartment building where Morris, the doorman, helped him through the lobby and into the elevator. He slept for fifteen hours. When he awoke at noon, he was confused as to where he was. But as the room, indeed his life, came into focus, he could see nothing but the past, his performances on British regional stages as a young man, his days at Stratford-upon-Avon, the applause, the adoring women, shooting films in exotic locations, the parties, the applause, the excitement of signing a new contract, and the applause, always the applause.

He consulted a small card on which the order of acts had been written. After someone named Diana Krall, it would be one of President Nash's favorite performers, Washington's venerable political satirist, Mark Russell, with Alan King functioning as MC between acts. It was noted on the card that King would do a six-minute standup routine toward the end of the evening, and those words seemed to be magnified as Bancroft stared at them. Alan King, funnyman, guaranteed to generate loud laughter with his one-liners and sage observations of love and life. Prior to him, Clarise was scheduled to say a few words.

He looked across the backstage area, saw Klayman staring at him, and stepped behind a flat to move out of the detective's line of vision. The presence of the officers who'd questioned him was disconcerting; he wished they weren't there. He took in others in his proximity. No one seemed particularly interested in him, for which he was grateful. It had been that way at Ford's Theatre since Clarise hired him, disinterest in Sydney Bancroft, dismissive of him, scornful, snickering behind his back. Who did they think they were? Ford's was a pathetic excuse for a theatre, mounting pedestrian plays with mediocre talent. He, Sydney Bancroft, had tasted what real theatre was meant to be, British theatre, great actors and actresses performing the thoughts and words of the world's best playwrights. He hated every one of them at Ford's Theatre, although that emotion had not been extended to Clarise Emerson—until now. She was worst of all, with her sophisticated facade and glib ease while mingling with the money people and bureaucrats.

Others backstage who obviously didn't belong there exaggerated his unease. Uniformed police, and men in drab suits and with nondescript haircuts, were there to protect the vice president, Clarise's friend, another politician, just another whore.

What was happening onstage was irrele-

vant to Bancroft. The music, and the audience's reaction, originated from another
place, vague and muffled, unconnected to
the moment. He realized he was sweating,
and felt light-headed. He made his way to
an exit door guarded by two Secret Service
agents and a uniformed D.C. cop. Bancroft
lifted the large badge dangling from his
neck, validating that he was entitled to be
there. "Feeling a little woozy," he said, forcing a smile. "Some fresh air will do the
trick."

The officer opened the door, and Bancroft stepped into the night air, where a contingent of police and agents were posted
outside the theatre. Tenth Street was cor-
doned off at both corners, but the Star Saloon across the street was open, sans customers. Bancroft displayed his badge as he
crossed the street and entered the bar
where the thoroughly bored bartender
lounged behind the bar. "Working tonight,
Sydney?" he asked.

"Alas, yes. Only have a minute, need
something to tickle the old throat."

"The usual?"

"If you please."

Bancroft consulted the list of acts again

as he downed the first scotch placed in front of him and indicated he wished a refill.

"How's it going over there?" the bartender asked.

"What? Oh, splendid. Yes, just fine." Bancroft placed money on the bar. "Keep the change, old boy. And remember me. Remember Sydney Bancroft."

The bartender laughed. "How could I ever forget you, Sydney?"

Bancroft retraced his steps to the theatre's rear door. A display of his pass gained access to the backstage. Mark Russell was finishing his performance, standing at the piano and delivering a final satirical ditty about Washington and its politicians.

Klayman had taken advantage of a break in the action to cross behind the sets to the opposite side of the stage, leaving Mo Johnson where they'd originally stood. He'd been looking for Bancroft but hadn't seen him. Now, he saw the actor come into the theatre and wondered where he'd been. Across the street at the Star Saloon? Like John Wilkes Booth fortifying himself before shooting Lincoln? That fanciful notion came and went as he observed Bancroft disappear inside a room; PROPS was crudely written on a sheet of paper and taped to the door, which closed behind the actor.

*"Ladies and gentlemen, please welcome the wonderful Natalie Cole."*

Klayman turned to see the singing star begin a song associated with her late father, Nat "King" Cole. He forced himself to redirect his attention to the prop room door, which was now open. He went to it and peered inside. No Bancroft. He scanned the myriad boxes on shelves. The boxes were neatly stacked, one atop the other, floor to ceiling, each carefully labeled. His eyes went to one box that sat on a small table wedged in the corner. He looked up to an empty space where a box had been. A few steps closer allowed him to read the label on the box on the table: FIREARMS.

He lifted the cardboard lid and saw the array of fake weapons piled inside. Why hadn't the Secret Service noted this when they'd swept the room earlier in the day? He looked up again. The box had probably been up there, high off the floor, when agents examined the room. Still . . .

Natalie Cole's voice singing "Route Sixty-six" reached him in the room. A Secret Ser-

vice agent looked in. Klayman motioned
him to look in the box.

"Where'd these come from?" the agent
asked, going through the array of stage
props.

"Up there, I think," Klayman said, indicating the space at the top of the shelving.

"All phonies. Plastic."

"Yeah."

"I'll take them."

The agent placed the lid on the box and
carried it from the room, presumably to
place it under the control of other agents
until the evening was over. Klayman stayed
behind for a few minutes, trying to put his
thoughts in order. Although every weapon
in the box was an obvious replica, why had
that particular box been taken down from
the shelf? Had Bancroft removed it and
placed it on the table? If so, why?

He left the room and took in his backstage surroundings. He spotted Johnson at
the other side and gave him a wave, which
was returned. Bancroft came into view. He
stood alone by the light panel, his back to
the lighting technician, head lowered, fingers pressed against his temples as though

to push a headache from his head, or a particularly onerous thought.

Bancroft turned and saw Klayman. He appeared to want to want to say something, but spun and disappeared behind a heavy vertical curtain.

"... *Someday my happy arms will hold you, and someday I'll know that moment divine, that all the things you are, are mine,"* Natalie Cole sang to conclude her set. The audience applauded enthusiastically as she took her bows and left the stage, to be replaced immediately by Clarise Emerson. She stepped to the mike, flashed a wide, dazzling smile, and began her scripted one-minute speech.

Alan King stood in the wings, poised to follow.

Bancroft stepped from behind the vertical curtain and followed the contour of the backstage wall to a position immediately to Clarise's stage left, out of view of the audience. Klayman saw the aged Brit make his move, reaching into the front waistband of his trousers.

Klayman narrowed his eyes and leaned forward to see better: "What's he doing?" he wondered.

Clarise was about to deliver her final line when she saw Bancroft out of the corner of her eye. She froze for a second, the smile sagged. But she delivered the line, smiling again, and finished with, "And now, ladies and gentlemen, one of America's comedy treasures, Mr.—Alan—King!"

As King strode to the microphone, Klayman looked into the audience. Vice President Maloney sat front-row center, flanked by two Secret Service agents. To her left, next to the agent on that side, were vacant seats President Nash and the first lady were to have occupied.

King launched into his monologue and immediately had the audience laughing. Police officers behind Klayman laughed, too, and a barbed comment about the nation's first female vice president adding Martha Stewart to the cabinet caused Klayman to chuckle, but only for a second. He watched as Bancroft, seemingly transfixed, his eyes boring holes into the front row, again reached into his waistband. This time, his hand emerged holding a handgun.

The sight froze Klayman for a moment, enough time for Bancroft to bolt from where he stood just offstage and take a series of stutter-steps to King's side. At first, the audience laughed at the sight of another person barging in on the comic's act. King turned, faced Bancroft, and said, "Who the hell are—?" The sight of the weapon silenced him in mid-sentence. King backed away as Bancroft faced the house, weapon raised. The audience now saw the gun, too, and gasps, mingled with female shrieks and male voices shouting, "No!" filled the theatre.

Klayman broke free of his inertia and rushed at Bancroft, and Johnson did the same from another angle. One of the Secret Service agents seated next to the vice president flung himself over her as Bancroft raised the weapon in two unsteady hands and squeezed off a shot. It was far off the mark, whizzing ten feet over Maloney's head and striking the front of the balcony.

"*Sic semper tyrannis!*" Bancroft shouted.

Klayman beat Johnson by a step and tackled Bancroft, sending him facefirst into the orchestra pit, where he landed on the percussionist's drum set, scattering its pieces in every direction, cymbals crashing, drums hitting other orchestra members.

Panic and fear filled the theatre. Some

people tried to run from it, but the aisles were clogged. Others raced to the front to better see what was happening. The Secret Service valiantly tried to extricate the VP from the mob but found it virtually impossible to move her to safety. Eventually, a corps of agents and uniformed police formed a V-shaped wedge and pushed people aside on their way to the lobby and out into the street.

Johnson, gun drawn, had scrambled down into the pit and had pinned Bancroft to the floor, a knee in his back, his weapon pressed against the back of the actor's neck. Klayman, with a uniformed cop, joined him, and Bancroft's hands were cuffed behind his back. Klayman saw the gun the actor had used jutting out from beneath a snare drum, pulled a handkerchief from his pocket, and retrieved it.

"You stupid bastard," Johnson growled at Bancroft, who whimpered beneath the big detective's weight, and the pain in his arms and wrists caused by having been handcuffed.

Mac's and Annabel's initial reactions were like everyone else's in the audience: shock, disbelief, then a need to take action.

They stood at their seats while the chaos around them developed and kept their attention on the stage where the bizarre, unrehearsed scene had played out before their eyes. There was as much bedlam on the stage as in the house. Some huddled together and cried; others came to the stage apron to peer down into the orchestra pit, where Johnson and Klayman had pulled Bancroft to his feet and were leading him into the hands of a dozen other officers.

"I don't see Clarise," Annabel told her husband, standing on tiptoe in search of her friend.

"She's probably backstage."

"No, I don't see her. I want to find her."

They left the area in which they'd been seated, and threaded a path through people in the direction of the stage. The front of the theatre was relatively empty now, most audience members having headed up the aisles toward the lobby. The Smiths skirted the orchestra pit in which musicians packed their instruments while discussing what they'd just experienced, came up an aisle that paralleled a far wall, and reached doors linking the theatre to the building in which Ford's Theatre Society's offices were housed. Before the incident, the Secret Service and MPD had been stationed at the doors, but had abandoned their posts in the aftermath of the shooting. Annabel opened one of the doors and prepared to go through it.

"Mac!"

The voice belonged to Dean Mackin, Mac's boss at GW.

"I need to speak with you for a minute," Mackin said.

"I'll go up to Clarise's office," Annabel told her husband, "and see if she's there."

"I'll be up in a minute," he said.

Annabel closed the door behind her. The turmoil in the theatre hadn't spilled over into the small, three-storey building that was home to Ford's Theatre Society. The short hallway in which she stood was dark, although lights from the street, many of them flashing, pierced the glass on the front of the building, creating a crazy quilt of light and shadow.

She walked in the direction of the entrance and was confronted by the park ranger who'd gotten up from his small desk and was looking out on the activity on Tenth Street. She'd seen him a number of times previously when she'd visited Clarise at her office. Her arrival startled him.

"What went on in there?" he asked.

"A long story," Annabel replied.

"Secret Service was here until they got a call to go outside. Something about somebody trying to kill the vice president?"

"I'm afraid so," she said. "Do you know if Ms. Emerson is upstairs in her office?"

"I think so," he said, his attention more on the street than on Annabel.

"I can go up?"

"Sure, Ms.—"

"Annabel Reed-Smith. I'm on the board."

"I know. I recognize you. Go ahead."

The stairs were illuminated only by ambient light coming from the street, and by lamps burning in offices off the landings. Annabel went up slowly—sirens, walkie-talkies, and shouts from the street punctuated the solitude of the staircase. She reached the first landing, the second floor, and paused, cocked her head, and listened. "Clarise?" she called. There was no response. She looked back down the stairs in search of Mac. No sign of him yet.

She crossed the landing and ascended to the third floor, where Clarise's office was located. She reached the top. Directly in front of her was the office. The door was wide open; every light in the office burned bright. She called Clarise's name again. A few steps brought her to the doorway. Her gasp was involuntary and loud. Clarise was in her chair, leaning back, arms akimbo, mouth open, her head flopped to one side.

"Oh, my God," Annabel mouthed as she entered, came around the desk, and examined her friend more closely. There was an ugly bruise on her left temple; the force of whatever caused it had broken the skin, and blood oozed from the wound. Annabel also saw blood forming in one of Clarise's ears. She didn't bother reaching for a pulse. She grabbed the phone and was about to dial 911 when Bernard Crowley, his girth filling the doorway, said, "Put it down, Mrs. Smith." When Annabel didn't immediately respond, he crossed the short distance between door and desk and ripped the phone from her hand, followed by a sharp yank that separated the cord from the wall.

"What have you done?" Annabel said, trying to control her breathing.

He was sweating profusely, and his round face was mottled, blotchy red. He took a step back, the phone still in his hand, and stumbled, back against the wall. His sudden loss of balance startled him, but not to the extent that he couldn't recover quickly and block Annabel's attempt to flee. She ran into him, a human wall. He grabbed her hair, pulled back her head, and looked down into her eyes. "I'm sorry," he said in a voice on the verge of breaking.

"Let me go," Annabel demanded. She tried to drive her knee up into his groin, but before she could, he released her, pushing her back across the desk. For a dreadful moment she thought he was about to throw himself on top of her. Instead, he retreated to the doorway, breathing labored, wiping perspiration from his brow with the back of his hand.

"I'm sorry," he repeated.

Annabel slid off the desk and circumvented it so that she was next to Clarise. She wasn't sure how to deal with him. Mac would be coming soon, she hoped. She had to placate Crowley long enough for him to arrive.

"You just don't understand what it's been like," Crowley said.

Annabel's mind raced. She knew she was

face-to-face with a possible murderer. Her
conversation with Clarise at the gallery had
been sobering, and frightening. According
to Clarise, the outside auditors of the theatre's books had uncovered a series of
misdirected payments to a fictitious small
company that never existed, except for
Crowley. He'd been issuing checks to the
company and cashing them, using an alias.

But that wasn't the worst of the CPAs'
findings.

Two bills from jewelry stores, and a
round-trip airline ticket to Florida purchased
through a travel agent, had been paid directly with Ford's Theatre's checks bearing
Clarise Emerson's signature. When shown
them, she told the auditors that she'd never
signed such checks; they were forgeries.

Obviously, Crowley had been embezzling
funds from the theatre's coffers, which was
bad enough. But one of the items purchased from the jewelry store, and the airline ticket, had been delivered not to Crowley but to a house on N Street, off Dupont
Circle. The store manager, and travel agent,
dug out their records, which showed that
both purchases were sent to N. Zarinski,

care of Mark and Laura Rosner at the N Street address.

Mac and Annabel had decided that while those facts uncovered by the auditors were startling, they didn't provide conclusive proof in and of themselves that Bernard Crowley was Nadia's killer. Mac and Yale Becker decided during their phone conversation to assign a private investigator to dig into the possibility that Crowley killed Nadia Zarinski, and to devote the next few days to seeing whether they could build a case sufficient to present to the U.S. Attorney and the court.

But Annabel didn't have any doubt at that moment, in that cramped office, standing next to the limp body of Clarise Emerson. The controller, with the pleasant facade and who'd earned Clarise's unbridled respect and admiration, was a killer, and Annabel knew he wouldn't have the slightest reservation about killing her, too.

*Keep him talking,* she silently told herself. *He said he was sorry. Ask about that.* "Why did you do this to Clarise?" she asked. "Was it an accident?"

"No, I—"

"You said you were sorry."

He looked away, eyes focused on the floor, and slowly shook his head. He wheezed with each exhalation, sounds from deep in his chest, expressions of the emotional pain he was feeling at that moment. He looked up with watery eyes: "I didn't mean to hurt anyone."

"I'm sure you didn't," Annabel said, more concerned with the role she needed to play than with her veracity. "You had an affair with Nadia?"

"You could call it that. She was—I never had affairs with pretty women like Nadia. You can look at me and know why. I've always had to pay for female companions, and she was no different. 'Buy me this, buy me that. Give me more or I'll never see you again.' "

A flash of pity came and went. Annabel looked down at Clarise, who'd moved.

"We have to get her help," Annabel said. "Please. I'm sure this can all be worked out, but if we don't get her to a hospital, you'll have her death on your conscience." She made a move toward the door, but he blocked it again.

"What had Nadia done to make you so angry that you hit her, Bernard?"

With eyes to the floor again, he muttered, "She said she'd tell people about me taking money from here."

"Clarise?"

"Yes. And others."

"And so you had to hit her to keep her quiet. Is that it?"

"She told Clarise."

"She—*when* did she tell her?"

"The day she—the day she died."

"But Clarise was shocked when the auditors discovered you'd been taking money from the theatre."

"She pretended to be. She's a good actress. She told me to take care of Nadia. She told me to clean up my own litter box."

The accusation hit Annabel in the stomach like a physical punch. He had to be lying. It was inconceivable to Annabel that Clarise would do such a horrific thing. It had to be a lie.

Clarise groaned and twisted in the chair; her hand went to the wound on her temple. Annabel reached down and grasped her wrist. "It'll be okay, Clarise," she said, not taking her eyes off Crowley, who leaned against the door frame as though the skeletal structure inside his big body were failing him. His chest heaved, and his eyes expressed, at once, anger and confusion.

"Bernard, don't you think it would be best for everyone if—?"

Annabel saw a shadow fall across the landing behind Crowley, and knew it was Mac. Her immediate concern was for him, although the fact that Crowley didn't appear to be armed provided some comfort. She wondered what Mac would do. Attack Bernard? She assumed he could see beyond the controller to where Clarise was slumped in her chair. He had to know something was terribly wrong.

Mac answered her questions by asking in a firm, even tone, "Are you all right, Annie?"

Crowley flinched at the sound of Smith's voice and turned in the doorway. Mac approached him and looked inside the office. "We need a doctor here, Bernard, and we need one now!"

Annabel had all she could do to not break down in tears and run to her husband. But she knew that might unsettle Crowley. Mac was steadying him by behaving normally.

"Get out of my way," Smith said, pushing past Crowley and coming to Annabel. "I'm fine," she said. He leaned over Clarise and said, "It'll be okay, Clarise. We'll get a doctor here and you'll be fine."

Mac and Annabel looked up to see Crowley leave the office and waddle toward the stairs.

"He killed Nadia, Mac, and attacked Clarise. He said—"

"He won't get far," Mac said, noticing the phone on the floor. "Grab a phone from another office and call 911. Tell them a murderer is leaving Ford's Theatre, and describe him. And tell them we need an ambulance here fast!"

# THIRTY-SEVEN

Mac Smith had coffee with Rick Klayman and Mo Johnson on Saturday morning following his Lincoln-the-Lawyer class at GW. He'd devoted the session to Lincoln's rise to preeminence as one of the nation's top lawyers when it came to resolving an increasing number of suits spawned by the rapid expansion of the railroads. Lincoln was comfortable taking either side of these disputes, and began earning enough to finally provide decently for his family. Still, he took on smaller cases for minimal fees when he felt a decent, honest citizen had been cheated.

But conversation over coffee didn't linger on Lincoln. The events of Thursday night dominated talk at the table.

"Crowley confessed right away," Johnson said. "Rick and I did the interrogation yesterday. I think he was glad to get it off his chest."

"What about his claim that Clarise Emerson told him to take care of Ms. Zarinski?" Smith asked. "In effect, he's saying she ordered the killing."

"He was still claiming that yesterday," Klayman replied. "You know her pretty well, Mac." They were on a first-name basis at Smith's request. "Think she's capable of doing that?"

"No," he said, "but that doesn't count for much. I've had clients over the years who did terrible things that I never would have suspected they were capable of. My wife and I prefer to think it's Crowley's attempt to shift blame."

Smith looked down at a copy of yesterday's Washington *Post.* An unnecessarily large photo of Sydney Bancroft, taken as a publicity shot years ago during his heyday as an actor, dominated the front page. Mac shook his head and smiled. "Who ever would have thought?" he said, standing. "I have to go. My wife is home packing. We're planning a trip to Paris later this fall, but we—she—decided we needed a long weekend away. We're driving out to White Post, Virginia. There's a lovely inn there, L'Auberge Provençale. Great restaurant, hot tub, no kids under ten, the perfect get-away."

"Sounds great," Johnson said.

Smith left them on the sidewalk in front of the coffee shop.

"What's up for you this weekend?" Johnson asked his partner.

"Not much left of it, is there? Rachel and I are having dinner tonight. I thought I'd spend Sunday trying to locate witnesses in the Marshall case, see if I can get them to remember things they might have forgotten first time around."

"It's your day off, Rick."

"I know. Been an interesting couple of days, huh?"

Johnson's laugh was low and rumbling. "You might say that. I told you Bancroft was nuts."

"Slightly skewed, that's all. See you Monday."

"Yeah. See you Monday."

\* \* \*

Had it not been for Sydney Bancroft's apparent attempt at assassination—since the president wasn't in attendance, it was assumed America's first female vice president was his target, a second-best victim compared to John Wilkes Booth's success at killing a president—and his spectacular failure in that leading role, the arrest of Bernard Crowley would have received considerably more media coverage on Friday. But Bancroft had succeeded at being center stage once again, his name on the tip of virtually every person's tongue. Crowley's arrest in the Zarinski case was Page Three news.

The corpulent controller had barely made it to the corner of Tenth Street before being apprehended in front of Honest Abe's Souvenirs, with dozens of Lincoln masks in the windows witnessing the event. Crowley offered no resistance, and was seen crying as the police placed him in the rear of a patrol car. He was held that night for his attack on Clarise Emerson; charges in the Zarinski murder would come later, after he'd confessed and other evidence had been processed and presented to the U.S. Attorney.

Clarise was rushed to the nearest hospital. Crowley's blow had fractured bones in her skull. Emergency room physicians stabilized her, and the prognosis, according to a neurosurgeon called in to operate that night to relieve pressure on her brain, was for a full recovery—with a headache now and then to remind her of her encounter with the controller in whom she'd invested so much trust. Once she was sufficiently recovered to travel, she sold the Georgetown house and flew to California, where she established a small production company to produce documentaries for public television. Annabel's contact with her quickly trailed off to virtually none. Clarise's former husband, Senator Bruce Lerner, abandoned his plans for a presidential run and was easily reelected to another Senate term.

Bancroft was held in a maximum-security cell and placed on suicide watch, which necessitated taking everything from him, including his shoe laces and belt. He was allowed to read the morning papers on Friday, and seemed pleased with the photograph of himself on the *Post*'s front page and the lengthy and detailed history of his career in the theatre that accompanied the picture. He looked every bit the leading man in the photo, and it appeared in newspapers across the country and around the world, as well as on TV screens in millions of homes. While court-appointed attorneys prepared his insanity plea—which they were confident would prevail—Sydney collected his press clippings and dutifully catalogued them in large scrapbooks. His British agent, Harrison Quill, interviewed by the London *Times,* stated, "Sydney Bancroft was a fine Shakespearean actor in his day. But I'm afraid he'd become a bit dotty in his old age and had lost his grip on reality. Sorry he's ended up in such a pickle. Dreadful shame, it is. Dreadful shame."

Once the police had Crowley's confession in the Nadia Zarinski murder, charges were dropped against Jeremiah Lerner. Because his mother faced a lengthy hospital stay and even longer convalescence, he'd spent a few days at his father's house before returning to his apartment in Adams-Morgan. He didn't accompany his mother to California, and seemed to drop out of sight in Washington, which to Mac and Annabel seemed only fitting. Whether he was the son of an ambitious U.S. senator, or a demented, aging British actor—or whether he was ever even made aware of the possibility that the senator wasn't his natural father—remained unknown to Mac and Annabel, nor did they wish to know. It didn't seem to matter.

It didn't take long for other events in the nation's capital, and abroad, to render that Thursday night at Ford's Theatre a dim memory in a city filled with memories, triumphant and tragic. But the publicity surrounding it was good for business at the theatre. Its shows were standing room only, and the number of tourists visiting the historic site reached all-time highs. Park rangers who conducted tours added something to their fifteen-minute spiel about Sydney Bancroft and the havoc he created the night he took the stage and fired that errant shot. "He thought he was John Wilkes Booth," the rangers said, usually adding a laugh when they said it. "But let's get back to Lincoln and the night he was shot. That's what's important about this historic theatre."

Bancroft was found not guilty by reason of insanity and was confined to a mental institution where, it was reported, he entertained other inmates with material he would have included in his one-man show.

A jury found Bernard Crowley guilty of second-degree murder and sentenced him to life; he would be eligible for parole in thirty years. It came out during his trial that he'd been dismissed from his former employment with the movie theatre chain in the Midwest for theft of funds, although no formal charges had ever been filed. Fearful of being sued for libel, the theatre chain's management would only confirm his dates of employment when asked for a reference. Ford Theatre's board of trustees contemplated suing the theatre chain for having foisted Crowley on them, but eventually dropped the idea.

Theatre, or real life?

It is often hard to tell the difference in Washington, D.C., where "real" people hide behind theatrical masks and speak the words of others more gifted in drafting them, and actors expose their souls on bare stages and assume roles other than those into which they were born.

Shakespeare said, a bit verbosely,

through his character Hamlet, that theatre should closely imitate life.

*". . . Suit the action to the word,
the word to the action; with this
special observance, that you
o'erstep not the modesty of
nature; for any thing so overdone
is from the purpose of playing,
whose end, both at the first and
now, was and is, to hold as
'twere, the mirror up to nature; to
show virtue her own feature,
scorn her own image, and the
very age and body of the time
his form and pressure."*

In Washington, it's too often the other way around, life imitating theatre. The "play" that is the nation's capital never closes, high drama and low comedy, villains and heroes, all the stuff of compelling theatre. And in true theatrical spirit, the show must, and hopefully will, go on.

# TO DANCE
# WITH THE
# DEVIL

Also by Karen Stabiner

INVENTING DESIRE

COURTING FAME

LIMITED ENGAGEMENTS (A NOVEL)